REIGN
OF
CLANS
&
GODS

ASHLEY MERDALO

First published in the United States of America April 2022 by Lake Country Press & Reviews

Cataloging-in-Publication Data is on file with the Library of Congress.

Publisher website: https://www.lakecountrypress.com

Editor: Samantha Costanilla

Cover: Emily's World of Design

Formatting: Dawn Lucous of Yours Truly Book Services

AUTHOR'S NOTE

Dear Reader,

Thank you for joining me on this journey through the land of Eiram. As a romantic fantasy, Reign of Clans and Gods contains a broad range of plot points and emotions. While this fantasy is not intended to be dark, to ensure ready safety, a list of potential triggers is available on https://www.lakecountrypress.com.

GLOSSARY OF TERMS, PLACES, NAMES

Name	Pronunciation	Definition
Beltane	Bell-tay-n	Spring holiday
Fiadh	Fee-ah	Willa's older sister
Sarai	S-air-eye	Scoutmaster of Clan Amongst the Rivers
Boannn	Bo-anne	Goddess of the River Boyne
Scian	Sigh-anne	Short sword
Faoladh	Fee-oh-lah	Wolf belonging to the Otherworld
Fianna	Fee-ah-na	Band of warriors
Sai	Sigh	Fiadh's husband
Meili	May-lee	Sai's mother
Lia Fáil	Lee-ah Fail	The screaming stone at the Hill of Tara
Calleach	Cal-ee-ahh	Goddess of winter
Cloch Oír	Clo-sh eh-ir	One of the standing stones
Clogher	Clo-her	Another standing stone circle
Cul na Móna	Cool nah Moan-ah	Haunted bog
Sheela na gig	She-la nah gig	Type of faerie
River Boyne	River B-oh-een	River
Ngels	nn-geh-l-s	Land where the Sectarians are originally from
Eiram	Air-em	The name of the island of the clans
Ráth na Ríogh	Raw noh ree-ug	Vast enclosure around burial of old kings and the Lia Fáil.

DEDICATION

To everyone who has dared to dream of more
Here's to your biggest strength

CHAPTER ONE

Willa

The bastard sword clattered out of my hands. Dust rose from where the weapon landed, tired and defeated. I stared at my opponent, at the cuts strewn about its figure, and shook my head in disgust.

My lackluster attempt wasn't good enough. Then again, it never was.

One by one, I pulled the daggers out of the straw dummy, sliding them back into their sheaths, guiding them home. I racked the blade on the weaponry wall. Hard as I might try, this practice in the ring wasn't enough to clear the echoes of last night's ghosts from my head.

I glanced at the silver band resting on my forefinger, a symbol of my gift from the gods, worn out and exposed for all to see. It was a tradition that gifts and accomplishments were displayed via these rings, so one always knew their enemy and the tricks they hid up their sleeve.

Since I was a child, gods and faeries always visited my dreams, the place between our world and theirs, a realm where the whispers of magic dwelled. At the age of three, my parents realized my gift, and I was anointed with the gift of prophecy and foresight, a ceremony beheld by all on our island. And so sat the ring, imprinted with the black eye of sight, looking on infinitely, taunting with the side of spirituality that had dimmed in me with recent years.

And yet, the murmurings of the gods had been growing louder for weeks on end. Sighs of their unrest rippled through the trees, their unhappiness echoing in the faintest of dreams. Try as I might to keep the gods and faeries and magick of the Otherworld out, they always found their way back in, sneaking through the crevices of my mind.

My attempt in the practice arena was a mere coping mechanism, hoping the sting of sweat and steel would be enough to lose the murmurings from my head. The whispers were a consequence of denying my nature, my gift; but I stopped finding answers in the gods a long time ago.

Even with their constant presence, I resented them, felt like they had abandoned me. As the days dragged on, I was beginning to feel more and more like I was losing myself, little pieces at first, but adding up quickly. Something about my reality felt like standing on sand, the solid foundation slipping out from underneath my feet, leaving me weak and vulnerable. The magick that threaded through our isle often raised itself in an uproar about my denial of the gods and my gift, screaming in outrage, begging me to find a way back to the person I once was– the gods reluctant to being let go. I refused to answer their call.

How could I trust in my gift from the gods, the gift of prophecy and foresight, visions that were supposed to be handed straight from them, when I felt like this? If the gods couldn't give me my own happiness, how could I trust what they told me? A world filled with malevolent gods was not one I would participate in. So, years ago, I stopped listening. I wouldn't act as their portal, their prophetic oracle. Not until the gods showed that they gave a shit.

The air in the practice yard was warm, and yet I shivered as I recalled my previous night's dreams: a nightmare filled with omens so realistic I felt my skin crisp and melt all at once, as flames crept into the forest clearing in my dream world.

The burning brush had taunted me to discover the answer, even if I already knew the dream held none. Panic bound ropes around me as my feet stumbled forward, tripping over the thick roots of the oak trees that clawed their way through the earth seeking purchase.

The clearing was unfamiliar, not one that lay within the Forest Clan territory. The homes and workstations should have been filled with life, the sound of clanging metal and the smell of rising bread, but what was clearly a village had been empty. No one was there to save me, but I was used to that, in this dream world and my own.

A sharp crack had echoed behind me as a giant sycamore caved into itself. The glowing trunk lost its structure and showered chips of bark and ember, and what was left of the leaves swirled down to the forest mulch. The sight was almost beautiful. It reminded me of the first fallen leaves of autumn with reds, oranges, and yellows returning to the earth. Desperation rose in my throat as I slowly realized I wasn't meant to escape this dream. My legs rooted to the ground as the heat crept into my body and flames met my skin. And then, as suddenly as the dream began, it ended.

A cool breeze twisted the untamed hairs at the nape of my neck, reminding me where I was and was not.

There was no exposed village here, only an arena shaded by the great oaks, creating a ceiling with their branches, sunlight peeking through. I picked up a longbow and strung the arrow with a slight hum. Maybe archery's meditative state would be better.

"Willow!"

The arrow flew out of my hands, landing far from the center of the target.

I winced, knowing exactly who it was. Only one person in the clan believed I actually enjoyed being called my full name. My parents may have had good intentions naming me after the trees that represented wisdom and thought to our clan, but the name only taunted me as I got older.

My betrothed hopped over the fence and into the training arena.

"Callan," I said, squinting up at his towering figure.

Callan was once whom I wished for. His blonde hair created a striking contrast with those sky blue eyes, and perhaps that was where I found fault with him. Something about him was too good, too perfect, that never quite fit right. Besides the fact that I barely controlled my own life, his presence felt like I was floundering more than usual.

Perhaps it was his attempt at compensation. Neither Callan nor his father was born inside my clan. They were emigrants, and while they were welcomed with open arms, intuition told me that Callan felt that he had more to prove than the men his age – a trait that never left as we grew older.

Callan and his father, Bowen, originally hailed from the cliffs of the eastern coast. Their people, the Clan o' Cliffs, were driven from their home when Callan was only a young boy. It was almost twenty years ago that the Sectarians landed on their shores and breached the cliffs that previously kept them safe. Eventually, their clan couldn't hold against the siege any longer, and the clan surrendered their land. Since those years, the remaining territory in Eiram stabilized, but there wasn't enough territory for Callan's clan to take for themselves. The remnants scattered across the other clans, and Bowen and Callan, along with a few others, chose to call the Forest Clan their new home.

My parents quickly became friends with Bowen. He was now one of their most trusted advisors. As such, the engagement seemed a natural match for their daughter given Callan's and my closeness in age. It was my parents' idea of providing for me, securing a good, strong match from a good and powerful family, ensuring I would never worry about the travesties of love.

The only thing to make Bowen and Callan stand out from the rest of their adopted clan were the black rings that sat upon their fingers. The black metal could only be found within the veins of the cliffs next to their seaside. Their respective rings sat upon the last finger of their left hand, marking the ending of where they came from, the last rings of their kind to exist. On the matching thumb from their right hand was a silver band, representing the metal of the clan they were now a part of.

Callan's blue eyes sparkled like the sun reflecting off chips of ice. There was no light or joy inside them, only a façade that served Callan as a mask.

"The wedding is starting soon."

CHAPTER TWO

Willa

M y head jerked up in surprise, thoughts swimming, startled by the idea of marriage.

"Willa... the clans are beginning to arrive for the wedding. Today is Beltane, remember?" Callan asked with a note of concern in his voice.

I blinked the shock away. The presence of my dream from last night was so consuming I had forgotten what today was and what it held.

Today was Beltane, a minor holiday for all of the clans. It meant that winter was no longer a threat over our heads and carried the expectation that the land would flow with an abundance of food.

Today was also my sister's wedding day.

My older sister, Fiadh, would be marrying the eldest son of the Mountain Clan's leader today, but their family would not be the only ones in attendance. Scouts heralded the news across the island for months, welcoming all clans and traveling warbands. All three clans would gather to see the occasion, the first intermarriage in years. All leaders and advisors were expected to attend, and it was likely that they would bring their strongest warriors and wily scouts. Everyone was on display, expected to exude strength.

Today was about more than marriage; it was about politics and power.

And somehow, the pressure was higher for the Forest Clan. Our land would be expected to provide for all three clans. Opponents and allies would see how well they were provided for, any traces of sickness in camp, any potential weakness. My clan – and my family, for that matter – would be putting on a show for dominance.

"Right," I answered with a quick smile.

"Are you alright?" Callan asked tentatively. He knew about my gift, the nightmares it sent me, but preferred to tiptoe around it. It might be that gifts were uncommon in his origin clan. In the forest, we were raised with the belief that every child had a gift bestowed upon them, no matter how diluted or plain. That excuse was better than the alternative; that Callan was simply uncomfortable around me.

"Fine. Distracted. I wasn't expecting to see anyone out here." I cursed at myself internally. Could I simply pick one excuse or did I need to provide several for him?

"Right. The training dummy is such a stunning conversationalist; I can't blame you for not wanting to see anyone."

"I never said I didn't want to see anyone," I replied, adding a slight bite to my words. The last thing I needed was Callan reporting that I was sullen and withdrawn to my parents, even if that might be the truth. "I just didn't expect anyone. Besides, I didn't think the clans would show until later this afternoon." I retrieved the arrow from the target.

"They must have traveled since dawn. I wouldn't expect the Clan Amongst the Rivers until later this afternoon. That will always be a few days' journey, no matter how fast you ride."

The words worked their effect, piquing my curiosity. "Why?"

I asked, looking over my shoulder at him from re-racking my weapons. Riding quicker should always affect a journey's time, or so any reason would leave one to believe. I wondered if Callan really knew all of the information he said with such authority, or if it was just his ego talking. I bit my lip to refrain from asking.

Callan picked up a sword and drew a map in the dirt. "The camp in the Riverlands is surrounded by a delta to the north. Once you make it out of that, you have to go around the bogs. It's part of the reason why our border with them is strong. It's so muddy the horses lose their footing. You're forced to go at a walk for the first day, at least."

"They better not bring that mud into camp. It's already wet enough with the spring showers." My words sounded cross, even to my own ears, instead of the cajoling tone I was aiming for. My words always seemed to fall flat, especially around Callan.

"Chin up, Willow," Callan replied cheerfully. "You don't seem to mind muddy training arenas; are muddy humans that much worse?" He winked.

I hummed thoughtfully, tilting my head up at Callan's figure.

"I suppose not, as long as you don't track the mud back to camp. I'll let you slide." I smiled, happy at the turn the conversation took, so close to the relationship we once had.

I placed the bow back on its stand. Brushing past Callan, not having the heart to look him in the eyes, I started on the path back to the Hollow, our village. Trees arched over the hardened trail, creating a tunnel with our village at the end. Hard as I might try to leave the thoughts of my dream in the training arena, it followed me back to camp, my gut screaming at me that I was ignoring an omen given by the gods. I feared it was delivered to me for a reason.

As we maneuvered through the undergrowth of the forest, Callan filled the silence with easy conversation. He reported the camp gossip, guesses for the wedding feast, and who in the clan would be betrothed next. For a warrior so highly regarded in the clan, Callan talked – a lot. I hadn't thought that many warriors were so concerned with marital plans, but I didn't bother pointing it out. Callan carried an easy brogue in the accent leftover from his origin clan, and some part of me still softened at it, remembering the shy boy I first met. His brogue added laughter to his words that helped set me at ease, which was no easy feat.

A broad grove of willows sprung from the land before us, protecting the village from the rain and occasional snow brought by the seasons. Our village was more visible than usual, wagons and tents filling the clearing. The Mountain Clan had arrived and brought half their clan by the looks of it.

The thought of feeding so many heads was worrisome, even if it was the end of spring. At the same time, I understood why so many came to this wedding. It was historic. Never before had such an alliance been struck between the clans. Callan had reported whisperings of similar betrothals being offered to the Clan Amongst the Rivers. Clan leaders believed this would lengthen the period of peace we were in, and after this marriage between the Mountain and Forest Clans, it was expected that the courtesy is extended to the remaining clan. I expected the weekend to end with at least one engagement.

Gossip faded away and Callan opened himself with a broad smile as we entered the large canvas tent near the middle of the village. Brigid and Fiadh sat in the center of the room, hunched over the wooden table and benches our father made.

My mother and sister were facsimiles of each other, both with auburn hair and eyes that smiled from within. If anything, I was a shadow of what Fiadh was, a muddier shade of brown in both my hair and eyes, lacking the fire that lit a room when she entered. Fiadh was a source of life, and now she was to be spirited away to the Mountain Clan, to live amongst the caves and snow. This is what she wanted, and what the clan needed, but it felt unsteadying to know she was leaving.

Brigid was handing blossoms and berries to Fiadh as she strung them onto a crown made of braided willow branches. It was an old tradition that symbolized the season of birth brought by spring, the birth of a marriage, and their new stage of life. The crown was only partially formed, but already beautiful, filled with blue forget-me-nots and white cherry blossoms. Fiadh would pass as a wood nymph at her wedding ceremony, and there was no better way to remember her.

"Willa! How you escape such tedious chores is beyond me," exclaimed Fiadh.

I smiled and rolled my eyes as Brigid slapped her eldest daughter's hand.

"And I suppose it's her wedding we're braiding this crown for then? I ought to make you finish it by yourself and scatter the remaining blossoms to the wind while I'm at it."

I laughed, my mother's outburst making it obvious that they had been working on this project for a while now.

"How was I supposed to know blossoms would be so delicate," Fiadh protested, "They're practically falling apart at my fingertips."

"Then you should have listened to me when I said to choose daisies," retorted Brigid.

"And have Sai confuse me with every other bride this spring? I think not." Fiadh sounded positively offended. Her eyes grew in horror.

"Because there will be so many other brides wandering about on your wedding day? We best keep a rope on you then, lest we forget which one belongs to us."

Fiadh continued to grumble underneath her breath as she picked up another bunch of blossoms to wind onto the crown.

"Brigid, can I help in any way today?" Callan asked.

My mother shot an exasperated glance over her shoulder. Annoyance briefly flashed in her gaze.

"I'm afraid not, dear, unless you would like to call in the nymphs themselves to finish the crown."

"Well, I'm not too sure I can do that," said Callan uncomfortably.

It was obviously an exaggeration. I rolled my eyes, knowing only Fiadh would see the action. Callan had the unfortunate tendency to take everything literally as if my mother expected him to draw forth the fae by hollowing out the trees themselves.

I was supposed to love Callan. He was the type of man that any girl in the clan, quite literally, swooned over. Maybe it was the fact that there was no chase in the relationship, never getting to experience the coy cat-and-mouse game that dictated the first months of courtship. Callan had just appeared in my life and assumed the role of my love, without any foundation. As much as I hated to admit it, I wasn't sure if I would ever feel that way about him, but I would be damned if I didn't die trying. If I tried hard enough, maybe this could be written in the stars. Maybe I could escape the misery it brought me.

I snapped out of my thoughts to see my mother shooing Callan out the front of the tent. I took the empty seat next to Fiadh, picking up the remaining blossoms silently, sorting them for the remaining spots on the crown.

"Something on your mind?" Fiadh asked without looking up as if she didn't care to know what the answer was. A well-honed trick to make people talk in the most unsuspecting way.

"Shouldn't I be asking you that? Are you nervous about the ceremony?" I arched a brow.

"Not really. I know what's going to happen in the ceremony, we've practiced it a dozen times. Gather under the oak, say a few words, exchange rings, spend the night drinking and dancing."

"And what about after?"

"Gods, Willa, are you asking me about the sex? I would be lying if I didn't say *I* wasn't thinking about it, but *you* on the other hand... Is there something I should know about you and

Callan? Any interesting developments lately?" I hadn't explicitly told Fiadh about the lack of spark in the relationship, but she could read the situation for herself, even if our blind parents couldn't.

I glanced nervously towards the door where our mother was still talking to Callan.

"Fiadh! Absolutely not what I was referring to at all. I meant going to live with the Mountain Clan, leaving home."

"I know," answered Fiadh. She fell silent, an infrequent occurrence for her. "I know that I'll be accepted, and I trust Sai. Not to mention that absolute stack of furs I've been collecting for the past year and a half."

"Do you really think that it will be cold enough for you to use all of those furs?"

"You cannot be too careful when it comes to frostbite," answered Fiadh firmly. "Besides, if I do get cold, I'm sure my husband will have no problem warming me up." Her lips wrapped in a coy smile.

"Fi, gross. There are things I don't need to picture."

"He is rather handsome, right? With those lips and that jawline, I think I'll be a happy woman." Fiadh wiggled her eyebrows suggestively.

I shook my head, laughing. Sai only visited our home a handful of times during his betrothal to my sister, but I couldn't deny she had a point. His jet black hair stood out against his skin, complimented by his sharp jawline and full mouth my sister had mentioned. The heir to the Mountain Clan was the closest thing my sister could find to a prince on this isle, and I had no doubt they would be a good match, this man who harbored no cruelty in his heart.

My sister propped her head in her hands, lost in a daydream, the flowers strewn across the table forgotten. I turned at the sound of a faint grumble, only to see our mother carrying armfuls of fabric. Brigid tried to avoid the draping pieces of cloth that twisted around her legs as she took teetering steps towards the table where we sat.

"Don't help your poor old mother, no, I'm fine."

My usually patient mother seemed rather quippish today, evidence of the stress the wedding placed on her with the threat of losing her daughter to a clan far away. It could be worse, though. I would rather our last days together be filled with jokes and laughter than sadness and tears, and it was only the teasing humor that was stopping me from breaking down on the spot. A wave of selfishness washed over me, filling me with guilt. These feelings must be insignificant compared to what my sister and mother were feeling, so I locked it away in a box deep inside me, never to bother them.

"What have you been up to," Fiadh demanded. "What is all this?"

Brigid placed her hands on her hips and smiled, proud of her efforts. "Did you really think I was going to send my child off without a new dress? I've had the seamstresses tailoring away at these things for the past month."

The fabric on the table was the lightest shade of blue, matching the pale buds of the unopened forget-me-nots in Fiadh's circlet. I couldn't imagine the hours of labor needed to concoct such a color; it had likely taken the seamstresses an entire season to prepare, toiling over the boiling color baths. My throat clenched at the thought of the care that went into it, the thoughtfulness of my mother.

Fiadh held the piece to the light, admiring it at full length. The gauzy material cascaded down to her knees, elegant and unassuming, designed to complement the owner. A separate piece lay on the table still, a skirt made to match the color, sewn to attach around the waist to give the illusion of a full gown. If I knew my sister, the piece was coming off the second the music started tonight.

As Fiadh picked up the second piece, my eye caught on a slip of fabric laying underneath it. My hands reached out, smoothing it against the table, running my fingertips over the silken cloth. The top was structured, corset bones giving shape to the square neckline. Loose, off-the-shoulder sleeves an opaquer color than the deep emerald hue of the bodice and skirt hung at the side, leaving the owner's chest and collarbone exposed.

"And that one is yours," Brigid said, smiling at me, proud of the secret she had kept hidden for months.

"Oh, Mum," sighed Fiadh, and I knew that if Fiadh cracked, all pretenses of cajoling were gone. The time had come to give my sister away, and the tears rushed down my face as I hugged my family.

"I'll be damned if I'm giving you away without my daughters looking like a sprite." Brigid blinked away her tears as she held us.

Even if Fiadh and I were total opposites, she was the person I was closest to in this clan. My sister had been my form of protection all these years, and now that she was leaving, I was vulnerable and exposed. My heart cracked open at the chasm of loneliness dawning before me.

CHAPTER THREE

Willa

J ust as Fiadh predicted, the wedding was held under the hollowed oak in the middle of the forest surrounding our village. Legend and elders told stories that sprites were born from the hollowed tree. When a warrior cleaned the trunk, it divided the tree's soul, and the faeries would spring forth. This one, and a few others, were sacred to the Forest Clan. It was a place of fate and spirits, and was honored as such.

The giant oak shaded the grass where Sai and Fiadh stood opposite each other, gazing into each other's eyes, hands clasped. Fiadh looked every bit a sprite, the blossoms intertwined in her shining hair, with a fiancé who looked like he could be a part of the fae. It might have been the clan's tendency to romanticize things and blur the cruelty of arranged marriages, but they looked in love. Perhaps they were. Love and adoration might be lingering in their gaze, and maybe in a world without the politics and alliances, they would have found each other anyway.

That's what we, the sons and daughters of chieftains, told ourselves.

The forest overflowed with people from each of the clans. Warriors stood, children hung from tree branches, scouts watched from atop their horses. Everyone waited with bated breath to see the intertwinement of two destinies, two clans, two people.

I leaned against a broad maple tree as the ceremony began. The couple was presided over by my father and Sai's mother. The entirety of the forest fell silent as my father threw his sword into the ground, marking the earth with his intention of a vow. A breeze wrapped its way around my neck as if the spirits were curious as to what today would bring them.

At the altar, Sai turned to his mother, Meili, who stood behind him. Silver streaked her black hair, her face austere and serious. Meili handed Sai a small package, one that was filled with honeycomb. It was a ritual from my clan – the bees representing the pain that Sai would endure for his love, honey being the sweetness that their union hoped to yield.

I wanted to laugh. As if eating a piece of honey would erase problems, that a bee sting was the most love could hurt the couple. Sai unwrapped the honeycomb from the linen and fed the dripping brittle to Fiadh. She ate the piece with a smile on her lips and honey on her tongue.

Behind them, Viktor began the next step of the ceremony, a piece from the Mountain Clan. The ceremony had been carefully manufactured, every piece of it planned and bartered and stretched from what a typical ceremony would look like in either clan. A bowlful of flowers and a mortar grindstone in hand, my father began to grind the plants together, creating a powdered dye inside the bowl. Meili took a pitcher of water and poured a gradual stream, turning the paste to paint, vivid with the orange of marigolds and poppies, even from afar. The custom was said to create the lifeblood of the marriage, bright and vibrant with hope and fidelity. Meili placed the pitcher behind her and grabbed a brush, painting the colors on Sai and Fiadh's hands, staining their palms orange.

When she finished, she gave a curt nod to Viktor. My father changed the words in the ancient language, *"Grá síoraí."* Love eternal. Sai and Fiadh repeated the oath, murmuring the words as one.

Sai grabbed Fiadh by the waist and held her close, staining the waist of her dress with the paint. He gripped her firmly as if he was afraid she was going to escape – or maybe that was adoration. Sometimes love and desire were too closely linked.

Fiadh slowly linked her arms around his neck as Sai kissed her. Fiadh's painted hand left an imprint on Sai's neck, while she was left with smudges of paint around her cheeks and chin. Their love, proudly displayed for all to see. A twinge of jealousy pulled at me, hissing at the obvious devotion while they gazed into each other's eyes. Callan and I would never share a look like that.

The paint quickly dried, cracking on their skin, and they were prepared for the next part of the ceremony – the exchanging of rings.

"Do you have your wedding bands?" Viktor asked.

Both Fiadh and Sai nodded, reaching into their pockets to reveal their wedding rings. Fiadh guided the ring onto Sai's left hand, just above the heart line, where everyone held their wedding rings. The band was thick silver inlaid with a chip of peridot, a reminder of the forest that Fiadh was leaving for him. A reminder of the vow Sai was making to my sister and our clan. It was a piece of political strategy, just like their marriage. Nothing in this family was accidental, especially when it came to matters like this.

When Fiadh finished, Sai revealed the golden ring that had been crafted for Fiadh. In the light, the ring looked minuscule, a necessity to fit Fiadh's dainty hands. My mother whispered to me a few days ago that the ring had to be refitted twice until it was perfect. She had whispered it because it was a sign of bad luck for a ring and its owner to refuse each other like that. The smiths had worked silently, mentioning it to no one, hammering the ring on all sides to mask the reshaping, creating a piece as dazzling as the wearer.

Sai pushed the ring onto Fiadh's finger and released her hand with a kiss. Tears gathered at the corner of Fiadh's eyes. Cries of congratulations rose from the crowd as Sai hooked his arm underneath Fiadh's legs, lifting Fiadh off the floor and carrying her down the aisle. They led the way back to camp, wife pressed to her husband's chest, and the marriage ceremony was over.

The crowd poured into the village to enjoy the night's festivities. A stage was constructed for the happy couple and their families, looking out to the clearing where a bonfire roared. A wild boar crackled over the fire, and tables overflowed with bread and cheeses. I beelined to a table stacked with beverages and surveyed the choices. My nose crinkled at the sight of beer, the smell of yeast and hops rising from the amber liquid. I quickly reached for a glass of cider, the need for the sweetened juice to give me liquid courage for the night. This celebration would take hours, and hopefully, this would keep a smile on my face and conversation on the tip of my tongue.

Today wasn't just a celebration; it was a display of family and power. Eyes were watching for possible signs of weakness, willing to exploit any crack in the façade.

Somewhere in camp, a team of minstrels began to play. Swaying gently to the music, I surveyed the crowd. Fiadh and Sai walked onto the dance floor just before the bonfire, and soon they were whirling effortlessly, every bit in sync. They were almost too perfect, and I resented myself for hating the sight of it all, my weakness flaring at the slightest sign of my sister's happiness.

The sounds of the minstrels rose and the brazier glowed orange as ash drifted into the wind, the air scented with spices and smoke. Wind carried faint embers out of the fire and onto the grass around it, only for them to slowly wink out and die. It would be too easy for one to land on a piece of dry underbrush, the right patch of grass, and create a blaze. With everyone dancing and the drinks flowing, no one would notice.

Again, my attention drifted to my dream the previous night, the wildfire that consumed the empty camp, destroying everything in its path. It wasn't our camp, yet my mind continued to linger on the thought of what if.

What if the gods finally had a message for me? What if it's meant to be our village? What if I'm killing everyone here?

Panic rose in my throat, choking the rest of my senses, numbing me to anything but my thoughts. Glass clinked against the table as I set my cider down, my hands heavy, the drink making me suddenly feel ill.

I need air. The corset in my dress was too tight as my chest heaved, struggling for breath. I pressed a hand against my collarbone, willing my breathing to slow, just so I could escape the clearing that seemed to be growing hotter by the minute. I needed everything to slow down, the dancers to stop spinning, the fire to stop carrying, the space to stop swimming.

All I could focus on was the blur of grass and the desperate need to escape, sheer will the only thing moving me forward as I walked from the clearing. Walked, not ran, because I couldn't be sure who was watching, taking note. Let them see, and I would forever be the girl with a weakness, filled with imperfections, unable to handle the pressure.

A gasp escaped me, and I choked down the crisp air in the meadow outside of the village. As I gulped down the air, I looked at where my feet had taken me, to the edge of land where it met the forest.

Leaning against a tree, I sank to my knees, and let out a sigh of relief at the escape. The night air was a small glimpse of freedom, and I feared it was the most I would ever see.

Today, Fiadh leaving, the inevitability of my marriage to Callan, the nightmares – it was almost laughable, my world turned upside down. I sat, weaving my hands through the tall grass, snapping off a piece at the root. Accompanied only by the rustle of the wind in the meadow, I picked other pieces, slowly braiding a chain, not unlike the one my sister was wearing somewhere in the village. I was utterly alone in the night, in life, and I wished I could disappear amongst the trees.

Except the swishing of grass grew louder, more than just the wind. Walking through the clearing was too telling, the grasses in the meadow fickle things, willing to betray the slightest movement. My head swiveled to see a figure making its way across the clearing to the forest, following the path that led to where I knelt.

The man was shouting something, calling out to someone as he walked towards me. And even though it was rare in our clan, I knew what could happen to women on nights like these, when the drinks had been flowing and men were shoulder to shoulder with their enemies. Women were always a consequence of those nights. The last case of assault left the man beheaded and a promise written permanently in the air if anyone should choose to follow in his path, but that might not be the case in other clans.

I could see two options in front of me. Hide, and pray this man was too inebriated to find me, or run, and hope he was too drunk to catch me, both of which relied heavily on the supposed consumption of alcohol. I looked down and silently cursed. There would be no running in this dress, or hiding, for that matter.

I pressed myself against the tree as I slid quietly around it, buying precious time. My hand traveled down the front of my dress, against the stitching and whalebone that created the rigid lines of the corset. A dagger slid out of the hidden panel, no longer than the length of my hand. Earlier that day, I was quick to argue with my mother that such measures were necessary, that if I was not safe in camp, then nowhere was considered a refuge.

Brigid had worn a small smile on her face as she listened to my naivety. "M'dear, for *who you are*, no place will ever be safe. Tonight, of all nights, you will be surrounded by many, each with their own calculated reasons why they should want you, dead or alive."

If only she could see me now.

I gripped the dagger in my hand, clutching it so hard my knuckles turned white, waiting for the suspect to turn the corner. He would have to duck under the low-hanging branch drooping from the tree, the limb too tired to stand tall like its brothers. It was a small window of opportunity to strike.

"Tad!" the figure called out with a deep voice that matched his tall stature. "Taaaddd!"

Company? Another person in the woods? What could they possibly find out here, tonight?

The branch shook as he slid underneath it, ducking to avoid catching his head. *Now.*

Cursing the skirt of the dress, I slid out from the tree, knife held in my left hand, angling the blade upwards, threatening the vital vessel in his neck that pumped blood through his body. One slice, one thin line, and he would be bleeding out instantly, dead within the minute.

With my dominant hand, I wrapped my arm around his waist, holding him close, avoiding letting him look at my face while blocking his access to his sword with my elbow. If he tried to draw his weapon, I would beat him to it, disarming him.

Swords never sat well in my hand, always too heavy, never quick and agile, tripping me in training and leaving me for dead in the countless practice bouts Fiadh and I ran through. It would be better to kill him with the dagger, cleaner. Lift the sword and I'm sure he would have no problem disarming me; but he didn't know that, yet. So I continued to block the sword, letting him think me lethal with it.

"Long way from camp," I said, aiming for curiosity and boredom at the same time. My heart thudded against my chest and I hoped to the gods that he could not hear it pounding against his back.

He was utterly still, a statue in the dappled moonlight streaming through the forest. His head turned, ever so slightly, acknowledging my presence.

"Am I somewhere I shouldn't be?" His voice was dry, rolling lazily over the syllables.

"Tell me where you're going, and maybe I could tell you." He wasn't from the forest, that I knew. *But then why would he be walking here, alone?*

"A bit hypocritical, no? When you're standing in the same place as me?" I heard the smile in his voice. "But who am I to judge."

I pressed the blade against his skin, irritated by his lack of concern. "Who are you, is the better question." I gritted my teeth.

"Drop the dagger, and I'll tell you."

My eyes widened at the audacity, the pure arrogance of the statement, to be standing next to death and not fear it.

He continued. "You can grab the sword, as well. And the knife, in my boot. I'll step away, answer your questions, and you can let me go. No one has to know. You can even keep the knife. Add it to your collection," he said, the corner of his eye darting to the one held at his throat.

Maybe it was foolish, even in my mind I saw the stupidity of my actions, heard my mother's warning chiming in the back of my head. But there was something about his words, soothing and understanding, that made me pause. The breeze whispered by my ear, urging me to listen and accept his offer.

The dagger traced around his ear, the freshly razored hairline that swept his neck, shaving the smallest of hairs that had begun to grow. I kept the pressure there as I slid it down his spine, a warning of what I could still do, the situation he was still in, as I reached low, my hand running down the hard muscles of his calf searching for a hilt.

I grabbed it and sheathed my dagger, small and weak in comparison. In one swift tug, I pulled out the sword from its scabbard, the iron turning liquid silver in the moonlight. I pressed the tip into his back, urging him forward and away, painfully aware of the danger I put myself in.

He took two strides forward and turned, arms raised, until he backed up against an oak, not far away. His hands slid down, until they were clasped behind his head as he leaned back. His eyes traveled, up and down, examining me slowly, curiosity in his gaze.

His mouth opened, and closed, wordless. Something in his expression changed, his eyes lighting up like he saw a challenge before him, and he shifted his weight forward, placing his hands in his pockets.

"My name is Dempsey. I'm out here looking for my wolfhound. I spend a year raising the damn dog and the bloody thing still can't understand a 'stay' command." Light danced on his face as it opened to a smile.

Curiosity tugged at me. "A wolfhound?" I echoed back to him amidst my surprise. In all the scenarios that ran through my brain, a dog never crossed it. Our last pack died before I was born. And just in case it was an excuse he was trying to peddle, I added "What does he look like?"

My shock was well-founded – the ability to raise wolfhounds was no small feat. The animals were flighty and seldom pack animals. The breed was well on its way to extinction, many deeming the negative attributes of the breed not worthy of the work for the positives. I hadn't heard of a warrior or scout who had the dedication to track down a pup, much less raise it.

"Taller than any dog you would be familiar with, gray with a shaggy coat. Not to mention his obvious inability to come when called."

I thought back to the name Dempsey was calling as he approached the tree. The story appeared to check out.

"Who were you expecting?" The question caught me off guard. I didn't know how to answer that without giving away who I was, an answer he obviously didn't know. I would like to keep it that way.

"Not... you." It was the most honest answer I could think of. I stopped, taking him in.

Dempsey was tall, a good head higher than me. His tan skin was a slightly lighter shade than his brown eyes, all framed by his brunette hair, the strands floppy – as if he had forgotten the last time he had a haircut. And despite everyone that came to visit my parents, on both official and unofficial business, he was unfamiliar, a total stranger.

"Lucky me, then."

I tilted my head, questioning his statement. "Lucky?"

"It's not every day I get a girl from the forest to help me find my dog in her woods." Dempsey sounded so sincere, I wanted to laugh.

"I don't remember offering that," I said. I crossed my arms, daring him to argue.

"I have a feeling you're going to come anyways."

Maybe it was the response to my challenge, or the underlying sense of danger. Maybe it was the way he looked at me, like I was undamaged and whole. But I found myself nodding, stepping forward to follow him.

My heart raced, blood thrumming in my veins. The sensation made me feel more alive than I had in months. Dempsey handed me the leather scabbard that wrapped around his waist, so I could holster the sword that still hung from my hands.

"Let's see what we can find," I said.

CHAPTER FOUR

Willa

We walked side by side further away from the meadow as the thick forest dimmed, the trees above intertwining together, forming a ceiling between us and the stars.

"How'd you know which clan I was from," I asked, breaking the silence growing between us.

Dempsey glanced at my hands. "Your rings are silver, the color of the Forest Clan. The same metal Fiadh gave to Sai today. His were gold, the metal of the mountains." Dempsey extended his own hand. "Mine are copper, the color of the Riverlands."

"I see." I realized that I had never seen a ring from the Riverlands, and how limited my sense of the world must seem to him.

"When are you going to tell me your name?" Dempsey turned to look at me before crossing the small stream cutting across our path.

He extended his hand to me, helping me across as I lifted my skirts, avoiding the water. I wanted to tell him my name. I wanted him to know me. Meeting him felt like racing on horseback, the air whipping around my face, the feeling of flying in my soul. It was dangerous, it made me feel alive, and there might have even been a small part of me that trusted him, for no good or obvious reason. But there was something about his questions that were frank and honest, a far cry from the delicate way I was handled at home.

Even if all of that was true, I still knew it was dangerous to tell him without knowing who he was.

"Maybe when you deserve to know." The answer came coolly off my lips, shocking myself. I looked up at him to see a flicker of delight pass.

"I shall strive to make myself worthy, then. It would be a tragedy, to not make your proper acquaintance." Dempsey gave a small bow that hovered between mocking and serious.

Hairs raised on my arms. His words were dripping in salacious flirtation, and I bit the inside of my cheek to keep myself from smiling.

I wasn't sure if I had ever spoken to anyone like this – easily, breathlessly; like I couldn't wait for what he was going to say next. There was some invisible line between us that we were strolling, here alone in the woods, far from the realities of life.

"What do your rings mean?" I asked, hoping to offer something to keep him talking, wanting to understand more about him and the potential threat that might be walking next to me.

Dempsey looked down like he forgot he was wearing any. He held out a finger. "My warrior band – but you already knew that; all the clans wear them."

He brandished another finger in what could be considered a vulgar gesture. "This ring is inscribed with runes. It was given to me at my anointing ceremony, years ago." My ears perked up, interested in what such a ceremony was for. Typically, they were reserved for major evidence of magick; my foresight, evidence of witchcraft, a prophecy revealed. I wondered what his was.

"What does it say?"

"It says that the power of storms lives within me."

I looked at him, shocked. To have a power of that magnitude was no small feat, and I was surprised I hadn't known this man before.

He continued. "The Oracle prophesized it when I was a child, and for a while it was right. Doesn't happen as frequently now though. Seems like I'm losing my touch." He didn't seem upset about losing his gift, as if he made peace with it a long time ago.

"And the last one?"

Dempsey held out his other hand. "Family heirloom. Claims to my birthright, and all that." He waved his hand in the air, making light of the ornate ring.

"What birthright?"

"You're terribly hypocritical when it comes to personal information, you know that, right? I'm expected to bare my soul while you keep yours tucked away."

"I can't help that you're so forthcoming with information," I pointed out. My mind lingered on the idea of his birthright, wondering what that could possibly mean to a man from the Riverlands. Leadership, advisory, naval officer all could be within the realm of possibility. Whatever it meant, he definitely had power. It was evident in the way he held himself, the way he talked.

We walked on, calling out for the dog as our search grew more desperate and the night lengthened. The path we were on split into two, diverging in the dark wood. I knew these woods like the back of my hand, well enough to know that we were far from civilization.

"The path on the left circles to a glen. The other one leads further into the forest, and it'll take you through the territory." I paused, thinking of the practicality of taking either. "I don't know if he would have gone down either." I turned to look at Dempsey to gauge his reaction, but he wasn't listening. His back was turned to me, his head moving as he examined the woods.

"Is there anything out here in the forest?" He asked the question nonchalantly.

I felt myself take a step back, my mind instantly wandering at the possibilities of what he meant. "Mountain cats, foxes. The occasional bear will stray down here, but it's too warm for them now."

Dempsey hummed in response, still studying the black forest. My heart thudded against my chest as I grew more and more uneasy at the situation.

"Dempsey, we should just go back to camp. The dog will come back when he's hungry; they all do." I tried to say the words firmly, instilling false confidence into the order.

His tall figure remained unmoving, silhouetted against the moonlight. "No – not yet."

"Not yet?" The question came out sharply, and I was aware of the tone in my voice. "I'm sorry, is there something that we're waiting for?" My hand traveled to the sword at my waist, wondering what I'd gotten myself into, if I would need to use it.

Dempsey turned, eyes scanning the edge of the forest. "We're waiting for Tad," he replied firmly.

For the first time, I began to wonder if the dog was real or if it was all a ploy by the charismatic man I met in the woods. I urged my voice not to betray me as I lifted my head high with false confidence.

"This is ridiculous. I'm going back. Surely you can find your own way once your dog returns." The words came out cold. He wouldn't be able to find his way out of the forest, I was his lifeline. The forest was easy enough to navigate in the daylight, but once the sun set, trees blended into each other while the faeries played tricks on unsuspecting passersby. I grew up hearing stories of invaders who went mad trying to cross as the forest protected our clan.

Dempsey's hand clasped my wrist with a flash of copper, his rings grabbing the little moonlight that streamed down through the trees. Despite the intensity of his grab, it was loose – I would be able to wrench my arm free if I chose. I could run. My body froze as my mind failed to make a decision. I looked into Dempsey's face, shocked and confused, uncertain at what was happening.

I was lost for a second in them. Those brown eyes held a warmth inside of them; his eyes felt like comfort. Callan's eyes were like chips of ice; there were never any emotions behind them. They were a fortress, hard and unforgiving. Dempsey's brown ones, on the other hand, made my soul quiver.

I glanced over his whole face, taking in the rest of the picture, trying to decide if I should trust him, if I should stay. His face didn't reflect what I was expecting; it was filled with worry and panic, betraying his cool tone.

A howl rang out, echoing across the forest.

"Do you know what today is?" His voice was low, barely more than a whisper.

"Beltane," I breathed, all bravado leaving my body.

"Right. Today is Beltane. In case they forgot to teach you anything in the Forest Clan, Beltane just so happens to be when the door between our world and the faerie world is the weakest."

"So?" And even as I asked the question, I feared the answer. This thing I'd walked into was bigger than me.

"So my wolfhound is currently patrolling your woods on one of the few nights of the year where we can be touched by the sprites, nymphs, and *other* creatures. *So*, I would bet that it is not, in fact, a wolf howling right now, but a faoladh, the very thing that wolfhounds are bred to hunt."

My mouth went dry. The faoladhs were fabled wolves, ancient and unpredictable. In the tales of the fae, they took the role of a guardian, appearing to warriors on a journey. But like all creatures not from our earth, they were dangerous, able to leave behind that small semblance of humanity and yield to their animalistic side.

"Do you think it'll attack?" Faoladhs were practically extinct in our realm, but long ago, they were feared by the clans, their bloodlust able to kill entire bands of warriors, poaching children from villages, stealing away women.

In their renaissance, wolfhounds had been in high demand, one of the few forms of protection we had. With the decline of the faoladh, the clans stopped seeing the use in the high-strung dogs, with few breeders existing.

"If you want to take into account Beltane, the wedding that is taunting them, drawing them forth with the sweet music, I would stake my life on it." Dempsey scoffed. "I don't know how your clan thought a wedding today was a good idea."

I bristled. In the old stories, music had been a draw to the faoladhs, attracting them like flies to honey. Dempsey was right, it was a foolish assumption for my parents to have made – but faoladh hadn't been seen in years.

Dempsey released my wrist, but wasn't finished with his lecture. "You can continue to walk into the forest, at night, in the dark, alone," I winced at every description of how idiotic my actions were, "or we can wait for my wolfhound to come and find us, and we go home then."

"Your choice, of course," Dempsey added.

I swallowed my bruised pride. "I can wait," I muttered.

And so we did. I studied Dempsey while we sat, backs against a tree, the trunk offering some small form of protection.

Copper rings shimmered, and I wondered what he thought of the bogs, if they were really as treacherous as Callan believed them to be. My mind wandered, looking at his strong hands, lean fingers. No evidence of a promise ring or a marriage band.

I cursed the second the thought ran through my head. *What would Callan think if he knew you were out here? No matter what he would think, what would he say?* That was one conversation I had no intention of having.

Tired. I was tired of the fighting. There wasn't enough energy to keep struggling against Callan, not enough fight to keep me afloat in the relationship.

Tonight, journeying into the forest with Dempsey, was the first time I felt anticipation in months. That probably had something to do with him, the way he spoke to me, the way he looked, and maybe it was wrong, but something about it felt like my last chance at freedom. Marriage would be on Callan's mind after today, and we were well above the age needed to marry. I didn't know if I could put it off much longer, my excuses growing feebler.

"So what was a pretty girl like you doing out here while there was a feast and dancing going on?" Dempsey decided to break the silence.

"I was hoping to be alone," I said, revealing the truth in more ways than one.

"Sorry for ruining your night." His hand dove into his pocket, pulling out a silver container.

"Is that a flask?" I asked.

"Whiskey," Dempsey nodded. "You look like you need it."

I laughed, not being able to argue with him. The swig from the flask tasted like oak and amber, licking my throat. I passed the flask back to him.

"I don't need to keep my wits about me for the faoladh?" I challenged.

Dempsey turned to me, grinning. His eyes studied me, hesitating on my face, my lips. I blushed, trying not to notice.

"You don't think I could protect you?" Dempsey asked, his voice amused but unassuming, like he wouldn't if I asked him not to. That wasn't the problem.

The problem was the way he said the word 'you', his mouth

worshipping the word, making it some holy thing he held in high esteem.

A breath caught in my chest. Looking the way he did, with that body, I was more than certain that he could, but he didn't need to know that. There the invisible line was again, both of us dancing around it.

I slid the dagger out from the sheath in my dress, the action somehow sultrier than expected. His eyes followed the movement, darting across the low neckline of my dress. The silver dagger twirled in my hand, the point looking like a sewing needle.

"I can protect myself."

His hand reached, skimming over my hip, my waist, tugging on the leather holster slung there. "Might want to use something a bit larger if you're going to take down a wolf."

Right.

I tried not to think about how close his face was to mine; the fact that his lips were mere breaths away. Part of me wondered if he was even real, if this was some elaborate fae plot to steal me away. Was it kidnapping if I went willingly?

"I know you can protect yourself. But I could protect you, too." All at once, his hands were gone from my waist, the skin feeling cold without him. "Tad's here."

The forest looked the same, undisturbed from the moment we sat down. I scanned the area, straining to see the giant dog Dempsey described as he began to stand. Bushes rustled, giving away the dog's location.

Dempsey kneeled, his arms open wide. A large, shaggy, grey dog bounded up to him, his size almost large enough to knock Dempsey over. Tad lifted his paws up excitedly, his tail beating hard from side to side. Dempsey tousled his ears, murmuring to the dog.

"My little Tadpole, where have you been? You mustn't run off like that. Do you understand?" Dempsey lifted the dog's chin, looking the dog in the eyes. I wasn't sure what was funnier, the warrior before me scolding the dog like it was a child, or the animal looking guilty.

Tad swung his head, looking at me. With a single bound, he was hovering above me and showering me with licks.

"Ferocious hunting dog you have here." I giggled as Tad began to sniff my ears.

"We're working on it," said Dempsey, clearly exasperated.

"Should we head back now?" I asked, standing up.

"We better, before it gets too late. I'm sure there's going to be someone looking for you, especially looking like that." His eyes flicked up and down my body.

If he only knew. I started on the path back to the village, too nervous to reply, unwilling to untangle the situation growing more complicated before me.

Dempsey and Tad kept pace, undeterred by the uneven forest floor unfamiliar to them. I fiddled with my rings, desperately wanting to say something, torn between the truth and the crooked grins that pierced my soul. My stomach deadened at the thought of what I wanted from him, what could happen if there was no engagement, the thoughts and feelings Callan never elicited from me.

The braided ring felt cold on my finger, a reminder of the relationship I was thrown into and the fiancé I never asked for. Anger swelled, frustration at the love I was trapped in without the chance to escape. There would never be a relationship with this man from the Clan Amongst the Rivers. There was never a chance for us to begin with.

"Stop," Dempsey commanded.

My body reacted to the authority in his voice, listening without thinking. It was evidence of that birthright he spoke about earlier. No mere warrior gave orders like that.

A low growl came from Tad, his grey hackles raised, teeth bared.

The faoladh found us.

In one quick motion, Dempsey stood in front of me, using one arm to keep me hidden behind him. He acted without thinking, and I knew he was standing between myself and death unarmed.

Trembling, I pulled the sword out of its sheath, wrapping it in Dempsey's hand. He would use it better than me. I grabbed his knife, the one I took from him during our encounter at the beginning of the woods. Throwing knives wasn't a skill of mine by any means, but I wouldn't be throwing this one at a target. The knife would be used to slice the faoladh's throat if Dempsey and Tad failed in their tasks. It was the last line of defense.

I wasn't quite sure how I got to that realization – that Dempsey and Tad would lay their lives down for me, a mere stranger they had met only hours before.

The wolf began to creep out of the ferns it had been lurking in, golden eyes piercing the darkness. It almost looked like a common wolf, so similar to the animals that typically roamed this forest. The snout was elongated, with teeth hanging snaggletooth over his lips. The faoladh was almost the size of Tad, with a larger torso, almost too big to be a product of nature. I noted the ribcage that protruded beneath his pelt, proving this faoladh was half-starved. From the look in its eyes, I bet that it had lost every essence of humanity it might have once had.

"If Tad goes down, you have to *run*. Get out of the forest and don't stop until you're in the village. I doubt the wolf will follow you to a crowd of people, but when it's just you and me out here… I won't be enough to stop him." Dempsey spoke urgently, each word carefully chosen.

"Okay." My words came out in a half-whisper.

"And don't drop the knife." Dempsey paused in between each word, stressing how vital this piece of advice was.

"Wouldn't dream of it," I answered breathlessly.

For a second, time stood still. We held the faoladh's gaze,

each of us unwilling to move. Sweat gathered on my palms, nerves fighting to get out. The ferns swayed gently in the wake of the wolf, betraying his gathering haunches.

Tad lunged forward, intercepting the faoladh mid-air.

The dog and wolf clashed, jaws open and locked. Despite his size, Tad was quick when they hit the ground, nipping at the wolf's hind legs and reversing to bite the soft underbelly before the creature could realize what was happening.

Whatever advantage Tad gained through his speed did nothing to deter the madness that came with the wolf's starvation. The hunger that rolled in its belly pushed it to the edge, fueling a desire for dangerous risks. It didn't recognize the threat of the wolfhound and a fully trained warrior standing in front of it; they were a welcome challenge in the face of dinner tonight.

"Do something," I hissed. Dempsey was still standing before me, one arm protectively extended around my body. He was just watching his dog get mauled by the rabid animal.

Anger rose inside me.

He gave a quick shake of his head. "This is everything he's been trained for. It's just as much a test for him. I'll step in but right now he doesn't need it."

I winced as the wolf's hind legs scrabbled against Tad's underbelly, scratching the soft skin there. Somewhere in the fight, blood began to flow. The two grey creatures were so evenly matched, intertwining at such a rapid pace, I couldn't tell where it came from.

A piercing yelp reverberated through the air. *Tad. It most definitely came from Tad.*

The faoladh broke free from Tad's grip and dove for Dempsey and me. Still only using one hand, Dempsey delivered a clean strike upward, aiming for the animal's throat. The wolf flinched back, almost in time, but Dempsey's sword sliced a wound across its face. Blood welled in one eye, staining the dusty fur.

Tad pounced on the wolf, his jaws locking around its neck. The wolf let out a whimper of defeat as its legs buckled underneath it, lowering its body to the ground before us.

"Tad, release," Dempsey ordered the dog.

Tad let go of the wolf's scruff but continued to stand guard over the dying creature. The wolfhound panted and grinned, tongue lolling out to the side, proud of his catch.

"The knife, please." Dempsey held out his hand, referring to the one in my clutches. I understood what he meant, without needing him to explain.

I placed the hilt in his hand, noticing how the leather length fit perfectly in his palm. The knife was custom work, crafted for Dempsey's exact requirements.

He knelt before the wolf, whispering silently before it. The knife glided into the faoladh's body, somewhere between his sternum and ribs. The wolf let out a low howl, one last cry to the forest. It was a hunter's blow, designed to put the animal out of its misery – an act of grace. He wiped the blood off his blade using the corner of his tunic and sheathed his weapon.

Wordlessly, Dempsey slung the animal over his shoulder, like a shepherd with a lamb. I looked at him, not understanding.

"The chieftains are going to want to hear about this," he said. Dempsey sounded tired, like this battle had stretched longer than just tonight.

"I don't understand. Faoladhs are magical, from the Otherworld. Why would this one attack us? He was clearly half starved."

"In the middle of spring?" Dempsey didn't look convinced. "Why? Why would an animal be half-starved when the prey is fat, and winter is long behind us?"

I turned his question over in my mind. "I couldn't tell you."

We started on the path back to the village, Tad trailing behind us with a slight limp. Reluctantly, I recognized that Dempsey was right. The eyes of the wolf and its protruding ribcage was evidence that it was starving, wasting away in a forest full of food. Any animal without a sickness should be healthy right now. The boar roasting over the spit at the wedding was evidence of that.

It was almost perverse, the idea that this encounter in the woods occurred while the rest of the clans were celebrating, blissfully unaware. Something about the traumatic event was bonding, it felt like I knew Dempsey on an almost intimate level. I never found this sort of easy friendship with anyone inside my own clan.

It was different for Dempsey, I supposed. He was funny, confident. He probably had friends at his home, maybe even a girl. He was everything my own life could have been but wasn't. A walking reminder of what freedom could do.

"Alright," Dempsey announced, "You have to tell me what's running through your head. You can't simply have a near-death experience and remain silent. It'll eat you alive."

It was almost as if he'd heard my thoughts, loud and clear.

"It's almost funny that we were nearly killed while everyone is drunk and dancing," I admitted, revealing the dark humor that was running through my mind.

"Nearly killed? I would like to think Tad and I are a bit more skilled than that."

I raised an eyebrow at him.

"Right, the dog's just walking with a limp because you executed flawlessly." My voice dripped with sarcasm.

"There isn't a scratch on your skin. That's all that matters to me." His gaze dragged over me as I suddenly became aware of my exposed collarbones.

I returned my attention to the path before us, the grasses that hung over the walkway, scratching lightly at my ankles. An owl hooted in the background. Thoughts of Dempsey seared in my mind.

"Willa."

"What?" asked Dempsey.

"My name is Willa. I think you've earned my name by now, no scratches and all." It seemed incomplete, for him to walk away tonight not knowing my name. I told him because I was afraid if I didn't, tomorrow I might wake up and think this all a dream.

"Willa," he repeated, savoring every sound. I nodded in response.

"Thank you – for saving me." I couldn't help but add, "Even if you were the one who dragged me into the forest to begin with." There was something about revealing my identity that made me surprisingly shy. I could no longer hide under the darkened archways of the forest and assume this out-of-body confidence that I found.

He glanced over at me, perhaps shocked by my sudden formality. "Tell me more. About you, your life."

And so I told him, every single piece of it. My horses, my family, my gift; all of it came pouring out as we walked through the canopied forest path. I stopped when I was explaining my rings, realizing I would have to explain the engagement band.

I twisted the ring, feeling it tighten and slide across my skin. "I'm engaged. Arranged since I was four."

He asked the question that gutted me ever so gently, not knowing he was hurting my heart by doing so. "Do you love him?"

If possible, the stars in the sky flickered at the darkness of his question – because that's what I associated with love. Darkness, emptiness. The dimming of light and laughter. My eyes surveyed Dempsey, his honest face, his casual ease. My body narrowed to the spark of connection that threaded between us.

"No," I said, admitting to the first person ever, that this marriage was something I didn't want. "I don't think I ever will."

"I see," he said.

Do you see me, standing here, on the edge of breaking? Do you see my soul dying? No one else does.

"Why not your sister?"

"What?" I asked, jerked abruptly from my thoughts.

"Why didn't they engage Fiadh instead of you? She's the older of you two, right?"

I swallowed hard, wondering how to explain it all to him. "Fiadh... Fiadh isn't like me. She's special. She's the one our parents have bookmarked for leadership. So why not marry the quiet daughter off, to a boy from a clan that no longer exists, so she can be safe and happy within her clan forever?" I didn't dare look into Dempsey's eyes; I didn't know what I would find there. "Fiadh needed to be saved for someone more – someone she could rule with."

The silence between us was deafening. There was something about the quiet that provoked the questions within me, and I couldn't help but want to gauge his reaction. I expected him to see me as broken, but his face didn't say. No – it was filled with some expression I couldn't read.

"I think they all might have misjudged you," he said quietly.

I didn't dare ask him what he meant by that, the words whispered that I might be worthy of something more.

"We're here."

The camp came into view. The bonfire still burned bright, with miniature dancing shadows circling around it. A pit in my stomach rose and fell as our outing had come to an end. *Would this be goodbye forever?* It might be better that way.

One last night of freedom before being locked in a castle where no key existed to let me out. I ruffled Tad's fur, knowing the moment had come.

"Join me for a drink."

I looked at him, surprised. Anxiety spiked within me at the thought of having a drink with him under the watchful eyes of my parents and Callan. Desire almost won the inner battle, my soul chanting for just a few more minutes of freedom. But that's all Dempsey was. An escape from reality.

I opened my mouth to tell him that no, I couldn't, that it was a bad idea, when footsteps sounded in the distance. I turned to Callan strutting towards us.

Shit. I grimaced.

"Willow! Where have you been? I've been looking all over for you." Callan called out, the few people lingering on the outskirts of camp stopping to turn and look at us.

So much for coming back unnoticed.

I took a deep breath. "We were looking for the dog in the woods. He strayed away from camp at the beginning of the feast." I quickly noticed that Callan was no longer listening to me.

Dempsey and Callan were eyeing each other, chests puffed out. Tad let out a low, warning growl.

"I'm sorry, and who are you?" asked Callan, taking in the blood and dead wolf around Dempsey's shoulders.

"My name is Dempsey. Son of Barra, heir to the Clan Amongst the Rivers." His birthright that he so vaguely referred to earlier, laid bare. The voice he used resembled something like the commands he gave in the forest, ringing with authority. Dempsey wanted Callan to know who he was, the power he held. He didn't care to ask Callan who *he* was, setting the power dynamic between the two.

"I see. And the dead animal hanging around your neck? There's plenty of food at the feast, and we don't eat wolves here." The coldness in Callan's voice echoed in my ears.

"The wolf attacked us. No need to worry, I took care of it. Your territory should be secure."

Callan furrowed his brow at this piece of information. "I'll let the next patrol know. If you will excuse us, I owe my fiancé a dance. Willow?" Callan asked smoothly, holding out his hand expectantly.

I began to reach out but was stopped by Dempsey's voice.

"Willa. I was under the impression her name was Willa." His words were pure arrogance, saying it as a statement, not a question. I held my breath as my eyes flicked between the two.

"It... It is." Callan stumbled over his words. The corner of my mouth twitched as I tried to suppress a smile.

Dempsey's eyes surveyed Callan with disdain.

"Good. Tad, come." Dempsey turned on his heel and strode towards the sea of makeshift tents in the distance, his grey wolfhound following along at his heels.

I could have sworn I heard thunder echo in the distance as he walked away.

CHAPTER FIVE

Willa and Dempsey

I watched Dempsey's fading figure as Callan and I stood there, standing in the party's shadows. Laughter and yells rang as the wedding feast grew wilder in the night.

A stare bore into me as Callan kept his eyes trained on my figure, marking the expression on my face. He was unreadable and I didn't want to know what he was thinking. A part of me wanted to walk away now, leave all this behind me as if it never happened and Callan never found out.

I supposed this night would only fester, so better air out the wound now.

Where to start? I could begin with why I entered the clearing, explain the anxiety, expose the lies I was hiding from him this morning. There was really no explanation why I trusted Dempsey and decided to walk in the forest with a complete stranger on the premise of finding his dog. There was no escaping the truth, no matter how I framed the night's events.

My thoughts were drowning me, any feelings of hope or happiness gone. After this incident, I was sure Callan would never let me out of his sight. I shivered, cold despite the night's warm summer air.

It was Callan who made the first move.

"Were you planning to tell me anything about the stranger you went into the woods with?" The accusation stung like a slap on the cheek. It was fair, but I grew determined not to flinch from the truth.

"His name is Dempsey," I said stubbornly.

"I know that." Callan was irritated, pinching the bridge of his nose, no longer making eye contact with me.

"I went to the meadow that touches the woods alone. I needed some air from this *event*," I motioned to the party around us, "and he found me there. There was no way he could have found the dog on his own, so I agreed to help." It was true, to a degree.

"Yes, well, I'm sure *the dog* could be very motivating." Callan rolled his eyes. "Have you stopped to even consider the danger of the little stunt you just pulled?"

My jaw clenched. "They protected me while we were out there." At this, Callan finally looked me in the eyes again.

"And what could have possibly motivated him to do that?" Callan's voice was scathing.

"That wolf was a *faoladh*. That's why the wolfhound got sucked into the woods in the first place. Dempsey and Tad both protected me, so you might try and sound a little grateful." As much as I didn't want Callan, he wanted me. I wasn't sure if it was the power I had, or who my family was, but Callan's desire was unmistakable. I knew for damn sure it wasn't because of myself.

Callan snorted.

"Willa, if you fucked him, just tell me. I won't even be that upset." His tone was bored, as if he no longer held any interest in the conversation. It was a strategy in the game he played, the sound covering the lie. We both knew where our minds had wandered.

"This isn't Ronan," I cautioned.

Callan's nostrils flared at the mention of the warrior I had an affair with the year we turned twenty. That year I slipped off my engagement ring, tucked it in the back corner of my room, and pretended like it didn't exist.

I spent the year trying to catch up for lost time, for the life I was never allowed to have. My parents had dismissed it as a harmless rebellion, but Callan saw it for what it was. My attempt at revolution.

By the end of the summer, I convinced Ronan to run away with me. The horses were saddled, food was stored, we had even plotted the area where we would build our home. The morning we planned to leave, a patrol of guards was there, accompanied by my parents, Callan, and Bowen. Fiadh sold me out, claiming she was afraid I would ruin my life.

Ironic, looking at the ruin staying caused me.

"Really? I saw the way he looked at you." Callan's eyes devoured me, and I could tell he was wishing he could hide me away. The girl in the sparkling emerald dress, a pretty jewel to be coveted.

"I couldn't imagine, why I might be so interested in someone who doesn't *suffocate* me!" I was screaming at this point, not caring who might see or hear.

"There it is. You see Willa, I want to believe you, and then you tell me shit like that."

Tears formed at the corner of my eyes, but I couldn't tell if they were from anger or my laughter at the maze of Callan's logic. *Was what I felt for Dempsey in the short amount of time I knew him that obvious?* It wasn't that Callan wasn't attractive – he was. I just couldn't *breathe* around him, couldn't get comfortable, not in conversation or physically.

"I didn't *fuck* him," I seethed. At this point, I wished I had if I was going to have this fight with Callan anyways. "This conversation is over. I have my sister's wedding to attend."

Without a glance behind, I left Callan standing there as I attempted to rejoin the party. I only made it a few steps before

Callan was at my side again, turning me around with a hand on my shoulder. His face was cold as he began to speak.

"We are not doing this. You will not make a scene. We will walk into that reception together and you will look happy, dammit."

I hated this. How did we get here? Alcohol rolled off Callan's breath, an explanation that was only a part of why he was acting like this. Overbearing, always, but controlling was a new level for him. An apology would be at the tip of his lips by tomorrow morning.

My will became iron, forcing myself to let this go, to not let it bother me. Determination was the only thing preventing me from falling into the pit of despair that was threatening to consume me. I looked at his handsome face and plastered a pleasant look onto my features.

"Of course. I'm sorry that my actions were so upsetting tonight." My words were tight, my tone cordial, thinly masking the building fury underneath my skin. Knowing these words were a lie to get me through the evening was the only thing stopping me from screaming right now.

Callan's face softened.

"It's okay, Willa. Gods, I hate when we're like this. I should work on my temper." He ran his fingers through his hair, his anger dissipating into the air.

My stomach churned with distaste. I pushed that feeling down, locking it away. This was my future. I needed to learn how to deal with it.

"Come on. Let's go." Callan outstretched his hand, and I took it like I was expected.

Dempsey

I stormed away from the couple who were talking amongst themselves. I was furious. In the few words I exchanged with Willa's fiancé, Callan was arrogant and calculated. The sense of entitlement that must come with being betrothed to the heir of the Forest Clan. A dull ache came from my hands, fists clenched with anger. One by one, I unfurled my fingers.

I don't understand how this girl caused such a reaction.

That was a lie. I knew why. The girl I walked away from was the only person I'd met within the last year who had managed to be a complex human being. She even liked Tad, something difficult to say with a dog who had drool hanging out his mouth. Some part of me thought she felt the connection too. There was no other excuse for her willing trust that could have easily led to danger with any other man, especially when she looked like that.

And gods, she looked breathtaking.

The wolf shifted off my shoulders and I began to shovel dirt over the top of it, a shallow grave in case the chieftains needed to see it. I walked over to the tent where I was staying, a white crest in the midst of a sea. Grabbing the long piece of rope sticking out of my bag along with a leather collar, I slipped it over Tad's neck, and tied the rope between a stake in the ground and a hook on his collar.

The forest of unfamiliar scents revealed Tad's weakness for adventure; I didn't think I would be able to convince Willa to follow me into the forest for a scouting expedition for a second time that night. With Tad securely tied, checking and double-checking my knots as the dog panted into my face, I set out to return to the wedding reception where I would be expected.

Gods, how far away the laughter and dancing seemed. In my

absence, the attendees had grown increasingly drunk, evidenced by the grins plastered on their faces and the wobbling steps they took. The wild boar was removed from the fire, and large flames grew in its absence.

Barra, my father, played drinking games with his friends, roaring with laughter. The kegs were flowing and I grabbed a tankard, knowing I would need it to get through the rest of the night. The beer was warm, and smelt stale, but I downed it nonetheless.

Following the beeline to my clanmates, I greeted the few that noticed my absence. I headed towards a warrior with broad shoulders and his curly black hair pulled back in a bun.

"Felix," I called out.

He turned around and promptly crushed me in a hug. The smell of whiskey rolled off of him.

"Dempsey, mate, where've you been?" he asked, his words running together. I tried to suppress a smile, knowing Felix was drunk, his normally formal speech slipping.

"Long story involving Tad running off and finding a faoladh in the woods."

Felix's eyes widened. "Shit. Little man knows how to find trouble." Felix tipped his glass to the nonexistent dog.

I snorted. "If you want to call a dog that's the same size as a small pony 'little'."

"Where's the faoladh?" asked Felix.

"You know; I didn't think it was appropriate to bring a dead wolf to the party. Thought it might put a damper on things." At this, Felix looked vaguely disappointed. "I dug a shallow grave for it outside camp; I'll have to speak to the clan leaders about it tomorrow."

Silence fell between us as we sipped our drinks. A man danced nearby, catching Felix's eye. I wanted to ask the questions that had bothered me since meeting Willa. Felix would know the answers to them, he always did.

Felix's parents were on the Council of Leaders in our clan; although they died when we were both young, the council always took a special interest in Felix. It was a soft spot for all of them, the little boy that grew up to look so much like his parents. I always thought it was guilt, knowing that Felix lacked parents due to their decisions, but it let him in on some very choice conversations.

There were only a few years between us, but I often felt like the younger brother. Considering I had no siblings, the two of us made a perfect pair.

A new tune carried across the bonfire and a wave of dancers began a slow, sweeping dance, skirts flaring as women were lifted into the air. My eyes landed on Willa as she twirled around the fire, a flash of emerald, the light catching her hair. My lip curled as I noted her dancing partner, Callan, as promised.

"The girl in the green dress, do you know anything about her?" I knew *who* she was, of course. The daughter of a chieftain with the gift of a seer is a piece of news in the clans.

The fact that she spent the majority of the night not wanting to tell me who she was, interested me. And her face, the sadness behind her eyes, interested me as well. It was obvious she was unhappy; you could hear it in her voice. But why would a girl who should have everything sound like there was nothing for her?

Felix noted the girl I was speaking about with a nod.

"This one seems to be very much taken given that very tall man holding her like *that*. What happened to the girls pining for you inside our own clan?" Felix replied.

I shot him a look, unhappy with his response. Felix sighed. "I'm not an oracle, brother. I'm going to need a little more than that. Name, parents, clan?"

"Her name is Willa. She's from the Forest Clan, and I believe her parents are Viktor and Brigid." I motioned towards the two seated at the head of the feasting table.

"Shit. You know how to pick them, but it sounds like you might know more than I do about this one." Felix saw the expression and my face and knew this answer wasn't enough. "I think, that she was engaged from a young age. I know that when we were discussing proposals with the Forest Clan, her name didn't come up once."

I took a long sip of my drink.

"Now him, on the other hand, I do know."

I raised my eyebrows, surprised. "The guy she's with?" I asked. Curiosity reared its head at the knowledge that he was important enough to be on Felix's radar.

"That's Callan. Son of Bowen, from Clan o' Cliffs – or I guess the Forest now. I've seen him at a few council meetings, but the man is so pretentious he wouldn't give me a second look. His loss, because I am an excellent friend." Felix said this last point with a jab of his whiskey for emphasis, managing to spill half onto the grass.

Felix was referring to the interclan meetings that occurred once a season. It was an initiative started after the Sectarians invaded the continent, and was meant to unify strategy and dispel any fighting between them all. Theoretically, they were attempting to gather strength from within when the inevitable attack came from the outside. For almost twenty years, the strategy worked.

"I'm sure a friend is all you want from him," I snorted.

"You wound me." Felix clutched his chest for emphasis. "Why do you care though?"

Felix had a way of aiming the most pointed of questions when a person was least expecting it. He had the most calculating mind in the Clan Amongst the Rivers, all perfectly hidden underneath a warrior's façade.

"The girl, Willa, helped me find Tad. I was so graciously introduced to her fiancé when we returned, and I don't think he appreciated our midnight jaunt."

"Bet he wouldn't, not with the way you're looking at her now."

I rolled my eyes but didn't bother protesting at what was the truth. The glass in my hand was suddenly empty, and I found myself wishing for more. Something to help forget her.

As if he could read my mind, Felix provided a solution. "Shall we join the dance?" A wicked smile grew on his face.

Clan elders forced us both to go through dancing lessons as young children, stressing that the ability to find marriage was directly correlated to one's abilities on the dance floor. This adage held little weight as we grew up, but the skill remained. A dance with either of us left girls swooning, and a waltz was enough to make a maiden blush. It was the way we lured people into our beds when we were teenagers, leaving a string of broken hearts the next morning.

The men around the bonfire were now leading the women through a flying dance, full of hops and lifts into the air, switching off partners as the women spun counter clockwise. The alternating circle of men took their partners by their hand with another tightly clasped around their waist, leading them through the footwork. We waited for a break in the music. As the melody began to swell from the minstrels, we made our entrance.

I bowed to the lady opposite me as she gave me a small smile. I took a large step to end with my feet next to hers, taking care not to tread on her toes. The tension was tight in our arms, creating the rope which both of us spun upon. She hopped into the air as I lifted her. Looking up at her dark curly hair, all else fell away except for the flying girl before me. Her face was pure joy while sweat beaded at her temples.

Normally, this would be enough for me to chase her for the rest of the night, but the ghost of Willa haunted me. I extended my arm, flinging her as she pirouetted her body, switching partners. This pattern repeated as I began to relax, finally enjoying myself. The music increased in intensity as I began to move my feet quicker, throw more life into the air, spin the women more ferociously.

Dancing was an art form to the clans. It was done at all holidays and feasts, after birth, before battles to celebrate the gift of life and death nature had gifted us. Some dances were light and airy, innocent and pure, other could be hedonistic and sultry. Some dances required strict pairing, chain dancing allowing anyone to join, and certain dances simply needed a partner, it didn't matter who.

A whirl of emerald caught my eye from across the bonfire. Willa was still dancing, and she looked *alive*. Gods, I felt like a teenager again, suffering from tunnel vision, unable to rid her from my thoughts. If we parted directly after the forest, I could have done that. Goodbyes would have been said and it would have ended there. Something on the way back opened between us, honesty baring our souls, and I suspected she felt it too.

Another change in the dance occurred, and it was Willa that had her hand on my shoulder, my hands wrapped around her waist. Cool composure settled upon me, and it was as if I was in another world when I began to speak.

"Couldn't keep away?" I saw the shock in her eyes as I asked my audacious question. Sometimes I wondered where I got the nerve to say half the idiotic things that came out of my mouth.

The corner of her mouth twitched and began to curl upwards.

"I think you're the one that followed me into the dancing circle." She was bold. Her assumption wrong – or maybe it was right. She might have been the reason I followed Felix out here tonight. Shock settled in as I realized the girl before me might know me better than I thought.

Willa glanced over her shoulder as I twirled her in the firelight. I could only guess that she was looking for her prick fiancé.

"What are you doing tomorrow morning?" The question

popped out of my mouth unchecked. I studied Willa's face, waiting for the answer.

"We have the bridal send off after breakfast." Willa looked nervous, but she continued. "Why?" The question hung in the air between us.

I gazed down at her. "Could I say goodbye tomorrow?" I answered honestly. If this was any other girl, I would have punched myself for saying it, but there was something about her.

I wasn't sure if Willa felt the same thing I was feeling, and I was well aware she had a fiancé, but what was the harm? I was sure in another life we might have found each other differently. For now, I would accept dancing with her this last time.

Willa

I was unsure how I spoke to Dempsey at all while dancing. My stomach was in knots as I checked over my shoulder for Callan's watchful eye. I knew that I should excuse myself from the dance, grab a glass of water, but I had the rest of my life to be miserably tied to Callan. What would a night of happiness harm?

"Could I say goodbye tomorrow?"

And just like that, I shattered down to earth. A dance tonight was one thing, but seeing each other tomorrow was another. The heat from the fire seemed to get hotter, just so the flames could watch me sweat underneath Dempsey's eyes.

Before an answer could be said, the music changed, signaling a switch in dance partners. Words left my mind as Dempsey answered for me.

"I'll meet you in the meadow at dawn."

A different set of hands grabbed my waist and repeated the steps I took just a few moments earlier. I made small talk with this man from the Mountain Clan, speaking of blessings and unions.

The marriage today proved to be a useful tool in brokering peace. There hadn't been this large a gathering between all the clans in a long time, much less one where with alcohol present no fights breaking out. Things were changing for the clans, and everyone was aware of it. Just like spring was becoming summer, the path of our entire future was changing with the season. Hope and promise lingered in the air.

Another switch of dance partners occurred as the musicians returned to the bridge in their song. This partner was mostly silent, and I didn't mind it. Although I wasn't shy, I was quiet. I never felt the need to fill the air with answers, instead always being comfortable in the silence that hung between two people. Most people found it unbearable to sit with their thoughts, but I was always swimming in mine.

Sometimes my mind was my best friend and worst enemy all at once. I preferred the days when it was my friend.

Again, a partner switch and the man twirled me out of his arms counterclockwise and another set of hands caught me. I swallowed as I noticed that I came full circle in the dancing pit, joining with Callan once again. A kernel of resolve bloomed inside of me. I couldn't live like this anymore. I wouldn't. There were only two ways I could go on this path, and one was no longer an option. The warrior before me may fight on a battlefield, but I was fighting for my life, even if it was to live with just a little bit of freedom.

"I saw you talking to the man from the forest again."

I scowled. "His name is Dempsey. Why can't you ever get anyone's name right?"

Callan looked shocked at my words. Irritation settled in his features as the music quickened. "What were you two talking about?" he pressed on.

"Gods, Callan. We were just talking. It's a dance, for gods' sakes, or would you like to tell me I can't do that either?" This outburst drew looks from the crowd as I grew louder.

"Look, I'm sorry about earlier. I let my temper get the better of me. I'm sorry I get upset when my fiancé is alone with a man who is very clearly interested in her."

Interested in me? Was it that obvious? Could he tell I was interested in Dempsey then, too?

It really was Callan just being upset at the obvious connection between Dempsey and me, something that never occurred between us. I couldn't help but note the pain in his features and disappointment in his eyes.

"It's fine. But Callan?" I waited until he was looking me in the eyes. "Never speak to me that way again."

I held my head high as I drew the line that got erased so long ago, even if it wouldn't be the last battle we faced. Demons were difficult to get away from with lovers. There was a glimmering hope, however, that the battles might get easier from here.

The song came to a close as we finished speaking, the final bridge concluding the melody. I walked to my sister and her new husband as they greeted guests and accepted gifts. I hadn't seen them since Sai carried off my sister after their ceremony. Frankly, I was surprised they weren't in a marriage bed by now.

Their union yielded many riches; swords and jewelry alike sprinkled the table at which they sat. The music and jewels swirled around the couple, the two of them oblivious to it all, noting only each other amidst the chaos of the party.

"Am I interrupting?" I wondered if I walked into a moment

that should be left alone. Fiadh was practically sitting in Sai's lap and lazy smiles were on both their faces.

"Not at all," Sai answered graciously.

"We were just discussing our life in the Mountain Clan. You need to come and visit us. Promise me, right now," Fiadh demanded.

I laughed at my sister's mercurial nature. "It would be my pleasure. Only not in the winter. I hear all you eat is icicles."

Fiadh's serene face turned into one of worry as she turned to Sai.

"A child's fairy tale, I'll have you know," scolded Sai. "It's better than eating moss and bark like I hear some people do." He gave Fiadh a pointed look.

"We do not!" Outrage echoed in Fiadh's voice, although anyone could tell the married couple were simply teasing each other. "Sometimes certain flowers, but they're edible."

"Willa, do you need anything? A glass of wine or perhaps a few flowers to whet your appetite?" Sai looked at me curiously.

I shifted the weight on my feet. "Actually, do you know where my father is? I've been meaning to talk to him but I can't seem to find him."

We needed to discuss the faoladh and what it meant before the night grew any longer and I had another glass to drink. Dealing with clan business was also another way of avoiding certain men out on the dance floor.

Sai pointed behind me and I turned to see my father walking hand in hand with my mother towards a table. I thanked Sai and Fiadh, and went to join my parents.

"Willa," my father said with a nod, "To what do we owe your presence? Shouldn't you be dancing or drinking or whatever your peers are doing?"

Eyes sparkling, Viktor took a sip of his drink. The clan leader normally had a somber yet intimidating atmosphere to him, but tonight lifted everyone's spirits.

Viktor wore his crown well. The old warrior was fierce in his younger years, earning his name on the battlefield. As he aged and fell into the chieftain position in his clan, he became more sage, although his daughters always showed his soft spot. My father was our polar opposite. He had near black eyes with a black beard and hair to match. Contrary to his daughters' relatively plain hands, his own held stacks of rings upon his fingers, boasting his triumphs of war over the ears, and the struggles that he bore for us.

Some clan elders liked to say that once upon a time, when my father was young, his hair was the lightest of brown. His hair turned dark with age, tarnishing with the pain he endured so his girls could beam as bright as the sun. I wasn't sure if this was true, but some part of my heart believed in the paternal love.

I cleared my throat, preparing my words. The crackle of the fire filled the silence and my parents looked at me expectantly. I dove into the story of how I was helping Dempsey search for Tad, and how we came upon the faoladh.

Viktor tugged on his beard thoughtfully while I braced for my parents' response.

"Gods above," was all my mother could say. "Are you alright? How did you come back to camp and only now just tell us?" A wave of concern washed over my mother's features as she grabbed my hand.

"I'm sorry," I stammered, "and you're completely right. I should have come to you first thing."

What was I thinking? Dancing instead of telling my parents of the immediate danger to the clan? What if there are more out there? Waves of guilt and regret hit me like an incoming tide.

"Willa, it's fine. What's done is done, no matter how quickly you were able to find us. No need to worry about it." My father dismissed my fears as if I said them aloud.

"We'll alert all scouts and warriors, let the nursemaids know to keep a closer eye on the children so they don't wander off," Brigid assured me.

"What would drive a faoladh to attack you?" Viktor sounded puzzled as he searched for an answer. "The gods must be angry if they sent one... but it didn't kill you. Perhaps a warning of sorts?"

We sat there, silently, pondering the implications.

"I want to speak with him," Viktor declared.

I cocked my head to the side, my father's statement taking me off guard. I scanned the area around the bonfire, unsure if Viktor was referring to one of his advisors passing by, perhaps Bowen.

"This man with the wolf dog. I want to discuss a few things with him." Viktor clarified his statement, but this did little to ease my mind.

"It's a wolfhound, Father. But I can find him and relay the message. Was there a certain time or place you had in mind?" I would be sure to let him know at our dawn rendezvous.

Ironic, that my father gave me the perfect alibi to meet Dempsey. Not that I was concocting an alibi, or needed one. I was unsure when I decided to go and meet Dempsey, but now that I had decided, there was no changing that choice.

"Anytime in the morning will be fine. Before the Clan Amongst the Rivers leaves to return to their home. I will be helping your sister pack her outrageous amount of luggage to travel with." He rolled his eyes.

I couldn't remember the last time I saw my father so nonchalant, but I supposed that was what the pint of beer in front of him would do to a man. My father seldom drank, citing the need to be prepared to ride into battle and make important decisions at a moment's notice, but he seemed to let his guard down tonight.

I bowed my head in response and swung my legs out from underneath the table, readying myself to leave. It had been a long night, and the bonfire was slowly dying down. Dancers lingered on the floor, the musicians slowing to the lilting melodies signaling good night. The chill of the night air started to set in, reminding the clans that summer had not yet arrived.

A hand caught my elbow. I turned to see my mother peering at me, those worried eyes still there. *Does a mother ever stop worrying about her child? Did my mother always bear that weight and emotion in her eyes?* I didn't know the answer to any of the questions that buried themselves in the corners of my mind.

"Are you *sure* you're alright?" Sometimes I could swear that my mother had her own gift of reading minds. Mother's intuition, Brigid would always say when I would ask her as a child. It was as if Brigid knew the monumental shift the occurred in my world tonight, the grating nature of Callan's love and the hope and freedom that Dempsey made me feel.

"It will all be okay, Mom, don't worry," I promised. The words registered, but I didn't know if I meant it.

I walked back to my tent, reeling from exhaustion and ready to climb into bed. The past day had been exhausting, and something in my world had shifted since this morning.

The night stars twinkled and winked at me, promising rebirth tomorrow.

I wasn't sure how tomorrow morning was going to play out, but something in my gut told me it was the right decision. My entire body, my mind and heart screamed at me to move onto this precipice and jump. I had a feeling that Dempsey might just be there to catch me.

CHAPTER SIX

Willa

The next morning came quickly, the sun painting the sky a pale pink. I hadn't been sleeping for the past hour but merely dozing, jolting awake every so often to make sure I didn't miss my meeting with Dempsey.

My stomach twisted itself into knots as I reflected upon the previous night, wondering why Dempsey really wanted to see me. The connection between us was palpable in my mind, but did he feel it too?

I twisted the rings onto my fingers, remembering the confessions that Dempsey and I made to each other walking out of the forest. Confessions of our lives, and powers. It didn't matter. Viktor had requested his presence this morning, and I would simply deliver the news.

By this afternoon, Dempsey would leave and life would return to normal. Routine would settle in.

I pulled on an extra layer of socks to fight the chill of the spring morning. Dew collected on the blades of grass just outside my tent, serving as a reminder that frost was never far away. Tempt the sprites, and they just might throw a cold spell over the forest. Beltane may have occurred, but clan elders liked to lecture that *Calleach*, the Queen of Winter, was always peeking out of her caves in the cliffs, hoping to paint the isle white once more.

The mirror in my tent reflected my unusually calm face. I never left my routine, never took chances. The sense of normalcy and routine was one I clung to, any veering path sent me into a panic. The unmapped territory that came with Dempsey should terrify me, a blank space of potential, but something in my soul soothed me and encouraged me to go. My feet obeyed these commands as I walked through the wet grass and towards the meadow, for once excited about what my future held.

Even from afar, I could make out Tad bounding across the meadow. Dempsey appeared to be throwing sticks, but Tad was refusing to retrieve them. As I got closer, I saw a stack of twigs and sticks next to him to supply Tad's fruitless endeavors.

"Not much of a hunting dog if he can't retrieve a stick," I called out. I placed my hands on my hips as I watched Tad lose track of yet another piece of wood.

"Willa. How many times do I have to tell you this? We are *working on it*. He simply needs to work on the retrieving part." Tad bounded up with a lazy grin on his face, his tongue sticking out to the side.

I knelt and gave Tad a hello as the dog pushed up against me, knocking me over, unaware of his own size.

"Sorry – Tad, get off. Big oaf. Here, go get the stick." Another piece of wood went flying, and Tad sprinted away, all interest in me forgotten. Dempsey extended his hand, offering me assistance in getting back up.

"Thanks."

"You're welcome." Dempsey looked at me. Perhaps staring was the better word for his action, his gaze unwavering.

"So, you asked to meet?" I prompted.

Dempsey cleared his throat. "Right. I did. Thanks for coming. I wasn't too sure if you would."

I was struck by his formality, and immediately I wanted to push the boundary between us, challenge him.

"Why wouldn't I?" A bold question on my part.

"A certain man with blonde hair and a small anger problem comes to mind."

I laughed. "That's a pretty accurate read of him if I've ever heard one."

"Does he normally have an anger problem with you?"

The question echoed in the clearing. I tugged at my rings while I saw Tad come to stand at Dempsey's side. I wasn't sure how to answer. *Did Dempsey hear our argument last night? Was that too personal to tell him?*

I wanted to share it with him, a chance to confide in someone. My mind wandered at the idea of him saving me from this doomed relationship. A more private part of me screamed that it was too intimate to share with a man I just met.

"I'm sorry. I shouldn't have asked that. I'm sure that you and Callan are very happy together." Dempsey answered his own question, assuming the answer from my silence.

"It's a fair question to ask," I answered, waving away the sudden awkwardness. "He wasn't exactly warm last night when the two of you met. I'm sorry for that. I think –" I paused, unsure if I should complete my thought. I looked at Dempsey, tried to read his face, but he kept it closely guarded. "I think he was intimidated by you, actually."

"By me or by seeing us together?" Dempsey finished the thought for me.

I sucked in a breath, shocked by his forwardness. "Both. Callan's never had competition here. He's always been an elite warrior. When it comes to me, he's never had any competition either. We were engaged so young, there's never really been anyone else."

Until now, my mind whispered.

Sure, there had been flings and indiscretions, on my side as well as his I suspected, but there was never a chance for anything real. There was nothing that ever felt genuine, that evoked feeling and passion and breathlessness. The feeling of being alive with someone.

"The pain of a large ego." His deep laughter filled the clearing, with my small laugh layering on top of it.

"I told my father about our little encounter in the woods yesterday." I felt slightly uncomfortable. Something about my statement made me feel like I was betraying his trust, as if our midnight adventure was something that happened in confidence.

"Did you tell him that you ran away with me into the woods or that we saw a faoladh while we were there?" Dempsey asked smoothly, pinning me with his stare. There was the flirting I'd been waiting for. Dempsey didn't open with it like he did last night, and it made me worry the connection I so clearly saw was imagined.

A smirk spread across Dempsey's face.

"The faoladh, although my father would have been thrilled to hear about you seducing me into the woods with you." I tried not to let my voice catch as I said it, but seducing was the right word. It was the act that he leaned into, that I craved from him.

He replied with a shrug.

"He would like to meet you. Apparently, he has a few questions to ask you, not related to the you and me in the woods detail." I bit my lip as I watched my words hit their mark, the subtle tug of his eyebrows at the idea of us in the woods. Conversation was so easy with this man. Connection was always out of grasp within my own clan, relationships elusive. Fate must be laughing at me today, to dangle him right in front of me.

"Well then, we shouldn't keep a clan leader waiting, should we?"

Dempsey fell into step with me and we walked back to camp.

"I'm surprised how beautiful it is out here," Dempsey said.

I glanced around the clearing. "It is, isn't it? Spring is my favorite, but we're just at the tail end. Something about the new leaves. They seem greener than they are the rest of the year," I admitted.

As if in response, a breeze ruffled the trees, as if the nymphs were agreeing. This year had yielded a particularly late spring, and the buds were just starting to burst into bloom. The clearing was filled with pale pinks and blue blooms, with wildflowers grazing our ankles.

"What's it like in the Riverlands?" I asked.

He smiled. "We still have trees. I don't think the Forest Clan is that unique of a moniker."

I had to admit he was probably right. Whenever I imagined the Riverlands, images of streams amongst marshes, shining shores, pebbled currents flashed through my mind. When I daydreamed about my sister going to the mountains, my imagination never conjured an image more complex than a rocky mountainside, slick with snow.

He continued. "The rivers are wide and low, and most of the year they're so clear you can see the stones underneath. It gets warm in the summer, and we hardly ever see snow. I can't imagine how you deal with it here."

"Snow is pretty," I objected. *Snow is pretty? Gods, Willa, work on your wit.* I cursed at myself silently.

Dempsey shot me a look, like he was thinking the same thing.

"What's your family like? You've already seen all of mine this trip."

"And you've seen all of mine. Barra is my father. My mother left us when I was younger, joined a passing Fianna when I was eight."

"I'm sorry about your mom." My voice softened, but Dempsey didn't want any of it.

"No sympathy for me, thanks," he replied tightly. I didn't

know I had walked into unspoken territory. "She didn't want us, and we don't need her. I think we've managed just fine."

"I know you have," I murmured, and I meant it. The past two days showed me that Dempsey was kind, considerate, and funny. His father raised him well. Sometimes, that was all a family needed.

I wasn't surprised. Sai had been raised by his mother after his dad had died in an avalanche when he was ten. Fiadh had whispered the story to me one night before bed. Occasionally, there would be children in the clan who had neither parents with them in this life. Sometimes, extended family would take them in or clan elders would watch over them. There was a sort of intangible strength that went into those children, I was certain. As if the gods had given them a little extra because they knew they would need it.

"Plus, we have Tadpole here, who is the most annoying little brother you could ask for." Tad looked up at the sound of his name, ears perked.

"I can't believe you call him 'Tadpole'." I laughed. I might always laugh at the sound of his name coming out of Dempsey's mouth.

"Maybe when he gets bigger, I'll call him Toad."

I rolled my eyes. "That was possibly the worst joke I've ever heard," I said seriously.

Finally, the village came into view. The clan had awoken in our absence, fires dancing with light and the smell of food wafting towards us. Children darted in and out of tents while cooks worked on breakfast at the boiling pot.

I steered Dempsey and Tad towards my father's war table. Even in peacetime, this table would always be called that. Viktor liked to say we were constantly at war, with the elements, with hunger, with the gods. Ever since I was a little girl, I could remember my father pulling up his great chair to this rock slab, where pieces of parchment and maps were spread out. In times of war, army figurines would dot the landscape, marking his troops and their movements.

Viktor looked up as we approached, always aware of everything around him. His face weathered a dark tan, and today his black hair was tied back as if his curly black hair was clouding his thoughts. He rose from his seat.

I sat in a chair adjacent to my father's while Dempsey kneeled respectfully.

"Viktor. It is an honor to share your table and offer my counsel."

"Rise, Dempsey, there is really no need for the formalities." I blinked at the lack of introduction between the two.

"Now, your father tells me that you have trained your wolfhound by yourself. Is that correct?" There was no time spared in going straight to business.

"I've had counsel from our Master of Hounds, sir, and the opportunity to travel to the Mountain Clan to speak with the master of their wolfhounds. They have a small breeding program there. My dog is the last of the wolfhounds in the Riverlands, though. From what Willa tells me, they have died out here in the forest as well?"

"They have, spare a few individuals who live outside the village," Viktor answered cautiously. "Most of the wolfhounds were lost when the Clan o' Cliffs were attacked. A few might have gone feral, I suppose."

Dempsey ran his hand through his hair, something clearly troubling him. His hands fiddled with the back of the chair he stood behind. Viktor leaned back, waiting for Dempsey's next words.

"I think the land is changing. That's the only reason why a faoladh would have attacked Willa and me last night. They're an animal that runs off the essence of magick in the land, there should be *no reason* for it to go hungry."

I blinked in surprise at his words, the frankness of them.

Magick was the lifeblood of our land, the thing that bound the forests and rivers together, that pumped the veins of leaves and whispers of snow. If the magick were to change, the land to change, where did that leave the clans?

"And you believe, what exactly? What does this have to do with your dog?" I winced at my father's concise words. I often heard tales of my father's ruthless nature, but rarely did I see it in practice.

This meeting was moving in a rapidly different direction than wolfhounds and breeding programs. Dempsey pressed on. "Our world moves between cycles, the flow of magic comes in waves and ebbs. Faeries and gods once walked the land and now we do. I wonder if it's happening again. If this faoladh was the first to transform into this bastardization of a wolf, I think there will be more to follow. Hence my focus on the wolfhound breeding stock. I would argue that this wasn't the first case. Haven't you noticed that the wolves have been more active of late? Bolder in stealing livestock and children?"

"So we set extra patrols." Viktor tugged on his beard.

"No." Authority rang in Dempsey's voice.

I glanced at my father. Dempsey might be heir to the Clan Amongst the Rivers, but I wasn't sure the last person who spoke to my father like this lived to see the next day. A dagger that was previously laying on the table was now dancing around Viktor's fingers.

"I can't say for certain, but the *land* is changing. Not just the wolves, but the land, the air, all of it. The gods we worshipped failed to protect the Clan o' Cliffs twenty years ago, and I think they're changing the isle on us now. I don't know how, or why, or how to stop it, but something is coming, and I think we need to be on guard for it." Dempsey finished and looked to me for support.

Viktor let out a low whistle. "I thought my daughter was supposed to be the one with the gift of foresight."

I found myself speaking. "I... I did have a dream of a fire a few days ago. A fire in the woods, with no explanation for why it started or with anyone in sight. I wasn't sure what it meant, but do you think it's related?"

Viktor hummed. "Fire can mean many things. It can mean destruction, or rebirth. It is what gives us life and makes us warm on winter nights. Truly, it could mean anything."

The three of us looked at each other, thinking, calculating. What had begun as an innocent conversation had turned into a talk about something much more. Somewhere, somehow, I decided I knew what it meant.

"It's a warning from the gods. Something is coming, and we must be on watch. Lose our focus, and we become the kindling." Confidence reverberated in my words. This message was coming from beyond, coming from my gift. The dream, the wolf, all of it had been a warning for me and the clans.

How much did Dempsey know before bringing this up? I wanted to trust him, but how did he fall into all of this?

Shock and curiosity was written on Dempsey's face, perhaps at the performance of my gift in action, but if his face was telling the truth, then this realization was new to him as well.

"We shouldn't speak of this anymore, not until the other clan leaders are present. Willa, if you could gather some advisors, that could prove helpful. We might as well discuss this while we have everyone together."

Viktor turned back to his papers, as if to dismiss us. Dempsey whispered to me that he was going to find his father, and would be right back. Tad padded away, following at Dempsey's heels, as always.

I waited until they were out of earshot before I turned to my father.

"Just how, exactly, are you planning to convince the leaders of the Mountain Clan and the Clan Amongst the Rivers that the world as we know it is about to change? Oh, and we don't even know how? And that this is all based off a nightmare I had and a wolf that Dempsey's dog – who can't even obey a 'sit' command – found lurking in the woods?" I fumed. The idea of using my dream for some political agenda felt wrong, my innermost workings laid bare. The possibility of what might turn into an expectation scared me.

Viktor looked unruffled at my outburst as he looked back up.

"I shall convince them just as you two convinced me. Besides, Dempsey basically *is* the Clan Amongst the Rivers leadership, and this is exactly the reason I allowed your sister to marry that boy from the Mountain Clan." Viktor smiled, as if pleased with the way his decision had worked out for him.

"Willa, please have faith in yourself. Firstly, it was not a common nightmare. You and I both know that. You have a gift given to you from the *Dagda*, the great god, and you need to start treating it as such. Secondly, don't insult the dog like that. I'm starting to think I want one for myself." Viktor chuckled to himself and I shook my head in disbelief.

"What are you going to tell them," I whispered.

"That, my dear, is a question for yourself. What are *you* going to tell them?"

I blinked away the angry tears budding at the corner of my eyes.

The audacity of my father to pin this on me. I was trying to warn him that something was happening out there, that the gods were threatening us to wake up, pay attention. Now he expected me to explain that to the rest of the clans? Last time I checked, he was *the leader, not me. I might have the gift of foresight, but I never asked to be a leader of this clan. Every bit of me grated against this role I was now being thrust into.*

Rising to the role of chieftain or an advisor was always Fiadh's plan, but not mine. There was something too calculating about it, playing with people's lives as if they were pawns. Having the weight of life and death on my shoulders was not something I needed nor wanted. So although my gift made me report to my parents, I decided a long time ago that was the closest I was ever going to get to their role.

I began to rise from the table, pushing the chair out from underneath me.

"Willa, my dear, when you go can you do me a favor? Make sure your mother, Bowen, and Callan attend the meeting? Oh, and let Sai and Fiadh know."

"Of course," I replied tightly. I turned on my heel and left. Somehow, I had fallen into my father's trap perfectly. Only he could take a situation like this and present it to me as an opportunity to better myself.

As I walked away, I shook my head at my father's scheming devices. I supposed this meeting was the perfect example of why he led our clan.

I reflected on what my father said about me, that I wasn't giving my gift the full power, implying that I was shielding it from the world. The Dagda was the closest thing our people held to worshipping a deity. The clan believed he was a father, god of all things good, and that his children were epic heroes who helped create the isle the clans now occupy. The Dagda was also the god of magick, and occasionally, he would gift a piece across the realm during a child's birth.

Clan elders believed everyone was born with a piece of it, but I knew the truth. Felt it in my bones. What I possessed was more than a talent or piece of trickery. It was power that came from within.

Maybe today was the day to let the power of the Dagda out.

CHAPTER SEVEN

Willa

I found my mother sharpening her weapons at the whetstone near the smith and masons' tent. Brigid took pride in the upkeep of her weapons, caring for them as if they were her own children. The blacksmiths welcomed her as if she was one of their own, and she practiced the way of the trade frequently, learning how to craft blades and weapons for her family.

Today my mother was working on a *scian*, a blade as long as a man's forearm. The design for this specific piece was similar to a knife but enlarged, perfect for combat with an enemy at close range. Brigid preferred scians compared to knives due to their strength and accuracy, all while still retaining their ability to throw if needed. In a pinch, a scian could take the place of a sword, and Brigid made sure both Fiadh and I were trained in the art of steel.

Fiadh was particularly skilled at the scian, but I found its exposed nature made me uncomfortable. In order to be effective at the long dirk, one had to be quick and bold, and I considered myself neither of these things. Instead, I preferred to arm myself with a series of darts. I kept them in a bag hanging at my hip, ready to be pulled at any moment. The darts were small enough to fit in my hand, and the shaft of bone they were constructed from made them light enough to land upon its mark.

I cleared my throat. From a young age I was taught to never surprise anyone working with a blade. Brigid looked up, surprised to see me standing before her.

"I won't be cleaning any blades for you, if that's what you're going to ask." I shook my head at the warm welcome.

"Wasn't planning on it. Father wants to see you – all of us. All of the clan leaders. He wants to have a conversation about what happened last night with Dempsey and me."

Brigid set down the scian. "I was afraid he was going to do that."

"Do you think it's a bad idea?" I was surprised. Normally, I considered my parents a pair. They rarely disagreed on anything, especially when it came to clan decisions.

"No, that's not what I meant. I was afraid what you told us last night was serious enough to warrant one of these meetings. The last time we had one of these... Well, you were hardly born."

"What happened then?" I only dared to ask the question because we were alone. My mother and father referred to the last time the clan leaders had an impromptu meeting like this, but never spoke about what actually occurred. My curiosity was piqued, but I was also afraid of what lay behind the question.

"The last time we had one of these was when Bowen brought the Mountain Clan to our doors. We were unaware that the Sectarians had invaded. The scouts fetched the Clan Amongst the Rivers, and we had a weeklong meeting discussing – arguing about what to do. The Clan Amongst the Rivers wanted to attack, run them off the isle or die trying. The Mountain Clan wanted to learn to live with it. Set stronger borders, fortify themselves within their caves. It was a risk they were willing to take. That was how Sai's father died, you see. He was part of the raiding party that attempted to help the Clan o' Cliffs, and he didn't make it out."

"Fiadh told me it was an avalanche. I knew that Sai's mother raised him, but I didn't think that was why. Gods, I can't imagine."

My mother shook her head, revealing that even Sai didn't know the true reason for his father's death. I thought of Sai's mother and how strong she always seemed, negotiating her son's marriage agreement and standing there at the ceremony.

"Yes and no. There was a battle in a mountain pass, and when springtime comes in the mountains, the snow is volatile. It can shift. The few that made it out alive told us... Sai's father sacrificed himself. Knew that he would be killing a large amount of their forces, but also some of his warriors as well. It was a calculated risk."

My stomach sank at the image of it in my mind, the bravery and sorrow that came with the decision.

"It came down to your father and me. We were the deciding vote. We saw the damage they could do, that they *did*. The Clan o' Cliffs was decimated, only a handful survived; the Mountain Clan lost a fourth of their fighting forces. So we voted against it. Without us, the Clan Amongst the Rivers didn't have enough force to attack."

My mother's voice grew quiet. "There were about fifty women and children who couldn't flee the cliffs, that weren't strong enough to escape. Callan's mother had stayed behind with them. They were all executed not long after the Sectarians realized there was no point in holding hostages."

"That's a massacre," I whispered.

Growing up, I spent my entire life thinking that my parents were these brave figures, willing to take on anything. Hearing them walk away from a fight – a battle that they *knew* they would lose shook me to my core.

The thought of the suffering the Clan o' Cliffs endured at the hands of my parents? It was barbaric. The sacrifice the Mountain Clan had made, and for what?

My mother continued, as if she had been holding back this story for years, waiting for someone to tell it to.

"So in exchange, we offered to take in a portion of the Clan o' Cliffs. It's how we met Bowen. Another half moved up to the mountains. A few went down to the Riverlands, of course. It's also how you became betrothed to Callan. It was intended to strengthen the bond between the clans, and satisfy Bowen when he wouldn't have his own clan to lead anymore."

My breath caught as words escaped me. I knew Callan had been here from a young age, that he was always promised to me. What I did not know, however, was that my marriage was an out. An offering instead of war. It was my duty to marry to help the clan, but *this* was a whole other level of sacrifice. Whoring myself to a man so an entire clan could die out. My mouth turned sour and my face betrayed my feelings.

"I – I see," I stuttered.

"It was time you knew the truth," her mother said softly. "I know you and Callan aren't quite in love yet, but you can get there. Don't underestimate the power of friendship and respect and where it can take you."

I let out a sharp breath. "I'll keep that in mind."

I backed away with tears in my eyes, still reeling from my mother's confession.

My marriage allowed an entire clan of people to be lost. My mind hyper fixated on that one thought, refusing to let go of what it meant, the dark ramifications of it. The fact that I was about to enter the same meeting in a different age did little to settle the sick feeling in my stomach.

"I'll see you at the meeting."

Brigid said nothing to my goodbye, letting me be. She knew I saw the truth for what it was, that I would need time to process.

I ran back to my tent before panicked breaths overcame my

being. The entire world was reduced to those few facts. *I am engaged to a man I cannot stand. I will be in a loveless marriage for the rest of my life. The only reason I am betrothed is so an entire people could die out. Because my parents did not see fit to help.* My sobs consumed me as I sank to my knees and tears blurred my vision.

I stayed like that for a long while, until I couldn't remember why I was crying and my thoughts ran into one another. Eventually, my fists unclenched, revealing half-moon indentations my nails left behind, and tears dried to salt on my cheeks. I let out a shaky breath, feeling incredibly fragile, as if the slightest movement could send me back to my previous state. More than anything, as I sat there in my tent, arms wrapped around my legs, gently rocking myself back and forth, I felt alone.

I wasn't sure how much time passed, but people must be gathering for my father's meeting any moment now. I walked over to my dresser with the small bowl and pitcher that sat upon it. Cold water poured out of the pitcher into the bowl, and I splashed the water onto my face, hoping to calm the blotchy spots on my cheeks. I quickly ran a brush through my untamable hair, the strands somehow refusing to both curl and remain straight, and twisted it into a bun at the nape of my neck.

A mirror stood at the back of my dresser, and I leaned in to examine myself. The face shown in the reflection looked hurt, confused. My skin was red, smarting from the cold water, but the pain from earlier was erased from my eyes. My brown eyes narrowed, looking back at me in the reflecting glance. There might be a hint of red from the crying, but no one would look that close. I smoothed the flyways back into my bun, tugging hopelessly at a brunette strand that refused to cooperate. One last deep breath in, and I promised myself that I could do this, whatever this meeting held for me.

Cursing softly, I realized that I never told Fiadh and Sai

about the meeting. I ran out of the tent and headed towards where my sister slept. There was no guarantee that the newlyweds would be there, but it was a fair place to start, although my steps slowed when I thought of the *activities* they might be engaging in right now.

"Willa!" A familiar voice called out to me, jolting me out of my thoughts. I turned around to see Sai, with Fiadh close by, holding his hand.

"I've been looking for you," I said, my voice tinged with relief. "Has anyone told you about the –"

"The gigantic meeting that everyone is attending and you neglected to mention to us? Yeah, thanks a lot, I did hear about it," interrupted Fiadh.

I rolled my eyes. Fiadh was exaggerating, although I did feel slightly guilty for forgetting about them.

"I meant to tell you, I just ended up talking to Mum and – and things came up." My voice faltered.

Something shifted in Fiadh's face, not enough to give away her thoughts, but enough to know she understood. Sometimes I thought that Fiadh could play the role of politics and people better than our parents.

"We should actually get going. I think they're going to start soon." Fiadh looped her arms through both Sai and my arms, and marched us to our father's war table.

As we began to approach our father's great stone table, I could tell there had been changes since this morning. The great willow that stood behind the stone slab cast a shadow over the benches and chairs that had been pulled up to accompany my father's seat.

This was what people meant when they said war table. This was a place of strategy and collaboration, meant to decimate enemies and reduce armies to rubble. Viktor sat at the head of the table, as always, looking the part. Rich furs draped his chair in which he sat, wearing a tunic of deep black and a silver circlet rested upon his head. The image was almost regal. To Viktor's right was Brigid, wearing a matching circlet inlaid with pieces of emerald, her crown looking as if a nymph had plucked it from a tree branch.

Bowen sat to Viktor's left. Bowen and his son were spitting images of each other, both possessing pale blonde hair and chips of blue ice for eyes. If there were any pieces of his mother in Callan, I could not find it, and gods knew I spent years looking. My eye landed on Callan, and sitting there at the war table, he looked too perfect. A lump rose in my throat while I wished I could erase the past day and everything that changed between us. Callan smiled at me and motioned to the open seat next to him. I released my arm from my sister's grasp, and took the seat.

Callan moved his hand to my thigh. Disdain spread through my body as I looked at it and the mark of ownership it entailed. I breathed in and out slowly, calming myself, willing my feelings back deep inside of me, at least for now.

Callan's eyes studied me before speaking.

"Is everything okay, Willow?" he asked.

"Fine," I whispered tightly.

Callan looked like he was about to say something, but instead chose not to. His attention focused on something in the distance as I turned to follow his line of sight. I let in a heavy breath, praying Callan didn't hear my audible reaction.

The Clan Amongst the Rivers had arrived. A tall man led the way, a thick copper crown nestled in his brunette curls. I assumed this was Barra, Dempsey's father. Behind him, Dempsey followed with Tad and a stocky warrior who I was unfamiliar with. Altogether, the group made a fearsome appearance, every bit of them screaming warriors ready for battle.

I looked around at the table. Sai and Fiadh had found Sai's mother, Meili, and the three sat around the foot of the table. There weren't enough seats for the Riverland's group of three to sit together around the unevenly shaped table. The stocky warrior who accompanied Barra and Dempsey did a double take, calculating the lack of seats.

Dempsey, however, didn't blink as he strode to my side and sat next to me, sandwiching me between the two men; one which I should love, and one who I thought I could. The irony of the situation was not lost on me, and I could swear I saw a smile twitch at my sister's lips.

All eyes turned to my father as he cleared his throat. Barra and the Riverlands warrior took the seats opposite me. Time paused as everyone felt the weight of what was about to happen.

The fate of our world hung in the balance.

"Let's dive in, shall we?" asked Brigid.

"Dempsey and Willa came to me this morning to discuss a finding in our own woods. They found a faoladh, half-starved and manic, who attacked them. Of course, you may be wondering, *why* would a faoladh, a creature that lives off magic just as much as it does the land, be starving in the middle of spring?" Viktor held every eye at the table, and no one dared speak.

"Willa also received an omen from the Dagda. We think it means -," Viktor paused, took a breath before continuing. "We think the land is changing, perhaps moving between cycles. The magick in the land that we are used to is changing, and the gods are trying to alert us to it."

"Now that we know this," added Brigid, "we must decide what to do."

I couldn't believe how my father had pieced my and Dempsey's ranting into such a logical and precise train of thought. That thought, however, was shattered in half a moment when Meili spoke.

"Forgive me, but what do you expect us to do? Send our scouts running around the isle chasing evidence of magick? I hate to be a bearer of bad news, but it's not as if we have a well of the stuff."

Just like that, the spell was broken and I crashed back to earth. I looked to Dempsey, wondering if he was thinking the same thing.

Viktor's eyes narrowed as if he was calculating his next move, preparing for battle.

"Thank you, Meili, for stating the obvious," Viktor said smoothly. "No, we cannot send our scouts to run in circles around the island."

"But it doesn't mean we should lower our guard." Heads swiveled to see Sai speaking, contradicting his mother. "That's how we lost my dad." Fiadh reached for his hand.

So he did know how his father died. If that was the case, then why did Fiadh tell me it was an avalanche? A half-truth was just as good as a lie.

"So we game plan it. What do we look for? Is there anyone with gifts that could look for a solution? Willa, could you maybe run a search?" Sai asked.

I blinked. I expected to listen to the discussion, yes, but I never expected to be asked to participate in it.

"Well, that's not how it works." I was vaguely irritated at this assumption. "I have a gift that gives me foresight and omens, but I can't just *call* upon it. The second something appears to me, though, you all will be the first to know," I added, looking at the group around me.

"Those are just dreams though. Don't we need something we can work off of?" Callan voiced this opposition, much to my annoyance.

Recalling my father's advice from this morning, I squared my shoulders. *I have a gift from the Dagda.*

"No, Callan, it isn't *just* a dream. They are images and prophecies given to me from the gods, and right now, they are the best thing we have." I snapped, my cool exterior forgotten.

I couldn't be sure, but I thought I noticed a glimmer of approval come from my father. Callan, on the other hand, radiated displeasure.

"Awareness is the best thing we have right now. Noticing changes, just like Willa and Dempsey did, is the only way we can prevent this change. Put everyone on high alert for the slightest of things. Let the elders tell their tales. Stories of faoladhs and faeries, the very fabric of our world is shifting. We all need to listen to it." The third Riverlands man spoke. His hair was pulled back into a sleek bun and his eyes told the truth just as much as his voice did. I didn't know his name, but my soul warmed at the fact he believed me.

"And you are?" Bowen asked, and although I wondered the same thing, I couldn't help but think the question rude.

"My name is Felix. Small counsel of the Clan Amongst the Rivers. And you?"

I had a sneaking suspicion that Felix already knew who Bowen was, but asked the question to irritate him anyways.

"Bowen. Pleased to meet you."

Felix ignored the answer to his question.

"So you want bodies, is it?" asked Meili. "Viktor, you give me your daughter and in return you expect what, exactly? My warriors and scouts?" Meili's expression matched her unhappy words. Little evidence supported that the Mountain Clan was going to give any aid to their cause.

Brigid and Viktor exchanged a glance. I was unsure where we could go from here; there seemed little tangible efforts the clans could put forth to shift the waning of magick.

Dempsey shifted in his seat next to me. I looked at him, frowning, wondering how he was going to fix this mess when he was the one to bring it up in the first place. "We set patrols around the isle. So yes, Meili, we will need bodies. Not many though." Dempsey's eyes twinkled as he made his request. "I think we have our patrols here, sitting at this table. Felix and I will volunteer from the Clan Amongst the Rivers."

Dempsey motioned to Felix as he, in response, nodded his head. I wondered if they had walked into this meeting knowing where this was going to lead, a thought that made me feel oddly left out and forgotten.

"Sai and Fiadh could represent the Mountain Clan, while Callan and Willa patrol for the Forest Clan." Hairs on my arm stood on end as I heard my name mentioned.

Dempsey planned every second of this, anticipated every interaction down to the meeting with my father this morning. A part of me couldn't help but admire him for it, the thought and cunning that had to go into planning an interaction like this. Dempsey was *planning* their futures, their destinies, rather than sitting by and accepting their fate. That sort of self-realization took courage and a more intimate knowledge of oneself than I cared to possess. This meeting was the stuff of legend, when history shifted before it was even written.

"What do you expect us to patrol for?" drawled Callan. By the sound of his voice, I could tell he wasn't convinced.

"I want to take the patrol and go to the Oracle of Clogher." Dempsey held Callan's stare, a challenge. The table erupted in talk.

"That's dangerous," pointed out Fiadh. "What do you expect to gain from speaking to it?" Her voice was incredulous.

"I want answers, and that stone is the only one that will give it to us. The Cloch Oír is too risky, the demon that speaks through it is too violent. The Oracle of Clogher is difficult, yes, but we can get answers from it." Dempsey surveyed Fiadh. "There's no need to join, if you feel unsafe."

If you feel you can't handle it is what Dempsey meant, the thought floating in the air.

My parents looked at each other, speaking their own

unspoken language. Meili looked unhappy, whispering quietly to her aid. Barra was the only chieftain who was quiet.

"This is a fool's errand." Meili sounded just as unhappy as she looked, but I'm not sure if she ever was pleased about an idea another clan presented.

"Where do we go without these answers? Attainable answers are within our grasp. We need them, otherwise we're just rowing without an oar." Dempsey held her gaze, something not many dared to do at this table.

"I don't see any other way," my mother said quietly. My father nodded at this sentiment.

"Why all of us then?" Sai asked.

"It's the way the Oracle works. You need to enter the hedge with as many people as there are stones. If you're out, tell us now, because we need a replacement." Dempsey said this information frankly.

"We're in." Fiadh said the words without a second glance. I didn't know when she started making decisions for the Mountain Clan, but Sai looked to be in agreement. Fiadh picked up a flask of wine before pouring Sai and herself a glass. Lifting it to the air, she announced, "To the Council of Clans and Gods."

The flask was passed around the table as every person filled their glasses with the crimson drink. Slowly, one by one, we each lifted our glasses, both unaware and hopeful of the future we decided to create.

CHAPTER EIGHT

Dempsey

The planning of our journey finished quickly, especially with Fiadh interrupting with every new topic. As quiet as her sister was, Fiadh was the polar opposite, in both looks and character. There was something between them, some familial bond, and I would never understand the connection and loyalty there – it was unyielding, unwavering.

Our route would take us to the western side of the isle, in the tiny peninsula between the Mountain and Forest border, the place that overlooked the sea. There, nestled between the rise of the seaside cliffs and rolling greens, lay the stone hedge that housed the Oracle of Clogher, one of the three speaking stones on the island. We would perform the ritual required to speak to the Oracle, and return to the Hollow with the news, where the Council would reconvene.

For all of the politics and strategy at the table, the clan chieftains stayed quiet. Meili swallowed her protests – a shock to all – and promised food and shelter if we needed to enter Mountain Clan territory. My father was silent, letting me speak for our clan in an uncharacteristic show of support. The three clans agreed to an unconditional truce until this came to an end.

Eventually, the conversation and plans slowed, until there

was no more to discuss. Shadows lengthened as the day slipped into late afternoon. Our party wouldn't be leaving tonight, taking the risk of starting our journey in the dark. I excused myself from the table as Brigid began discussing the matter of a hunting party for tonight's dinner. As I turned away from the table, I heard the voice of Callan volunteering for the task.

Of course. Kiss ass.

I forced myself to click my tongue and call Tad, walking away from the table. Willa sat there, her eyes darting between Callan and myself. I wanted to go to her, whisk her away. Be alone in the forest where I might just be a man and she could be a woman, with no titles or expectations. But that was in the past.

Felix silently fell in line with me, his sword swinging at his waist.

"The girl's a piece of work." That earned him a glance. Annoyance must have been written across my face because he hastily added, "Fiadh. Not Willa."

"It's not her I'm worried about."

"Are you talking about the blonde, brooding one?"

I gave Felix a curt nod, not wanting to discuss further. This journey, this group of people, was a mistake.

My hand went to the knife at my side as a figure rolled out from behind a tent, nearly knocking into me. A half second and gut reaction later, my hand stretched out, reaching for Willa's waist as she gained her balance.

"Shit, Willa. Why do you always have to startle me like that?" I couldn't help the twitch of amusement from my lips as I remembered the previous night in the meadow, the cold blade of her knife against my throat, her frustrated anger at my nonchalance.

Somehow, I felt the gaze of Felix standing there, analyzing us.

"I need to talk to you," Willa said. Her eyes darted to Felix.

There were no words, but I could hear the innate distrust in her voice. *Why are you so wary?*

"You need to talk to me? Talk more, even though we just spent hours talking?"

Willa folded her arms. "*We* did not just spend hours talking." And I couldn't help but agree with her – she didn't say a word at that table. "Can we go somewhere private?"

The idea of the innuendo that didn't lay there brought a smile to my lips. "Well, I do like the sound of that. Felix, I'll catch up with you later. Take Tad with you."

I didn't turn my head, or bother to gauge Felix's reaction. There would be opinions to hear later. Felix called Tad and they both walked away, back to their tents, I presumed.

"C'mon." Willa said it as an order, not a question. She took my hand and started to pull me through the sea of tents, cutting across the rows until we reached the end of a row near a grove of willow trees that stretched the circumference of the village.

"Go," Willa ordered, pushing me and motioning towards the grove.

It wasn't until I was halfway to the grove when I realized that she wasn't following me. Instead she stood there, checking over her shoulder, until darting to follow me. I walked underneath the hanging branches and Willa followed, arranging the branches to provide a thick curtain of anonymity.

There was so much force in her, a frustration that leaked out. I wasn't sure what I did to make her this angry, but it clearly was enough to warrant a conversation. My back hit the tree and I began to roll up the sleeves on my tunic. I dared to glance up at her.

Willa stood there, the dappled light creating a pattern across her hair and face. Both hands were planted on her hips, a fighting stance.

And there came another smile, perhaps more this weekend than I had in a year. "You know Willa, I was intrigued when you asked to go somewhere private, but now, I'm really curious as to what you have in mind." I pushed off the tree and started to walk towards her, the grin spreading as I watched her jaw tick.

Her hand reached toward her neck as she said, "Don't get too excited there. Did you really think I was bringing you here to make out?"

Sinking disappointment hit me, even if I knew it wasn't why we were standing here.

"Among other things," I responded flippantly. "Why did you bring me here?" I asked, flipping the focus back onto her.

Willa placed her hands on the back of her hips like she was bracing herself. "Back there at the council meeting, how much of it did you have planned?"

The question bewildered me. "Willa, I obviously wasn't going to bring my idea to the leaders of all three clans without a plan in place. Felix helped me think it through after we spoke to your father this morning. Why?"

What was she thinking? Why bring me here, ask me this? Does she really mistrust me that much? Did Callan make me a villain in her eyes?

"I just…" Her voice trailed off. "It all sounded like you had it worked out perfectly, like it was exactly how you wanted the meeting to go. I felt like… like you used my relationship with my father as an opening." And as much as I prepared myself for the worst, I wasn't prepared to hear that. How alone she sounded, how she automatically expected the worst.

Willa cleared her throat. "So how would I know that the faoladh wasn't planted? That you wouldn't expect to speak with my father? Flirt with me so you knew you had an in?" Her voice sounded like she aimed for nonchalance, but I heard her voice hitch, the evidence of emotion.

Is that what she thought that was? The connection between us, chalked up to a political scheme? And it hit me how much she hurt, because I had access to her father. Barra being chieftain gave me audiences in other clans, ensured my words were listened to – but that didn't mean anything for her, like she was used to being used for personal gain.

"Willa, is that what you think of me?" I asked softly. It took all self-restraint to not go to her, when I wanted to have wrapped my arms around her, have nestled her under my chin so she felt some sense of security.

"What am I supposed to think? When the handsome warrior is kind to me?" Willa cast her eyes to some point behind me, somehow not seeing how my heart lurched at the sentence.

"Willa. We're on the same team here. I think we want the same thing." And I watched her eyes return to me.

If only she knew what I wanted. I laughed silently, doubting she wanted the same thing from me.

"You'll be included from now on," I assured her. "If Felix and I ever need to make decisions, you'll be there. It's been you and me since that moment in that meadow, and that won't be changing."

I wondered if she heard the promise that hung in the air.

"Okay. We're in this together," she agreed.

"Do you need a ring to signify that promise for you?" I crooned, lightening the mood.

Important promises and contracts could be sealed with rings as a token of the exchange. There were some in my clan who obsessively hoarded those promises and favors, stacking the bands on their fingers, hoarding the power and pull.

"I think I'll be okay without it, thanks."

Idiot. How's she supposed to explain a ring to her fiancé?

I answered quickly to cover my mistake. "Then we should probably get back. Unless there's something else you'd like while we're out here," I asked with a raised eyebrow, innuendo written across my face.

And it cracked her exterior as I watched blush color her cheeks. "You're incorrigible, you know that?"

I chuckled. "Live a little, Wills," I said as I flicked her hair over her shoulder and walked past.

Willa followed me out from under the tree, trotting to keep up with my long strides.

"When will the Clan Amongst the Rivers leave?" she asked. "We leave tomorrow at first light, but the Clan Amongst the Rivers couldn't possibly be waiting here until we get back."

"Tomorrow as well. It's a fairly long journey back to the Riverlands."

"Because of the marshes?" Willa blurted out.

I looked at her curiously. "Have you been to the Riverlands before?" Why was she speaking about the marshes?

"No," she admitted, "But I've heard stories. Reports of horses twisting their ankles in the bogs."

No one should be riding through the bogs on a horse. It's asking for a death wish.

"Well, they're probably just poor horsemen then. I've heard you handle your clan's entire herd." The fact slipped out of my mouth and I don't know how to take it back.

"How'd you know that?" Willa tilted her head, no doubt wondering if I was stalking her.

"I like to do my recon on the people I ask to save the fate of the clans with, Willa." I winked at her.

She hummed. "I'm sure. Interesting band of characters you've picked then."

A pair of newlyweds, my best friend, a warrior I hated, and whatever Willa was to me. I had no clue how this journey was going to work, or even come close to being successful. It was pride and arrogance that fueled me at the war table, and I regretted it.

"I think your sister tops the lot of them. The Council to Clans and Gods, indeed." I snorted at the pompous name.

A fire lit in Willa at that. "It is accurate; you can't argue with that."

I tilted my head in concession. I stopped walking as we hit the edge of camp. The sea of tents was finally behind us. The sun slipped in the sky, quickly hiding behind the stretch of trees that surrounded the camp, casting long shadows. In the distance, there were yells and the smell of cooking. Dinner must be on the fire, and the hunting party would return soon. We couldn't be found like this, but I didn't want to leave her.

Willa looked at me, and I knew she wasn't sure what came next. I opened my mouth, and then closed it again.

"See you tomorrow morning?" I reminded her gently. I was afraid it would break her if I said the wrong thing with the way she looked at me with the pain in her hazel eyes.

It's okay. Tomorrow I'll see you again. We have time. It's not goodbye yet.

"See you tomorrow," Willa said, equally as gentle.

She stood there unmoving, until I knew that I needed to be the one to walk away. I would be counting the hours until I saw her again.

CHAPTER NINE

Willa

My horse stamped its feet, impatient to leave. We gathered by the bonfire, the camp grey and filled with mist.

Meili whispered in her son's ear, his head nodding dutifully. My own parents spoke with Fiadh, my mother pressing bags of food into Fiadh's hands. I looked for Barra, but he was nowhere to be found, his son speaking with Felix over their horses.

I had nothing to do but saddle my horse, wait, and let my nerves eat at me. Fiadh had been right to raise concern about the Oracle yesterday. It wasn't just a speaking stone, ready to tell the story of destiny, but a judge of sorts. Tales ran wild in the countryside, intensifying the horror associated with the story of the souls that had been sucked away. Theoretically, there was nothing to worry about – if your intentions were pure.

"Ready?" Dempsey walked over to me, his mare in hand.

"As I'll ever be." My voice was dry with sarcasm.

"It's really not that bad. I've heard the scenery is beautiful." Without having to say it, he knew my fears.

"Oh, well then it's all worth it for a bit of scenery." I didn't know why I didn't say something yesterday, speak up when I had the chance.

His face grew serious. "Willa, we're doing a good thing here. We *have* to do this."

I sighed and nodded.

My horse started, jumping slightly as her eyes darted sideways. Callan came around her side, trailing his hand lightly over the horse's rear so she wouldn't kick, until his hand was at the small of my back. It was all I could do to keep from squirming in the saddle at the possessive signal he was displaying.

"Are we spending all day talking or were we hoping to hit the road sometime soon?" asked Callan. His eyes traveled from me to Dempsey.

I looked around. In the five minutes I'd taken to speak with Dempsey, everyone was ready and waiting for us. *Perfect timing.*

I nudged my horse forward. "Let's go," I said, effectively ending the conversation.

Cries of goodbye echoed from camp as the six of us rode out, leaving the village behind as we started our journey through the forest, the trees turning into smears of green. Callan and I led the pack. I urged my horse faster, hoping for some distance between us.

I'm sure he matched my pace out of spite.

We rode for hours without stopping, despite the picturesque glens and lakes we passed. The pace was hard and fast, our destination the only goal in mind.

When we finally did rest, camp was nothing more than a few bedrolls beside a fire. The aroma of pheasant roasting over the fire made my stomach growl.

Pride got the better of me today; I refused to be the one who made the pack stop on our travels for lunch. That decision felt foolish now. Sitting in a circle, we ate quietly, just as we had been all day. The silence echoed, and I wondered who would be the first to break it.

Callan was unlikely, as was I. Not that I was being

unfriendly, I just wasn't sure what to say. Everyone else seemed to know what they were doing here, having been groomed to inherit leadership from their parents. It was our future we were designing, but I felt like a passerby.

Fiadh's soft whispers carried across the fire, and I noticed it didn't pique solely my interest.

Felix chose to break the silence.

"Care to share?" His voice was coy, innocent, even if the question was anything but.

Fiadh looked up from the crook of Sai's neck, annoyed. She gave a tight smile. "Not really."

I raised an eyebrow, now genuinely intrigued. "C'mon Fi, if you can say it in public, it's not that bad." I could only imagine the flirtatious comments coming out of her mouth.

Her mouth remained firmly closed, but it was Sai who spoke. "The Oracle gives judgments. What will ours be?"

We sat there, pondering. Considering each other, trying to assess what truly lay underneath. Weaknesses, strengths, fears, and promises. Hidden secrets. Hidden feelings.

"A group that has no clue what we're doing?" Callan sounded bored when he answered, irritated to have been dragged on this quest in the first place.

My body turned to him only to see his mouth set tight in anger. He ran a whetting stone over the blade of his dagger, the sound ending a sharp cry.

"A group that knows there's something going on out there," Dempsey answered, all too ready to fight.

I glanced between the two, already sensing where this was going. There was a derisive snort across the fire, and our heads swiveled, following the sound.

"People who decided to go on some crusade together but can't even get along." The way Fiadh spoke, it sounded like she thought we were going to fail. That deduction shocked me – Fiadh wasn't content with failure. She was raised to accept nothing less than achievement. If we didn't have her confidence, this mission was doomed.

"Some of us were volunteered to go and talk to a rock. Forgive me if this wasn't how I planned to spend my time." Callan's voice was dry, full of irritation.

Another scrape of the whetstone. The tip of the dagger gleamed in the firelight, the tip honed to the size of a needle. I could only imagine what he was planning on doing with it.

"Gods forbid, we do something proactive about the problem at hand," Dempsey said, his voice full of challenge. His body was tight, muscles coiled. *Gods, if they start a brawl here...*

"You know nothing about the problem." Callan made a smooth stroke over the piece of stone. "You come here thinking you know best when you're just as ignorant as the rest of the clans." His hand clenched around the hilt.

Not just a shot at Dempsey, but a shot at me, my gift. Across the fire, Dempsey's hand tightened on the hilt of his sword in response.

"The Oracle is going to see a shitshow." Callan threw the whetstone into the saddlebags at his feet, finishing the conversation.

Felix fixed his gaze on Callan and smiled, his expression more polite than anything. He raised the skein of wine in his hand to his lips. "If the shoe fits."

Dangerous territory for Felix to venture into. This might have been a mission for the clans, but I had never seen Callan this on edge. It wouldn't take much more to push him over, invite his anger out to play. *That* could be more dangerous than the Oracle.

We all fell silent once more.

"Talk like that, and the Oracle isn't going to let us walk away favorably," I said, my mind reverting back to the worries from this morning. Our minds would be held by that ancient magick tomorrow. Our bodies and will would submit, and if the spirit of the stones didn't like what it saw, then there would be no tomorrow.

Dempsey held my gaze from across the campfire. "No. No, it won't."

I stood up, tired of the animosity brewing. "Look, we all chose to come. You're either in it or not. Go home, if that's what you decide."

I stalked back to my bedroll, sliding between the rough sheets. There was no point in peeking over my shoulder to see their reactions. The crackling of the fire lulled me to sleep, but I wasn't sure if I was ready to face what the morning held.

⋄

T he next morning as the mist settled, my sister sidled up next to me. I glanced over to see the expression on her face, one I recognized immediately from when we were children. The reins tightened in my hands, slowing my horse to walk beside hers, hanging back from the group as we skirted a group of pines.

Fiadh looked me square in the eye. "Willa, are you sure this is something you want to do?"

The question shocked me. "What makes you think it's not?"

"I can tell when something is off, even if I don't have a gift from the gods. If you don't want to do this, say it. We'll go home right now."

Her words should have reassured me, but they did anything but that.

"Fiadh, I'm starting to think you're the one that doesn't want to go to the Oracle. What are you so afraid of?"

The accusation hit her and she flinched like I landed a blow. If any of my words resonated, she didn't show it. "The Oracle is dangerous. It could very easily go wrong. I'm giving you an out." The words were rational, but they infuriated me. I didn't ask for her to protect me from this thing I willingly walked into.

My blood started to boil. "Fiadh, if you had a problem with this, you should have said something back at the Hollow. You know we need six people, and if we turn back, we've wasted an entire day's journey." My voice sharpened. "Don't try and pin it on me."

She thinks you're weak. The thought came to me, unwelcomed, but it rang with truth. If my outburst last night after dinner didn't show my support, I didn't know what would. Why Fiadh was so hesitant was beyond me.

I clicked my tongue and my horse shot forward, leaving Fiadh behind as I caught up with the group. The stares from the men burned into my back, but I kept my gaze stony. I was tired of being the weak little sister.

Despite the anger, despite the conversation I kept playing over and over in my head, our surroundings did little to let me slip into a fury. My conversation with Dempsey the day before proved true, the journey to Clogher absolutely gorgeous. Since the woods dissipated earlier this morning, the entire ride had been along the cliffs. Great white walls met the sea, filling the coves with white breakers, a striking contrast to the green grass on top. The dark sapphire waves stretched as far as my eyes could see, not another isle in sight. It felt like we were alone, like there was no one else in the entire world, and we wouldn't know. A moment of peace before the storm.

Even from miles away, I could see the great standing stones. They loomed tall in a circle formation, six elongated boulders equidistant from each other. The rocks were bent at an incline, paying homage to the pillar, known as the Oracle of Clogher, firmly rooted in the middle. We approached from an angle, the rising sun appearing to dart across the sky, radiating from the western stone, like the circle birthed it itself.

It was strange, but the atmosphere felt sacred – almost

divine. The circle was built long before any of our peoples roamed this land. The elders told tales of the faeries and gods living there, holding their councils, each standing stone a seat for the mythical beings. With the structure coming into view, I believed it. There was no way a man could have moved those stones, even with the aid of clansmen or horses. The boulders and the center stone towered feet above us, stretching towards the sky, larger than any rock I had ever seen on this island. It was like the gods brought them here from the Otherworld before retreating.

My heart began to race in anticipation, my body feeling the bizarre static of the magick that filled the air here.

One by one, our horses slowed sensing the powerful magick, unwilling to travel further.

I shook my head. "We leave them here. Walk the rest of the way on foot." Out of the corner of my eye, I could see Callan opening his mouth, preparing to protest, but it was Dempsey's voice that spoke.

Feet hit the ground. "Let's tie them to this tree," Dempsey said. He roped the reins around a slim pine.

We each followed suit, gathering our horses amongst the young trees that bordered the stones. The trees and brush stopped within a certain distance of the pillars, something unknown holding them back, a force around the holy ground.

Up close the stones were smooth, any imperfections washed away by centuries of rain and wind. I ran my fingers over them, feeling the slight pebbling, feeling their ancient presence. Little flecks of black and crystal ran over their grey surface, dotting their appearance. The rest of the group spread out, each choosing a stone for their own, the air heavy with silence.

"So what happens next?" prompted Fiadh. We all looked to Dempsey, not knowing the answer. It dawned on me how unprepared we were for this.

He sat down, leaning his back against the stones, tilting his head back so his face faced the sun. Light washed over his features, highlighting the brown stubble that was beginning to grow around his mouth.

"We sit, listen to the world, and wait." The breeze lightly ruffled his hair.

Callan snorted. "That's it?"

Dempsey opened one eye, looking bothered like Callan woke him from a nap. "Is that too difficult for you?"

Callan quieted, sitting down against the stone.

I watched as my companions slowly closed their eyes, one by one. I knew I should follow suit, but I wanted to savor this hallowed place, take it in by myself for just a second. It was so beautiful and wild it almost broke my heart, this place that could have been straight from the Otherworld. My soul felt quiet as if my gift could feel it too. *Home.*

I shuttered my eyes, darkening the golden light that filtered in around the stones. A few seconds stretched into minutes while I waited. My imagination ran wild, wondering what Dempsey meant by "listening to the world". I could hear birds in the background, brightly chirping, the whisper of the wind across the grass. The cool stone pressed into my back and sent a chill through me despite the sweater and leggings I wore.

Thunder rumbled in the distance, and as I faintly registered it, I began to worry about rain soaking us as we sat here. The lightning might spook the horses, too.

Then I heard it.

It was a voice that sounded familiar, like the embodiment of a rushing river or the gentle waving of flowers on a breeze. It was both young and archaic, and although I should have been filled with fear I, instead, felt curiosity course through me, wanting to learn this mystical being.

"Welcome to the seat of Clogher." The voice echoed around the circle, bouncing off the rocks. "And who do we have here?"

It felt as if there was someone at my side, peering down at me, scrutinizing my person.

And yet, I opened my mouth, ready to respond to this thing that somehow *knew* me.

"We are the Council to the Clans and Gods. We hail from all of the clans, hoping to share in your omnipotence." It wasn't my voice, but Dempsey's that spoke.

A chuckle came from the stones. "Oh? I don't remember inviting you." I could picture the cruel smile snaking across the Oracle's face, lambs falling into the lion's lap.

Silence.

I waited for Dempsey to speak again, but he didn't. My heart began to race, not knowing if this was part of the game we needed to play. I desperately wanted to open my eyes, but I was afraid of the consequences. The stories of warriors going mad at the stones, men walking away without a sense of reality, women losing their souls, all rushed through my head.

Somehow, I spoke. "You didn't invite us, but we hope you welcome us anyways." I held my breath, waiting.

The wind shifted in response to my answer, and the image of the Oracle in my mind's eye swung its head to me.

"Pretty little thing. But what have you brought me, Dempsey of the Clan Amongst the Rivers? A seer, a prophet, a portal to the gods. How positively tempting."

I didn't want to ask what I was tempting it for, but my palms began to sweat. I pressed a hand against my heart, willing myself to calm.

"Don't worry, little one. I don't bite. Why *have* you all come to see me today?" The voice crooned, singing to me.

The voice was both hell and high water, the promise of absolution and deception of sin. This being was death and life in the infinite place where they both lived together. It was a monster, not of the world that lived by sunup and sundown; it was an entity that was immortality and fate.

"The land is changing. We know something is wrong. We were hoping the gods might have answers, the truth." I offered it all to the Oracle, knowing that there could be no secrets kept here.

A chuckle. "I'm afraid answers and truth are often different things."

I gritted my teeth, frustrated. "We need to know how to protect the isle, and what the gods are trying to tell us."

"Big questions. Big answers."

My hands drifted down the earth, my fingers weaving in between the grasses there as I willed myself to think back to the peace I first felt arriving at this place. *It's a test. The Oracle needs to see if you are worth the answers.*

You are the portal to the gods. You are the same as this thing. Let it judge that.

"We are here to protect the isle," I repeated Dempsey's words. "Judge us, and see for yourself."

Curiosity shifted in the wind, the breeze wrapping around us. The Oracle's essence was everywhere as if it was the breeze, the sun, and the sky all at once. It was the grass that wove in between my fingers and the soil pressing into my palms. It was everything and nothing, and it cradled our souls at that moment, weighing us in the balance of things.

The Oracle spoke again. "I see good in you all. I see hope, and protectiveness, selflessness. But, I also see jealousy, anger, cruelty. There are two sides to every coin, and this is yours."

Nothing more was spoken. I waited, but nothing came. No judgment, no answers, no soul-ripping.

"Everything has life and death, good and evil, winter and summer." I hesitated, feeling the earth beneath me. "I hope our good outweighs the evil, that you see our intentions which are pure." Magick tugged at the roots of my hair, and although my eyes remained closed, I felt the strands wave in front of my face.

The world went still, the breeze that was the Oracle dying

suddenly. "I don't know if your good outweighs the evil. That remains to be seen. But I do see your intentions, and they are whole."

I breathed, relief flooding through my body.

"I will tell you the answers you need." I nodded at this, my hands pressed to my lips in gratitude. "Fortunately for you, the answer to both your questions is the same. You were right to open your eyes, Willa, the prophet to the gods. An old foe is returning, and they are not yet done with the isle. You hold the fate of us all in your hands."

"You need to be more specific. What do I tell our parents? What am I supposed to tell the clans?" As soon as the words were out of my mouth, it occurred to me that demanding things from the Oracle was a mistake.

"Careful now, before you get greedy. Your parents will know. Tell them to look at their pasts, they will understand. Tell Viktor and Brigid that I say hello." The Oracle said this last sentence like they were old friends and it meant to invite them over to dinner.

I shuddered, but committed the words to memory. Slowly, the presence retreated, nothing more between us to be said. It was gone, the judgment passed, the answers given. Still, I didn't want to open my eyes, just in case it returned. In case it wanted to tell me more. I didn't want to leave this place, this glimpse into the Otherworld.

A hand landed on my shoulder, warm against my body. I realized that I was freezing, my body like ice.

"Willa. It's over now. Come back to us."

I kept my eyes closed, knowing that I was back in my world.

"It's gone. Leave it be. You don't belong there."

My fists uncurled as I slowly began to let the light in, accepting that I was in this version of reality.

Fiadh, Dempsey, and Callan were standing in front of me – except that it was Dempsey speaking to me, not

Callan, as I originally thought. My forehead wrinkled as I looked for Felix and Sai, immediately worried. The boys were standing on opposite points of the stone circle, refusing to look at each other, both vaguely watching me out of concern.

I went to reassure them all, tell them that I was fine, but my voice felt like gravel. I might have thought it hadn't been used in years, and I wondered if this was what hermits felt like when entering a piece of society.

"I'm fine," I whispered.

Fiadh looked cross at the slight stretch of the truth I offered. "You are absolutely not fine. We've been waiting for you for an hour."

"I'm sorry – what?" I knew I'd ignored their voices for a few seconds, but an hour was absurd, and Fiadh always tended to over-exaggerate.

To my surprise, Dempsey's concern matched Fiadh's.

"I don't know if it was an hour, but we have been waiting for a while. I was getting worried," he admitted. There was something soft in his tone, and I forced myself to ignore it.

"But... Did you not hear the Oracle?" I asked, pressing myself into the rock behind me, suddenly scared.

The three of them looked at each other.

"The Oracle never responded to me," Dempsey said. I furrowed my brow.

"Yes, it did. And then you never answered it, so I spoke." I looked at their faces, worry growing on each of them.

"The rest of us woke up after that, Willa. What did it tell you?" asked Callan.

I took a breath, realizing what had happened. The Oracle only spoke to me. It knew I was the portal to the gods. That was the only reason why we were judged, the only reason why we received answers.

"The Oracle said to go back, that whatever is harming our

island is in our past. It said our parents would know the answers."

Fiadh lifted a hand to her mouth.

"Shit," said Callan.

And for once, Dempsey agreed. "Deep shit."

"It has to mean the Sectarians," Fiadh said, her hands pressed to her hips.

Sai looked across the circle, ready to correct her, but she didn't let him. "What else could it be? What's the *only* thing our parents have dealt with that's harmed this island? I don't think they're talking about the rabid fox outbreak from a few years ago," she said defiantly, daring anyone to disagree with her.

This was the leader my parents had groomed for so many years, leaping into action. This was why my father had tapped her as heir, decided to wait to betroth her – Fiadh was the strongest, out of all of us. She held the most potential. As a child, my parents hadn't wanted to hold her back, limit her possibilities so young. It was only in recent years that they decided that Sai was her best option. Right now, in the stone circle, I saw why.

"You're right." It was Callan who spoke. He was so quiet today, I almost forgot he was there, the only one of us who had seen the Sectarians in real life. For him, they were real warriors, not some nursery tale. I wondered how traumatic this must be, stirring up old ghosts.

"Congratulations, you figured out the riddle," rasped Felix. "What do you win?"

"Felix, we're not *finished* here," Fiadh snapped, exasperated at us not understanding what she obviously saw. At this, my ears perked up.

Felix raised an eyebrow in response. "We're not?" His voice was empty of curiosity, he stated the question, refusing to play into her games.

"There's only one way to find out what the Sectarians are planning," Fiadh said.

"Fi," I breathed, knowing what must be running through her mind. "That's too dangerous."

"Let everyone make their own decisions, Willa," she retorted.

"What exactly are you proposing?" asked Dempsey.

Sai ran a hand through his hair, as if being married to Fiadh was already aging him. "She wants us to invade their camp. See if there are any preparations for battle, stockpiling of supplies, any war plans." I could have sworn I saw Sai look at his wedding ring, reminding himself of the vows he made only a few days prior.

"The chieftains only ever sit around and talk. You saw them trying to decide what to do at the last council meeting. Someone needs to make a decision, so it might as well be now," Fiadh declared, pacing as she explained. Dangerous. My sister was brilliant, but dangerous.

I glanced at Callan. His face was drained of all color, his eyes unreadable. In recent years, I rarely felt anything for him, but now all I could feel was pity. Dragging him to his lost home, to the people who killed his mother and destroyed his clan, formed the cruelest type of punishment. I stood up and walked to Fiadh, not wanting the boys to overhear what I was about to say.

"What about Callan?" I whispered.

"What about him? If anything, he should be jumping at the chance. Vengeance, and all that." Her voice was flippant and it curdled my stomach. The lack of compassion made me want to scream.

A broad hand touched my shoulder. "Willa, it's fine." Callan looked Fiadh in the eye. "I'm in."

She gave me a saccharine smile. "See? Everything works out."

"What if we get caught?" I asked.

"Then don't," Fiadh said, as if it was that simple. Growing up, Fiadh and I trained with warriors, each of us mastering the various weapons and learning hand-to-hand combat, but walking into an enemy's camp and expecting all six of us to leave was naïve. Unfortunately, none of the boys shared that sentiment.

Callan's hands settled on my shoulders. "It's fine," he whispered in my ear.

"Do we know how to get there?" asked Dempsey.

"I do." Callan spared no words. I couldn't bring myself to look at Dempsey, knowing how Callan and I looked right now.

Fiadh furrowed her brow. "Callan, the last time you were at the cliffs, you were six." She said it gently, as if explaining something to a child.

I looked up to see Callan fixing her with that cold stare of his. "Fiadh, I regularly patrol the borders of our territory. It's not that difficult. We follow the cliffs." I wanted to shrink and hide at my sister's ignorance. I wondered if Callan had ever dared to venture closer on those rides on the perimeter of our land, if he ever dared to risk seeing his home once again.

Fiadh held her hand out to help Sai up from where he sat, still leaning up against a standing stone. She held everyone's gaze, looking around the mossy stone circle. "Let's go then. No point in wasting time."

I watched as one by one, they started to leave the circle. I traced my hand once more over the standing stone, not wanting to leave this place.

"Everything alright?" Dempsey asked lingering behind.

With a start, I realized it was only us two left, the rest of our group traipsing through the long grass, back to the young pine trees where our horses stood.

A smile faltered on my face. "What could I possibly have to worry about?" I asked, sarcasm evident in every syllable.

His brown eyes darkened. "If you don't want to participate in this raid, no one will blame you. What you did here, today, none of us could do. Trading riddles with the Oracle – that's no small feat." He tilted my chin up with his hand, forcing me to stop avoiding those eyes I knew I would drown in.

My heart skipped a beat before I stepped back, breaking eye contact. A stray hair blew across my face in the wind.

"We should probably get going."

His face was unreadable as he nodded his head, motioning towards the moor before us, letting me walk ahead of him.

I wasn't sure what was more dangerous, walking into the Sectarians' stronghold or the games I was playing here with Dempsey.

CHAPTER TEN

Willa

B lackpool sat on the cliffs that once belonged to the clans. It towered over the sparkling half-moon bay that left them so vulnerable to attack in the first place. Hundreds of years before, it was said that the fae carved the caverns and roadways into the side of the cliffs, and the great stone wall that shielded inhabitants from the threat of invading clans. The wall proved futile when the Sectarians surrounded them by sea and land.

In the present, that great stone wall eroded away, covered with vines and grasses that waved in tufts from its tip. The stones were crumbling and there were no warriors to watch when we approached it.

The space between the topmost caves and the grass plain at the top was too great for anyone to notice us immediately, and we crept forward, wiggling slowly on our bellies, no one daring to breathe.

We'd tied up Tad and the horses a while back to keep them hidden from any unwanted attention. The camp of our enemies was in plain sight below, people and warriors hard at work constructing some kind of formation. There was a great wooden structure pushed up against the cliffs, but I couldn't discern whether it was for their camp or for war. Few ships docked in their harbor. On the far side of the cliffs, a large sigil was erected, a sign of an offering to their god whom they called the Father.

Even when not at war, the Sectarians dressed differently from the clans. Their clothing was large, restricting, full of garish colors and ruffles. It was beyond me how they moved and lived like that, stuffed like a goose before a feast. And yet, for all their differences, they weren't that different from us with this distance. Warriors trained and I spied cooks preparing food. Children darted around the yard, no doubt playing games and make believe.

It was almost enough to make me wish we weren't about to go forward with our plan. *Almost.*

On our way, we passed a peat bog, a small one that bordered a nearby village. They knew who we all were almost immediately, and swore their allegiance to us on sight. All it took was one request, one explanation of Fiadh's plan and they gladly handed over several clumps of dried peat. Light danced in Fiadh's eyes as she explained to us what we were using the substance for.

Callan, Felix, and Dempsey took their positions flanking the east side of the cliffs while Fiadh, Sai, and I matched their position on the west. I laid between the two, keeping watch. Something inside me whispered that this was a bad idea, and when Fiadh asked me for the final time if I was in for the plan, I shook my head no. In this headspace, I would be a liability.

Hurriedly, Callan took out a piece of flint and stone and began to strike sparks. A few bright orange sparks landed on the thick grass and fizzled out almost immediately. The surrounding moor and the sand below would be unlikely to catch fire, but as Fiadh pointed out earlier, the Sectarians were hell-bent on expansion. The burning of any lumber or ships would be detrimental; and there they were, proudly displayed down below.

A large spark landed on the dark peat and caught almost immediately. Callan picked up the block, letting the flames catch a little more, so it would have the strength to travel. It wasn't until the fire was almost licking his hands did he throw it in a large arc. The piece of peat became a glittering jewel tumbling in the sky, reaching further and further. Across the camp, Sai did the same.

The fire worked quickly, eating the wooden structures, greedily consuming anything it touched. As fast as the flames worked, my sister worked quicker. She secured herself in a sling fastened against the cliff. Fiadh paused, waiting for Sai to grab the other end. Once he did, she began to lower herself down slowly, leaning back into the air and bracing her feet against the sandy rocks. She climbed down, lower and lower until her feet hit air, and she knew that she found the first cave in the system.

Fiadh gave a tug on the rope to let Sai know she hit it, and then she let her hands go from the rope and took the scians from her waist. She stuck the daggers into the soft stone of the cliffs to test it. The dagger slid in and out of the cliffs easily. One last tug, and Sai gave her slack on the line as she hung onto the daggers and slowly began her descent into the cave.

The only thing we could do now was wait. Fiadh planned to go in, gather as much information she could, try to locate a war room of sorts, and leave. We gave her ten minutes to look around, and then she had to get out. Any longer put us at too much risk of being uncovered in enemy territory, especially at the top of the cliffs. Fiadh tried to argue for twenty, but Callan insisted those caves were a labyrinth, and she was likely to get lost, with no hope of recovery, if she stayed too long.

Gravel crunched as Callan, Felix, and Dempsey crawled over to me, hoping to get a better view of the fire and Fiadh.

"Do you think anyone noticed?" asked Felix.

"I didn't see anyone," I answered truthfully, but how accurate could I be? I couldn't see the inside of the caves. Images of sentries lying in wait around the corner conjured in my mind and my stomach tightened.

Waiting for Fiadh, I daydreamed about the stories I had been told as a child, the stories of their cruelty. Rumor had it that they had outgrown their own land, the island of Ngel, and were rapidly turning to other isles, different places to conquer and subjugate, killing anyone in the land who refused to cooperate. They brought different ways of life, refusing to acknowledge our gods, massacring people in the name of human sacrifice. That was what happened to those at the Clan o' Cliffs – sacrifice. An offering to please their gods, naming ours as backward and unnatural. But what was more natural than the earth, the air, the sea? The Sectarians held no understanding, no willingness to negotiate. There was only brutality, a parasitic relationship working to smother us so they could live.

Ten minutes came and passed without notice. The fire kept burning, supplied by the endless amount of fuels the boats and scaffolding provided. Judging by the number of people, their entire settlement was working to douse the flames, running back and forth from the sea glass bay. I hoped the diversion was enough to buy Fiadh the time and access she needed. I looked at the boys, wondering if they noticed the time.

Felix was checking his timepiece, frowning. He closed it with a click, sliding it back into his pocket.

Callan spoke what Felix was thinking. "It's been too long."

I nodded, the same thing on my mind. My fingers dug into the sandy cliff as fear grew.

"I can go in after her," Callan said. Maybe Callan still knew the layout of the caves, assuming that the Sectarians didn't change things. Foolish hope ran through my body.

"No, you can't," Dempsey said. I looked at him, alarmed and confused, but he continued. "You're too heavy. We won't be able to haul you back up the sling. Fiadh was small, that's why we needed her to go down." His head turned, looking at me.

"No," I said firmly. There was no way I could go in there. If Fiadh hadn't returned, if she wasn't able to make it out then how was I? I was less than Fiadh; she was faster, stronger, more cunning. It was a death wish.

Dempsey pinned me with his gaze. "If you don't go, there's nothing more we can do besides wait up here."

I bit the inside of my lip, torn. Maybe if I was able to find her, then we could make our way out together. The smell of ash floated up from the cliffs, a silent reminder that our time was running out.

I cursed. "Fine." Checking down below to make sure no one was watching, I ran over to Sai, not wanting to wait another minute.

I barreled into Sai, surprising him in the process. He tightened his grip on the rope he was holding, checking the stake in the ground before looking at me.

"Shit, Willa. What if I let go of the rope?" He shook his head as I realized my mistake.

"Sorry," I whispered, but thankfully he didn't seem mad about it. "I'm going in after Fiadh. She's been gone for too long, and we're all worried."

Sai nodded in agreement. "I was wondering the same thing." He began to pull up the sling, making light work of it now that it was empty. There didn't appear to be any damage – a good sign. The Sectarians didn't grab her out of it.

I checked the daggers around my waist before strapping myself into the sling. I rolled to the edge of the cliff while Sai nodded, letting me know that he was ready. Closing my eyes, I took a deep breath in, steadying myself, listening for the roar of the waves. I dug my hands into the cliff and swung my legs down, dangling. How Fiadh did this freely was beyond me.

"Grab the rope, Willa. I got you. The sling will grab you even if you don't grasp the rope right away," Sai reassured me.

The braided rope hung in front of my face, and I slowly

shifted one hand onto it, and then the next. For a split second, I swung against the rocks as my feet scrabbled, trying to find a cleft in the rocks to balance against. The toes of my boot slid against a foothold, and I stilled.

"Okay, start to give me slack," I called up. Slowly, I began to lean back as the rope grew in length, taking vertical steps down the slopes.

A pattern emerged, syncing my breaths with the steps down the cliffside. Soon my feet hit air, and I'd arrived at the entrance of the cave. I followed in Fiadh's actions as I gave a tug on the rope one last time. With this much slack, there was no saving me if I fell. Sliding my daggers into the loose earth of the cave, I leaned my weight on them as the rope dropped, giving me enough room to begin my climb into the cave.

Looking around, I gave a sigh of relief. It was empty and seemed to be used only for storage. I checked the amount of rope I had left, and wrenched my daggers free, dropping to the floor. Fine sand and dust rose around me as I landed with a thud. My fingers trembled while I untied the knots of my harness, and I stepped out of the makeshift seat.

Peering around the corner, I darted into the hallway. I picked up my pace, walking as quickly as I could to the next cavern in the system. The room was packed to the brim with pickled vegetables and salted meats, confirming my previous assessment that this entire level was only storage.

Our plan never accounted for going deeper in the levels, but it looked like Fiadh deemed it a necessary step. We foolishly assumed while planning that we would find what we needed on the topmost level. No wonder Fiadh didn't arrive back at the mouth of the cave in ten minutes. I eyed the staircase warily. The peat fires would only last for so long outside; eventually, people were going to be returning to the cave system. It was now or never.

Taking a deep breath, I started down the staircase, taking the winding steps two at a time. If there was a place I was going to be killed, it was going to be here. There was limited visibility, and I wouldn't be able to draw my sword in such a narrow stairwell.

The steps beneath me turned to a landing and I was on the next floor. Voices floated down the hall. I retreated further up the steps, holding my breath and hoping the source of the footsteps didn't decide to climb the stairs.

"Do we have any suspects?"

"No, but the scaffolding was completely destroyed. I don't know how we'll be able to support any more soldiers at this rate."

My eyes narrowed as the footsteps got softer until they faded away entirely. Dashing out into the hallway, I followed the path of where the Sectarians emerged from. I slipped around the corner into the room, and I knew I'd found the motherlode.

The map room was laid out before me, ready for the taking. The table showed the outline of Eiram, just like I saw countless times on my father's war table. The land the Sectarians now occupied was highlighted in red, with the rest of the isle – clan territory – a drab grey. Ready for the bright color to sweep through.

I scanned the battle map, hoping to count ships, troops, anything.

There were a few red dots scattered across the table, most likely representing spies, in every territory. There were larger figures pushed to the side of the map – battalions. I tried to memorize their locations, but time was ticking.

I peered out the window to check the status of the fire. Most appeared to be put out, but there was still a blaze spreading across the odd wooden structures near the water. I estimated I had mere minutes before the Sectarians figured out how to contain the fire and returned to the caves.

Hurrying, I opened the pouch of supplies I'd brought with

me. What remained of the dark peat stained the inside of the bag, leaving traces of dirt behind. I scooped my hand around the corners of the bag, in search of anything that might have been left by the peat bricks I carried for Callan earlier. The dark peat left a trail around the room as I shook it out, across the table and maps. Running towards the door, I took out my piece of flint, ready to strike and go, when a hand caught my wrist.

A girl, not too opposite my age, stood across from me. My skin crawled as I looked into her watery blue eyes. There was no kindness within them, only harsh cruelty as her nails began to dig into my wrist.

We stood there like that for a second, sizing each other up, assessing strengths and weaknesses as we were immobile.

"I don't think you belong here," said the girl in a slow, grating voice.

"Funny, I could say the same to you." My eyes blazed in silent fury.

I twisted my arm, knocking the girl's hand against the wall, hard enough to get it open. The Sectarian girl lashed out with her other hand, trying to get a grip on anything she could use to hold me.

Dancing backwards in the room, I drew a scian, fitting the hilt to the palm of my hand. The Sectarian's eyes widened and gave a half glance around the room. I recognized it for what it was – a tell.

The girl didn't have a weapon. Luck and the gods were on my side that day.

I lunged forward, moving to dip under the Sectarian's arm, but the girl swung towards me first, low and hard, catching me in the rib. A cry of pain echoed through the room, and I dully recognized that it came from my own mouth. My body reacted, and I lashed out with the scian.

Scarlet rippled through the air, and I knew that I struck true.

A large rip appeared on the Sectarian's upper arm, and blood soaked through her sleeve.

She didn't advance, unwilling to risk herself with a blade involved. My eyes shot towards the door.

"Don't," the Sectarian warned. "It's useless. They're going to kill every last one of you heretics." She spat at the last word, cleansing it from her mouth.

At that, I saw red. I took the flint out of my pocket again, and struck it, hard and fast. A spark landed on the peat that was sprinkled around the room. Almost immediately, a violent column of flame erupted. I turned and ran, knowing the entire room would be on fire in a matter of seconds. I sprinted up the staircase, desperate to get back to the harness and haul myself up the side of the cliff and back to safety.

Just when I could taste freedom, could see the air outside of these cliffs, my entire world shifted. For a second, my vision went dark and my ears were ringing. My body skidded across the floor, scrapes stinging at my palms. I gazed up to see a Sectarian guard standing over me, this one definitely armed.

From behind, another force pulled me up, a thick hand at the back of my neck. The scian was wrenched from my hand, and I felt the tip of it dig into my back.

"You don't think we have eyes everywhere?" The guard across from me leered.

The knife trailed down my back, lovingly scraping over the knobs of my spine.

"How stupid must the little mouse be, to run into the viper's nest?" mused the guard from behind me. Panic flooded my veins as I marked the exits, blocked in every way by the guards around me. Silently, I counted the weapons on them that I could see. One sword, one dagger. I almost laughed at the complacency.

A handkerchief entered my mouth as a makeshift gag while the other guard took a piece of rope to fashion handcuffs. I was trapped and contained, with no escape from the viper's nest I'd willingly crawled into.

"Perhaps we'll make you sing, and you can tell us what brought you here." The guard was in front of me again, his dagger pointed directly towards my chest.

Lower it dipped, ripping a tear in my shirt. Contempt filled his face as he scoffed at me.

"Where are your gods to protect you now?" he sneered. His knife dipped lower still, hovering over my navel. I took a deep breath in as he pushed the scian in deeper, pricking the skin of my stomach. Tears started to spill out of my eyes, even though I was unaware that I formed them.

I began to pray to those same gods the guard mentioned, the ones that spoke to me for an entire lifetime though dreams that filled me with soft whispers and messages, to the Dagda, to the Clan o' Cliffs members who previously walked these halls.

As if summoned, a dart appeared out of mid-air whizzing through the hallway, slicing into the guard's eye. Blood gushed from his face, and his features were drowned in a red sea.

I drove my heel into the Sectarian behind me, crushing his instep before whipping around and aiming the sole of my foot for his groin. I drew ragged breaths through the handkerchief, wildly spinning around to find Fiadh slitting the throat of the other guard. Screaming through my bonds, I wordlessly begged Fiadh to cut them instead.

She obliged, hurriedly sawing through both gags. I rotated my wrists, cracking my joints as I bent down to grab the scian that had clattered out of the guard's hand. With my other hand, I slipped a dagger from my belt, and charged at the remaining guard.

He brought his sword down, aiming a blow for my shoulder. I sidestepped, jabbing the scian upwards as I slashed, drawing blood from the sensitive underside of the man's arm. He lunged forward, anticipating the advantage of size and proximity, but I moved backwards just as quickly, almost slipping on the pool of blood spreading from his companion.

I parried forward, meeting his sword blow for blow, slicing at his arm and stomach with the scian. There wasn't a thought running through my head but vengeance, anger for my homeland and clan warriors who died at the invaders' hands.

The guard feinted, driving the hilt of his sword straight for the underside of my ribs. The blow was unforgiving, knocking me off balance and I fought to right myself. The guard took advantage of this moment of weakness, his sword becoming coated with blood on his next stroke, drawing a thin line across my back.

"Willa, we need to go!" screamed Fiadh from the threshold of the stairs. I ignored her for a second, wanting to finish this, craving the feeling of this man's death on my hands. I aimed my scian for the base of his blade, where I knew it would hold. Eyes locked, both of them unmoving for a second, knowing this fight was going to end in one way.

My brown eyes didn't remove themselves from his weak blue ones as I swung my blade upwards, cleanly severing wrist from hand. Blood spurted from the stump as the man's face transformed into pure chaos beholding his dismemberment. I moved to leave, but turned back for one second to see the man rushing towards me, both arms outstretched.

A dagger flicked and tumbled across the air, finding its mark in his throat, slowly drowning him in his own essence. I turned to see Fiadh at the stairs, arm still cocked in throwing position. The last battle noise of his life died in his throat as his soul faded from his eyes. Knees folded forward, and the Sectarian hit the ground. It was only at this, after that satisfying dull thud, did I allow myself to join Fiadh in the cave.

Outraged shouts began to fill the hall from the stairwell. We ran up the stairs, flying into the storage room. I slowed as I understood the problem before us.

Fiadh took one look at me. "Go." It was an order, with no room for negotiation.

"Fi, I'm not leaving you here!" I was outraged at the thought, all we'd just risked, just for me to leave her behind.

She rushed towards me, untangling the rope and seat for me, holding it out. "Get your ass up the cliffs as fast as you can. Then drop the rope down for me. I'll hold them off here for as long as I can." She saw the protest building in my eyes. "*Go!*"

My bloodstained hands trembled as I struggled to finish the final knot. My fingers kept slipping off the rope; there wasn't enough time.

Delicate hands brushed aside mine with a single sweep. Quickly and efficiently, Fiadh finished tying my knots for me, before giving my trembling hands one last squeeze.

She pushed me out the cliffs, screaming up at Sai to haul me up. I don't know if I said a single word during it all. Slowly, I rose in the air, clearing the side of the cliff. I took my blades out of their sheaths, sliding it into the rock, the cliff crumbling slightly. Somewhere, I became faintly aware of the sting of the cut across my back and the ache in my shoulder. But there was no stopping now because the only way was up, to freedom and air and the land of my island.

Hands were waiting to pull me over the top as Callan and Dempsey seized my shoulders. I gave out a faint cry, my cuts beginning to open again. Dempsey's eyes were shining, and I could tell he thought the worst while I was down there.

I gasped, trying to force air into my lungs.

"Lower it back down," I said.

Felix looked at me, confused. "What?" he said.

"Lower it back down!" I screamed. "She's still down there, there's only one seat, she needs to climb back up," I kept repeating over and over while Sai dropped the rope and all three of the men hauled Fiadh up.

Judging by their struggles, she was safely in the seat and the Sectarians hadn't found her.

"We need to go. *Now.*" Callan turned to the horses waiting. They must have gathered them while we were in the caves.

We took off, racing against time. It wasn't until we reached the outer limits of the Cliff's territory that we allowed ourselves to slow.

I turned to Fiadh. "What happened in there? What the *hell* took you so long? What happened to the plan?" I demanded.

Fiadh blinked, caught off guard by my anger. "The... the top floor was only storage so I decided to do a more thorough search."

"Fi, you *stick to the plan.* You were in *enemy territory.* They could have killed you. You risked us all, waiting there for you to return. I almost got myself killed going in there looking for you," I fumed. I couldn't believe her recklessness, her need to play hero. It would be the death of her. "Ten minutes. What happened to ten minutes?"

"I went to the bottom and worked my way up, I had to find what we were looking for —"

"Yeah, well, no need. I did it for you." I shook my head.

"You what?" asked Dempsey. His voice was incredulous – and before going into those caves, I would have had the same reaction. Now the only emotion I registered was annoyance and the faint tinge of fury at my sister, for her reckless actions, her inability to think of us while in enemy territory.

So I explained it all, the story of how the Sectarian girl found me in the maps room, our fight, trapping me in a room that was surely up in flames. I described how I'd sliced off a man's hand with my scian. The dark and ugly poured out of me, exposing me for what I was.

I didn't say the worst of it all, that I wanted to kill that man, that I knowingly lit that girl on fire, that I craved the violence.

That the entire experience felt like retribution. I looked up towards the horizon, refusing to meet Dempsey's eyes.

We rode on for a while, not speaking. Slowly, the pack fanned out and I trailed towards the back, not wanting to be seen or spoken to. I watched as Dempsey's pace slowed, done with enough ease to go unnoticed by Callan.

I didn't say anything as he walked next to me.

"Stop."

I glanced at Dempsey, surprised and uncertain. His eyes traveled over me as I looked back to the group. Fiadh and Sai were in deep conversation, neither of them appearing happy. I'm sure they were talking about Fiadh's decisions, so close to the people who killed Sai's father.

"You're hurt," Dempsey elaborated.

I looked down to where the breeze grazed my skin, my shirt flapping in the wind, threatening to expose me with the rip down the front. If I was being honest, I completely forgot it occurred, adrenaline wiping my memory.

"It's just a rip," I said, beginning to dig in a saddlebag for a change of clothes.

"Your back, Willa."

Shit. In that instant, the cut along my back began stinging, reminding me of the lengthy swipe the Sectarian drew along my spine. I stopped the horse completely, hopping off. Dempsey did the same, grabbing a kit from his saddlebag.

He opened a skein of water, soaking a rag with it. Goosebumps appeared on my skin as he slowly reached under my shirt, beginning to wipe the blood away that must be soaking the linen. Even though we had been on the road for days, I could still smell him, like faint cologne, whispering of water and salted shores.

My shoulder relaxed, and I enjoyed this feeling, the feeling of being taken care of, not having to fight to survive, even if it was just for a second.

There was the faint smell of something cool, similar to rosemary or mint, and a faint tingling along my spine as Dempsey smoothed a salve onto my skin.

"This should help it heal. I don't think there will be a scar," he said, removing his hands from my back.

And I missed them. I missed the presence of him, and I knew I was going to miss him hell of a lot more once this journey was over.

"Dempsey?" I asked, waiting for him to look at me. "Where do we go from here?" The question held a double-meaning, both of us understanding it.

"We go home," he said quietly, answering both of the questions I had.

"Right," I said, because what else was there to say at his answer? A heavy sigh escaped me. "How do I begin to describe to my parents what happened in there? Talk about what I did?" The bloodlust echoed through my mind.

"You're a fighter," he said, as if the matter was plain and simple. "I knew it from the beginning, and I'm *glad as hell* that you are. You won't be able to survive this if you aren't." He grabbed the reins of my horse, halting it before grabbing my hand. "You just aren't used to being out here on the front lines. It's hard, yes, but change always is."

I withdrew my hand hastily, not wanting Callan to see, but the words soothed my soul.

"I wanted to kill them. The entire time I was down there, I could only think about the ghosts of the people who were murdered twenty years ago."

Dempsey nodded simply. "You were fighting for your people." He made it sound so easy. "But if you can't be more careful, you'll be watching the horses instead of Felix."

I scowled. "Oh, I'm sorry for dropping into the heart of enemy territory for you. Let me be a little more discreet next time."

"Quite literally what I'm asking for," quipped Dempsey with one of his crooked smiles.

I shook my head as I dug into the side of my horse, urging her on. When we were within earshot of everyone, I cleared my throat. "We need to go back to camp as soon as possible."

"Care to elaborate?" called out Felix.

"I saw their battle map. They have spies positioned all around the island. They're watching us."

Sai and Fiadh's heads jerked back to look at me.

"The fucking audacity," whispered Callan.

"How are they wandering the isle without us noticing?" wondered Fiadh aloud.

I squinted at the idea. "I'm not sure if we want to know," I breathed.

CHAPTER ELEVEN

Dempsey

"Y ou did what?" Meili's voice cracked like a whip when we reported the answers from the Oracle and our subsequent journey. I couldn't tell what alarmed her more – that we took matters into our own hands, or that we endangered her precious son.

Across the stone table, Viktor and Brigid exchanged guilty glances. "We aren't sure that's what the Oracle meant. You should have come back here –" Brigid started to say, but Meili cut her off. *Were the Forest Clan chieftains honestly trying to redirect our answer to the Oracle's riddle? Why don't they want us looking into the Sectarians?*

"Brigid, I don't want to hear it. The Sectarians are the one thing we all dealt with, that affected each and every one of us. And then they left twenty years ago, just as quickly as they came." Meili swiftly laid to rest the Forest Clan's misdirection.

My father spoke, voicing his own opinions for once. "We didn't bother the settlement they took over at the Cliffs, and perhaps that was a mistake. We let them think they could take and take."

I examined the rest of us at the stone table, the children of the chieftains silent, our parents stewing. If we weren't there, it could have been a scene twenty years ago, when they decided to leave the Clan o' Cliffs behind. What happened, all those years ago? I felt it grating against our parents.

"Well, we've already decided to dissolve one of the clans," said Bowen bitterly. "What's one more?"

Brigid reached for his hand, to reassure him, but he jerked back.

"We can't let them take any more territory," Viktor said.

"We don't know when or if they're going to attack," pointed out Meili. "We're sitting ducks."

Coward's words.

I looked to where Willa sat, a few seats over from me. She sat there, tugging at the rings on her fingers. The words of the chieftains eventually looped in circles about what could and could not be done, the futileness of our journey dawning upon me. *What was the point of it all?* The differences between the clans, between the leaders, seemed insurmountable. *What happened to the fearless leaders I worshipped as a child?*

"I know what I saw," Willa spoke suddenly. "They had spies across the island. No, it wasn't a warship, but are we really going to just sit here? Let them sink their claws in?" Her voice was incredulous.

Anger vibrated in her words, the fight that was buried so deep leaking out. *Was this what she was like before? Before Callan invaded her life with his demanding presence?*

"They said something, while I was down there," Willa continued. "A girl. She said they were going to kill every last one of us. And it didn't sound like an empty threat." A specter of the memory haunted her, that much was obvious.

Brigid and Viktor exchanged another glance, communicating in the silent manner of theirs. I shifted in my seat, unsure of where to go from here. The movement earned me a frown from Willa, and I could already envision the words she would berate me with – as if it was my fault. Maybe it was. The council was my suggestion to begin with. But this was all a fault of the past, a consequence of history and bad decisions. It was our parent's fight that turned into our war.

"We set patrols around the isle. Not many though," I said, my voice firm. "The patrols are here, sitting at this table." Although the solution was ready in my mind, I questioned my sanity as I locked eyes with the group that was dysfunctional at best.

Fiadh opened her mouth, ready to protest. *As assertive as ever.* I'm sure this was far from how she planned to spend her year.

"What was it you called us, Fiadh? The Council to Clans and Gods?" I met her eyes, reminding her of the commitment she was so eager to make, however performative it may have originally been. "There are three pairs of us. There are three moons until the harvest festival. If that isn't a sign from the gods, I don't know what is. We'll each take a month, patrol the borders, check on evidence of Sectarians. This council will meet again at the end of the summer." Felix nodded along to my instructions as if it was decided.

I dug into my pocket and cast my fist over the table. Half a dozen shining rings tumbled out onto the table, dancing and clinking until they all finally settled. Solid silver bands, commissioned here in Forest territory while we were gone. An insurance policy. A reminder of what we each agreed to.

Each ring was embossed with a rune, three lines equally intersecting. The *Iodhadh*, the symbol of druids, meaning justice and council. Three clans, three months, three lines. A representation of us at the table. One by one, the rings were passed out and slid onto fingers. Each of us tried to fit the rings onto one finger, the silver bands not being custom fit. I watched as Willa stacked the ring above her foresight ring. A finger to show who she was and what she was a part of.

Fiadh rose from her seat, pointing to the map spread across

the table. "We can start at the edge of the cliffs, skirt around the edge of the marshes, up the moors on the eastside bluffs, and end at the mountains. We'll cover the entire isle that way, even the Sectarian stronghold."

Viktor nodded in agreement, stroking his curly black beard.

"If there's significant news, a full council meeting with clan leaders and advisors will be arranged," Sai added.

And so the planning went, gradually piecing together ideas and suggestions, mapping out the most comprehensive path around the isle, taking care to add enough rest stops at outskirts and villages for the patrolling couple. Once Fiadh and Sai returned to the Mountain Clan and settled in, they would start their round. Sai estimated it would take them at least a fortnight to finish their patrol, but could take more.

As quickly as the matter began, the planning was finished. Tad grumbled at my feet when there was a movement out of the corner of my eye. Willa's seat now sat vacant, a girl who wished to disappear into thin air.

It was stupid. It was a death wish to play politics around this girl, knowing I would do anything to get closer to her. I organized the damn patrols so I would see her over the summer. There was a ring on her finger, so why was I chasing her? She had no interest in me. Her fiancé looked like he wanted to kill me half the time, and I could easily return the favor.

Death was rapidly approaching our isle, and my concern for living wasn't focused on *my* life.

I watched her figure from a distance, the Forest Clan's training ring appearing in view between the thick trees. Willa was hacking at a training dummy, wisps of straw being carried away on the wind. The bastard sword twirled in her hand, and she hit an offensive combination. Again. She repeated the move until it blurred together, ducking and whirling.

With each of those precise movements, honed to kill, it was clear that Willa was no stranger to the training ring. Yet she seemed to hate war, and certainly wanted nothing to do with talks of strategy. Odd, to say the least.

"Need help?" I called out as Willa raised a foot to the straw dummy, attempting to yank out the sword she buried there.

She didn't respond, didn't turn around, simply pulling harder at the sword.

"Want a sparring partner?" I asked again. I grabbed a sword from the deck of them, and let it hang lazily from my hand.

Noting her silence, I tried again, searching for that sweet spot. Somewhere in between teasing and arguing, where the smiles were easy and quips were fast. "I could use the practice – never know how many faoladh I'll need to defend you from."

That got her attention. Willa spun, her hair flaring out behind her. "Your move," she said, her voice betraying nothing.

I paced, my feet slowly dancing across the training yard, lovingly tracing the dust. The movements were as light as they were when we danced at the wedding. *Gods, I hated how my brain went there.*

Pain twisted across her face, and she attacked. Her sword delivered a slice at my weak side. Shock slipped through the mask I donned the second I picked up the sword, and I pulled at myself to regain composure.

"Am I playing a one sided game?" Willa asked, nodding towards where my sword was held. Low, at ease, no sign of a battle to be fought with it.

My feet traced the dirt. There was a flash of silver in the air, and the sword stopped mere inches from her face, blocked by her own. Her eyes darted down, looking at me, before meeting my own.

Willa grabbed my wrist, pulling the sword away while she

slipped under my arm. Her blade slid against my spine, and I wanted to lean into it, into her.

"What, no fight today? Remember the last time I had you in this position?" Willa teased. The taunts were designed to illicit a reaction from me, make me fight back – give her what she wanted.

I smiled, breaking that cool composure. "Thought a lot about us in certain positions?"

My hand jumped, and I turned back to face her. Steel sang as our swords clashed in midair. I moved through offensive maneuvers, timing each one perfectly. Blink and it could take off a hand – and let Willa see that I came to play her game.

The explosion of force backed Willa to the edge of the training enclosure, the fence pressing into her back. I aimed the tip of my sword to her throat, one I wanted to kiss and bite. My other hand held a dagger, poised to make a killing blow at her heart.

"Care to explain the attitude today?" My voice was nonchalant, but I cared. I wouldn't have bothered to ask otherwise.

Willa stared down the plane of the silver sword.

"You should go back." There was an alien tone in her voice.

"Are you going to tell me what's wrong?" Something had to be wrong. This couldn't come out of nowhere. She felt it between us too, right?

"Am I under duress?" Willa frowned at the weapons.

I lowered the sword but kept the dagger aloft. Willa's head turned a fraction toward the village.

"People are going to think things if they see us here like this."

I blinked. "I don't give a fuck what they think."

Willa gave me a beautifully pained smile. "I care. I'm the one that has to deal with Callan's jealousy. They're all going to start asking questions if they catch us here like this."

"I can deal with Callan for you –"

"Dempsey, you can't take care of me. I don't know what this is between us," Willa said, motioning to us, "But it needs to stop. It isn't good, for either of us. I'm stuck in an engagement that I can't break, and you're trying to what? Save me?" Her voice threatened to break. "I'm not a thing that can be fixed. Go find someone you can actually have. Shouldn't be too hard."

She stared at me. I took my time studying her, savoring the curves of her face, the sweep of her lashes. There were so many words left unsaid between us. It was foolish to think that we had more time.

It felt like a battlefield, raw and broken. I hated myself for causing it, for only bringing damage when she was already so hurt.

Slowly, I tipped the blunted edge of the knife and pressed it into the soft underside of her chin, tilting her head up. I knew what we looked like right now, the torn lovers. This thing between us promised to be so sweet. Willa's sword clattered to the ground. My hand moved to cup her face, and I wanted to kiss her. *Did she want me to kiss her?* Just for a moment, even if it might break my heart afterward?

We were breaths away, and I could smell the perfume of her. Our scents mingled, the smell of salt and storms and sea with earth and lavender and mist. I stood there, studying her like that. But I didn't kiss her. Couldn't kiss her. The invisible line that we waltzed around so often was there, a firm divider. An ever-present reminder.

I wanted to say something, but there were no words to explain, to apologize, to make this better. Maybe there wouldn't ever be words for what was in between us, the story of what could have been.

Instead, I turned on my heel and left. There was no looking back – otherwise, I would be on my knees in front of her, begging her to run away with me. Offering to bring her to a new life.

CHAPTER TWELVE

Willa

I don't know what Dempsey said to the rest of them, but no one came to find me the rest of the evening. Eventually, I made my way out of the thick forest and back to my tent, where I fell asleep, exhausted.

The next morning, I woke early, hoping to see him once more, offer some sort of apology, an attempt to explain... whatever yesterday was. His tent was already deconstructed, horses saddled. The closest I came to goodbye with Dempsey was watching him leave on horseback, next to Felix and his father. I didn't know what I was expecting, but I still felt oddly disappointed, even if I was the one who pushed him away.

The rest of the morning was dedicated to helping Fiadh pack. After several tears, Fiadh managed to fit her clothes into her trunks, with space to spare for her wedding gifts. Fiadh and I were raised knowing that eventually, we would be separated, but that didn't make parting any easier. I always viewed my sister as the louder, brighter version of myself. I wasn't sure what I would do without my defender.

So many goodbyes today. Outside of my own sorrows, I worried about my parents. Dark circles and red puffy cheeks haunted my mother. Viktor, on the other hand, spent the morning attending to all tasks possible, stacking and restacking the wagon in every configuration possible. It broke my heart to see them this way. The fearsome warriors, reduced to fretting parents. It spoke to their hearts and soul, the essence of humanity inside of the cool and calculating exterior. I wondered if that humanity lived there before children, or if it came as an adaptation after.

"By the end of summer, when the council rotation is over and we're settled, you'll come and visit, won't you? It won't be snowing by then. Willa, are you listening to me?"

I was jolted back to reality at the sound of my sister's voice. I glanced at Fiadh's face, trying to remember what exactly had been asked of me.

"Fi, of course, I'll come and visit you, even if it snows. Save poor Sai a heart attack, thinking he needs to control the weather." Of course, I knew a man who could, but it probably wasn't an appropriate time to bring *that* up.

"Girls, I'm going to pack some food for the road. Any requests?" asked Brigid as she whisked into the room.

"The summer plums, please!" called Fiadh. "Oh, and some of the goat cheese if there's any left over," Fiadh added in response.

"I'll see what I can find," answered Brigid with a smile.

She grabbed a burlap bag to place her finds in and left us to ourselves. It took all of one glance and my sister's eyes began to fill with tears after our mother left the room.

Fiadh was calculating and aggressive, but she was also the most emotional person I knew. She never hesitated to share any of her thoughts or feelings, and I respected her for it. It was why the entirety of the clan loved her. With those tears welling in her blue eyes; she meant it.

"I have something for you," she said. My curiosity piqued.

My entire family got Fiadh a wedding gift, a matching set of the scians she loved so much, one for her and one for her newly wedded husband. The blades were finely crafted steel, hand-measured to balance perfectly with their owner's strength. The pommel was made of a rich, auburn leather with a singular emerald inlaid into the center. They were beautiful and extravagant, and fit my sister perfectly.

Wedding presents were customary, but gifts for the sister of the bride were unheard of.

Fiadh pulled out a small woolen bag cinched at the top with a drawstring. My breath caught at what I thought it was going to be. Hands trembling, Fiadh poured out the contents, revealing two silver rings so delicate and small I marveled at the skill that must have been needed to make them.

"They're rings for us. To keep us together, always."

I picked up the delicate band. The ring was so impossibly small it could only fit on one finger. I slid the ring onto the last finger of my right hand, the same finger that Fiadh and I used to hook around each other's and make our promises to each other as kids. My eyes stung as they filled with tears.

"Promise?" I asked, my voice wavering slightly.

"Promise," Fiadh answered, and enveloped me in a crushing hug, all of the thoughts and words running through our heads going unsaid. Although my sister was leaving today, I would never lose her, not truly.

"Fi, I hate to interrupt, but my mother is insisting on leaving now. She says if we don't make it to the pass before the sun starts to set, the mountain cats *will* eat us alive, and I'm not entirely sure the way she said it was a joke." Sai entered the tent, and although he looked remorseful at breaking us apart, his mouth was set in a firm line that told Fiadh there was no room to delay their exit.

The three of us walked towards the center of camp where horses were being saddled. Brigid was there, handing the bag of food she promised Fiadh to a woman in a wagon. At the sight of us, she brushed her hands on her dress and folded her arms.

"Are you off?" she asked, although the sorrowful tone in her voice indicated that she already knew the answer.

Fiadh opened her arms in answer. As the two of them embraced, Viktor walked over, finally done with his list of endless tasks for the day.

With one last round of hugs for everyone, dozens of promises to visit and send letters with scouts, and a handful of warnings from Meili about the ravenous mountain cats waiting to ambush them after dark, Fiadh and Sai mounted their horses and set off at a canter.

I watched my sister's figure grow smaller and smaller in the distance, hair billowing in the wind as she journeyed off with her husband. I half hoped that she would look back, but she didn't.

Fiadh was too strong for that, and she had places to go.

CHAPTER THIRTEEN

Willa

T he next month passed slowly. The trees in the forest grew a deeper shade of green and the flowers in the meadow finished blossoming. The night chill and morning dew was chased away by the heat of the upcoming summer and the days grew longer.

I buried myself in working with the horses, training the yearlings, and breaking them to be ridden. Sometimes it felt like this work was the only thing keeping me sane. Since Fiadh's departure, I felt more and more withdrawn. I saw my parents in the mornings for breakfast and at night during dinner, occasionally taking a ride to patrol the boundaries of our territory, but I couldn't shake the feeling that I had a hole where I previously had a best friend.

Callan got no better during the time since the Council departed. If anything, he gave me more space than usual, but whenever he deigned to speak to me, his words were overbearing and cold. I worried if he saw Dempsey and me in the training arena on that last day. It felt like the fates were laughing at me, balancing the overly full and friendly wedding weekend with a month of bleakness – taunting me with the world in full bloom around me, but leaving mine a desolate landscape.

So it was routine that kept me going. That, and the promise of adventure at the end of the month. Even if I was going to be accompanied on the trip with Callan, it was a price I was willing to pay.

Maybe during the route along the marsh, we could stop and see Felix and Dempsey in the Riverlands. See Fiadh and Sai on our trek up to the foothills of the mountains. My heart pined to see those faces that set my anxious mind at ease.

I passed the weeks preparing for the trip. I woke early, claiming the training ring as my own, practicing not just my darts, but also the scians and the bastard swords as well. There was a healthy fear within me that the weight of the swords would prove too much for my arms and shoulders, and they would give out halfway through a fight. It was a mental block, one that I spent years trying to overcome. I grimly decided after seeing how the Sectarians fought, the possibility of having to defend myself in the future was too great, and there was only one way to beat that fear. Much to my chagrin, the muscles in my arms never appeared to grow, but my endurance when holding the swords felt longer, and my thrusts and parries became stronger.

The only disturbance in my preparations came from my dreams. Nightmares probably were a more accurate term. My dreams turned increasingly dark. Vivid images of a fire crackling around me, burning me alive while the smell of burning skin and hair stung my nose, the scent lingering long after I awoke. My parents knew about the increase in frequency and intensity of my dreams, but neither of them held any answers for me. So, night after night, my dreamscape was filled with haunting omens screaming at me that danger was drawing closer and closer, and all I could do was prepare.

A few weeks after receiving word that Sai and Fiadh started their rotation patrolling the island, I was greeted at night with a new vision.

A welcome respite from the usual fires I found myself

trapped in, I was on a moor. Green grass stretched as far as I could see, gently waving in the wind. A broad, winding river babbled and flowed over rocks, filling my ears with a soothing roar. The grey sky overhead shielded me from the beating sun of summer, and for the first time in weeks, I felt peace.

A woman wearing a blue flowing dress appeared as if she'd emerged straight out of the river and onto the banks, walking straight towards me. She had long, brunette hair and wore an expression of serenity on her face while a wolfhound walked by her side. A small smile grew on my face, thinking of Tad. I didn't know this woman, but something about her felt familiar.

"Hello, Willa. I was wondering when you might decide to come to visit me." The woman's voice was soothing, as melodic as the call of the river. She wore an easy type of beauty, although there were no cosmetics on her face, only the evidence of a light tan and smile lines etched into the corners near her eyes.

"Where are we? Who are you?" I asked, the questions not coming quickly enough. I didn't know how much time I had with this woman, and I rarely, if ever, got to speak to someone who might know the answers to the cryptic messages I received so often.

The woman smiled as if amused by my curiosity. The wolfhound lay at her feet, clearly attached to his owner.

"My name is Boann, goddess of the River Boyne. I've been keeping an eye on you." She spoke slowly, ignoring the urgency of the questions that flowed from me.

So I waited, somehow knowing that Boann would reveal the reason for her midnight visit if I was patient enough.

"You're not listening to what we're trying to tell you, Willa." I was shocked at this piece of criticism. The trauma of the horrors in my dreams was with me at every waking moment. There was no respite.

"What do you mean I'm not listening? I'm quite *literally* being forced to listen. Every night, in my dreams, I am forced to watch myself and the forest around me *burn*." I let out a harsh laugh. "What else can I do? We've created a council to patrol the isle, what more could you want from me?"

Again, another smile.

"The Council to Clans and Gods, no?" The ears of the hound perked up at the mention of the Council. I wondered if the gods really did watch us that closely. "Willa, you are seeing what we are telling you, but you need to take *our* council. Listen to me."

I snapped to attention at the sharp tone of Boann's voice, a sound almost unnatural to the ear.

"The flames will burn you all if you aren't careful. Go to the river, that will be your savior."

My mind started to race. *Did she want us to relocate the village? Go to the river – the River Boyne? The river might help with the fire, but it won't stop it. She said burn you all – are people going to be hurt? Which people? Mine or the other clans?*

Before I could ask any more questions, Boann stepped forward and placed her thumb upon my forehead. The touch of her thumb brought instant peace to my soul, erasing all feelings of panic and anxiety, washing away the fear I lived with since the beginning of my recurring nightmares. I knew immediately that I would never feel this at peace again, nor would I ever find this moor on my isle.

"Your time has come, Willa." And with that, Boann walked into the river, her hound following her and the two disappeared.

I woke up gently, awareness slowly spreading back into my limbs. The entire dream was so different from my nightmares, even down to the jolt awake that I normally felt. Boann had given me important information, but I laid my head back down on my pillow. Rest tonight, with the small bit of peace Boann gifted me. I would tell my parents about the message in the morning.

CHAPTER FOURTEEN

Willa

Light filtered into my tent, the soft golden tint of morning instead of the cool rays of dawn. My eyes opened and adjusted to the brightness; I could tell I slept for far longer than I intended. Stretching out in my bed, I moved my aching limbs, sore from the rigorous training from the day before.

Rising from bed, I began to get ready for the day, dressing for the hot weather that was unescapable this time of year. I threw my hair up in its usual knot and looked myself over in the mirror. With a deep breath, I began to remember the details of my dream last night. The visit with Boann.

Although I wasn't well versed in religion and rituals, I knew who she was. Boann was the secret lover of the Dagda, a love that was held so dear that the Dagda stopped time so Boann could bring their child into the world without drawing near their enemies. The gift of foresight I held was always considered a portal given by the Dagda; what I hadn't known was that it was a gateway to the rest of their gods and goddesses as well.

The warning I received the previous night brought a chill to my bones despite the heat outside. *The flames will burn you all if you aren't careful*, Boann warned. The damned flames felt like they could erupt at any moment, hovering around my dreams like a dark cloud. Exhaustion seeped into my thoughts and body, the sheer energy it took to be on guard at all times finally wearing upon me.

Go to the river. The advice seemed useless to me. There were countless brooks, rivers, and streams inside our territory; not to mention the unknown rivulets that led into the mountains and the Riverlands themselves. To station a scout at every mouthpiece and delta was insane. My clan didn't have the numbers and I doubted that Barra or Meili would be willing to give numbers to our cause. Meili was already reluctant to send her son on the council's patrol, I couldn't expect her to be much more willing to give without a solid piece of evidence. Unfortunately, I didn't think my dreams qualified.

I set out to find my parents, hoping I could catch them together. They needed to know about the prophetic words the river goddess had given me; gods knew I couldn't comprehend them by myself. For half a heartbeat, I wanted to stop, go to the meadow and lay amongst the daisies, as I had countless times before when I needed a breath. Almost twenty years passed since my gift started to manifest, and I was no closer to knowing the answers my dreams held than when I was a small child.

Out of the corner of my eye, I saw Bowen rushing past. He looked stressed, but that wasn't unusual for my parents' friend. Bowen liked to worry about every possible thing that could go wrong; I assumed there must have been a wayward blow at arms practice this morning or perhaps a hunt returned empty-handed and now Bowen was going to lecture the cooks about how to properly ration food. I couldn't blame him, really. The home of his entire clan had been taken out from under him. The man endured the loss of his wife while taking his five-year-old son and finding a new home. Preparation was something Bowen did to get by, a survival technique.

"Bowen, wait!" I called out. Bowen swiveled towards me,

urgency written on his face. My eyes traveled to his hand lightly touching his sword hilt, made of the same blackened iron that ran through the veins of the cliffs he once called home.

I stopped, my entire body stilling, the rise and fall of my chest the only reminder of time moving. Without saying anything, I knew something was wrong – really, truly wrong. Knots began to curl in my stomach as I waited for Bowen to say something, anything.

"Willa, where have you been all morning?" Noticing the confusion in my eyes, his tone softened. "Has no one told you?"

"Told me what?" I asked. My voice sounded cold, foreign to me. Chills raced down my arms as dread set in.

"Your sister – Fiadh and Sai – they're here."

"Already? But their monthly patrol hasn't ended, why are they so early? I wasn't expecting them for another month." I searched for any evidence of explanation Bowen might offer.

"Come. I think you need to speak with your family," murmured Bowen gently. I allowed him to usher me to my father's war table, where I found my entire family sitting.

Viktor sat at the head of the table, his posture rigid but some emotion seated on his face, betraying his regal demeanor. My mother was wrapping a thick blanket around Fiadh's shaking body.

As my eyes fell upon Fiadh, my heart broke a little. My sister's normally immaculate hair was in knots, lacerations crisscrossing her arms, and a larger, swiping cut fell across the high point of her cheekbones. Not that Sai looked much better. The man looked as if he had seen a ghost, his rich skin unusually pale and his eyes held bags underneath them as if Fiadh and he rode day and night to get to the Forest Clan by the morning.

Sai took a sip from the goblet that lay before him. I couldn't be sure, but there was a flash of a bright red mark peeking out from underneath his cuff.

Was that a burn?

"What –" My voice faltered, drawing the attention of those at the table. I swallowed hard, willing my fear to be pushed aside for the moment. "What happened?" I asked, my voice stronger this time.

With this question, Fiadh's eyes welled with tears as a shaking hand pressed to her mouth. Sai placed a protective arm around her as he looked at me to answer my question.

"When we finished our patrol of the island, we decided to go back to the mountains, just for a week. We wanted time to settle in, and the patrol went faster than we expected. There was nothing unusual, no evidence of the Sectarians, even in the spots we saw on the maps."

At this point, Fiadh wiped the tears that were streaming down her face and raised her head high. "Things were normal, for a few days. We planned to wait a week and then report to you and Callan. Sai was afraid the clan might be slow to warm to me if we were away after being married – but it was a decision we made together." Fiadh finished her explanation with a touch of defiance in her voice as if daring someone to argue with their logic.

I nodded. "Of course. There's no problem with that," I said, knowing that was what she needed to hear.

"Last night, we woke up to an ambush. The Sectarians had made it across the pass and invaded camp. We didn't see them on our patrol. Their forces must have docked at Blackpool and continued on foot, it's the only explanation. Our patrol route took us to the cliffs first, and we saw their settlement from afar, but no evidence of them raising an army or a fleet. It all seemed so normal." Sai's voice trailed off, realizing that he could have prevented this all if the timing had been different.

Fiadh placed a hand over Sai's, reassuring him that they had done all that they could.

"What of the fight? Your clan?" I dared to ask the question, only because I needed to know.

"We fought. Their forces were great, and they outnumbered us. They were prepared to lose a large number of their men."

"Which was accurate," added Fiadh, a spark of confidence returning to the surface.

"Fiadh and I led a large portion of the clan through some tunnels in the mountain. We hid everyone who couldn't fight, and then we went back ourselves." I understood that not everyone in a clan could fight. For as many scouts and warriors the Clan of Forests had, there were just as many farmers, gatherers, cooks, all of whose work was equally important to have a properly functional clan. Some healers refused to even touch weapons, leaving themselves utterly defenseless in the throes of an attack.

I was shocked at the mention of the tunnels that ran through the caves in the mountainside. It wasn't surprising; rumors had long run rampant that the Mountain Clan had some secretive hideaway or second camp in their caves, but there had never been evidence to support such claims. With the decimation of their clan, I supposed, there was no point in keeping the secret any longer.

"When we came through the tunnels, the forces were completely gone. Vanished without a trace. Before they left they'd set fire to the entire camp. We helped evacuate the remaining warriors, but the whole camp is ash now. Even the sycamores, that have been standing for centuries, fallen."

Time slowed as Sai finished explaining what happened to his clan.

"It – it had to have been because of our raid on Blackpool. It was the tipping point," said Fiadh with a sob. Tears filled her eyes as she began to cry silently.

My stomach heaved like I was going to be sick. It all clicked in my head now, all the omens that had been sent to me in the past month. They had only been increasing in frequency and intensity because the time had been drawing closer and closer.

The gods were trying to warn me of the Sectarians and their return. I had been *burned alive* in the Mountain Clan's camp, died with their warriors in my dreams.

I was right all along. The Sectarians invaded, twenty years later, and they were out to destroy every piece of the clans left. Burn our homes and relics to the ground. The gods may have been trying to protect us, but they needed us just as much, if not more. If our clans died out, who would be there to remember the gods and the story of the land?

When the Sectarians had originally landed on the shores of the cliffs at Blackpool, Bowen and his clanmates had brought fearsome tales of the invaders. There was no respect for the forest or its nymphs and faeries. Perhaps the most fearful of all, they didn't recognize the same gods as the clans, using that as enough of an explanation to fill their hateful hearts and launch their invasion of the Clan o' Cliffs.

But there had been no more attacks after Blackpool, and the clans decided to let it be. Coexist peacefully, if there could be such a thing after a massacre. Obviously, that wasn't possible. The Sectarians had returned to finish the job.

I looked at everyone sitting at the table. My parents, Bowen, Sai, Fiadh, were all watching me expectantly. Part of me couldn't bear to explain to them, but the other part of me screamed Boann's warning. *The fire will burn you all if you aren't careful. Head to the river.* Boann had been right. If it wasn't for Sai and Fiadh – hell, if Sai and Fiadh *had* followed the route perfectly, they might not have been there to evacuate half their clan. They could have all been burnt.

"My dreams make sense now. The visions of the fire, they weren't in a forest. I was in the Mountain Clan's camp. I've never been around that many sycamores before, and they were all in that ring you described." Sai nodded as if everything I was saying was making sense.

"The visions have been getting worse this month because we

were drawing nearer to the date. The gods were trying to make me listen. And we didn't. Maybe that's my fault."

"Willa, nothing is your fault. We all gave input as to what we thought your dreams meant," reminded Brigid.

I turned on her, at her inability to comprehend my *guilt*, my complicit, silent nature in the ambush. I looked around the table at the hopeless, exhausted expression on many of their faces.

"Last night the goddess Boann visited me. She tried to explain it all. She gave me another warning. She said the flames will burn us all if we aren't careful. Go to the river, that will be our savior."

The breeze wrapped around my neck, the feeling of magick making my hairs stand on end. *Rectify it*, the wind seemed to whisper. *Rectify the past.*

"I don't think this is the end of the Sectarians. It's the only reason why they would have retreated. There will be another battle, another day, and we will need to be prepared to fight it. We can't do it alone though. We need all three clans, especially if the Mountain Clan has already suffered losses. We can't survive what the Clan o' Cliffs went through; I won't tolerate it." And just like that, I found my voice and put my foot down.

I knew my parents and Bowen were entitled to their own opinion. Based on the grimace on Viktor's face right now, he might even disagree with me. These were my dreams, however, and the Dagda and Boann and whatever other gods watching were speaking with me. It was my duty to interpret these prophecies, and this time, my heart and mind screamed that this was what they wanted.

I waited for someone to say something, anything. Bowen started to nod his head slowly, agreeing with me.

"The forces of the Sectarians are strong and brutish. There is no mercy in their battle, and they make every blow to kill. There is no honor in what they will try to do to us," Bowen warned. "Willa is right. We will need the Clan Amongst the River to join in this war as well as the Mountain Clan. We need Barra and Meili to agree otherwise it'll be like walking into a suicide mission."

I nodded. "That's what Boann meant, I think. To go to the Clan Amongst the Rivers. I can be there in less than a week to gather troops and support. The way back might take more, but the whole journey can be done in less than two." I spoke with confidence I didn't know I had. Something about the invasion pushed me into a fight or flight mode, leaving my body to take over. Fight, until the very end.

"Barra may seem like a jolly giant to you, Willa, but the man is much more complicated than that. I've never seen him agree to something that didn't benefit him first. You will need to be prepared to bargain. Horses, land, what have you. He will ask, so you need to be prepared with an answer."

"Surely he'll understand the importance and necessity of what we're asking him to do, though?" I asked incredulously.

"He will, just as he will understand the effect his choice has on you and your family. Willa, you are playing with politics now. Power comes in the form of self-interest and strength. You need to show yours in order to gain theirs," advised Brigid.

Shivers ran down my spine, but I didn't care.

"Okay. I'll leave for the Riverlands right away." I got up, ready to start packing and preparing my horse.

"Willa, dear, have you ever been to the Riverlands?" asked Bowen.

I looked at him with wide eyes. "No, but I can read a map just as well as anyone."

"I think it might be smart to take Callan with you. Of course, if that's alright with you, Bowen," my mother interjected.

My heart sank slightly. Callan was a piece of the journey I never factored in. To be on a journey to the Riverlands, with him, a journey entirely guided by a gift that he delicately tiptoed around at best; I shuddered at the thought. This journey would be difficult, for entirely different reasons than I previously thought.

"Okay. Callan comes with me. Anything else I should know before I go and pack?" My fingers tapped on the table impatiently.

Neither of my parents answered me. I approached Fiadh and Sai from behind and wrapped my arms around the front of my sister's chest before I leaned in and whispered.

"I'm glad you made it out okay. Both of you."

Fiadh's answer lay in the slight squeeze of the arm. My heart sank at the thought of the horrors my sister must have encountered the previous night to quiet her so. A silent promise filled my mind, a promise of revenge, as I twisted my pinky ring around my finger.

I left the group at the table and returned to my tent, my mind already reeling at the idea of packing. Once inside, I opened a leather satchel and began to select items for the ride. Loose breeches, warm leggings, light tunics would all be necessary for the journey that lay ahead. I surveyed the contents of my bureau. My mother told me in no specific terms that I was going to have to play the game of politics.

I picked up a summer gown, one made of nearly transparent material placed over a shift with gauzy, drooping sleeves and a tight, straight neckline that bound across the chest. The dress reminded me of the River Boyne I dreamt of last night, an impossibly calm and peaceful shade of blue that almost bordered on a stormy grey. I wasn't sure where my mother kept finding the seamstresses to make such dresses, but I had never been more grateful. I folded the dress carefully, so it wouldn't crease during the travel I had ahead of me. A few more items in my bag, a hairbrush, a pair of shoes, and a quick collection of the weapons laying around my tent, and I was ready to leave.

By the time I arrived at the pasture to saddle my horse, I found Callan waiting. The bay mare was already packed and saddled, and Callan had picked a near-black stallion for himself. I shook my head. *Of course Callan would pick the most finicky horse of the whole lot.* I didn't like traveling with mares and stallions mixed to begin with. Males were too aggressive and temperamental, reluctant to listen to their riders at the most inopportune moments. I didn't think Callan wouldn't respond well to me critiquing his choice. Regardless, I did just that.

"You're really going to pick that horse for this journey?" I wasted no time in pretending to win Callan over with flattery. With every second we wasted, the Sectarians could be preparing their next strike. *Gods, their next strike might even be on the Riverlands.*

Callan looked up from buckling his saddlebag.

"He's the only one that's able to keep up with your horse, Willa." I did a once over of the herd and recognized, begrudgingly, that Callan might be right.

"You know I don't like traveling with stallions," I warned.

"It's only a few days' journey. We'll be there soon. I think it will be fine," Callan cajoled.

I wasn't sure whether I should be bothered or let it go. I kept telling myself Callan had good intentions, that he had the same goals as me. Any bickering now was just going to make the journey miserable.

We had a common enemy in the Sectarians, but I couldn't shake the feeling that he was coming to watch over me, to take note of my actions when I was around Dempsey.

"Should we ride through the village? Say goodbye and grab a bite for lunch?" I asked, wanting to get on our way.

"Yes, let's go through camp, but only eat if we can on horseback."

I agreed, and with one swift motion, I swung myself onto my mare's back. With a slight nudge of my heels, my mare started forward with Callan's stallion not far behind.

Despite the gravity of the situation, I couldn't help but feel jumpy, as if energy was pouring out of my body. Part of me wondered if this was truly my calling; this journey right here, right now. This was why I had been given a gift from the Dagda. My heart and soul soared at the idea of having fulfillment, at long last. The clans wouldn't ever be the same after this attack, regardless of what happened when I went to negotiate with Barra. But the idea of preventing history from repeating itself, wiping out another clan, something that my own engagement led to; I felt a sense of duty and fate.

Callan and I trotted into the camp's center where our parents waited beside the large bonfire. I smiled at the bag of food I saw clutched in my mother's hands. Without dismounting from our horses, I accepted the food, tucking it into one of my empty saddlebags. Callan and I said our goodbyes, promising to be back soon.

"Willa," my mother called out. I looked down at Brigid's face, full of concern.

"Remember what I told you about Barra. Even if you are there as a courtier, you will be in enemy territory. Expect it."

I nodded silently, but a shiver ran through my body.

What happened with Barra so many years ago that my mother felt the need to warn me so? I wasn't sure of the answer, and perhaps it might have been a good question to ask, but now there was no time. The only way to understand her message was to experience it firsthand. I gritted my teeth and nudged my horse into a gallop.

We ate up the ground, running through the meadows before encountering the path to the forest. I had studied the map in my bedroom, memorizing the trail and important landmarks to look out for. Nevertheless, I reached into my pants pocket and pulled out the map to check, just one last time. I pulled Callan's horse next to mine before I showed him what I was looking at.

"This is the right way?" I asked, looking to Callan's face for confirmation.

"Lead on." We took a path to our left that cut through the bottom half of the forest. It was clearly a worn trail, marked fresh by the horses and wagons that had traveled it weeks ago.

As we left the edge of the Hollow, I made a silent promise to myself. *This has to work. We have to convince Barra to pledge his forces. If not for my own clan's sake, then for my sister's new clan. For the sake of the gods, too.*

CHAPTER FIFTEEN

Willa

Callan and I had been riding for hours but the forest appeared unchanging. The trees became a blur and I resigned to the fact that I would be continuing this until nightfall. The journey so far had been a far cry from the epic adventure I had been expecting, but part of me was glad for the lack of excitement.

Even though there was nothing to cause alarm, I twisted in my seat every few miles, anxious about the things the forest could be hiding from us. At the last check over my shoulder, Callan let out a sigh.

"Are you expecting someone else?"

"I'm sorry – what?" I asked, confused.

"You keep looking around as if you're expecting someone to join us. Is there a third in our party I was uninformed of?"

I blushed. I hadn't realized how paranoid I was until Callan brought attention to it. But to explain my fear of the faoladh, and *other* things, seemed silly.

"I was just keeping watch," I replied curtly.

"For?" prompted Callan.

"There could be more faoladh in the woods. Not to mention

the invading Sectarians, and any other being, magical or animal. I'm just being safe," I protested.

Callan smiled. A part of me raged at that smile, brushing off all of the very real problems I'd just mentioned.

"Willa, I think we're fine. Nothing is going to attack us and these horses, and we would've noticed if the Sectarians had made it this far inland."

"We also didn't think the Sectarians had left the cliffs at all. Plus, Dempsey and I were with his wolfhound when we got attacked, so I think it's safe to say all bets are off the table at the moment." As soon as the words left my mouth, I regretted it, bringing up Dempsey to him.

Part of me still hadn't gotten over the guilt of my feelings towards Dempsey. I lived in fear that Callan knew and I couldn't imagine the implosion that would occur if we discussed it.

"Fine."

A beat passed. I scrutinized the back of Callan's head, trying to understand what was going on in there. I expected him to engage, to respond with intensity and control. At least a whisper of the anger he had shown on my sister's wedding night.

"Fine?" I blurted out.

Callan looked back at me, his face perfectly smooth, unbothered.

"Fine. Keep checking for the faoladh and the Sectarians and the bears and the faeries." Callan shrugged and turned back around.

I spurred my horse on so that I was walking in tandem with Callan and his stallion. He gave a sideways glance towards me.

"What is it?" he asked, keeping his words clipped and short.

I wasn't sure how to begin this conversation with him. We never talked about our emotions, and I certainly never asked him to confide in me. I wasn't sure what bothered me more, his strange response at me mentioning Dempsey or his lack of his typical jovial nature.

"Did I do something?" I asked.

"I don't know Willa; why don't you tell me?" He shook his head as I searched for words. "You weren't even going to tell me that you were leaving for the Riverlands. My father told me, and then had to tell me that *he* was the one that volunteered me to come."

He continued. "Willa, you don't like to go further than the meadows. You get out of patrols whenever possible, and you've never been to the mountains or the Riverlands. So," he continued, his voice harsh and grating, "what about this journey is so different. You tell me."

I went silent as my mind began to race. *There it was. All of it, just stewing underneath the surface.*

"I came because of my duty to my sister." This was partially true, even if my brain refused to admit it. *That was partially false*, a cruel and small voice in the back of my head taunted me.

"You came because of your feelings for that Riverlands warrior. Don't lie Willa, it isn't becoming."

I felt like I'd been slapped. But there was the second half of the truth, laid out and bare between us.

"Callan, I've told you. Nothing happened between the two of us. I can be friends with other men. I know you like to keep me on a tight leash, but at least let me have a little freedom." A lie, but what other choice did I have? Death by his strangulation of liberties?

Callan raised his eyebrows, surprised at my courage.

"As you wish. Just make sure you don't forget the promise sitting on your hand." I twisted the engagement ring on my finger in response. I let my horse take the faster pace, putting steps between us, letting our argument fall away.

I spent the day's remaining few hours on the trail in tears. My stomach twisted at the thoughts running through my mind. *Callan must think I'm horrible. He must dread the marriage as much as I do, especially considering my behavior recently. Gods, and all he's ever been is nice to me.*

It was true, at least in my eyes. In the past twenty years, I could only ever remember Callan being there for me. A constant presence at my side. And yet that was where the death of the relationship lay.

Night fell fast and in as few words as possible, we agreed to make our camp for rest. We chose a bank underneath a ledge, giving us something solid to lean our backs against, one less direction to guard.

We laid out our thin bedrolls silently, divvying up the blankets. Callan went to find something to eat while I started a fire. As I struck the blaze into life, coaxing the faint timbers into larger flames, I thought about the dream I had not too long ago. The irony of it all, to be making a fire in the woods not long after the Mountain Clan had been burnt to pieces. I sat like that for a while, staring into the flames until Callan returned with a rabbit in hand.

We cleaned the animal and fashioned a spit over the fire to roast it, cleaning the meat off its bones and burying the entrails to cover any scents a nearby predator might pick up. While Callan may have doubted that an animal would attack us earlier, he didn't want to take any chances, especially while we were sleeping. After cooling down the horses and feeding them, I slid into my makeshift bed for the night. Callan's breaths in his own were already deep and slow.

We placed our beds in one long line, with our heads pointing towards each other. I looked up at the stars twinkling above me as I pictured Callan's face.

"Cal?" I asked. I hadn't used my nickname for him in such a long time. At least since I was a young teenager, still believing he was my hero.

"Willow?" he responded. I bit the inside of my cheek, thinking about what I was about to say.

"Do you think we ever had a chance? Of truly falling in love?" I whispered.

"Can you fall in love when you're forced into it?" He went silent, the sound of crickets filling the air. "Maybe we still have a chance."

I appreciated the lie he told me, even if it was just for the night.

CHAPTER SIXTEEN

Willa

I opened my eyes to an unfamiliar section of thicket. For a second, I tried to piece together what had happened before I remembered yesterday. I pushed myself up from my bedroll and looked to the empty bed next to me.

A quick scan around our makeshift camp told me that Callan was nowhere in sight, but both of our horses were still there. *He's probably just trying to find breakfast.* As I waited, I busied myself with the horses, strapping back on the packs and saddlebags, rolling up the blankets to place underneath the lift of the saddle.

Heavy steps sounded from far away. I knew it was going to be Callan, but I drew darts from the bag that hung at my hip just in case. If it was a Sectarian, or whatever else the woods had to offer me today, a quick throw to the eye would leave me with enough time to jump on the back of my horse and return home.

I shook my head, remembering the conversation I had with Callan the other night. Was it normal to always expect the worst, one eye always checking behind me? There was a sense of survival within me that told me being on edge might save my life one day. I hoped to never find myself in that position.

"Where have you been?" I asked as soon as Callan's blond head came into view.

Callan looked around him. "I was out looking for breakfast and scouting our route for the day," he answered smoothly.

His answer was so flippant, like he couldn't care to think of telling me. "Next time let me know. You scared the shit out of me."

Callan's lip twitched, amused by my choice of words. He raised his eyebrows. "Okay, I will."

"What did you find for breakfast?"

"Honestly? Nothing. It's like this part of the forest went quiet."

Shivers covered my arm. It was never a good sign when the prey went running, and as of late, more and more occurrences revealed themselves as omens.

"We have some fruit and cheese that my mom packed. I'm sure the Clan Amongst the Rivers will feed us once we get there."

"All the more reason to hurry up," smiled Callan.

Using the sharp edge of my knife, I unwrapped the hard cheese and sliced the apples. I looked up at Callan standing over me.

"So where does the route take us today?" I asked, making small talk. Something between us felt easier, lighter than it was yesterday. I was in no rush to see it leave.

"The path I'm used to taking down to the Riverlands is blocked. I thought I heard Barra mention it to my father when he attended the wedding. Looks like there must have been a big rain down here; there's a giant oak blocking the path, and I don't think either of the horses could jump it."

I cursed under my breath. *What luck. The only journey where time actually mattered and we were going to have to find a way to move the damn tree or go around it.*

"Is there an alternate route?"

"That's what I was looking for. There looks like there's one on the map. It's a little overgrown, but it should take us down to the marshes and fens. From there we can follow the delta to the Riverland camp."

I remembered about the warning Callan had given me months ago, about the dangers of bringing horses around those marshes. I squared my shoulders, thinking to myself there was no other way. We would be extra careful and surefooted.

"Let's go," I agreed.

The two of us ate our small breakfast and finished cleaning up the rest of our makeshift camp. Somehow the horses seemed to have even more energy than the previous day, taking to the rest of the road quickly. Normally, I would have worried about exhausting them when there was an entire day of travel ahead, but I reasoned we would probably end up walking the majority of the way once we hit the wetlands.

Despite Dempsey's opinion that the forests weren't unique to the Clan of Forests, I saw the difference. The lands here were wooded, yes, but they weren't the forests I had come to know and love. The trees here grew shorter and had thick roots that curved into the ground. It looked like a place where dryads might live. Tall grasses replaced the thickets of underbrush while unfamiliar flowers grew in the gaps.

I hoped we would reach the Riverland camp today. If we were stranded out here and Callan couldn't find any prey to eat, we would be reduced to what was left of the cheese and fruit, which wasn't much. Even if the flowers here did look like cousins to the ones in the forest, that was the difference between a bite to eat and poison.

Slowly, but surely, the path started to transform, turning to a short grass filling the trail and divots every few feet. We slowed our horses to a walk, knowing the path was a twisted ankle waiting to happen if we pressed the pace any further. I noticed the roots of the tupelo trees were exposed and clumps of soil hung around the edges of the path as if it had flooded recently.

The trees started to break and a waterline appeared in front of me. My eyes filled with dismay looking at the vast amount of water before us. The wetland spanned the horizon, dipping deeper and deeper until I saw groves of trees popping out of the waterline. Tall grasses curved out of the perimeter of my vision, allowing a gauge for where land stopped and water began.

There was no doubt in my mind that Callan told me the truth. It wouldn't be easy for a horse to just break an ankle, but if it were to panic and get stuck? The horse and its rider could drown.

I looked at Callan nervously. "What does the map say?"

"To our left. It looks like if we follow the waterline enough, there's eventually an inlet that will let us cross to their camp. Should only take an hour or two." Callan gave me a reassuring smile.

An hour. An hour to navigate the murky waters. An hour until I could see Dempsey. An hour until I would have to negotiate with Barra for the future of our clans.

We picked our way across the narrow path, eventually dismounting our horses to continue on foot. I wasn't sure how stable the ground was here, and didn't want the horses to sink with our added weight. Walking on foot added even more time, and to my dismay, we would be arriving at the Clan Amongst the Rivers dirty and reeking of peat.

The sun was beating on our backs when a splash came from the water. I lifted my head from watching the placement of my feet to scan the bog.

"Did you hear that?"

Rather than dismissing my worries once more, Callan stopped. "I did," he answered quietly.

"It's probably just a fish, right? Or maybe some sort of fishing cat or beaver?" My voice rose as my heartbeat thudded against my chest.

"Willa, beavers only live around running water. Who taught you your animals?" Callan's voice was light, trying to joke it off.

"Callan, I am not joking." My voice cut like a knife in between each word.

He paused. I didn't dare ask once more what was going through his mind.

"Let's hope it was a fish," and he kept walking.

Hope? What else could it be? What isn't he saying? The heavy air threatened to swallow me whole, making me feel as if I was sinking into the greedy silt of the bog.

He's not saying what it is because he knows you can't handle it. Because you're pathetic. I tried to breathe, fill my lungs with air, but it wasn't working. The air hung rancid around us, refusing to give life, ready to smother us. I knew by now that I was starting to hyperventilate.

Callan stopped once more. He let go of the reins he was holding and sidestepped around my horse until he was firmly grasping my shoulders. He had learned the hard way not to get too close to me while I was panicking.

"Willa, look at me. *Look* at me."

I looked up into those crystal clear eyes that always sent ice down my veins. My hands stopped shaking.

"Willa, I am going to tell you something because I trust you, okay? Because I know you can handle it."

He thinks I can handle it. I am not weak. I am not weak. I will handle it, I repeated in my head, over and over again.

"This bog is marked as *Cul na Móna* on the map. I decided to take us through here because there was no other way to get us to the Riverlands."

A frenetic laugh escaped my lips. Cul na Móna wasn't just a piece of marshland. It was a place where the bog bodies rested, and I prayed to the gods we did not wake them. Anger surged through me, making me momentarily forget the panic that suffocated me moments earlier.

"You took us through the most sacred and deadly bog on the isle?" I whispered in a voice so low and urgent I could see Callan lean in to hear me.

"It was the only way!" Callan insisted.

I tied my cloak to my horse, leaving my sword free to grasp as I wielded my scian in my hand. I would prefer not to see a bog body close enough to need a scian, but if I carried the bastard sword during the remainder of this journey my arm would grow tired before the battle even began.

"Callan, shut up. You will wake the dead." I motioned for Callan to keep moving, that we were done here, and I didn't need his comfort anymore.

At the moment, I couldn't comprehend what Callan had been thinking this morning when he decided this was a better route. Warriors never crossed this bog unless they had a death wish. It was legend that there were once creatures and people too broken, too dark and evil to enter the Otherworld through the tombs where spirits normally resided. The castoffs that hell didn't want became trapped in the murky waters of the bog, willing to pull anything and anyone into their depths.

Gods, no wonder today has been so strange. The lack of prey – the lack of animals throughout our trip, the strange plants, they were all signs we've been on the path to something unnatural, where we clearly don't belong.

All matters of politics and negotiation left my head, my only focus on leaving the bog alive. My mind raced, trying to recall any stories of warriors or scouts who had escaped the bog's clutches. Certainly never in my lifetime. Someone had once lived to tell the tale, I supposed, how else do legends begin?

A ripple in the water moved the still image before me. I watched as a creature slowly rose out of the water, mud sloughing off its body. *It* was definitely the right word for the creature standing before us, I decided. The figure was the size of a large man, with skin so warped it resembled leather. The twisted and pockmarked skin clung to its emaciated frame. The bog body looked to be in the midst of some decaying phase, yet preserved, because for as dead as it looked, the body had not decomposed as a corpse would.

The beast still had its hair and the eyes were dark pits, but skin stretched tight over where a nose normally sat, and that is where the similarities to humanity ended. The creature was missing its bottom jaw, and the lower half of one of its arms hung off, tendon and sinew exposed at the elbow. Whatever – whomever – this body once belonged to, it had not entered the bog in a peaceful manner.

I sheathed my scian slowly and drew my sword instead, deciding the further this creature stayed away, the better. To my side, Callan did the same. The horses began to panic as fear crept into their eyes, whinnying nervously. I prayed they didn't spook and try to run. That was the last thing we needed right now.

Slowly, the bog body stepped towards us, sending waves through the water.

"Stay back," called out Callan, brandishing his sword.

Nervous laughter threatened to escape me. Every part of me was certain that the bog body was not going to listen to us. The dull, black pits for eyes reflected only one need – to kill and bring us to our watery grave.

Boann, river goddess, if you have ever been at my side, be here now.

Some part of me hoped the water goddess would be able to see me, help me, even if I wasn't at the River Boyne. The other part of me knew it was futile, that only dead things ruled this bog, that there was an absence of good and light associated with a god's touch, and there was no reach for them here.

The bog body was almost upon us. It waded towards the path, the trail being so narrow that we would be within arm's reach of the bog body. I swallowed, knowing what we had to do, certain that it wasn't going to be easy. The bog body might move slowly, but it didn't seem stiff or broken. It was as if the creature was biding its time, knowing it would kill us eventually. The atmosphere of the marsh made me wonder what other types of dark magick were at play.

The face of the bog body shifted, the withered face's expression lifting upwards. Even without the bottom half of its jaw, without a mouth, I could tell it was smiling at us. My feet rooted in place as the body's remaining arm reached to its side and drew a large broadsword.

The sword glinted off the sunlight, but it did not shine. Rather, it couldn't shine, not with the rust and corrosion and peat hanging off the piece of steel.

Callan charged forward, moving off the path and into the bog, the water going up to his shin as he made for the first blow towards the body. The bog body blocked with surprising ease, returning a brute blow for Callan's head. Callan shifted back, missing the blade by a hair's length. The mud was sucking around his boots, anchoring him to the spot, slowing him down as the bog body advanced. Callan was rooted to the spot, using pure strength to fend off the advancing corpse.

"Callan!" I screamed, breaking the spell on my silence, running to the point in the path behind Callan, taking great care not to enter the murky waters. The mud was a death trap, and I didn't have Callan's strength to fight off the bog body.

Maybe I would be able to distract the body – maybe buy Callan enough time to get himself unstuck and out of the murky water. There was a small part of me that felt guilty, guilty that I was unwilling to enter the waters, fighting at Callan's side.

I picked up a stone by my side, throwing it at the bog body, doing anything to get it to break concentration. A large rock landed on its skull wiping a strand of peat off of it, grazing the bone.

And then the bog body was upon me, striking blow after blow, seeking blood. The corpse took long steps towards me, still staying within the water, but the path wasn't wide enough for me to stay out of reach. I blocked each strike, gaining strength from the knowledge that the body couldn't leave the water and enter the narrow sandy path.

I watched out of the corner of my eye as Callan struggled against the mud, moving behind the bog body to sandwich it between me and him. The body raised its sword above its head, ready to bring it crashing down on me. I would be helpless once it struck. The creature had an unlimited power drawn from the bog, and I would be crushed beneath its broadsword.

Callan thrust, and his sword went straight through its chest cavity, breaking that perfectly wrapped skin. It stopped, the sword still hung above its head and went completely still. I wondered for a moment if this was it, if we had defeated the bog body.

Those thoughts vanished as the bog body swung into motion, swiftly rotating and bringing the sword down, crashing the blunted end into Callan's golden hair. Callan had a look of surprise on his face as he crumpled into the water, falling with a splash. Blood leaked from him, staining the muddy water scarlet. His face never shifted from that look of surprise, the disbelief at being beaten permanently etched there.

The body turned around, refocusing on me. A rattling, wheezing voice came from the thing's chest as it began to speak.

"The tribute has been paid. You are free to go, my lady."

I didn't dare move a muscle as the bog body slowly turned around and sunk back into the water, taking Callan's body with it.

Gasping, racking sobs heaved from my body, my screams hanging in the air, disbelief echoing in the air.

I began to cry, something I never thought I would do for Callan, but even until the end, he was my protector. The thought of him decaying in the marsh made me feel sick.

Our future was ripped out from under us.

My hand rose to my throat trying to quiet the hysterics rising from within me. A cool piece of metal touched my throat, and I knew what it was. I grabbed at the band, pulling and twisting to move my engagement ring off, the feeling of it constricting on my finger too much. I was trapped in this heavy air, *trapped in this bog, Callan trapped in the bog.*

I ripped the ring off and let it fall from my hands.

And except for me, the bog was quiet, as if the violence never occurred. The only thing to mark the fight was the pool of blood in the water, the burgundy stained tide now lapping against the shore. A bird flew by, and I finally registered the return of animals to this ancient place.

The thought of the body coming back was enough to get me moving again, knowing I couldn't fight it alone. Knowing that Callan's sacrifice couldn't be for nothing.

Gods, that's what he was. He was a human sacrifice to whatever hell this place is.

Before the body could come back or change its mind, I swiftly mounted Callan's horse. It was stupid to ride it through the wetland, but I wasn't staying here a second longer than I needed to. My horse would follow. I clicked my tongue and the stallion started forward.

I looked back once more, to the spot where I once stood. A piece in the dirt shimmered, where my engagement ring would rest for eternity.

CHAPTER SEVENTEEN

Willa

T he stallion's legs stretched out, galloping at a hard pace, wanting to leave this place of evil and death as much as I did. I spared a glance behind me to confirm my mare was following. Around us, the bog swung back into life, dragonflies flitting above the water's surface and a chorus of toads bellowing as if the bog was happy with the sacrifice it took.

My stomach churned at the thought. I looked at my left hand, now completely bare as it gripped the reins.

I'm free. The thought bubbled to the front of my mind, unable to help myself. A part of me didn't know whether to laugh or cry. My fiancé died, and I should be grieving, but it was as if the universe knew we weren't right, as if fate had another destiny for me. Dully, I recognized these thoughts as a symptom of shock, not being able to comprehend the weight of what just happened.

The bog body called me *my lady*. As if it answered to me, responded to me. The creature simply could have been ancient and polite, but I wondered if it had meant more.

Gods, Callan. His body would turn into that same kind of leathery corpse cursed by the magick that haunted the swamp.

His golden hair would fade into the same straw color and the dimples that he liked to flash would become warped and twisted. A sob escaped my body. Callan would not have a burial, wouldn't be laid to rest in the wedge tombs reserved for the warriors of our clan. And maybe the worst part of all was that he deserved it, deserved that honor. Even until the end, he was good, chasing these lofty goals with me, traipsing across the island at my request. This was my fault. Perhaps I didn't want a future with him, but I never wished for *this*. I didn't know how I was going to tell Bowen, or what was going to happen to the negotiations now. I wiped at the tears, wondering how Barra was going to take me seriously when I was crying.

I cursed, realizing the only map I had packed was the one I gave to Callan yesterday, which he used to scout out the paths this morning. The stallion slowed to a walk as I searched hopelessly in the saddlebags around me, double-checking every pocket. The only map we brought was in Callan's pocket, sinking beneath the water.

There was no way I was turning back for it. It would be a fool's errand. Desperately, I tried to remember all that Callan had said about reaching the Riverlands camp. *Follow this path and it will eventually turn into an inlet. That inlet will take you straight to camp.*

Gods, how could I have been so stupid to have not asked a single question? But there was nothing I could do except keep going, hoping Callan was right.

I thanked the gods an hour later when I saw the waterline dropping away and the narrow path widening. A clearly cut, green footpath lay in front of me, a hint of civilization nearby. As the horses and I stepped upon the path, a weight lifted off my shoulders. We had to be close to camp, I felt it in my heart, and I dared to be optimistic, hoping I would be in safety soon.

The path stayed like that until nightfall, the muddy water next to it turning into a clear stream. I knew I was alone, and that there were so many things to be afraid of out here, isolated, in the dark, but I couldn't bring myself to worry. In the face of flight or fight, there wasn't room for it.

For two nights, I traveled like that, walking in the daytime, taking dips in the river to stay cool in the heat that became increasingly unbearable. There was little game, but I hunted what I could, but not nearly enough to fill my belly. I didn't dare to eat the plants that grew around me, each one more unfamiliar than the next.

Callan and I had finished the food my mother sent on our second day, and I wouldn't have a proper meal until I reached the Riverlands. The idea of their camp was starting to sound more and more like salvation. My days and nights were spent thinking of Callan, thinking of his father, remembering those few good moments we had and cherishing them. The shock wore off, and instead of crumbling with grief, I simply kept going, forcing my body through the motions, the only thing I could do when reality became too painful.

On the third day, I laid my head on the black stallion and prayed for him to follow the path. My head ached from the sun, and I couldn't sit upright without getting dizzy. The stream was widening, and I was afraid I was going to have to cross it sometime in the near future. The scenery around me blurred together, and I wished for time to pass, to move quicker, for the day to be over already.

Life felt so far away, losing Callan felt so far away, and I knew that my body had no more tears left for him. I might have been saving them for myself.

At some point, the inlet started to slope upwards. The horses turned around a bend, and I gasped. A great ringfort stood before me, larger than any I had ever seen. Stones were stacked and cobbled together, creating an enclosure around the top half of the hill. The wall protected the life within the enclosure, and I could barely see faint smoke rising, giving hint to the prosperity there.

Below where the wall started, I saw tents and huts, signaling the presence of a normal village. I had underestimated the power of the Clan Amongst the Rivers, and I wondered if this was what my mother had warned me about.

As soon as I came into view, torches lit around the tents. Bonfires sprang into action as a gate was lowered across the entrance to the ringfort. It was as if the village switched on with my arrival.

The ringfort was sounding an alarm.

If the Mountain Clan hadn't been prepared for the Sectarian attack, the Clan Amongst the Rivers certainly would be. I slowed my horse to a walk, looping a rope around the horn of my mare's saddle, so she wouldn't be spooked for what was about to happen. I stilled myself and the horses, and waited.

It happened slowly. The small figures of people retreated into their huts, and the space inside the ringfort cleared. It was as if a back door opened, because soon horses poured out from around the ringfort, enveloping the sides of the building. I knew they were coming for me.

Just in case, I slipped my pouch of darts inside a hidden pocket in my cloak hood and drew it over my hair.

The first group of horses rode towards me and I counted ten men. The rest of the pack stayed at the top of the hill outside the gate entrance, claiming their vantage point.

A powerful voice spoke out.

"Declare yourself." The horses stayed a good distance back from me, far enough that no weapon would reach except for a bow. These warriors were trained as a unit, mimicking an arrowhead formation, similar to a pack of geese flying south for the winter.

A light formed in my eyes, a feeling of hope seizing me once more. Unlike my bubble of optimism from a few days ago, this feeling might be here to stay.

"Willa, from the Clan of Forests, member of the Council to Clans and Gods," I announced.

Let them tremble to hear my name and my story. I always thought that the clans were honest. Our life's work and accomplishment represented in our rings, allegiances spelled out in our names. But sometimes a name doesn't equal an explanation, and I didn't know if I could ever explain what truly happened in the bog to anyone. The bog body killed Callan and set me free from my engagement, yes, but it also freed a part of my soul that was trapped.

There was a monumental shift in my form, my essence, in that moment, moving me closer to what might be my fate.

CHAPTER EIGHTEEN

Dempsey

I stepped out of line, breaking rank.

"Gods, Willa, you just couldn't stay away." A lazy grin filled my face.

She's here. She's here. She's here. There was no fiancé to accompany her, no ring that sat on her finger. Was she a ghost? A figment of wishful thinking and imagination?

"Obviously not, Dempsey," Willa responded. She swung down from her horse and walked towards me. The horse looked almost emaciated, clearly having seen better days. And Willa... while she still held her beauty, there was something different about her. Exhaustion etched across her face, and her face looked hollow. Something had happened – but what?

"We have a lot to talk about. A lot of things have changed." Willa gave a pointed look to the warriors that stood on either side of me.

"Of course," I said, understanding immediately. I turned to the warband that flanked me. "It's fine. Go back up to the ringfort and lift the alarm, please. Let everyone know it's okay to come out." My warriors sheathed their weapons and turned back to the hill. This conversation needed privacy.

"Felix," I called. My friend appeared at my side. "Tell my father we're to have company."

Felix gave a curt nod. "Nice to see you, Willa." He gave a wink and a smile before walking away.

Willa and I looked at each other, alone for the first time since our almost kiss – and fight – in the training ring. That was her last attempt to push me away, so why come here? Why seek me out? A rush ran through me as I remembered the feel of her next to me. I swore I heard Willa sigh as I stepped closer to her.

"Are you going to tell me why you're here? It isn't time for the handoff." Reluctantly, because it needed to be said, I added "Where's Callan?" as I searched her face for answers.

Willa opened her mouth, but no sound came out. Instead, she shook her head no.

"I'd like to tell you and your father at the same time if it's alright with you."

In mere seconds, my stupid, foolish hopes came crashing down. Something was stewing underneath the surface, and it didn't have to do with her feelings for me. This was bigger than us.

"Okay," I murmured. "But Willa?"

"Yes," she breathed in response. Perhaps I imagined it, but it was there, that shimmer of connection that ran between us.

I took a step closer to her, so close she could reach out and touch me if she wanted. I would let her. But never the other way around – those kisses weren't mine to steal. I guided a hand towards her face, slipping it around to the back of her head. I gave a tug at the hood of her cloak.

"Would you at least tell me why you're carrying a pouch of darts inside your hood?" I asked, furrowing my brow.

Willa's hand flew up as if she couldn't believe the pouch of darts I held were hers. I wanted to roll my eyes in disbelief – if only she knew there was a dart feather tangled in her hair.

Anyone would have seen it a mile away, but I had to admire the courage.

"It's better safe than sorry," she said. "Are you going to tell me when you got so good at pilfering things?" Willa asked, raising her eyebrows.

Another grin, the second I'd experienced since she arrived. "A light touch is the trick," I winked.

A blush colored on her cheeks. I could practically hear her thoughts: *Did he mean...?* I let amusement spread on my face, to show her that yes, that was absolutely what I meant.

I walked back to my horse. "My father will be expecting us. Let me show you to his chambers."

Our horses ascended to the ringfort. While we walked, I watched Willa take it all in. Her head swiveled between the village, the garden patches that colored the walkways, and the bonfire structures with giant cauldrons for cooking. Curiosity weaved between us. It was rare to have someone from another clan visit the Riverlands, much less the ringfort. In many ways, the marshes and rivers left us ostracized from the other clans. Travel was often difficult, especially when the weather let nature run wild.

"What determines who lives out here and who lives in there?" Willa's head bobbed between the village and ringfort.

"The ringfort has been in my family for nearly a century. It's the strongest hold on the island and is impenetrable. My father's household lives inside, along with our top warriors. There is space enough inside that if there ever was an attack, the villagers could fit, for a while at least." It didn't go unnoticed that my father kept his best warriors close by, unwilling to extend their reach to the outer limits of the Riverlands.

"What if you were caught unawares?"

The question asked for secrets that were not meant to be shared. But I found myself answering anyway – if not to brag about my clan's strength, then to share with her that there are other ways of living.

"Youngest warriors sleep in a tent down here, pay their dues. If they earn it, then they can move up to the ringfort. But most enjoy it out here anyways. Something about being out in the open. So we let them choose their destinies."

Willa nodded. "Seems like your clan has thought of everything. I could understand that – wanting to choose."

I decided to not push. Instead, we rode in silence until we reached the gate of the ringfort. The metal grate slowly raised, and our horses padded underneath. Willa took it all in – tilting her head back, examining the murder hole above her head, the guards at the gates.

I led us to the small set of stables to tie up the horses before setting off to my father's quarters at the far end of camp. Willa staggered slightly as she hopped off her horse, but righted herself quickly enough that I didn't point it out. She tugged on her rings the entire walk there. *What are you nervous about?*

My father's tent swept the back expanse of the yard, a rich maroon color that made it look like the great stone walls were bleeding. The Riverlands crest waved on a flag above it, claiming the land. Inside the tent was my father, surrounded by mounds of books and maps, a platter of food, and a goblet of wine at his side. He smiled as we entered, the greeting he would give a friend he hadn't seen in a long time. Barra stood from his chair that was covered in furs and moved aside a pile of books from a lounge.

"Please sit, my child. You must be so tired from your journey. Although I might say it wasn't one we were expecting."

Willa blinked, clearly taken aback by the jovial nature of my father. But that was Barra – cunning and clever, so friendly by nature that his enemies forgot the threat of him. It was a multi-faceted nature, and I couldn't advise Willa on which side she would receive. Half the time I never knew what I was walking into.

"Thank you, Barra. I'm pleased to make your introduction." The words sounded wooden, the pleasantries of court life.

"Oh, please do drop the formality, Willa, there is no need." His back turned to us, busying himself at the table. "Wine? Beer? Cider?" He called out over his shoulder.

Kind, compassionate Barra it is then.

"Cider, if you have any," Willa answered in a surprised tone. Probably wondering what other tricks my father kept hidden here – although my father probably should have offered Willa food and not drink. Her face was pale, and I wondered when was the last time she had a proper meal.

Barra returned with a pint glass filled with amber-colored liquid, closing the trunk he had been reaching into with his foot.

"Dempsey, help yourself. Now, Willa, please indulge us in the story of how exactly you came to visit today." Barra settled himself back into his chair, prepared for a traveling minstrel show. I rolled my eyes, familiar with my father's antics, and helped myself to a beer.

Willa took a deep breath. "Four days ago, my sister and Sai arrived at our camp, early considering that the handoff between council patrols should have been much later. They told us that the Mountain Clan had been attacked, their camp burned to the ground. They were able to save the majority of the clan, but they sustained major losses."

"Shit," I muttered, and even Barra looked stunned. Willa continued.

"The Sectarians left after *they* were finished with the battle. They didn't kill every last warrior, or make some declaration of peace, or have demands of war." She took another breath, steadying herself.

"It was the first point of attack, to weaken and surprise.

They'll be back," answered Barra, stealing the thoughts out of all of our mouths.

"Yes," Willa said, nodding. "It's the only explanation."

"Why now? After twenty years, why did they choose now to attack?" I asked. Two decades, an entire generation had passed – and yet their old grievances lingered.

Willa turned to me. "Honestly? I don't know the answer. Maybe it was our attack on their camp? I'm confident I didn't see any troops on the map when I was in the caves," she concluded solemnly.

"Ironic that they struck in the middle of a great peace, when we're intertwining all our clans through marriage." I snorted, taking a sip of my beer.

My father had been particularly insistent on *that* when we returned from the wedding. *It's your duty to offer alliances and continue the family. Find a girl, any girl. She's yours, I'll be sure of it. But you need a wife, and soon.* Easier said than done when the woman I wanted was promised to another.

"It's not funny," Willa turned on me, her temper flaring.

"Objectively, I think it is. Given the context of the situation, no, probably not." I waved away her anger, knowing I should have expected it.

"How did they attack? Where from?" questioned Barra, returning to the subject at hand.

"We think they must've had forces dock at Blackpool. Spies have scoped out the colony at the cliffs, and it's not large enough to support the host that attacked in the mountains."

Barra swirled his wine in its cup. He looked up at Willa, locking eyes. "So you're telling me that the island could be crawling with them."

The room fell silent. The idea of unseen eyes, watching and waiting, made my skin crawl.

"I cannot speak for a clan that isn't mine. The Forest Clan has strength in our patrol numbers, and I can assure you that we do not have invaders camping on our land. Can you say the same for yours?" Her head straightened as she spoke, temper turning into something far more regal.

"Easy there, Willa. We weren't accusing you of anything. I was simply drawing a conclusion." Barra looked at me, utterly unbothered by the news that just broke.

He turned his gaze back to Willa, scanning her face before he asked his next question.

"And your parents allowed you to travel here alone? It can be a dangerous journey, especially with invading forces at work."

The question landed like a blow, Willa looking like someone threw a punch at her. Her fingers drifted to her opposite hand, where her engagement ring should have sat.

"No, they didn't." Her voice was soft, losing all of its muster from earlier. "Callan, my betrothed came with me, except –" She looked down at her hands. "He chose the wrong route. He took us through the Cul na Móna and he paid the price." Willa lifted her head and looked Barra dead in the eyes. "The bog bodies took him as payment. He's dead."

The statement hit me, even though I hated the man. Willa's face blanched, obviously remembering the trauma she witnessed, the death of a man she was meant to be bound to. *Gods, I feel like an idiot.* My first thought when seeing her was that she was here because of her feelings for me. How wrong I had been.

Grim determination set in. No more. I wouldn't push my feelings onto her any longer. No innuendos, or flirting. She didn't want it, and I didn't deserve the hope that came along with it.

"Oh, dear child," whispered Barra. "I'm sorry." His voice shook with conviction, and I could tell he meant it.

"That's something no one should ever have to witness. We haven't lost someone to the bog in such a long time…" Barra's voice trailed off, making me wonder who the last victim had been. It wasn't anyone I remembered.

"Well, I've heard enough for right now. We can discuss this later. Dempsey, why don't you help Willa settle in. I'll check in after dinner." And just like that, Barra dismissed us.

Willa followed me out of the tent, blinking at the late afternoon sun.

"Where to now?" She asked faintly.

"By the look of you, I'm thinking to the kitchens. You look like a ghost, Willa. When was the last time you ate?"

Willa paused for a moment. "I caught a squirrel a day ago."

I raised my eyebrows. "You caught a tree rat and haven't eaten since?"

She didn't answer but nodded in confirmation. I ran my fingers through my hair, deciding what to do next.

"Stay here. I would bring you with me, but I think you'd fall over on the walk there." I gave her a nervous glance before heading off in the direction of the kitchen.

I hadn't walked for more than a minute when I heard the sound of footsteps behind me. I glanced back to see Willa trotting after me, the effort clearly strenuous.

Gods, what had she gone through that she can't sit with herself for a few moments? Not that I was judging. I just wanted to know what was running through her head, the echoes of the monsters she fought.

"Couldn't stay away?" I teased. My earlier resolution flooded back to me. *No flirting.*

"Can't get rid of me," she answered, her voice dripping with sarcasm.

We approached a stone building, smoke escaping from the top, the smell of fresh bread and roasting meat heavy in the air. Willa's stomach growled in response. I leaned up against a window, raising the pane of glass so my head could duck in. A rush of heat escaped, giving clue to the hot fires within.

"Dinner's not for another couple of hours, sorry love." A

large woman with a brisk voice shooed me away, closing the window from the inside.

The window held at an angle, kept open by my forearm. I tilted my head, trying to look remorseful. "Ofie, it's not for me. It's for my friend. She's journeyed for the past week, and she's hardly had anything to eat. I'm just trying to show her some hospitality." I lowered my voice to a theatrical whisper. "She looks like she's about to break in two."

I glanced back to Willa, while she tried to look remorseful.

Ofie looked her up and down.

"Fine. But don't go telling any of your friends, especially not Felix." She walked away grumbling about men and appetites.

"You looked very cute," Willa teased, referring to the show I put on.

"I know how to work it, what can I say?" I grinned wide.

Ofie appeared at the makeshift counter with a basket in hand. I didn't dare open the wicker clasps in front of her, but I thought I smelt roast chicken. I murmured my thanks and began to walk towards the gates.

My steps led us toward the same portcullis we'd entered through, walking on the gravel path that intersected the inner circle of the fort. I looked back at Willa, checking to see she was still upright. "I think I know a place, if you don't mind walking a little." My tone was soft, afraid she might break if I spoke too loud.

Willa nodded and followed me out of the ringfort. At some point, Tad came bounding out of the bushes, the shaggy dog walking by my side. We picked our way down a winding path that brought us to the backside of the fort, facing the opposite direction of Willa's arrival. I trotted forward, running off the last bits of the downward sloping path before turning to Willa and extending my hand, helping her do the same.

A shallow, broad river extended before us, glittering in the sun. The water was clear, mirroring the stones underneath.

Several islands dotted the middle of the water, with straggling trees clinging to them. I savored the clean smell of the water and the rush of the river in my ears.

I walked towards a tree rooted in the sloping bank, sitting against the trunk in the shade. Tad followed, turning in a circle before choosing his spot.

"It's nice, right? You would never know there's an entire isle with problems behind it."

"It's peaceful. Beautiful, really," Willa admitted. She tore into the food. The smells of roast chicken and fresh bread filled the air while she ate. She was starving and I immediately filled with guilt at not filling her needs earlier.

"The River Boyne feeds into it. People say it's blessed with the water of the gods." I tilted my head back, closing my eyes.

"Do you come out here often?" Willa tilted her head, as if picturing me here.

"No."

She scrunched her brow. "No? Then why are you showing me? Why are we here?"

I struggled to find the right words to explain it. "This place is too pure, too good. I don't want it. It's a place of the gods, and I'm not worthy. But you," I opened my eyes to look at her. Her hair caught the light, shining as her eyes were cast out to the water. Her profile was beautiful, as was every part of her, her hands cradling her cheeks. "You seemed like you needed it."

Willa's head whipped towards me. "*I'm* worthy?" She spoke the words carefully.

I looked her over once more, shocked. "Of course you are." I couldn't think of anyone who would feel more at place here, amongst the rushing river and the raw gift of nature.

Willa swallowed. "I don't know if anyone has ever told me that, gift from the Dagda or not." Tears splashed upon her cheeks. "I'm sorry I'm a mess," she muttered as she furiously wiped away the tears.

Rocks slid down the bank as I moved closer to her. "You're not a mess. You've just been through a lot." I reached out to her slender hand, letting my touch linger before withdrawing it.

Willa didn't respond as she stared out towards the water. *Tell me. Tell me all of it. Let me help carry your burden.*

I continued, sitting close enough that she could feel my presence but not so close that we were touching. "First person I've ever seen speak to my father like that. For all the kindness he shows, the man can be a real bastard." I observed her silence. "Are you upset? About Callan? I can stop the chatting if you want, but if you want to talk, I'm here." I didn't know what to give her, what I should offer.

For a moment, I thought she wasn't going to say anything. That we were going to sit here in silence – and that would have been okay. Grief appears in different forms.

"I hated him," she said quietly. "I've been engaged to him since I was two years old, and I couldn't stand him. He was overbearing and loud and rude. He never truly cared about me. Or my gift, or what it was doing to me."

I remained quiet, letting her speak.

"And the worst part of it all? No one noticed. No one saw that he didn't let me speak, or that I was overwhelmed and miserable. No one could tell when I was pretending to be happy. They didn't hear the panic attacks when I couldn't take it." My chest stopped rising, stopped working as I absolved her confession, listening solemnly as I beheld her hurt and darkest secrets. I didn't think her darkest secret was how much she hated Callan, but what that unhappiness brought her to, the low that she had been attempting to climb out of.

"It didn't happen all at once. It got worse when we were teenagers, when boys stopped being my friend, and girls became jealous he was mine. As if I wanted him." Willa's voice wavered, lingering on the edge of amusement and sorrow.

"And all I knew was duty. For my family and clan. So I let

them think the boy with the golden hair was perfect, and now he's dead. I get to go home and look his father in the eye and tell him that."

"I can't help but think Callan chose that death. He chose to go through the bog knowing what it meant. But watching the bog body sever a part of his head? I feel traumatized." Her voice dropped to a whisper, as if she couldn't bear to say what came next. "But mostly, I feel guilty, for finally being free from it all."

I let her lay there like that, staring up at the sky with tears streaming down her face. I laid next to her, close enough so she would know I was still there. At some point, she fell asleep listening to the lapping of the river on the shore, at peace with the freshwater of the river and the saltwater tears on her cheeks.

CHAPTER NINETEEN

Willa

"Willa," Dempsey whispered.

Hairs tickled my nose. I opened my eyes to see Tad standing over me, staring down, waiting for me to wake up. A smile blossomed on my face as I reached up to scratch Tad on his scruff.

"Dinner should be ready soon if you're ready to go."

"How long was I asleep for?" I asked, disoriented. Sure enough, as I looked around, the sun was setting and the river glowed orange with the reflection of the sun.

"An hour or two. I figured you could use the rest. Do you feel better?"

I nodded. There was something about the nearness of the river, washing away all shock and grief. Something told me the gods foresaw this or at least knew that it would help. What happened was terrible, but I undeniably felt like a chapter of my life was now closed. Opportunity lay in front of me.

Dempsey offered his hand to help me stand and we turned to make our way back to the ringfort.

"Do we dine inside or down below?"

Dempsey laughed. "We dine inside. Although I wouldn't be surprised if my father has concocted some scene instead."

"Why do you speak of him like that? I thought you were close." I didn't know if it was too personal of a question to ask, but I couldn't wrap my head around the father-son dynamic they had.

"My father has a way of using... *power dynamics* to his advantage, which is something I am getting irritated by. The whole jovial, kind, you-can-tell-me-anything act is nice for a while. It also tends to gut you when he tires of it." Dempsey shook his head and continued. "I mean, even where we live, those in his good graces get to be inside the ringfort. With enough work, you can move up. Out of our goodwill, we protect the village; it's all bullshit. My father has created a meritocracy to profit off people's hard work and dreams. Instead of providing them a better life, it fuels his power."

I paused. "I didn't realize it was like that here."

Dempsey shot me a glance. "Well, that's the thing, isn't it? We never know how it is on the other side. People rarely switch clans. Since we were children we're trained that our clan is the greatest and the rest are invading warriors and that loyalty is bred and rewarded in our clan." Dempsey stopped walking, conscious of the ringfort wall we were drawing near.

"My father is a good man. He isn't cruel or violent. He means well and everything he does is to keep our clan working. I'm just saying that maybe what we see on the surface isn't the full story. That's why I have a hard time blindly following him like everyone else."

I was shocked at the depth Dempsey had analyzed his father's leadership in the clan. Perhaps it was his duties that led him to see things with such clarity, but I could never remember a time when I didn't think of my parents as great heroic figures.

"Maybe our relationships with people aren't always supposed to be easy," I replied softly. "I think that's okay."

We locked eyes, unspoken understanding passing between us.

"C'mon, I can smell dinner already, and if the warriors have anything to do with it, there will be nothing left."

Dempsey extended his hand, helping me climb up the rocky slope that enwrapped the ringfort.

"Is there somewhere I can clean up? I still smell like the bog."

Dempsey looked back at me. "Right. Yes, we can do that." I raised an eyebrow. "You can do that," he clarified. "I'll take you to a guesthouse."

We entered the ringfort where all of Dempsey's assumptions had been true. A large bonfire roared in the center of the yard and minstrels were setting out their instruments. Several large kegs were getting hauled in, and from what I could tell, many warriors were already drunk. A slab of venison was being cut on a table, the smell wafting towards us.

"Are all your dinners like this?" I asked.

"Unfortunately, only when we have guests," Dempsey grimly replied.

Dempsey guided me to a carriage house behind the stables of the ringfort. He quickly excused himself to find my saddlebags, leaving me alone for the first time. The carriage house, obviously a stable hand's quarters, was nice. Even if Dempsey hated the way people were invited to stay and work here, it was obvious Barra took care of those in his household.

The door creaked open and I turned to Dempsey with my saddlebags over his shoulder and his hands full, carrying two buckets of steaming water.

"There's a hot spring that runs underneath the ringfort. The well's easy enough to access, so let me know if you ever want more."

I nodded, thanking him. He stood there for a second longer,

like he was planning on saying something but couldn't bring himself to.

"I'll leave you. You can find me at my father's quarters when you're done."

I smiled in response.

He looked me up and down, hesitant to leave. "I'm glad you're here." There was something unreadable in his eyes for the briefest of moments, but he left before I could decipher what it was.

Safe. For the first time in a very long while, I felt safe. It wasn't Dempsey, or that Callan was gone. Maybe it was the River Boyne. But all I knew was that I could take care of myself, I was safe and no one could take that away from me. I reveled in that feeling as I dragged the buckets of water to the shallow tub in the corner, letting the heat wash over me as I scrubbed away the caked dirt and mud from the bog, becoming clean in body and spirit.

Please be in here. I furiously rooted around in my saddlebags. The leather pockets were stuffed with random articles of clothing, and I held my breath as my fingers brushed against a wispy article of clothing. I tugged, and the periwinkle dress with the grey overlay came out. If there was ever a night for it, it was tonight. I was going to need all the help I could get with Barra, so I might as well look the part. The dress fit perfectly, my mother somehow knowing my exact measurements. The top cut across my chest, walking the line between coquettish and demure, while the sleeves billowed and gathered at my wrists, the material still light enough for a summer night.

I quickly combed through my hair, not bothering to place the pins that my mother would have expected if she was here, and exited the carriage house. The yard was dark, night fast approaching, and the warmth of fires and torches filled the circle.

Tables were set every couple of yards, warriors crowded at

each of them, crowing over their latest triumphs. As different as this territory might be, it was the same as my own, people never changing. I walked straight through the center, my boots crunching on the gravel path, aiming towards the head table where I saw both Barra and Dempsey, and from what I could tell, the majority of Barra's advisors. I became faintly aware of the political waters I had been dropped in – but I didn't plan to drown.

My skirts rustled as I dropped into a kneeling curtsy before the head table, my head bowed, waiting for Barra's command.

"Willa, please, your manners are impeccable, but you really shouldn't. Take a seat at my table, dine with us," Barra called out.

Dempsey rose and walked to me, extending his hand. He dropped me at a seat towards the end of the table, far enough to prevent any discussions with Barra. The smell of roast venison wafted toward me and my stomach growled, not content with the lunch from earlier.

As Dempsey walked away, I sat there, painfully aware of my gown amongst the men at the table, feeling distinctly removed from any real conversation occurring. Insecurity clawed at me while I sat there alone. Even if I had never grown up with many friends, there was always someone at my side. My parents, Fiadh, and Callan were always there, and now I sat alone, watching the night unfurl around me.

"He's a fool to leave such a precious jewel here unguarded." A raspy voice spoke over my shoulder. I jumped slightly, pressing a hand to my chest.

I turned to see a middle-aged man taking the seat next to me. I forced a smile on my face, trying to hide the fright he gave me.

I drew my shoulders back. "I think I am quite capable of guarding myself." I wasn't sure what game this man was playing, but to insinuate I was defenseless bothered me on some level.

Tonight I was going to be questioned and tested, and something told me this was only the first of my trials.

"Oh, of course. I'm confident your parents wouldn't have let you leave the forest if you weren't."

Distinctly bothered by the mention of my parents, I studied the man's face. There was nothing malicious about the faint grin on his face, but his gaunt face and deep-set eyes made me want to shift in my seat.

"I'm sorry, I didn't catch your name." I took some pride in knowing that I had a semblance of power that he knew who I was but I didn't know him. The thought struck me as foolish. How many times had I learned that in the game of politics, knowledge was power? My first night of playing this game, and I was already a half step behind.

"Fintan. Advisor to Barra and the Clan Amongst the Rivers. But there is no need for you to introduce yourself Willa, gifted with foresight and Council to the Clans and Gods." Fintan's eyes gleamed. I wasn't sure if I should be bothered or on alert that Fintan was so well acquainted with both my gift and my seat on the council.

I looked at his hands, clasped together on the table. They were pale and slightly wrinkled, with bulging veins hinting at both his age and his past as a warrior, crisscrossed with scars. Guessing by both his hands and the wrinkles set around his eyes, he was older than both Barra and Viktor. There was something inside him that seemed full of youth, too quick-witted and all-knowing to be considered an elder just yet. His finger bore the same warrior ring that Dempsey's did, along with a stack of rings that resembled the ones my father received for accolades in battle. There was no evidence of a gift or marriage, just a man who was obviously trusted by his clan for his achievements and legacy.

"So, Willa, what do you foresee for our clans?"

I scanned his face, trying to decide what he meant. My

parents taught me at an early age there was a fine line with my gift, that I was never to be considered a fortune teller or a witch.

Witches were something else entirely, something separate from the clans. Those that did have the gift to control and transform forces of magick were often excluded from clan life, living alone and only appearing when called upon. Although it was a noble gift, the power associated with it was also feared, and Viktor and Brigid worried that one day it might be misunderstood.

"I'm not a witch. I cannot read your palm or peer into the future at will." Fintan looked at a loss for words, and I wondered how often anyone dared to correct him. "I am granted access to a portal with the gods, and I receive omens from there." My voice was cold, haughty, transformed into an instrument of politics.

"Of course. I did not mean to assume or misconstrue. It appears I have gotten off on the wrong foot, perhaps." He chose his words carefully. I stared at him, my eyebrows raised. For the life of me, I could not understand his motives. That, perhaps, made me more unsure of Fintan than Barra.

"I have been *shown* that the magick on the isle is changing. And I *know* the Sectarians are invading, and I do not believe they intend to stop. What we do, as an entire people, is yet to be decided." I fought the urge to twist my rings underneath the table.

Fintan nodded. "It seems we have many important choices in front of us. We can only pray to the gods for our safety."

I breathed a sigh of relief. I wasn't quite sure what just transpired, but I had a feeling I navigated it well.

"Fintan, please tell me you aren't boring our beautiful guest. Why do we all look so serious on the night of a feast?"

Felix took the seat beside me, and I smiled at his arrival. He placed a glass of wine in front of me and set one for himself on the table.

"The world isn't always a party, Felix. You can't drink your way through conflicts," Fintan sighed as if this was a conversation he'd repeated many times.

Felix raised his glass in the air, toasting to Fintan. "I beg to differ." He took a long swallow of the dark liquid in his cup.

I had to admit that Felix fascinated me. I could tell he was best friends with Dempsey, yet there was an authority in his voice that made people listen. The interaction he had with the old warrior on my other side sounded as if they were equals, both advisors to Barra and Dempsey. The only obvious difference between the two was the large age gap.

Felix must have to be very powerful to command respect at such a young age, I decided. My mind was stuck on the question of how he did it. Felix turned the opposite direction, his face full of distaste, apparently done with the interaction.

"Well, we don't always have a Forest girl in our presence." Felix turned his glass in his hand, examining me. Something in his voice told me he was calculating why I had come and what I planned to do while here.

I took a sip from the wine he'd handed me. "You were all just so enchanting when you came to visit last month, how could I stay away," I said, my voice dripping with dryness. I gazed out at the tables feasting before us, amused at the drunk warriors across tables. There were groups with arms around each other, attempting to sing in tune with the musicians who played their songs. A few were in argument about a drinking game, but all were in good spirits.

At the table closest to the head table, a warrior belched loudly and Felix winced.

"Oafs, all of them. You can train them to kill a man and disembowel an enemy, but they can never remember table manners." He shook his head.

"Some things never change, no matter which clan you're in."

"What was Fintan asking you about?" Felix attempted to make the question sound nonchalant, but I saw the hitch in the way he swirled his wine glass, the pointed glance away from the table. I looked at the seat next to me, now unoccupied, as if Fintan had disappeared.

I decided to take a chance and tell Felix the truth. "He asked me what I foresaw for the clans, as if I hold our destiny in my palms." I snorted and took a sip of my wine. "Which is not how it works, before you ask."

Felix rolled his eyes. "Between you and me," he whispered conspiratorially, "Old Finty is a little conservative. Doesn't like change much. He probably wishes you could tell him what he will eat for breakfast every day for the next year."

I laughed.

Dempsey appeared, his arms filled with plates as he took the spot next to me. "Has Felix been harassing you?" Dempsey frowned.

"Quite the opposite. I saved her from the clutches of Old Man Fintan." A smile curled on my lips at the endless amounts of nicknames he had for Fintan.

"Never a good sign when he takes interest, trust me, Willa." Dempsey dug into his food, but I turned my head at this piece of advice.

"You don't think he's going to back the movement against the Sectarians, do you?" I asked quietly. I was taking a risk by asking, but I didn't come here to play games of flattery and flirting. At the end of the day, I needed to walk out of here with an army behind me. I hoped that Dempsey trusted me enough to tell me the truth about it.

Dempsey and Felix shared a glance. "No, I don't think he will," Dempsey replied grimly.

"But, on the bright side Willa, you have Dempsey and me pulling for you. So wipe the glum look off your face. This is a party and I hate worrywarts." Felix took his wine glass in hand and motioned for me to do the same.

I took a sip, mulling over Dempsey's answer.

"Okay, up." Felix rose from his chair. "We're going dancing, Dempsey, and I will not be returning your friend here until she is in a proper feasting mood." Felix took my hand and directed me towards the dance floor. We approached the clearing in front of the minstrels, my skirts swishing, and I looked back at Dempsey.

He was smiling, his entire face lit up.

Felix paused, waiting for the band to strike up a new tune, before pulling me in with tension tight in his arms, and taking me through the steps. Both song and dance were unfamiliar to me while I let Felix lead, praying I wouldn't falter.

But Felix, on the other hand, was living for each step. His eyes gleamed like he had been set free, running for the first time, infinite possibilities around him. He navigated me with confidence, before dipping me low and whispering a question in my ear.

"What is your endgame?" Felix's lip barely moved.

I froze. I glanced at his face, but Felix's features betrayed nothing.

He leaned in. "This isn't safe for us to discuss at the table. So *what is your endgame.*"

I was keenly aware I was walking in dangerous territory. There was a split second for me to decide whether or not to fully trust Felix with everything. For me to decide if he would help me achieve the goal I had walked in here with, or if he was going to use it against me.

I cursed before reciprocating the closeness to Felix. He clutched my back and I rested my chin on his shoulder as the dance slowed. "If the clans are to survive, Barra needs to pledge his legions."

A smile played on Felix's face as he twirled me in a sweeping motion. "Well, you don't ask for much, do you?"

I ignored the joke. I was here to play the game, with or without Felix on my team. I spun into his arms before answering. "The Sectarians can kill us, clan by clan. I'll assume you'll hold out longer than the rest with the ringfort, but they'll beat you, eventually."

Another four steps, another twirl out of Felix's arms. "So you can draw it out, or you can join us. And we stand a fighting chance." My voice quivered with the need for him to understand.

"Okay."

Okay? My head spun as I tried to control my facial expressions. My heart sank as I waited for Felix to pledge his support. I wasn't sure what other moves there were to play in this game, but it was a calculated risk to tell him everything. Felix could very well tell Barra it was a suicide mission, to prepare for a siege and pray the Sectarians never marched south.

My mind ran through every interaction, every mention of Felix, trying to understand what motivated him. I landed on a memory of me and Dempsey, underneath the willow tree near the Hollow. The promise that Dempsey made me, saying that I would never be left out from another strategy session between him and Felix.

"So this is me letting you in, leveling with you. I think I can do it, but I need your help, your support. The three of us, until the end of this."

I waited, hoping to the gods that I had made the right call.

"Welcome to the team."

CHAPTER TWENTY

Willa

B y some grace of the gods, I'd gained admittance to the highly selective boys club inside the Riverlands, and it emboldened me. After our dance finished, I let Felix guide me back to the head table where Dempsey was waiting.

"I want to speak with your father," I announced.

Shock passed on Dempsey's face. He raised his eyebrows, looking to Felix, who simply shrugged.

Dempsey looked out to the night-filled ringfort, illuminated by the large bonfire in the center. He seemed to be debating briefly in his head before he opened his mouth to reply. He stood and motioned to Felix and me, walking toward the same tent we found his father in earlier.

Dempsey let Felix take the lead as he fell in step with me, pressing a hand lightly to my back. He leaned in.

"Are you sure about this?" I could hear the tension in his voice as we walked behind the head table.

"As much of a nice visit this has been, Dempsey, I came here for a reason," I reminded him.

He looked uncomfortable. "Before we go in here, I need you to know, my father is a difficult man. I can't promise that my or Felix's support will mean anything."

I wondered what Dempsey had seen, to warn me so about his father. I placed my hand on his arm.

"I know," I replied softly. "But I came here to fight."

Barra's tent lay before us, flickering with shadows and candlelight. Felix opened the flaps to reveal Barra and Fintan, along with several other men. Judging by the few words that were flying from their mouths, they were arguing about something before Barra, who sat in the same chair he was in this morning, the darkened leather framing his figure.

The men fell silent as we entered the tent. The air felt uneasy, the men afraid of being overheard. My tongue felt heavy, and I suddenly wished I hadn't had that glass of wine with Felix before.

Fintan spoke. "To what do we owe the pleasure?" His voice was calm, calculated. I remembered Felix's warning from before, that Fintan was loathe to change, and I made the decision that this man could not be an ally.

Before I could speak, Dempsey responded to the question hanging in the air.

"I supposed we might be asking the same thing. Why were we not notified that there was a meeting of the advisors?" The challenge stood bare-faced in the air, staring and waiting for someone to answer its call. His arms crossed over his chest as he awaited an answer.

I studied the faces of each man in the tent. This unsanctioned meeting was most definitely about my presence in the camp. The feast and dancing outside was a mere distraction, to keep me from listening in to what occurred behind closed doors.

A tall man with a thick head of hair cleared his throat. "You were all busy, and we know how draining today was. We didn't want to bother anyone," and he offered a small smile in apology.

Felix's eyes narrowed. "No need to apologize, Shang," although no formal apology was offered. "Mind filling us in on what we missed?" Shivers ran down my back at the cunning revealed in Felix's voice.

"Swords away, boys," chastised Barra. "I was simply filling them in on the information Willa shared with us today. Unless you would prefer to share instead?"

I jolted when I noticed Barra addressing me. My mouth went dry as I began to speak.

This is it. Now is the time to ask for the allegiance, for the warriors, for support.

A cleansing breath went through my body. I prayed to every god I knew of for their support, and in response, I caught a whiff of the smell of the river, as if Boann was over my shoulder, guiding me towards this.

"I won't bother repeating what brought me here. I assume that was already shared, but correct me if I'm wrong." I paused, stopping to meet the pairs of eyes in the room. No one spoke, so I continued. "The Clan Amongst the Rivers has already agreed to the original finds and formation of the Council to Clans and Gods."

I looked at Barra, holding his gaze. "*You* agreed there was trouble on this island, acknowledged its magick is changing, and that we need to do something about it."

I paused again, but there was no emotion on their faces, nothing for me to interpret, no hints of approval. I prayed what I was saying struck home.

"If the three remaining clans don't partner together and fight back, we will all die. And I say that with knowledge directly from the gods. So I come here to ask you for your support in fighting this war. I ask for your leadership and your troops. I'm asking you to help finish what they started twenty years ago."

The room was silent as the yells and music outside the tent grew louder. There was no sign of approval on Felix and Dempsey's faces, only cold calculation.

Felix avoided my eyes but spoke instead. "Willa speaks the truth. I think if we want to survive, it is our only hope."

Someone in the back of the smoky room snorted. Shang looked apologetic but spoke for his colleague. "You three are so young. You only know peacetime. You don't know what the Clan o' Cliffs went through all those years ago, the horrors they spoke of."

Anger flared inside of me. "We know enough. We know the Sectarians have dared to wipe out an entire clan. We know the Mountain Clan and the Forest Clan refused to fight back. And *I* know if we repeat that mistake, we will all die."

"That is precisely why we have fortified the ringfort. Added an extra layer of stone, a system to notify of any invaders, increased our stores. So we don't have to fight again if faced with it." Fintan spoke this time, and even though his tone was polite, Felix's words earlier rang true.

Disgust crept into my voice. "So you would let the clans be killed off, one by one, rather than leave your great stone prison?"

A ripple moved through the crowd before me. Hysteria crept up on me in this suffocating tent, rich with the scent of candles and alcohol and the faint smell of paper. I saw the fight conclude before it had even begun and I realized that everything had been in vain.

A voice spoke next to me, Dempsey, if I was right. Tears began to blur my vision and my mind refused to process the words he was saying. Yelling, actually; Dempsey was yelling at his father and his advisors. The only thought I could focus on was that it was all for nothing. The Mountain Clan dying, Callan dying, all for nothing. My sister's crying face, begging for help, for nothing. All because these old and cruel men couldn't open their hearts to care for anyone outside this miserable compound.

My mother's advice ran through my mind. *Barra will want something in return.* But what did I have to offer him? The

Riverlands had security, they had strength in numbers and food storage.

I began to speak, still in shock and disbelief. "What happened to Clan Amongst the Rivers? What happened to the men who craved war all those years ago? Who had a duty to protect their land and their gods?" I paused before delivering my final blow. "You've all turned into cowards." My lip curled at the men before me, who had no right to lead a clan like this.

Barra cleared his throat. "Please leave us. I would like to speak with Willa alone."

The advisors rose and left their places, keeping a healthy distance from me as they exited the tent.

Barra massaged his temples before he spoke. "Willa, I want you to understand that I never intended for this conversation to happen like this – happen tonight, even."

"And you were all just discussing it in here tonight, for what reason?" Dempsey challenged.

"Unfortunately, son, I do like to make agreements with some thought behind them. So yes, I decided to discuss the matter with the rest of the advisors who weren't aware of what had happened."

"This wasn't a discussion. This was a decision. There was nothing I could say tonight that was going to change your minds."

Barra nodded, confirming what I was thinking.

"It's just too risky. It's unnecessary for us to put that much on the line for such little reward."

Gods, how right Brigid had been. Barra – not the rest of his council – wasn't willing to risk anything that wasn't going to benefit him. I cursed at Barra, cursed at the damn ringfort inside my head. I laughed at myself, how foolish I must have seemed, playing games with Felix and Fintan in the name of achieving my goal.

What proposal would get Barra to agree? Perhaps there was

hope, now that the advisors had left and it was just us within the tent.

"What is it you need then? Do you want a piece of land? Livestock as payment?" I was reduced to the level of bartering, aware of how desperate I sounded.

"Willa, it isn't a matter of what I want," Barra reminded me gently.

"Well, then *why not. What is stopping you?* " I growled.

"We only stand to lose power if the clan joins the others. I understand why this means so much to you, with your sister's new clan at stake as well as yours, but frankly, it isn't a concern we share. If there is any displacement from what is to come, maybe you can take comfort in knowing we will take in any refugees." Barra gave me a kind look, as if his statement had made it all better.

But it hadn't. It only added fuel to the fire that was burning inside of me. I wanted to scream. I was tired of other people deciding my fate for me, of picking the wrong side and the wrong option, and being too blind to see what is right.

Everything fell away as I spoke, my shoulders drawn back and my voice clear as I figured out Barra's riddle. "My hand in marriage."

Barra stopped pouring himself a glass of port and looked up at me. "I'm sorry?"

"I offer my engagement to you. I will marry Dempsey, enter into a formal alliance with your clan, in exchange for your support and troops." This was the key I had been looking for. This way, Barra was given power in politics. I offered him the Forest Clan's youngest daughter, an offer that was too tempting to refuse. I hoped it would be enough.

Barra examined both me and Dempsey. "You two will live here. And there will still be a dowry involved."

"Of course," I answered, aware that I was speaking about the rest of my life as a transaction.

"You will have my troops and my public support."

"And the lesser villages in the Riverlands? What about them?" I knew enough about the Riverlands to know there were a few lesser settlements in the area, each equipped with warriors.

"They stay."

I opened my mouth to object, but Barra cut me off. "If the Sectarians send a force to the south, it would be foolish to leave the coast unguarded."

I couldn't argue with that logic. "Deal."

"There is a condition to this all, however."

"And that is?" asked Dempsey dryly, speaking up for the first time.

"I have no qualms about the marriage, but the advisors will, I'm sure. I will send my troops up to the Forest Clan to meet as one host, to begin battle preparations, but you two will not join them."

I glanced at Dempsey while Barra continued to speak.

"You will journey to the Lia Fáil, at the Hill of Tara, and if the gods do not bless the union, the deal is off."

I covered my mouth, shock settling on me. The Lia Fáil, also known as the Stone of Destiny, was placed there by the faeries, and served as a connection to the gods. When there was a prominent marriage, or when a man claimed legitimacy to his right to rule over the clans, they would take the oaths over the stone, and the gods would make their verdict known. No man or woman in living memory had dared to approach the stone.

I stared at Barra. I was well aware that my engagement had just ended, and a political alliance was the reason for it to begin with, but something about this one was different. Maybe it was my connection with Dempsey, or the knowledge of what this alliance would bring my clan. Either way, I had no choice. This was the only way I was going home with an army.

"I agree. To all of it."

"Should I be the one to tell the advisors or would you rather, Father?" asked Dempsey, his voice cold.

"I will," answered Barra with a smile on his face. "I do enjoy reminding them who the leader is for this clan. Felix, care to join me?"

Barra left the tent with Felix walking after him, with an apologetic look on his face. I took a deep breath and felt my stomach jump as I turned to look at Dempsey. I looked into his eyes, hoping to understand what he was feeling. I braced myself for the worst, well aware that I had trapped him in this marriage without any input.

The rings on my hand had grown tight from tugging at them when Dempsey took two long strides to appear right before me, dangerously close. He slid one hand onto my cheek and held my eyes with his own before leaning in to kiss me, long and deep.

CHAPTER TWENTY-ONE

Willa

E very thought in my mind dissipated as I was drowned in that kiss, all my focus on the electric intensity of Dempsey's lips, the same pair I had thought about for so long, that had smiled and teased me. My hands rose up to rest against Dempsey's chest, feeling the muscles underneath his tunic, grabbing the thin fabric underneath my hands. His scent filled the air around me, the smell of water, salt, and soap.

Dempsey pulled away, looking at me once more. He rested his forehead against mine, as if afraid to move, afraid to break the spell that was weaving around us. My body screamed at the proximity of him, if I just tilted my head a fraction, our lips would meet again. I dully recognized the tenderness with which he held me, contrasting the ferocity of our kiss.

I dared to look up at him. "You don't hate me?"

Dempsey laughed, a sound that was dark and rough. "No. Gods, no. Willa, I've been waiting to do that since the moment I saw you. I've wanted to kiss you like that since I found you in the woods, hiding amongst the trees like you were one of the fae." He ran a thumb across my lower lip.

I slowly pieced together what he was saying, trying to put my fears to rest. "You don't think I trapped you into a marriage that I never even asked you about?"

Dempsey raised his hand to smooth out the worry lines on my forehead. "My father has been waiting to marry me off for at least half a decade. I just never thought it could be you." His voice lowered. "I never dared hope for you."

His words raised the hairs on the back of my neck. He spoke to me as if I was someone to be cherished. Some small part of me whispered it wasn't true, it was lies, but I pushed that spiteful voice deep down, ignoring it for once.

"I should be the one asking you if you're okay. Willa, you just got out of an engagement you hated. Are you so sure you want to be trapped in another?"

I paused. Dempsey had a point. What was so different about this political engagement I'd just landed myself in?

"It's a choice I made for myself. It's not something my parents chose. It was my own free will, my own power, that led me to this decision." A faint blush crept over my cheeks. "It helps that you haven't left my head from the moment we met."

Dempsey held back, obviously waiting for something to be said. I studied his face, worry knotting back into my features before he spoke.

"Even if you decided this engagement was something you're okay with, something that has to happen, do you want *us?* Because if you don't, we can change the oaths tomorrow. We can change the level of marriage, and make it purely a union of law and country. Say the word and we never bring *us* and a relationship into it."

I blinked, bewildered by what he was saying – at the *out* he was giving me. My heart nearly melted at the thought of what he was giving me. Although rarely used, it was common knowledge in the clans that marriage could be considered *only* a contract. Sometimes it was a contract of love, and the oaths pertained to agreements in the relationship.

Other times, it was a contract of offspring, of land sharing, of political unity. If a lesser level of marriage was invoked, the parties involved would be free to love elsewhere. In the case of my engagement with Callan, it was simply never an option. A union of law and country opposed to a full-fledged marriage was weak, one that did not hold the promise of heirs or stability. I had never thought to ask my parents for the approval of one, and I was touched that Dempsey would be willing to negotiate that with Barra.

Dempsey stood there, silently waiting for my answer, his brown eyes churning. He was still maintaining his distance, unwilling to impose himself on me.

I shook my head. "I want you. I want all of it." My voice was scarcely audible, and I was afraid Dempsey hadn't heard me, that he would just stay there standing, staring at me. I was unable to breathe until he moved again, one of his delicious grins spreading on his face, the smirk that made me think of wicked things. Dempsey ran a hand through his thick hair, and he closed the distance between us again, this time allowing no space between us.

My fingers tangled in his curls, pulling him closer to me. Dempsey's hands roamed my back, sliding down to my ass before lifting me up into the air. As a smile grew on my face, I wrapped my legs around him.

This was what love was supposed to feel like. Not oppression, not control, not desperation, but freedom and optimism and euphoria. His mouth went to my neck, and all I could think about was him, sucking and biting at my neck, tugging at my ear.

Something hard was underneath me before I realized Dempsey had set me down on one of the tables, and by the sound of it, he chose the one covered with maps. I struggled to put words together before spitting out a jumbled sentence.

"We're... we're going to ruin the maps."

Dempsey's nose, then mouth brushed against my ear. "Would you like me to stop?" he asked, his voice a low rumble.

"No," I breathed, tugging on his tunic to bring his mouth back to mine.

He tipped me back, laying me down with surprising ease. His hands roamed my body, gripping my hips, my waist, feeling the curve of my ribs before finally cupping one of my breasts.

Something in me groaned. I bit at Dempsey's lip, wanting more, *needing* more. My legs were still wrapped around his back as I dug my feet into him, spurring him on, letting him know I wanted this.

Dempsey took a ragged breath. "Fuck, Willa," he panted.

I stopped and looked at him. Savoring every second I unabashedly studied each feature of his face. He ran his hand through his hair, curled strands falling into his eyes.

Dempsey cupped my chin with his thumb and index finger, slowly turning my head towards the side, exposing my jaw and cheek. He very softly kissed the skin underneath my chin, somehow moving even slower to the next spot. His kiss lingered as he nipped the skin, and I tried to hide the thrill of excitement that ran through me.

Dempsey continued to make his way up to my ear. "Willa, I don't just want you, I *need you*. But unfortunately," Dempsey paused to leave a lingering kiss on my lips, "I'm afraid my father might be returning soon."

Right. Shit. I had really been ready to have sex on Barra's desk? A shudder ran through me at the thought of getting caught. I pushed myself up off the desk, the maps crinkling slightly underneath me. My hands went to my hair, quickly trying to tame the victim of our activities.

"Right," I answered briskly. As if I hadn't been nearly suffocated by my need for him moments earlier.

Dempsey's hands wrapped around my waist. "But, trust me when I say I have plans for you later." My heart jumped in anticipation.

I looked up at him, at this man I could now call mine. Our fingers intertwined. "Should we go face the masses?"

CHAPTER TWENTY-TWO

Willa

Dempsey led me back into the ringfort, the scene before us looking so similar to when we had entered, but everything now changed. I couldn't help but steal glances of him. There was an undeniable charge of fate between us, a hint of the gods' planning. If that was the truth for us, I would willingly, gladly accept the darkness of my previous relationship, with the hope that this one, already so different, would last.

We marched together, onwards, for the wooden table that we ate from earlier. It was now full of Barra and his advisors on the raised platform, eating and drinking, engaging in merry talk. Pure shock struck their faces at the sight of us. I bet Barra had told them the promise of the union, but the sight of Dempsey and me together, the force of a united front, was what brought them to their knees.

I followed Dempsey along the backside of the advisors whose hearts had been so full of disdain moments earlier. The strong ones kept at their meal, their faces a wall of stone, refusing to acknowledge us. The weak ones, however, strained in their seats to get a look at us, and I could laugh at them, for all their planning and hatred had been for nothing.

Barra rose from his seat, holding a pint of beer. The minstrels fell silent as a hush went over the crowd, warriors showing respect for their leader who had shown them through the season.

"As some of you may have guessed, tonight was not simply a feast for good behavior." A light round of laughter echoed through the crowd.

"Tonight we are gathered in honor of a guest. Willa, daughter of Viktor and Brigid, from the Forest Clan, bearer of the gift of foresight and Council to Clans and Gods, graces us with her presence." Barra paused, his lips curled upwards like a cat playing with a mouse, waiting to pounce.

"But luckily for us, we will be seeing more of her. I announce her engagement to my son, Dempsey, from our Clan Amongst the Rivers, Bearer of Storms. They leave tomorrow to seek the approval of the gods from the Lia Fáil."

A roar came from the crowd, with lifted glasses and clinks from the tables. Cries for a toast rose from the masses. Although this engagement was unexpected, it was not for lack of enthusiasm, I noted.

"A toast you say?" The people yelled back their approval.

"Willa. Dempsey. For the rest of your journeys, in this life and the next, may the road rise up to meet you and the wind be always at your back. I hope the sun will always shine upon your face." Barra's eyes were shining, and I suspected it was all genuine.

"And may the leprechauns dance upon your bed tonight!" someone yelled from the crowd. I allowed myself to blush and laugh with the rest of them, to enjoy the happiness of it all, while the people around us echoed our names and took long drinks.

The chairs next to Barra were empty, reserved for us, a seat of honor in any clan. Barra turned to us, his cheeks ruddy, and I wondered how much he had to drink since leaving the tent.

"Now, you both may be upset at me, but I feel that the gods are whispering something in my ear about destiny." His eyes twinkled, although I couldn't say if it was from amusement or the copious amounts of alcohol.

Dempsey snorted. "I think you will find both Willa and I are pleased about the union." I noted his hand on my thigh, his thumb tracing circles.

I bit the inside of my lip, begging myself to focus.

"Good. I'm glad you came to your senses. I already sent out the announcements."

There was a frown etched upon Dempsey's face, the firelight throwing shadows across the valleys of his face. "We've not yet been engaged for an hour and you've already sent out an announcement."

"I – I haven't had a chance to tell my parents yet," I said.

Barra didn't shy from the fact. He nodded vehemently. "It is a bit rude to let them know on such short notice, but I think they'll be understanding given the situation."

I swallowed a laugh given the fact that Barra was *not* joking.

"If you have another messenger to spare, could I write a letter to my parents?" I prayed they didn't die of shock at the news that in the span of a week, their daughter had lost a fiancé, gained a new one, secured an alliance, and was traveling to the Hill of Tara. All in all, a very eventful trip.

"Of course, Willa. I do want you to know that I now think of you as a daughter of mine, and you will be treated like family."

"Thank you, Barra, for your hospitality and kindness."

Barra said nothing in return but gave a small smile before turning his attention back to his beer and the advisor on his left. Dempsey rolled his eyes before turning his attention to me.

"Would you like to stay, or call it a night? I know tonight's been a lot."

I nodded. "I would like the chance to rest before traveling again tomorrow."

"C'mon," he murmured. Dempsey took my hand and guided us out of the center of the ringfort. Our hands intertwined, just as they had been when entering the feast, together as a team. The simple gesture whispered more than words, spoke of his admiration and care for me. Us holding hands was different from when Callan did it. With Callan, it had been aggressive and territorial. A mark of ownership, dictating where to go. With Dempsey, it was a symbol of cherishment. A gentle presence, telling me that he was by my side, come hell or high water.

Dempsey guided us out of the ringfort and we approached the grated portcullis. My steps slowed as I tilted my head, gazing out at the black outdoors.

"Where are we going?"

"I told you the ringfort is my father's household, but not all warriors like to live there. Some, like myself, prefer to be a little more open where we live as opposed to feeling like you live in a prison, as I think you called it earlier?"

I cringed when I heard the words I hurled in the heat of the moment when I was looking for any kind of ammunition. The words to apologize formed, but Dempsey cut me off.

"Don't bother. I agree that's what it is. Keeping people in. A physical manifestation of our society's restrictions. An empty promise that with hard work, you can curry the favor of the Great Barra and be invited in." Dempsey scoffed. "But there will never be enough room for everyone in there. Hard work will only get you so far. He still considers you a pawn, as you were witness to tonight." My heart broke as fear rose inside of me, worrying that he thought of our engagement as no more than a necessary step in the game.

"So I choose to keep my residence out here. With the help of a few friends, we built a small house. Or maybe it's a hut. And it's rickety and tiny, but it's mine, and my father doesn't rule over me here." Dempsey explained, baring a small bit of his soul.

Dempsey was right, it was a modest-looking house. It had wooden walls, and a thatched roof that a tarp stood over, as if the roof wasn't strong enough to expel the elements on its own. I smiled at the sight of the windows built into the side, even though glass was a frivolous expense in an area with so many storms. As if Dempsey valued light so much he couldn't bear to be without it.

The door creaked open as Dempsey silently welcomed me inside. I stepped through the narrow door frame and looked at the cabin. It was only one room, with a small wash table off to the side. A bed took up the majority of the space, with a trunk sitting at the foot of it. A wardrobe, obviously taken from his father's camp with its extravagant carvings, stood in the corner. There was a space for a fire underneath a chimney along the back wall, while a table and a pair of chairs stood in the rest of the empty space.

"This is it." Dempsey said the words simply, and I knew he was expecting me to be disappointed. "When we get back and everything is settled, I can build us a new home – one that's larger. I can make sure it's nicer, now that I've finished one and know the tricks of the trade." He laughed with some semblance of bravado.

I smiled at him. Not laughing along with him, but showing that I appreciated the space. That I understood what it meant to him – to us.

"If you want. I'm fine with this." *With this being ours.* The idea of it was so near it was almost tangible. The possibility of true happiness being so close almost scared me, as if the feeling would disappear when it was within my grasp. As if joy was allergic to my very essence.

"I had your bags brought here from the carriage house during the feast." When he realized how presumptuous that sounded, he hastily added, "I was going to offer you the cabin tonight. Sleep in my quarters at my father's." Dempsey's hand rubbed the back of his neck, an attempt to act nonchalant.

He sounded nervous. Nervous of me? Of being with me? Or

maybe just nervous like I was, at the idea of finally getting to be together after all the barriers were lifted.

"I'll let you get ready for bed. Your bags are in the trunk." Dempsey looked around the room, realizing that the one room left little chance for privacy. "Do you want me to – I can wait outside if you want."

"No," I answered, slowly walking towards him, the floorboards creaking as I moved.

"No?" Desire gleamed in his eyes.

I placed myself in his arms, letting him wrap himself around me. "I think you mentioned some plans you had? For later?"

Dempsey lifted a brow, his eyes full of mischief.

"You have no idea the plans I have for us." Dempsey wrapped his hand in my hair, tilting my face towards him.

He leaned in and kissed me, and I surrendered to him. One by one, I let my guards drop, knowing that my heart was utterly open to damage. My back arched, trying to reach out to meet Dempsey fully, always wanting more. Dempsey's arms were there, wrapped around my back, supporting me as we both leaned into the kiss.

Dempsey's face scanned my face as we broke from the embrace, before darting down to my lips. He kissed me again, this time more urgent. I could never tire of this feeling, of this want building inside of me, the feeling that I was both safe and standing on a precipice at the same time.

We took steps, him guiding me, never letting his lips leave mine for more than a moment. With a soft thud, I was pinned against the wall, the wood of the ramshackle cabin surprisingly sturdy.

His hands gripped my hips, keeping me in place as I squirmed to get close to him again. "Patience," he murmured against my neck. "I don't want this to end, not yet."

My chest rose and fell as I waited for Dempsey's next move, while he looked at me like he was the predator, waiting to play games with his prey. I liked the sight of him like this, knowing that I was the reason for the animal before me.

I raised up on my toes, tilting my head up so I could reach his ear, meeting the height difference between the two of us. My hand trailed down the front of him, my fingertips tracing the hollows of his muscled stomach down to the waistband of his pants, before tugging at the laces that held them up.

"Do your worst." I tugged at his ear with my teeth, letting him know that I was here for all of it. Dempsey's eyes lit up at the command as if I gave him permission for things he had been dreaming about.

Time slowed as Dempsey grabbed my hips, spinning me so I faced away from him. One by one, he unclasped the buttons of my dress, placing a kiss on my spine, moving lower and lower as his fingers dropped. Cold air caressed my back as the dress fell away. Dempsey cursed softly at what lay underneath, at the sight of me in my corset. "Shit, Willa."

I spun around, worried I made a mistake. "What?"

"You're devastating. All of you." *Gods, this man was hell-bent on breaking me tonight.*

I took his hand, leading him to the bed before climbing up on it myself, resting on my knees so I was his height. Silently, I unlaced the rest of his pants, leaving it loose at the waist to sag, hinting at the perfect V-shape that lay at the end of his torso.

I tugged at the bottom of his shirt, knowing I wasn't coordinated enough to take it off by myself, not wanting my hands to fumble and ruin the moment. He smiled at my fists, kissing each of them softly, before pulling the dark tunic over his head and throwing it on the floor.

Shit. That was all I could think as I gazed at the god-like creature in front of me. Dempsey's golden skin rippled with muscles, twisting and curving across his arms, divots and shadows spreading across his stomach. I wanted to explore every piece of him, and I found myself reaching behind me, pulling at the laces on my corset, wanting to be skin to skin with him.

How in the world did I get here? Did I deserve it? I didn't want to know the answer as Dempsey held me closely, like he never wanted to let go. He shrugged off his pants before slipping my corset over my head, and he tipped me back onto the bed.

I propped up on my elbows as Dempsey's head drifted down, showering me with kisses as he dipped below my navel, across my hip, down to my thigh, before coming to the place where he had intended to land.

Shit, I thought again. In that second, I understood what Dempsey meant by *plans*. I squirmed as he grabbed my ankles, exposing more of me to him as he feasted on me. My back arched off the bed as Dempsey slid a hand onto my stomach, holding me in place as his tongue did lazy circles, mimicking the same pattern his thumb wrote on my thigh earlier. I slid a hand into his hair, needing more pressure, needing more of him.

I finally broke the heavy silence that had been filled with our ragged breathing. "Dempsey, please," I begged. "*I need you.*" I echoed those same words he said to me earlier.

Wild eyes looked up at me before Dempsey ran a hand across his mouth. He moved up the bed, the bedsprings creaking under our combined weight, looking me in the eye as he repeated those words back to me. "And I need you." It was a promise, and somehow I knew he would always need me, entirely, in this life and the next.

Dempsey guided himself inside of me, groaning. I found myself next to his ear again as I whispered a single word. "Fuck." I wasn't sure if it was a statement or a command or a murmuring of agreement.

Either way, Dempsey replied as he thrust inside of me, one hand on my hips as I rolled to meet him. Our breaths became pants.

I placed a hand on his chest, telling him to wait, wanting to savor the feeling of being with him longer. I rolled to the side and pushed him down onto the bed before straddling him and beginning to move. Dempsey pushed himself upright, so there was no space as I ground up and down on him. There was one hand on my back supporting me, as the other roamed my chest. My soft cries grew louder as I got closer, before intertwining my fingers with those gorgeous curls.

Dempsey warned me. "Willa."

I nodded silently before tilting my head back, welcoming the release as Dempsey finished, burying his face in my chest.

We stayed still for a second before looking at each other.

I tipped my head down lightly to kiss him. I cocked my head as the sound of soft rain began to fill the cabin.

Dempsey smiled. "Happiness," he clarified. "That's the sound of happiness."

I laid there, content in this man's arms while his storm echoed quietly outside, feeling more complete and content than I had ever known.

CHAPTER TWENTY-THREE

Dempsey

Willa and I lounged there, exchanging kisses and telling stories of our youth. At some point, my head strayed into her lap, and she absentmindedly braided my hair. Peace coursed through us in that one-room cabin. There was something about the smell of pine and rain and the warmth of the blankets and *her*. It felt like home.

Willa opened her mouth, about to ask me a question when the cabin door opened. I grabbed a dagger from where it lived under my mattress while Willa yelped and grabbed the comforter to her chest.

"It's me! It's me, gods damn it." Felix raised his hands, no evidence of weapons in either of them. Tad, who was at his side, barked as if verifying this information.

"Shit, Felix. It's the middle of the night," I said. I pulled on my pants that were lying on the floor from earlier.

"Oh, I know," answered Felix in amusement, his eyes coolly sliding over to Willa.

She made a small noise of indignation and gripped the bedsheet with both hands tighter. Her eyes dipped to the dagger that laid on the bed, no doubt contemplating using it.

"No need to worry Willa, when I'm looking at you, I'm not looking at you like *that*. Unless you're about to turn into a man, and even then I don't think you'd be my type." Felix rolled his eyes and turned back to me.

"Sarai is here. She came with reports from an outpost that the Sectarians are here and marching inland," Felix reported.

I cursed, turning to Willa to explain. "Sarai is... Honestly, I don't know what to call her. One day she appeared and never quite left. She now runs the scouting program for the outer villages." I stopped to run my hands through my hair. "*Shit.*"

I paced back and forth, picking up the rest of my clothes. Somehow understanding the urgency of the situation, Willa decided that it was no time for modesty, hopping out of bed. She rifled through her bags, looking for clothes. Even though I just had her in my arms, it took all self-restraint to not shove Felix out into the rain and lock the door. It was an urge to stay in the realm of happiness we fell into, to ignore the world crashing down around us.

Willa fixed Felix with a stare. "What are they doing?"

Felix scrunched his brow. "Excuse me?"

"The Sectarians," she clarified. "What are they doing?"

Felix was deadpan with his answer. "Invading, Willa. They're invading."

Willa looked up at the ceiling, obviously willing a semblance of calm onto her face. "No shit. Are they just marching straight here? Are the outlying villages holding their hand while they do it? *What is everyone doing?*"

A dark chuckle escaped me. As much as Willa hated to play the role of general, it was one that fit her well. Her mind was cunning, strategic. The kind that thought five steps ahead in battle and kept one eye on the enemy.

"It's a good question," I said, defending her. "C'mon, let's suit up and head up to the ringfort."

Felix and I systematically opened my cupboard and drawers.

Dozens of weapons flashed in response where linens and cutlery should be found. We strapped them to our bodies, handing each other a weapon when we noticed an old favorite. The sound of metal clanging filled the cabin, and I caught Willa looking on in wonder.

"Gods, you're like a crow with shiny objects," she noted in disbelief.

Felix turned to her with a grin. "Would you like one?"

Willa went silent for a second. Then – reluctantly, "I like that scian."

The hilt spun in the air as I tossed it to her. *Scian. The favored weapon of both her and her sister. Her mother, too.* I pulled out a leather bound parcel and laid it out on the table, revealing her weapons from the journey.

"Thief," she muttered underneath her breath.

"Safekeeping," I crooned in response. Willa shook her head in exasperation.

Willa's mouth moved silently as she counted them, but a spot laid empty. *It must have been lost in the bog.* She strapped the scian and bag of darts to her hip before slinging her bastard sword across her back.

Once ready, Felix opened the door, and we began our trek to the ringfort. Next to me, Willa scrunched her nose at the soft rain that fell around us. "Could you stop the rain now?"

"Sorry, can't. Too happy." I tapped the tip of her nose with my index finger. *It was true.* I couldn't remember the last time I felt something this strong that the weather, my gift, responded to it.

"That's a cute way of saying you don't know how," called out Felix.

Truthfully, I was glad for the rain that I summoned. The ringfort lay before us, the imposing black shape looming. The slope up the portcullis was slick with mud. It would be difficult for the three of us to climb up without slipping, but an army would make the mud worse. The Sectarians would be hard-pressed to meet the gate. Small footsteps patterned the mud; the villagers had already made their way in.

"Will they let us in?" Willa asked. The portcullis was already dropped, but it was easily raised – for the right people.

"The Sectarians are off by maybe an hour at most. Half hour if we aren't lucky. They'll spot the host coming before we see them. Once they see the troops is when they stop letting people in," answered Felix.

The portcullis raised and permitted us to pass through once we were within clear sight. The three of us briskly walked towards Barra's tent, the mud sucking at our feet. The ringfort was brimming with people, men and women, young and old. The brazier from earlier had turned into a holding pen, the air smelling of desperation and fear, the people clustering inside knowing this was their only line of defense.

The sight inside my father's tent wasn't much more organized than the throng outside of it. Barra stood at his table of maps, and I remembered what almost occurred there earlier today. I drifted a hand down Willa's back, noting her gaze to the same spot. Goosebumps raised on her skin as if to say *I remember too*. The advisors argued over what sounded like the placement of the cavalry. And in the midst of it all was a girl who sat in Barra's chair, legs slung over the arms, smoking a pipe.

A grin broke out on my face. "Sarai," I called out.

She turned to us, blowing a cloud of smoke as she cocked an eyebrow. "Dump. What do we have here?"

My childhood nickname – one that had never been funny, or clever – rang in my ears. My grin vanished as quickly as it appeared. "I told you to stop calling me that. I bought you a new set of throwing knives to get you to stop calling me that."

Sarai shrugged, jumping out of the chair and walking towards us. She reached up to ruffle my hair, despite our obvious height difference. "I forgot." She gave me a saccharine smile. "Felix, always a pleasure."

"Oh, likewise." Felix's tone said otherwise.

Sarai stopped pacing in front of Willa. She leaned in, bowing at the waist. The smell of tobacco wafted off of her. Willa stood rooted to the spot, unsure. Sarai gave a sharp, audible sniff.

She straightened and looked at me. "Smells of trees. Whatever are you doing with a Forest girl?" Curiosity crossed her features.

"Sarai, this is Willa. My fiancé. Willa, this is Sarai." I moved to stand behind Willa, one hand around her waist as I pressed a soft kiss to the nape of her neck.

"Nice to meet you," Willa offered.

Sarai grabbed her hands, examining the rings on Willa's fingers. In most circles, the action would be considered rude. One could piece together what they knew based on the common ones, but sometimes there were parts of life that were too private, despite being on display for the world. A warning that not everyone or everything was as it seemed.

Despite Willa's polite nature, I noticed her eyes skimming over Sarai's hands, taking in the rings there. Her hand held a scouting ring on her index finger, one ingrained with the impression of a map, as well as a band that came to a point in the middle, like an arrow. An advising band, like on both Felix and Fintan's hands. The copper rings played off her dark skin, dancing as she moved her nimble fingers across Willa's hands. Another intricate ring sat on Sarai's left hand, the one she never spoke about, the loops and curls making a thick cuff.

Sarai flipped Willa's hand over, patted it twice, and dropped it. "We'll be friends," she announced. *No small feat there.*

Felix placed a hand to his temple. "Oh, good. I was *so* worried," he said, his voice dripping with sarcasm.

I leaned in close to Willa's ear, watching the hairs on her

neck raise as I did so. "Felix is upset because Sarai has never said that to him."

She smiled up at me. "I like her," Willa said, respect reverberating throughout her voice.

"Now that we've got you three here, Sarai, could you please go over your reports?" Barra called from his pile of maps.

Sarai gave a winning smile. "Gladly." She dragged over a chair next to Barra and stood on top of it, towering over the crowd.

"Crones." She silenced the advisors with one word. Willa's lips twitched upwards. "I received word around midnight from a scout on the south coast outpost. He reported that a fleet had docked underneath a cliff, and by the time the patrols discovered the ships, they were completely abandoned." Her voice was brisk, businesslike.

She continued. "That tells me that they are marching straight for the ringfort. Messengers were dispatched to the remaining outposts, letting them know to take cover." This was no small raiding party if the entire network of outposts had been notified. One by one, a messenger would deploy to notify the next in line, a system used only for the greatest of threats.

"I took the liberty of splitting the host at Harborpoint, sending a force from behind to pressure them upwards. I routed the smaller troops to here – they should be arriving any minute. I think we will send a wave of warriors from here down to meet them, sandwiching them between the two. Then my second force can either join in for reinforcements, or stay back here to help protect." Sarai said these last words with such fervor that she somehow brandished a knife, slicing at the air to emphasize her words.

"With your leave, of course, Barra."

Routing my father's troops was bold. The Sectarians must have been moving at such a pace that there wasn't enough time for my father to make the decision. The invaders were intent on raising hell, not creating a healthy campaign. Then again, perhaps the greatest way to take the ringfort was by surprise.

Barra was either used to her antics or simply not amused. Either way, he continued to stare at the map before them. "Thank you, Sarai."

Fintan spoke. "The timing won't work. The river is too wide with the rain and the clearing you're thinking of will be underwater, and by the time we go around, the Sectarians will be knocking at our door."

The room fell silent. Sarai whispered a string of curse words underneath her breath, eliciting a look from Fintan.

"The land bridge," I spoke, my voice authoritative. "We take the land bridge out, and intersect them on the far side of the river. If we're assuming the river is too high to cross, they're going to face the same problem as well. Their host will have to curve to their left." My finger traced the direction on Barra's map. "And they'll have to meet us eventually."

"But if the river doesn't raise enough, they'll be left with a wide opening to the heart of our territory." Fintan shook his head as he spoke.

"Which is it? The river too high or low? Either way, it's better than sitting on our asses." I crossed my arms, daring anyone to argue. If my idea was shit – fine. But I wasn't going to let our clan be stunned into sitting by because we believed there was no option. It was surrender by another name.

Fintan was stunned into silence, refusing to answer my question.

"Shang, prepare the forces according to Dempsey's plan. You four. Stay put." We hung back as the rest of the advisors exited the tent and prepared for battle.

Barra looked up, and for a second, my father looked a thousand years old. Every worry was etched into his face, and the burden of leadership clearly weighed on him. Barra rubbed at his eyes.

"You will not be joining us."

Both Sarai and I opened our mouths to object at the same time, but Barra silently held up a hand. "Willa, if you want to send that letter, I would suggest you write it, quickly." My father slid a pen and paper over to her.

"Leave now for the Lia Fáil. Say your vows as soon as you get there. If we survive, we will meet you at the Hollow. If we are not there, do not come looking for us." *Because we will be dead.* No one dared to say it, that the troops preparing the ringfort were weighing the deaths in their hand. Because they would rather die than live under an invading force.

"No. You need us. You need every hand you can get." My mouth was in a flat line, unhappy and unyielding. I studied too much battle strategy to know how this went. Numbers were essential, especially when caught off guard. Forces raised must match the potentials of invaders. Otherwise, it's a quick fall to abdication.

My father looked at me, his eyes cold. "*I* do not need you." Hurt slapped me in the face. "Your clan needs you. Your isle needs you. Your *gods* need you – both of you, all of you. If we die, you are the last. If you cannot see that, then you are too foolish for your fate anyway," Barra snapped.

Willa tugged at my hand, but my eyes refused to leave Barra's face. Anger and frustration surged through me – what good could the Lia Fáil do for us? Our gods had already cast their judgment by allowing the Sectarians to have a resurgence. *Why couldn't my father accept my hand in battle? What of the forces I've trained, commanded? Are their efforts futile? Why can't the Hill of Tara wait?* But my father's face held no answers, only an expectation to obey. His face held betrayal, a refusal to let me aid my clan in the time of greatest need.

"We should go. Grab horses and food and a few pieces of clothing," Willa murmured. There was hesitancy in her voice – at this ugly monster rearing its head between my father and I. She folded her letter neatly, handing it to Barra, then looked at me expectantly.

"Go. She will be your victory." Barra nodded towards the door.

I held his gaze before nodding and obeying. There was no point in arguing further if his mind was set. I didn't look back, didn't say goodbye. Hurt settled like a viper in my stomach.

Willa tugged on my arm, falling back from the crowd as we exited the tent.

"Are you okay?" She paused, waiting for an answer, keeping silent until I provided one.

How to begin? How to explain the shit relationship of my only family left?

"It's my father. What's not fine about it?" My tone was acrid and biting. *Was I taking it out on Willa? Does she deserve this?* Regret was no doubt coursing through her, at her involvement in another broken person.

"You realize your father just said that you are the only person he would have lead his clan? That his advisors could die, and if you were left he would know your people would still be safe?"

"My father just said that he couldn't care if I was there to fight for my clan. My father is walking into his death and doesn't want his son by his side."

"Because he wants you to *live*. He's willing to risk the edge that you add to the battle so you can survive."

Fuck. Willa was right – I had a feeling she always would be. That piece of wisdom somehow bridged the gap between my father and me, providing the perspective that was never quite gained. The emphasis of Willa's words made me think she saw something else in our interaction, something more meaningful than words.

I faced Willa. Tears danced in my eyes, and I didn't bother to wipe them away.

"Do you think I'm foolish?" The words were raw, hinting at the chasm inside of me.

"I think you're loyal and caring and compassionate, but never foolish. If those are the things that make you a fool, then I hope we all are." Her mouth was stubbornly set, and she crossed her arms, daring me to argue.

I swiftly kissed her, cutting off her last word. The kiss lingered on our lips. I couldn't bring myself to break it.

"Oi! No kissy-kissy when we're racing to escape the invaders, eh?" Sarai yelled, causing us to break apart with flushed cheeks.

"I see why she's in charge of the scouts," Willa commented.

"She's been like this since we were five. It hasn't gotten better, so it's best to get used to it." I grimaced at Sarai's petite figure, standing there waiting for us with two hands on her hips.

We raced to catch up to our companions, ignoring the jokes hurled at us by Felix and Sarai. Felix looked at me.

"Did you swipe the map?"

I gave him a winning smile. "Of course."

"Felix, did you remember the spearhead?" asked Sarai.

"You wound me." Felix clutched at his chest.

Willa looked at us three, her head clearly spinning. And yet – it was too crowded. I couldn't explain here, not while we were in the ringfort. It was too dangerous. Explanations would have to wait.

I raced ahead, Sarai and Felix not far behind me. As soon as we left the gates of the ringfort, I swerved left, finding the same path that took us to the river earlier today.

"Is – is the cabin not in the other direction?" Willa voiced her concern.

"We're not going to the cabin, Willa," Sarai explained, as if she was speaking to a child.

Please be patient. Please understand. Just give us a few more moments, and I'll explain everything.

Irritation scrawled across Willa's face, but she didn't say anything further. She simply gave me a look as if to say *this better be good.*

I jogged to an overhang in the path down to the riverbanks. Sarai grabbed a stack of wood behind a pile of stone, ensuring it was the least waterlogged of the bunch.

Sarai struck two rocks together, creating sparks that flew onto the stack of wood. I watched out of the corner of my eyes as Willa's shock grew. The fire before us roared to life, casting illumination upon the cave walls. Flames leapt and shadows danced as the fire began to radiate heat and grow.

Felix handed me the spearhead he had hid within his cloak. I unwrapped the map and placed it in the middle of the parchment before folding it to fit the shape of the weapon. I set the package in the rain, just outside of reach from the dry climate of the cavern. The soft rain from earlier was pelting down, bleeding through the map and running the colors together.

"Can someone explain what is going on?" Willa demanded. Her gaze swept the three of us. Both Sarai and Felix looked to me, asking for permission. I gave them a swift nod.

Please understand. Keep this secret like I've kept yours.

"When my storm magick started to wane... or if I found I needed a reason to call forth more power, I discovered offerings help. If they aren't accepted by the gods, it can also signal that whatever action or decision we're about to make isn't a good one. It's our way of confirming it's the right path." My eyes widened, imploring her to understand.

"You're asking the rain to fall harder, to make sure that the river widens, so you can fight them in the right path?"

"Yes," I breathed. But it wasn't just that. Magick that was outside the sanctity of recognized witches was taboo. This was dangerous, and if my father found out... I shuddered to think of the repercussions. The accusations that came along with using the gods for our whims and desires. Bending the elements to our will, outside the realm of gifts. The greediness of asking for more, then taking it.

"And the map and the spear?" Willa asked, beginning to piece it all together.

"The map represents the location of the battle, and the spear is to call to the war gods. I'm charging the offering right now, with the rain that's already been created by a gift from the gods."

"And now, we place the sopping wet parcel in the fire and hope it burns," finished Sarai cheerily.

I tossed the wrapped spearhead into the center of the fire and shielded my eyes, praying that the gods were listening.

The fire sprung even higher, leaving scorch marks on the top of the cavern walls. Defying all logical sense, the map's edges crisped and curled. Burning, just as I described. Pieces of ash began to float in the air, like the red leaves of autumn swirling on a breeze.

Sarai clasped her hands together, dropping to her knees. Her mouth silently shaped words as she stared into the depths of the fire.

I caught the realization in Willa's eyes. I could practically see the whites of them when it hit her – *Sarai's a witch.* I gave her a warning glance before raising a finger to my lips. A sign that said 'I'll tell you later'.

Just as quickly as the fire flared, the flames started to drop, lower and lower. The last of the blaze licked around each other, playing and tangling amongst the dark. I found myself wanting them to last, not to shy away from the night. I wanted them to keep us company amongst the fears faced when alone with thoughts in a dark wood.

With a hiss, the last of the fire went out, leaving a perfect outline of the map in the middle of the fire pit and a scorched spearhead in the center. A grin broke out on Sarai's face, her pride beaming ear to ear. I watched as a spray of rain whipped off the surface of the river, and knew that the offering worked.

"Let's go before it gets too bad," Sarai announced. She blew the ashes into the wind and scuffed dirt over the fire site, making sure no stray embers would get caught in the breeze, even if there was a storm.

I fell into step with Willa as we exited the cavern. "I'm sorry for not explaining earlier, but I wasn't sure how you would react. It was easier to talk about it while we were doing the offering."

I knew that she would understand as she stood there nodding. Gifts from the gods were a powerful thing, and they could also bring a pile of fear with them, through no fault of the bearer. It was the reaction of the unfamiliar.

"And Sarai?"

"A witch."

Willa opened her mouth to ask the next question that popped into her mind, but I stopped her. "She likes being around people too much. Thrives off it, really. She's good at leading the scouts, likes advising my father – she loves her life. Is she to be punished for something she can't change?" I looked around me and continued. "We didn't think so, so we keep her secret. But occasionally, she chooses to practice in front of other people, and I need her help to make the offerings, and she uses me as sort of a conduit."

"Your gift is quite literally her portal to the gods," Willa noticed.

"Call me a doorway," I answered with a wry smile.

Willa nodded, letting me know she understood all of it. And I could tell she did – understood the level of sacrifice that we were making for Sarai. Gods, if I didn't love her more for that.

As we approached the cabin, it became clear why I placed the tarp over my home. Water sloughed off the top, practically creating a moat around the entrance.

"Never said it was well built," I whispered into Willa's ear.

Felix turned to us. "Dempsey and I already have our go-bags ready. Willa, what else do you need?"

"My clothes. They're in my saddlebags in the trunks."

"Perfect," answered Sarai. "After that, we'll go to the stables on the outer limits of the village, that's where I left my things."

We dipped inside the cabin. Willa hurriedly grabbed her things and cast one last look around the room. *Reluctant to leave so soon?* The idea of her being so attached to this ramshackle home pulled at something inside me. Felix and I opened another one of the hidden cabinets, strapping packs to our backs and pulling on thick, waterproof coats made of sealskin. I wrapped a smaller, grey one around Willa's shoulders. Through many versions of trial and error, we discovered that sealskin was the only repellent strong enough to withstand one of my storms.

"Unfortunately, you're going to need this if you're going to be hanging around much longer."

"So the rainstorms are going to become a habit?" Willa asked with a grin, wicked delight mixing there.

I leaned in. "Oh, most definitely." *That was a fucking promise.*

"Dirty. I did not need to know that," chided Felix.

"Alright. Are we ready?" I looked at everyone. Felix and Willa gave me nods, while Sarai simply started for the door.

Tad whined. The hound had been shockingly quiet, padding along throughout our various stops that evening. I bent down to scratch his ears. "It's okay, boy, we'll be back soon." I stood, puzzled.

"Does the dog not like the rain?" Sarai looked bothered by the inconvenience of the thought.

"No, normally he's fine with it." I hummed. Tad ran out the door without warning, and I gave one last glance to my friends before following.

Outside, the forest was pitch black, somehow darker than when we entered the cabin. The sound of rain filled our ears, the rest of the world quiet. The wet earth muffled the sound of our footsteps as we grimly set forth, the rain rolling off our cloaks.

A howl echoed through the forest, unmistakably belonging to Tad. I frowned once more. "Tad!" I yelled, trying to recall the wolfhound.

"I feel like we've been in this situation before," Willa noted. Her voice sounded light like she was trying for a joke – but I heard the quiet worry.

I slowed my footsteps before drawing the broadsword at my side. "It's not a faoladh. He's trained not to howl at animals."

Sarai blinked at that. "Then what is he trained to howl at, exactly?"

"People."

The entire forest went silent, even the rain sounding softer. Our group spread into a circle, all of us drawing our weapons. Felix held a sword that was a twin to my own, and Sarai held a throwing knife – no doubt from the set she claimed to have lost. As for Willa, she drew the scian she selected in the cabin. I glanced towards the sword at her side, wondering why she wouldn't use the large weapon.

Tad bayed again, this time closer. Squinting into the distance, I saw a faint outline of him standing on a ridge, his body formed into a perfect point. My head swiveled, tracking the movement of the dog until my gaze landed on a group of strangers.

Sectarians.

The invaders walked forward and fanned into a half-circle, pressing us into the bunch of forest. *An attempt to separate us. They think they can beat us through one on one contact.* I sized them up. There were four of them, matching our numbers perfectly. The only difference in their group was that they held both Sarai and Willa at a considerable height difference.

"Reveal yourself," I commanded. My voice boomed across the forest, stopping the Sectarians in their tracks.

There was a pause, and not a single creature in the forest dared breathe. And then a harsh, grating voice said, "We are the people from the Ngels, and we bring you your death." The man that spoke leered at us, revealing a mouth full of brown and rotting teeth framed by the silver of his helmet.

Some silent command spread through the group and the invaders rushed forward. Their swords were held high as they charged, a foolish act of defiance. Then they were upon us, slashing and cutting, driving us into separate corners of the forest.

I turned towards Willa, about to tell her to run, when there was a flash of silver. I jumped back and beheld the Sectarian before me. I couldn't tell if it was the one who spoke – they all looked the same. But this one was out of shape, his body stretching past the plated armor hooked upon him – and I knew my greatest strength.

Agility was an underrated skill in swordplay, but it was important as the skill of dance in politics. That was to say, it was essential.

I traced a circle around him, taking care to dodge errant swords from the other duels occurring. Anger flared in the Sectarian's eyes, and he rushed forward, making broad, cutting motions. I blocked his sword in a three-step parry, alternating the direction of my sword with each footfall, before deflecting at the base of his sword. I took a long, sweeping step back, reassessing the fight.

The Sectarian loomed opposite me, waiting, watching. Unwilling to move, he kept his eyes trained on me like a cat toying with his prey. Rotating my sword in a circle with my wrist, I dove in, letting each attack linger, allowing the Sectarian to feel the strength of my blows.

Our swords met, both of us refusing to yield.

"We will kill you all," the Sectarian said.

I spat in his face for even suggesting that. That moment of anger caused the warrior to react without thinking, his spare hand moving off the blade to wipe at his face. The weakness in his grip was enough for me to break the stalemate. I pushed the blade off mine, letting my other hand dip to my bandolier and grab a hunting knife, before dancing towards the Sectarian one last time and plunging it into his neck.

Blood sprayed as I wrenched the knife, ensuring I cut the life-containing artery that lived in the neck. The spray turned to a river as I pulled back, and the warrior slumped to his knees, then the ground.

I was wiping the blade on the edge of my tunic when I heard the voice. It was the same one that spoke earlier.

"Should I kill the little girl with a blade, or with my bare hand?"

I spun to see a Sectarian throwing Willa to the floor, aiming a kick for her ribs. She curled into her side, protecting those vital organs as a wheeze shuddered through the air.

I sprinted, not caring about the other battles around me, unable to think about anything save for getting to Willa in time. Fear paralyzed her as she stared up at the Sectarian – I didn't see her chest rise or fall.

Blood spattered the ground as the Sectarian's neck was split open and blood drenched his chest. My sword entered and exited through his neck, and all I felt was satisfaction as I withdrew the blade and kicked the body to the ground. Rage coursed through me, and I fell to where Willa laid, still curled up in pain.

I grabbed her shoulder, assessing the blood that stained her clothes, the bruises that were caressing her skin.

"I'm fine, I'm fine," Willa quickly reassured me. It wasn't until the second time she repeated the phrase that I dared to look her in the eyes, afraid of what would happen if it wasn't true.

Felix watched, the warrior he fought already dead. Sarai had her opponent on his knees, the tendons of his ankles sliced. Two hands lay in the grass next to her, and she held a knife to his throat.

She pressed it gently against his skin.

"I will only be asking one more time. *Why* did you find us?"

The man's words were nearly unintelligible, marred by the sobs racking his body.

"Orders... orders from our Father and our King to kill clans." A faint odor filled the air as the man soiled himself, the front of his breeches darkening.

"No. Not the clans. *Us.*"

"They – they told us to," he sobbed.

"Who?" Sarai yelled. "Your commander?"

The man whispered something as his face went white and his body folded.

Felix walked over and surveyed the body. "Dead," he pronounced. "Bled out too quickly from the looks of it."

Sarai scowled. "I knew I should've left him with a hand."

Felix patted her on the shoulder. "You live and you learn."

I scanned the rest of them for injuries. Besides a scratch across Felix's forearm, they were all relatively unscathed. Even Tad made it out clean – if that was the right word for it. We were covered in mud, and our cloaks were caked in it.

"How did they find us? How did they cross the river so quickly?" Willa asked, turning to scan the forest, looking for any Sectarians that might be in a second wave.

Sarai stepped over the body in front of her. "I bet they sent the team by boat up the river. With the ringfort virtually undefended at the moment, no one would have stopped them as they crept around. Smart, for a bunch of idiots."

"But why us?" Willa asked.

"I don't know," I responded. "But if they attacked our group, intentionally, we have bigger problems."

The group fell silent as we exchanged glances. Knowing that if the Sectarians intentionally sent a group for us, then the invaders had more intelligence on the clans than we were comfortable with.

And potentially, a spy.

CHAPTER TWENTY-FOUR

Willa

S arai looked back at the ringfort. "If they really do know that much, we need to leave. Now." She broke into a run, setting a brisk pace for the rest of us to follow.

I slung my bag back over my shoulder and followed as they made for the stables in the distance. My lungs burned with the added weight of my baggage, I was grateful for the month of grueling training I put myself through. Disbelief filled me as I watched Sarai's tiny figure outpace the pack, running as if she was weightless.

Once we arrived at the stables, Sarai and Felix saddled their individual horses. I stopped at the sight of my chestnut mare and Callan's black stallion.

My mouth went dry. There would be no one to bring Callan's horse back. It felt wrong to ask Felix or Dempsey to do it, and I was sure Sarai would laugh in my face if I asked. I stepped close to the giant animal and held the horse's face as I blew gently into its nose.

"Remember me?" I whispered, knowing that the animal did. "I'll come back for you one day, but for now you have to stay here," I promised. I gave the stallion one last look before turning my back on him, forcing myself to leave those memories in the past.

I noticed Dempsey watching out of the corner of my eye, but I didn't say anything. There was no need to. I was allowed to have the feelings of grief still ebb at me, no matter how miserable my relationship may have been. Grief and trauma were funny things, I decided. Most would consider grief accompanied by sadness and pain, but its friend was guilt, a more heart-wrenching feeling than anything I had known. I hoped that day would come soon when I would lay it to rest.

I grabbed the saddle off the wall full of tack and buckled the clasps, securing the saddle and bags to my horse. Unhooking the gate, I swung it open and guided my horse out of the small set of stables. My companions were waiting just on the other side of the door. We were ready for the adventure to begin.

❧

I wasn't quite sure when we stopped riding. The group pushed through dawn, riding until the sun started to warm our backs and the rain had dried off the trees. Slowly, we shuddered to a walk, each step becoming more painful for the horses. It was a silent agreement when Dempsey swung off his horse and prepared a campsite hidden away in the thick brush.

Sleep was fleeting. Sarai shook me awake and I stumbled over to the horses. There was no time to eat and conversation was little. The air felt tight with tension – Dempsey and Felix worried about the clan they left behind, Sarai worried about her forces, and everyone's mind on the Sectarian invaders.

Trees began to reach for the sky, stretching out their limbs in search of sunlight, their broad leaves creating dappled patterns on the ground. We edged out of Riverland territory, with the trees becoming taller, intermixed with meadows and no marshland in sight. The path we were on was joining with another out of a different branch of the forest.

"Do we go right or left?" I croaked, speaking for the first time in hours.

The three Riverland warriors looked at me.

"Left. The other will only take us back into the territory." Sarai dismissed the question.

Dempsey peered at me. "Willa... the other road takes you to the bog," he answered softly.

Half a dozen memories flashed before my eyes, each of them more vivid than the last. "It can't," I murmured.

"But it does. It's ingrained in our heads as children to avoid at all costs. We only take this path that we're on right now." Concern passed over his features.

"That's impossible," I said sharply. "On our way to your camp, Callan said *that* very path was the only one open. He told me that this one was blocked later down the road by a fallen tree."

Now all three were staring at me, wordlessly.

"So this path can't be the only one used, because there is no fallen tree." My voice raised in pitch as I saw the disbelief written across their features. I gripped the reins even tighter, my knuckles turning white as the leather bit into my hands. "That means that we went through the bog for no reason and he *died for no reason*."

Tears started to swim in my eyes. Out of confusion or anger or shame, I wasn't sure.

"It means that he lied." Sarai supplied the words that I couldn't bring myself to say. Shivers ran across my body. I pressed a hand to my mouth in horror.

"Why," I asked, but no one had an answer for me.

Felix shook his head. "Maybe he was told the wrong

information. Maybe he thought that the bog would be faster, and didn't realize the risk."

"Maybe he was a fool." My voice was cold. Callan's death appeared to be more of a mystery than ever, this piece of the information tarnishing his memory. Foolish choices ignoring the will of the gods. *What a tragic and senseless way to go.*

I spurred my horse on, taking the lead, needing space to breathe. Stares peppered my path, my companions obviously concerned at the revelations I just discovered. Hooves thundered behind me, and I looked back to see Dempsey catching up to me. If I was being completely honest with myself, I wasn't sure I could talk to Dempsey about it, the evidence of the engagement I had so easily traded staring me in the face.

"Sometimes we'll never know why people do the things they do." Dempsey offered the piece of advice, letting it hang in the air.

I shot him a glare. "Does that make it any better?" I frowned at the discontent stirring in me, the yells and screams at the unfairness of nature that refused to order itself.

"No. But it doesn't change the fact that we have to accept it."

"I hate him for leaving this piece unanswered." I laughed darkly. "I hate a dead man for something he can't change or answer to. Does that make me pathetic?"

"I don't think any part of death makes sense. The entire being of Death leaves something that we will never understand or be able to speak to, because no one will leave the Otherworld. Our very nature can't sit with it because humans need answers."

I looked at Dempsey, this piece of advice comforting my soul. "You're very wise for a young man."

He gave me one of his winning smiles. "Send me to live with the elders when we get back."

"We'll call you Old Man Dump," said Sarai. Dempsey winced while I gave a slight giggle.

"She really does love her nicknames, doesn't she?" I asked with a smile playing on my lips.

"No matter how many times I ask; she won't drop it." He shook his head solemnly, and I could only imagine the work he had put into that very cause.

"Why would I stop, when it brings me so much joy?" Sarai's eyes sparkled as her horse fell into step with Dempsey and mine.

"Someone has to put you in your place, brother," chimed Felix, walking in line with us.

At that moment, a sense of family clicked into place. I looked at the line of warriors and down to the dog who trotted behind them, tongue lolling out the side. There was a word in our clans for it; the bands of warriors that would patrol the forest across the ages. *Fianna.* The legendary bands would act as justice across Eiram in times of strife, and the webs of magick shuddered around me as we slid into importance. As if the gods knew the magnitude of the quest we were embarking on, attempting to hold together the clans against the invasion of the Sectarians.

"Fianna," I told my friends, not needing to explain the rest.

Dempsey and Felix looked surprised, but Sarai nodded. She understood. "Yes, I think so too."

"Glaine ár gcroí," said Felix softly. *Purity of our hearts* in the old language.

"Neart ár ngéag," replied Sarai. *Strength of our limbs.*

"Beart de réir ár mbriathar," Dempsey and I said at the same time. *Action to match our speech.*

The words of the Fianna, their battle cry. The words that also represented the oath to uphold all that was good and just, putting weight behind our plan. Binding us all together as one.

"Well, it looks like we might need to get a new set of rings forged," Dempsey pointed out.

We made camp that night full of smiles and laughter, our hearts lifted at the prospect of our futures and destinies. We found a crop of ruins, half-cobbled stones that were once home to some hermit. The structure was falling apart and vines tore at the roof, but it was more solid a shelter than we could have asked for, giving us rooms and a hearth, protecting us from the elements.

Tad ran down a few rabbits into snares that Dempsey had set, and we all ate well that night. I was able to find a mass of vegetables and the old hermit had bushes of potatoes growing in what was once a garden. We knew we wouldn't always have the chance for dinner like this on the road, so everyone ate their fill and then some.

I wandered into a back portion of the ruin and laid out my bedroll, slipping off my boots and into my thin nightgown made for hot summer nights, relishing the feeling of the soft materials instead of the tight pants I wore while riding. There had even been a well out back so I could wash the mud still dried on my skin from the fight with the Sectarians. I almost cried at the feeling of being clean. I slid into my bed, unbraided hair framing a halo around my face.

My eyelids were lowering in lazy blinks when a figure appeared around the corner, leaning against the wall. Instinct told me to grab the knife I hid under my pillow; one second more and my mind told me that it was Dempsey.

"Didn't mean to startle you." His eyes took in my setup, the bedroll, and the nightgown I was wearing.

"No, it's fine. Did you need something? Do you want me to

take the first watch?" A yawn broke out from me, revealing my offer as a hopeful lie.

"No," he murmured. "You should sleep." He went to turn away, not wanting to bother me, but he hesitated.

I waited for what he wasn't saying, knowing that it would come out eventually. Dempsey took short strides to my bedside, kneeling down so he wasn't towering over me.

"I have something for you," he said softly. Dempsey took out a pouch from his pocket, a small drawstring linen bag. I pushed up from my bed, fully sitting up to see what it was.

A copper ring fell out into Dempsey's palm. At the top of the band was a stone, clear in color but flecked with black inclusions, looking like an ink splotch in water. The dim light of the cabin caught and glinted off the stone, highlighting its brilliance. It must have taken a highly skilled craftsman to make; the delicate claws that gripped the stone in place were unlike anything I had ever seen. Most marriage rings held gems that were pressed into the metal, creating an unbreakable bond between two elements.

Dempsey held the kite-shaped diamond ring to the light.

"I promised you a ring a while ago. I had it made the second I got home, and was always going to give it to you. Even if you couldn't be mine." His voice echoed with the knowledge of what had almost been.

Shock ran through my body as I recalled the memory of Dempsey and that vow underneath the willow tree after the first council meeting, where he promised me that it would always be us. A pair, fighting the world together. I had never understood the depth of his promise to me – until now.

I studied the man kneeling before me, so compassionate it almost broke me. For the life of me, I couldn't understand how he felt drawn to me, what I did to deserve him, or why he felt equally responsible for me. How could he love me when I had spent half my life hating my own being?

"It's been you and me since the moment in that meadow." I softly repeated the vow he once told me many months ago. Dempsey nodded in agreement.

I held out my hand in response and Dempsey guided the ring onto my ring finger, where it sat above my heart line. It was bold and beautiful; everything I hoped to be, and everything I hoped that Dempsey saw in me. The ring that was once a promise of his vow now represented our betrothal and our chance at a new life if this journey went according to plan.

It was a ring for love and life, shimmering with camaraderie and family. It wasn't just a vow to me but to him and our clans. "I don't have one for you." I looked at his eyes, searching. They twinkled back in response, dismissing my worry.

"I'm a patient man," he crooned. His answer told me we had time; we would be able to get that time because this would go to plan. We would be walking amongst the forest with rings on both of our hands one day.

I wrapped my arms around his neck, savoring the feel of his skin against mine, how he felt strong and secure. His love was so opposite of what I had always known, but there it was, shining with hope. I kissed him, my lips and body remembering the last time we were in a bedroom alone. I savored the feeling and the freedom of it all.

"Well then, I'm glad you waited for me," I whispered. "Do you want to sleep here tonight?" I wriggled over into the corner of the cot, knowing the two of us would barely fit on it together.

Dempsey blew out the lantern in the corner of the room, plunging us into darkness. I blinked, letting my eyes adjust as I made out Dempsey's dark shape before me.

Dempsey took off his shirt and boots before sliding into my cot, sliding his hand onto my waist. His warmth radiated from him. Nerves leapt in my stomach as I gathered the courage to continue my kiss with the man next to me.

I swung my leg across Dempsey, straddling him as my

nightgown rose up around my hips. I placed my hands on his cheek as I bent down to kiss him, guiding his face to mine in the dark.

Dempsey's hands roamed across my back and down to my hips. I flattened myself against him, wanting more of him and his body.

In one swift motion, Dempsey had me against the ground and the cot. I let out a squeal in surprise. I looked into his brown eyes.

This connection between us – *this* was living.

"Shhh," he hushed. "We should be quiet so we don't wake anyone." His eyes glimmered with mischief.

I bit my lip in response.

Dempsey grabbed my hands, pinning them over my head. He rubbed his hips against me. "Do you think you can do that?" His voice deepened with desire.

"Yes," I breathed. Part of me doubted that answer.

Dempsey kissed at my neck, nipping and biting me as I was pinned there, at his mercy. I lifted my hips to meet his, wanting more.

"Patience, dear Willa." He gave me a lingering kiss on my collarbone. "A virtue."

Gods, the fact that he is talking about virtue *of all things right now.*

Dempsey released my hands, making his way down my body, slowly moving his hand up my thigh instead. He pushed my nightgown further and further up, running his lips against the inside of my thigh as he exposed it. The night air was cold against my bare skin, but Dempsey was so warm.

I lifted the shift up and over my head, exposing the rest of myself to him. Begging him for more, now. Dempsey grabbed my breast in one hand before turning to the other.

He bent his head and bit at my nipple, eliciting a gasp from me. Amused eyes looked up at my face, and an almost feral smile spread on Dempsey's face.

"You enjoy that?" He waited for my response, his fingers toying with my hardening nipple, waiting for my permission to continue.

"It feels good," I whispered so softly, my words surprising even myself. *This man is causing me to throw out all semblances of modesty.*

"Fuck, Willa." Dempsey lowered his head to suck on it, teasing me with his teeth, pinching my other breast with his hand, grabbing and kneading at it.

My breaths grew heavy in response, and my hand darted across my stomach, wandering to give myself more.

Dempsey grabbed my errant hand. "Is there something you want?" His head dipped to kiss the point where my ribs knit together.

I wanted him at this point, having no patience for his teasing games that he delighted in.

"Dempsey, I want you. I want to have sex with you, right now. Please." My voice wavered. I said it both as a request and a command, and Dempsey listened.

I could hardly think straight as Dempsey slowly slid into me, making me gasp. I pressed my hand onto his lower back, pushing him further. I looked at Dempsey's face and locked my gaze on his gorgeous brown eyes, the eyes that always felt like home.

His mouth claimed mine as he picked up speed. A moan escaped from me, and I hoped that no one could hear us. I grasped his arm, feeling the strength that was so soft around me, reveling in the feeling of it all. Dempsey slowed his pace, grinding against me so tantalizingly slow, and frustration and desire began to build in me.

I tried digging my hands into his back again, but he resisted. He was in complete control now, and I could see on his face that he was going to make me beg while he savored it.

He drove into me, slowly, pushing his entire length into me before withdrawing and repeating. I let my hands roam across his arms, his abs and lower, sucking and nipping at his forearm, trying to bring him to give me more. A smile snaked across his face as he held perfectly still.

Dempsey withdrew completely as he pushed me onto my side and laid down behind me, holding my body against his. I held my breath, waiting in the silence for what he had planned next.

He spread my legs before entering me again. Dempsey's arms wrapped around my body, holding me tight. I ground against him as he gave me what I wanted, complete control. Our breaths, panting with desire, filled the air, the sound leaking from us. I wanted to stay in this feeling forever, the feeling of us, of desire and safety. The entire world could fade away and we wouldn't notice.

We lay there like that for a while, holding each other tightly, unwilling to let go, knowing that this was more real than anything either of us had experienced. Fingers trailed absentmindedly across my shoulder, marking the outline of my spine before running back up it again. I pressed my lips to Dempsey's hand before resting it across my hips, as I leaned into him and finally closed my eyes.

"It was always us, from the beginning." He whispered into my ear as my lips curled in a lazy smile. That night, I dreamt of home in our clans, surrounded by my parents and my sister, Barra laughing with Sai over a beer. Sarai and Felix were there too, mercilessly teasing each other. It was a dream of hope and one tinged with fear that it would never happen, that we wouldn't reach the Lia Fáil in time and the Sectarians would claim the isle and we had left the Riverland warriors to unknowingly reach their death. The dream that had started out so sweet had taken a dark turn into a nightmare, familiar in concept but brought to a new level of terrifying, the stakes now heightened.

Now, there was more on the line than ever before.

I woke in the middle of the night, the darkness curling around me as I hoped that it wasn't just a dream, but an omen. A way of the gods silently whispering to me that we would be successful, that montage of scenes from home being our future. I turned and looked at Dempsey's peaceful face, relaxed with sleep. In that moment, I vowed that I would fight for this, my Fianna, my family, and my clans. To death, if needed.

CHAPTER TWENTY-FIVE

Willa

The next morning began with a letter. A hawk intercepted us as we left the ruins to return back on the road. Tied to the ankle was a small scroll, the inside detailing the victory of the Clan Amongst the Rivers. Barra reported being able to win the battle with minimal losses, thanks to Dempsey's plan. If there was any pride in Dempsey at that, there was no evidence on his face.

While the fighting occurred, Sarai's scouts were able to intercept the location of the majority of their ships. One bold scout named Ophelia managed to light their docking stations on fire, leaving many vessels burned and a few completely destroyed. Sarai let out a devilish grin at that, proving that her scouts were more than whispers on the wind and eyes on the horizon for Barra. I suspected that Sarai had turned them into a destructive fighting force, and was waiting to unleash them.

With the knowledge that the clans were succeeding in battle, it appeared that the Sectarians were retreating for the moment. Eyes on the colony in the cliffs showed that there weren't enough soldiers to continue the battle after the skirmishes against the Mountain Clan and the Clan Amongst the Rivers. Felix guessed that they were going to need to send word to Ngel, their homeland, and ship in the troops. Mercifully, the gods had bought us time.

On the clan side of things, there were minor losses, mostly belonging to soldiers from outposts who hadn't been trained at Barra's hand. Shang was the only noticeable absence that I recognized; it seemed that the young advisor had disappeared. Whether that was due to a violent death or being taken as a prisoner, no one was sure. Apparently, the carnage had been bad enough that senior warriors were spread thin in an attempt to strengthen battle lines.

At this piece of information, Dempsey shook his head. Sarai dared to question him.

"You think that was a bad call? That his death could have been avoided?" She looked up where she was sprawled in the small courtyard, her hands interlaced behind her head.

"I've studied the war between the Sectarians and the Clan o' Cliffs for years. Everything tells us that they fight organized, using front lines and formations. When we match their fighting style, that's when all hell breaks loose." Dempsey leaned forward in the chair he was sitting in, his intensity growing with this subject he was obviously passionate about.

Felix continued for Dempsey as he walked about the courtyard, commanding an invisible court. "We think that we should fight in war-bands. Similar to a fianna, if you will. When you use point attacks coming from a wayward point, they don't know how to handle it and it tears them apart. At least that's what we hypothesize." Sometimes Dempsey and Felix spoke like two voices for a single mind, like twins with the same mouthpiece.

"But of course, my father doesn't seem to care about testing these ideas."

I opened my mouth from the corner of the courtyard in which I stood, the words escaping before I had time to truly process the implications. "When it comes to life and death, doesn't it seem a little brash to test out new battle formations during the war?"

Dempsey turned to look at me, standing from his chair, while Felix attempted to master the shock that settled on his expression.

"You think we're wrong?" From the way he spoke it, I could tell he rarely faced opposition on these ideas. I pressed my back into the cold stone of the house, squaring my shoulders before answering.

"I think you might be right, but that we shouldn't gamble with lives. Maybe if it was a border skirmish, yes. But not war."

Dempsey studied me for a long time while Felix and Sarai waited for him to pass judgement.

"Maybe you're right." He turned to Sarai, perhaps the most dangerous of all. "What do you think?"

"I think it's a brilliant idea, and you know it's how I've trained my own." Her voice trailed off. "But I also don't have the best reputation for responsibility and having my head screwed on straight." Felix let out a snort behind her.

"That's one way of putting it." With her eyes still closed, Sarai flicked out a leg, leaving a bruise to blossom with a well-aimed kick to Felix's shin.

"But if the losses are really that bad, maybe you're right, it should be the correct option." I shrugged. "I'm not an expert in battles or armies. I was just trying to think of it from your father's point of view."

"No, you're right," Dempsey admitted.

Felix whistled. "That's big for him to admit. You must really have him wrapped around your finger."

Dempsey threw a punch at his shoulder.

"You guys, I *bruise*." Felix scowled at his friends.

"Because you don't in any way invite it." My voice dripped in sarcasm as I kicked off the wall and leaned down to grab my saddlebags. We went to prepare the horses while Dempsey fed Tad the leftovers of the previous night's meal.

"So where to today?" I asked, unsure of the path that lay ahead of us.

"The foothills," Sarai said. The Hill of Tara lay in between the Clan of Forests and the Mountain Clan, where the trees turned evergreen and the air became alpine.

"All the way through?" Even if I was no cartographer, that was a massive distance to cover on terrain that wasn't easy for the horses. But part of me saw the answer coming from Sarai's mouth before she even said it.

"If we can. But more likely than not, we're going to have to stop for another night." Sarai didn't have to specify where. We all knew it was dangerous no matter where we slept, and the closer and faster we pushed for the Hill of Tara, the closer we were going to get to that capital outpost. "I want to stop at Kelz's house. It's pretty much halfway, and he'll give us a roof over our heads."

"Kelz?" I asked.

"Witchy friend," Sarai explained.

Felix, however, looked less than understanding. He pulled out a rolled-up map from the holder at his waist, spreading out the parchment before him.

"Show me where," he said. "I'm not traveling hours in the wrong direction just so you can exchange some rocks."

Sarai rolled her eyes. "They're crystals, not rocks, and it was an enriching experience," she glowered.

She pointed to a spot on the map. "Happy?"

Felix narrowed his eyes. "Fine. We'll go there today," he said, apparently approving of the location.

T he forest beckoned to us, its branches welcoming us into the innermost layers. The Clan of Forests might claim this territory, but I had no memory of ever reaching this patch. The idea of once being afraid to venture past the camp filled me with regret, regret for being the girl who flinched at her own shadow and trembled at the corners of the world. Part of me wondered where she went, and if she would ever return.

But somehow, Sarai knew the way, her footing sure and without hesitation. This house did not lay on a map, nor did it have a name. When Sarai spoke of it, it conjured a murky image implanted in my mind, one that I had never seen before but was familiar all the same.

The strangest thing of all was that the idea of the house matched the thing in daylight. The weathered hut was filled with vines, plants exploding from every orifice. The structure itself was built into the tree that towered over it, the architecture spanning around the mass of roots through which the walls crawled. There was nothing to mark that a person lived there, yet it was alive all the same. Sarai told us to wait while she went within first, to ensure their welcome.

Time passed, just enough for me to shift in my seat. Felix and Dempsey were better composed, showing no worry on their faces. Silence can sometimes be a better tell than voice. But nothing dared escape their mouths, and the horses walked no further, as if waiting for permission to exist in this place.

After a long while, Sarai finally emerged, this time with a person in tow. They were even shorter than Sarai, with round cheeks and a flat expression on their face. They walked up to me and looked me in the eyes.

Their eyes were green, not quite the same earth color I was used to, but not the cold blue that scared me so much. It was as if there was a depth to them, an inner working that hadn't been revealed yet.

"Kelz," said Sarai, "this is Willa. Willa, this is Kelz."

Kelz took my hand and flipped it over so the palm was facing the golden light that streamed through the trees. They traced a finger down the seams of my palm, marking the spot where the gods had stitched me together.

"You don't remember me?"

I tilted my head, shocked. I had never been here in my life, and Kelz held no familiarity with me either.

"Do you remember me?" I asked softly.

"Daughter of Bridgette and Viktor, with the gift of foresight. Who do you think was the one that figured it out? It certainly wasn't your bumbling parents." Kelz snorted.

"You – you were the one to figure it out?"

"Honey, the Dagda told me himself. Good thing too, you were the shiest little thing I had ever seen, and I think it frightened your parents to see you talking to trees."

A chuckle escaped from Felix.

"And you." Kelz moved over, repeating the same exercise, tracing the lines of Felix's palm. "A warrior who is cleverer with words than his sword. That's a dangerous place to be. I would keep your guard up if I were you," they added with a wink.

"Dempsey, son of Barra, don't think you can hide by standing there being *respectful*. Honestly, the very thought is shameful." His behavior earned him a slap on the wrist from Kelz, whose face twitched as they examined Dempsey's palm. "Such a deep fate line," they murmured.

Kelz closed Dempsey's hand with a short tap. "Well. You have all passed the Judgement. Tea?" As quickly as Kelz had appeared, bringing life into their garden, they left it, striding back to their home which looked so impossibly small I wasn't sure how we would all fit.

The door opened, revealing a house that was both tidy and

stuffed to the brim. Kelz walked over to a kitchen table and patted a few stacks of books before seating themselves on the only chair. I wondered if Sarai knew what she was promising when she said we could stay the night here.

"Sarai mentioned you might have a hawk we could send out; we were hoping to get some updates back to the clans." Felix tried his hardest to sound business-like, clearly off-put by his reading in the garden.

Kelz's eyes sparkled. "Oh yes, she did mention that. Of course. Although I am convinced that squirrels are a better method of communication."

"Squirrels?" I asked. I had never heard such a thing in my life. This visit was getting stranger and stranger.

"Squirrels indeed. They're incredibly quick creatures, and the best part is that no one suspects them. I'm training a legion of them myself." All emotion dropped from Kelz's face. "You mustn't tell anyone," they said, tugging on my sleeve.

"Of course not," I stammered in response.

Kelz walked to the kitchen not two steps away and began to prepare the tea they promised. Dempsey, Felix, and I all studied Sarai's face, hoping to gain some sort of context, but she had pulled out the book she was sitting on and begun to read. Underneath the table, Felix tried to deliver a well-aimed kick, but Sarai simply shifted her weight, tucking both feet under her in a cross-legged position.

"So what is the grand plan of things?" asked Kelz, calling over their shoulder while placing a kettle on the stove.

Dempsey cleared his throat before answering. "We plan to travel to the Lia Fáil, to declare our marriage and receive the approval of the gods."

"And you think that will go over well?" Kelz asked, one eyebrow cocked.

"I do," Dempsey bristled.

Kelz sat four mismatched cups on the table before setting a floral teapot on the checkerboard tablecloth.

The kettle whistled, and Kelz hurriedly poured the steaming water in the floral teapot.

Once poured, I hesitantly sniffed at my tea. As far as my senses could tell, it seemed normal. I gave it the smallest sip, rolling the liquid around my mouth, testing for odd textures and taste. Across the table, my companions weren't being as careful, with Dempsey drinking his like normal, most likely afraid of seeming rude.

Felix, on the other hand, took a long sip of the steaming beverage and almost immediately let it fall out of his mouth and back into the cup. Dempsey let out a chuckle while I thanked the gods Kelz seemed to be talking to their plants at the windowsill, apparently forgetting about their guests.

"Kelz, we can stay here tonight, right? You still have that loft?" asked Sarai.

Kelz whipped around with a surprised look on their face. "I do! I almost forgot about that," they chuckled.

They walked up to yet another shelf of books, transporting them by the armful across the room. Slowly, a curtain was revealed, which Kelz whisked aside, revealing a ladder.

"You can stay here as long as you would like. Although if it were between you and me, leaving would be better sooner rather than later."

"And the hawk? Could we use the hawk for a message?" asked Felix, gently reminding them.

Kelz simply motioned for Felix to follow them and led the way outside.

The moment Kelz closed the door, Sarai shot out of her seat, opening a small wooden panel behind her. The door appeared to be carved out of the wall, a hidden compartment. Ducking her head, Sarai squeezed through the door obviously made for a much smaller person. Out of the corner of my eye, I caught a glance from Dempsey, concern, and curiosity written across his face.

The teacup clinked softly as I sat it on the table, moving to follow Sarai. As I stooped to look through the doorway, I gasped. The door led to a sort of atrium, the outdoors somehow held inside Kelz's cottage. Somehow, we were nestled against the roots of the tree, the trunk gathering a good foot above our head.

Light bounced across the small yard, the plants adorning the room like jewelry. I squinted, looking closer at the vibrant flowers. They weren't plants. What appeared to be miniature daffodils and daisies were actually crystals, growing in bunches across the roots.

I only recognized a handful of them, the varieties extending far past what we used for daily life in the hollow. I recognized the vibrant color of citrine, the sparkle of clear crystal. In the far corners, hiding underneath the shade like night roses was black tourmaline.

Vaguely, I remembered Felix chastising Sarai about trading crystals the last time she took him on a journey. It was clear that you could spend hours in this place and find a new burst of gemstones, hidden and waiting to be found.

Climbing on top of the serpentine roots, Sarai had half her hand buried in a knothole, reaching for something out of eyesight.

"Lose something?" I asked, too many questions swirling in my mind.

Sarai looked behind her with brief annoyance, as if she hadn't realized I followed her.

"You shouldn't be here," she replied flatly.

I scrunched my brow. "Should you? Does Kelz know we're in here?"

Shoving a handful in her pocket, Sarai hopped down, narrowly avoiding crushing a smattering of chrysocolla. "No. Kelz does not know we're in here, and if they do find out, we will not be invited back for a few lifetimes." She motioned towards the door, ushering me to leave.

My feet stayed rooted to the spot. "What did you grab?"

"Something he'll never miss. Something that *you* will not be telling him about." Sarai moved to push past me, but I grabbed her arm.

I jerked back, hurt by this change in attitude from Sarai, someone who I had considered to be a friend. Friends weren't something I had in abundance, and immediately I wondered if I had misread it, if it had all been a façade.

"Sarai, I don't do secrets. Maybe Dempsey and Felix know what you're up to, but we can't operate like that. It doesn't work here."

A murderous look crossed her face before her other hand reached in her pocket. For a second, I thought she was going to show me what she took; come clean about it all.

A pocket knife flipped open and pressed against the crook of my elbow.

"You'll let me go, and I won't hold this against you. But I don't respond to threats or people who condescend." Her nostrils flared, fight flaring in her eye.

And as much as I wanted to press her about it, I stopped. Enemies in a close circle was a dangerous thing to have, and I couldn't afford any, especially with Sarai. I held her gaze briefly, softening my grip.

"Okay," I said simply.

My hand went to the hidden pocket on the inside of my cloak as Sarai turned around, turning the smooth stone I had plucked out of her pocket.

We ducked out of the small door before returning to our seats at the table. If not for the crystals in our pockets, there was no evidence we moved from our spots to begin with.

But I wasn't finished. "Are you going to tell Dempsey?"

Dempsey frowned. "Tell me what?"

Sarai flipped the pocket knife still in her hands. "I needed a few crystals. Kelz has more than enough. I am simply taking out a loan. I'll give them back when I'm finished," she said sweetly, although her voice was tinged with annoyance.

"Sarai, you did not." His voice bordered on chastisement, and I could already see Sarai brewing from it.

"I don't question your decisions, Dempsey. I let you fall in love with a girl you don't even know, and now you're rushing off to talk with the gods, who might not even want to speak with you." Her words cut like a knife, and I knew I felt the sting just as much as Dempsey did, if not more.

Dempsey opened his mouth to speak once more, but Sarai cut him off. "I never knew you to act so much like your father. Careful, otherwise she might run off, just like your mother did." Sarai threw back the rest of her tea. She stormed out of the room, not bothering to close the door behind her.

I wrapped my arms around myself, unsure of what wire I had triggered. A long whistle came from Dempsey. "I haven't seen her pull a number like that in a while."

I opened my mouth to speak, but nothing came out. If I was being honest, I didn't feel like talking much either. But something in me reached for the wounds Dempsey should be nursing right now, ones that would have ripped me open.

"Are you okay?"

"I'm used to playing the bad guy. Something must be going on, and she'll tell us in due time. Just have to wait until she's ready to open up. I suspect she had other motivation for coming to Kelz's because hospitality is not an offer that they make lightly."

"You don't think she has an obligation to tell us what that might be?" Part of me was outraged at the hiding and the lies that I didn't realize I was participating in. Lies that had weaved themselves in what appeared to me as a family. It wasn't about the stealing, that I didn't care about. It was the disregard for the mission we were on right now, the disregard of how that stunt could potentially put us off course.

"I don't think it's within our realm. It's between her and the gods and her witchcraft, and we aren't entitled to that."

Dempsey read my face, where my discontent was written. "I can try and talk to her." He got up and left the table, leaving me alone.

And so I sat, ruminating in my thoughts, a dangerous place to be. Wondering what the hell I was doing here, with people I barely knew, in an area of my territory that even I had never been in. I might be the only person in the room, and I had never felt more alone.

It wasn't just Sarai snapping at me. It was this entire place, this whole feeling it brought on to me. As if I was one of the oddities sitting on Kelz's shelves. My life wasn't one I belonged in, not ever, and especially not now.

This thought echoed through my mind, inescapable. I felt myself slowly sinking back into that hole I had been so proud of climbing out of, except that it wasn't even Callan who put me there this time. This time, I only had myself to blame. My demons had simply shifted forms.

Jostling at the door broke me from my spell. Kelz walked in as I quickly wiped the tears from my face.

"Oh, dearie. It looks like we need another cup," said Kelz kindly, deftly lighting a fire for the kettle. They sat, waiting for the whistle, and took my hand. This time, however, it wasn't for a reading. It was simply a gesture of kindness; a touch so tender, it nearly sent me into tears all over again.

"I'm sorry. I'm not sure what's wrong with me." I managed to heave a self-deprecating laugh, but it only sounded tired and sad.

"It's the magick. It can... *exacerbate* things. Emotions are heightened because you are closer to nature and your truest form."

The explanation sounded so reasonable I wanted to laugh at the idea that this feeling was normal. It was like Kelz dealt with crying women in their kitchen every day.

"And what is my truest form? Saltwater?" My voice dripped in sarcasm.

Kelz shook their head. "No. Willa, you are the in-between, the portal to the gods. Your form is not of this world, or the next. You are barely more than air, but cannot stand the heaviness of magick. You are grace incarnate, and the gods did not flinch when they created you with their gift."

They continued. "When I first saw you and your gift, I knew that your life would not be without its struggles." They lifted my chin. "But who is to say it is not without its rewards as well?"

I nodded, my soul oddly comforted by these few sentences. It felt like Kelz had stared directly into my being and was able to understand it fully.

"The gods admire your fight, and I believe they will be there with you when the time comes."

I blinked in confusion. "What time? When will they be with me?"

Kelz looped around me to grab the kettle that was now screaming in a falsetto. "I meant figuratively, my dear. You must have misheard me," they said smoothly.

"Do you think Sarai is okay?"

The kettle let out a thud as it was set on the table. "I think Sarai will always be okay. You should not worry so much, it will give you wrinkles."

Kelz gave me an odd look. "Why don't I make you some food and you can go upstairs and sleep? Sarai told me about your ordeal, and I'm sure you must be tired."

I wasn't sure what shifted in the air, but I agreed. Kelz sent me upstairs with a platter of meat and cheese and a toasted chunk of bread. The food was a welcome presence, and at some point shortly after, I fell asleep.

❧

I was dreaming, but I didn't know it. Grey mist filtered through the air around me, creating a cocoon. It blinded me, there wasn't anything else I could see besides the thickness of it. A high-pitched scream filled the air, an eerie sound unlike anything I had ever heard before. Frantically, I looked around, looking for Sarai or Felix or Dempsey. They must be hurt, but I couldn't find the source of the screaming. It echoed in my ears until I couldn't think straight, there was nothing but the screaming. It never stopped, never took a breath, just kept screaming, on and on.

A figure loomed overhead. It was shaking me, and I opened my eyes to a barely lit room.

"Willa," the voice hissed.

"Sarai? It's not dawn yet," I said.

"Willa, you have to listen to me. I'm sorry about what I said earlier. But you can't go to the Lia Fáil. Just lie, and tell Barra you did, and we can go to the Clan of Forests straightaway. Right now, if you want." Sarai's voice sounded frantic, as if she was trying to convince me between life and death.

My brow knit together as I tried to piece together what was happening. "Sarai, we have to. It's a part of the betrothal agreement. Why don't you want to?" I wouldn't doubt Barra's ability to figure out what exactly happened at the Hill of Tara, and I *needed* those troops he promised, the whole island did.

I couldn't be sure in the dark, but something in Sarai's expression changed. "I just don't think it's smart. I saw it in my vision with the summoning stone." I briefly thought about the crystal she insisted on taking from the garden.

"So the rock told you this?" I asked doubtfully. I hated the disbelief in my voice, the same sound I myself had faced so often with my own visions. *But wouldn't the gods tell me something? Why would they speak to Sarai and not me?*

Sarai hushed me. "Talk much louder and you'll wake up the entire house. The stone was a gateway to speak with the gods. I don't think we'll make it out if we go to the Hill of Tara."

"Sarai, it's a rock. How much damage could it do?" I pushed myself fully upright as I grasped how concerned Sarai was. "We'll go there and say our vows. We won't summon the gods or do any sort of rituals, and I won't even speak to them. Then we'll leave. Immediately."

"Okay," Sarai nodded.

"Get some sleep. We'll leave early tomorrow."

"Willa? I'm sorry about earlier," said Sarai.

"It's okay," I murmured.

"Willa?"

"Yes, Sarai?"

"It's really weird how you casually speak to the gods," Sarai deadpanned.

I nearly choked on my laugh in the dark, and Sarai let out a giggle as well. I held out my hand, reaching for Sarai. A small hand grabbed mine and gave it a squeeze, a reassurance that she would always be there. When I fell back asleep, it was a peaceful one.

The next morning, Kelz ushered us out of the house, their hospitality seemingly at its end. We set off, making the final leg of our journey, at last seeing the Hill of Tara in the distance. Even if making it past the Hill of Tara meant the start of a war, something in me sparked with excitement. Dempsey looked over at me and gave me one of his grins.

Today was our wedding day, and we would say our vows before the gods. For hundreds of years, vows and marriages and pacts had been said over the Lia Fáil, and our words would blend into the unbreakable promise there. The Lia Fáil wasn't just a monument to the gods, but a symbol of eternal verity. I didn't dare let my mind wander to what would happen if the gods didn't give their approval. It simply wasn't an option, and I would lie to Barra through my teeth if I had to.

We had entered the Ráth na Ríogh, the enclosure that enveloped the Hill of Tara. The ancient burial site loomed before us, with the buried kings of old entombed within. But we were not there to visit the dead. The air around us shivered with power, and the greenery of the meadow we were in fell away. I looked at my companions to see if they noticed that we were no longer in Eiram, but in a different dimension on our land. We were entering the land of the gods.

CHAPTER TWENTY-SIX

Willa and Dempsey

O ur group approached the beginning of the hill and dismounted to tie our horses. If we were to go any further, we were going to need to be on foot, to feel the ground underneath our feet. Stone walls surrounded the innermost working of the hill, with a single, unmanned gate facing us.

Felix went to open the gate, but it did not move. The bars were stuck, rusted with age, and unwilling to respond. He took out his greatsword, ready to saw the brittle bars in two, but Sarai stopped him. She placed a cautionary hand on his shoulder and gave a smile.

"This is no longer our realm. It operates under a different kind of law." She looked at the gate, her eyes shining and bright. "Did you never listen to stories about the Hill when you were a child?"

Felix shook his head.

"Of course not," she sighed, moving to sit cross legged on the grass. "The Hill of Tara is where the faeries and the gods used to live. This was their capital. Some argue it still is, and you can feel it in the magick in the air." She ran her fingers through the wind, as if feeling it herself.

"Every being that has ever entered the Hill is completely unique in their aspect. It's a condition of being a god. And in order to be in there, with them, you must prove your worth."

She fixated her gaze on her friends. "My name is Sarai, scoutmaster and witch of the Riverlands. I am the only witch to have ever lived inside a clan and allow our magicks to combine and cohabitate. You will find none like me." The words weren't her normal speech; instead she spoke them like a spell.

Sarai rose from the grass and walked towards the gate. A slight tug, and it creaked open. The world went silent as she entered the monument, and the door closed behind her as she walked deeper within. The only evidence of her ever being there was the sound of the gate jostling back into position.

Felix shook his head. "I don't have a connection to the gods like you three do. I can't go in there; this is no longer my journey. I'll stay here, watch Tad, in case anything goes wrong." He turned to Dempsey. "I'll be waiting on the other side for you."

Nerves began to fill my throat, but part of me knew the gods would welcome me into the labyrinth that was beckoning me home. *It was now or never.*

"My name is Willa, daughter of Viktor and Brigid, Council to the Clans and the Gods, gifted with foresight and the portal to the gods." When I moved to open the door, there was no resistance or hesitation. The gate swung open, as new as the day it was soldered into the rocks it guarded. I couldn't see Sarai, didn't know if she had gone left or right, and I discovered a whole new fear of getting lost in the Hill and never finding my way out.

I kept one hand on the grate, for fear of wandering without noticing. I looked at Dempsey through the iron bars, where he stood on the land of mortality, his shape outlined against the grey mist that was seeping in.

"Dempsey, you need to say it. Out loud."

He gripped the hilt of his sword – fear, perhaps. "I am Dempsey, son of Barra, and heir to the Riverlands." He approached the door, placed his hand on it while I withdrew mine, but nothing happened. Confusion settled in his eyes as he rattled the gate once more.

"Willa – Willa, it isn't working."

Anxiety set in, making me question what would happen if Dempsey wasn't allowed access to the Hill. And if that meant I wouldn't be allowed out of it. I swallowed my fear, and forced myself to breathe, just as I had done all these years, forcing the breath in and out of my body.

"Try again. Say something else. Your father was an heir to the Riverlands, too."

Dempsey examined the gate, as if he would rather take it off his hinges. He ran his fingers through his hair before stepping back and trying again.

"Dempsey, son of Barra, and I am one of the Council to the Clans and Gods and a member of the Fianna that patrols our isle."

The gate held true again, even as we rattled against it. Even with my hands on it, the gate didn't swing inward to let me out. This place wasn't just a capital for the faeries but a jail for living, and if there was no way to outsmart it, we would rot in here.

My mind whirled, trying to think of Sarai's instructions. "There's already a member of the Council and the Fianna in here. I took that. It isn't unique. Sarai said you must be *one of your own kind,* like the fae and the gods."

I wanted to call out to the gods, thinking that Boann would know what to do, that she always had the answer. Grimly, I thought of my conversation with Sarai the night before. I had made a vow that I wouldn't call on the gods while we were here.

Was Sarai right? Were we to never leave this place? Was this what she warned of?

"My name is Dempsey, and the power of the storms runs through my veins."

"No, Dempsey! *Think!* There are already storm gods that inhabit here. There are already fae and nymphs with the power of water. What makes you *singular*, what is your fate that makes you different from every gods-forsaken soul on this isle," I said.

Dempsey was pacing now, his hair falling out of place as his expression darkened.

"I am Dempsey, son of Barra, Council to the Clans and Gods, member of the Fianna, who has storms running through his veins. I am a warrior and a fiancé, I raise wolfhounds, and dance at feasts. I laugh and I fight and I love and I *live*. Which is more than the gods can say. There are none of you within there that can say the same, you are none of what I am." A fury settled in his eyes.

"If there is another in there like me, you can take me to the depths of hell, right here, right now." He paused as a crooked grin spread across his face. Part of me wondered if the Hill had pushed him too far. "But if there isn't, you better open this damn gate."

A click echoed through the stone walls as the gate swung open, as if moved by its own accord. An incredulous laugh escaped from me, and Dempsey swept me into his arms. He sighed with relief.

"I thought I was going to have to leave you here," he murmured.

"You would never dare." Light danced in my eyes.

He smoothed back my hair. "No, I wouldn't," he said in agreement. He leaned down and kissed me, the briefest of things, a reminder of the task at hand.

"Where's Sarai?" he asked.

I shook my head. "She wasn't waiting when the gate opened for me. I think she's deeper in, but I wanted to wait for you."

Because I was afraid of losing myself within this maze. Can you feel it too? Tearing at your mortality?

"Well then, we better find her." Dempsey took my hand. "Right or left?" The hallway before us diverged both ways, leading into tunnels only lit by flame from torches that must have started long ago.

I hesitated. "Left."

We walked, hand in hand, until the darkness threatened to devour us whole. The torches were meaningless flames, hardly illuminating the ground underneath us, much less a way forward. Our feet clicked on the cobblestones underneath, reminding us that something far greater had built this place thousands of years ago. The walls began to fill with tombs, coffins carved from stone lining spots in the walls. It was a great mausoleum.

The road sloped downward, and the temperature dropped around us. Puddles lapped at my feet, and the sound of rushing water filled my ears.

"Do you hear that?" I asked.

Dempsey's eyes widened with wonder. "Look down." We were standing on a bridge, one I didn't realize we had entered. Underneath flowed an underground river, somehow cool and sweet-smelling, filled with light and whitecaps as it tumbled down the underground path.

"Welcome to the Hill of Tara," a smooth voice intoned from behind us. I whipped around and beheld Boann, standing there in all her beauty.

She held up a hand. "There is no need to explain, I see all. We have been waiting for you for a long while. I believe you are looking for the Lia Fáil?"

I nodded. "Can you show us the way? And we had a friend with us, a witch named Sarai. Have you seen her as well?"

Boann laughed. "Sarai is fine. She is meeting some of the others as we speak. Come, and join her."

I wondered if Boann's message for me all those weeks ago

had a different message, if she had meant to follow the river to the Hill. I grabbed Dempsey's hand tighter as the goddess walked us deeper into the Hill.

It was a land of both beauty and death, one that intoned the ancient and yet seemed to be full of life. Along the banks of the river, wildflowers grew to the point of abandon, and there was a somber beauty along the meadow that flanked our path. Among the walkway Boann led us upon sat small homes, unlit, waiting for people to return to them and give them life.

Somewhere before us, the cavernous overhead brick ended, and a sweeping blue sky started, twinkling with stars, even in the daylight. It was the perfect color of blue, and yet I had never seen it before, being both blue and purple at the same time, the deepest form of periwinkle, too vibrant for my mortal eyes to comprehend.

The meadow was a perfect circle, and I could tell, could feel, that we were at the top of the Hill of Tara. Green grass skimmed my legs as I moved forward, my eyes set on only one thing. The Lia Fáil. The towering pillar of stone was erected in the center of the meadow as if everything in this world revolved around it. Spreading out from the base of the monument were bricks, shooting out like the rays of the sun, spreading into the meadow until they were covered with mosses.

Sitting directly in front of it, her back to us, was Sarai, her neck bent upwards as she stared in childlike wonder. I wondered if she could hear the power vibrating from the stone as well. I walked up and kneeled next to Sarai. My friend's face was shining in admiration, and tears streamed down her face.

"It's incredible," she whispered. I touched her back.

"I know. But we can't stay here for long," I reminded her gently.

Sarai nodded and stood up in one fluid motion. She looked to Dempsey, who was now standing alone, Boann nowhere to be seen. The entire meadow went still, not a breeze moving a single blossom as we all waited for what came next.

Dempsey offered me his hand. "Are you ready to get married?"

I smiled, all of a sudden feeling shy, like this man hadn't seen all of me and heard my deepest secrets and fears. I took his hand and stood, looking at the Lia Fáil. It wasn't the wedding that my parents had, not the elaborate celebration I had seen my sister endure, but it was *ours*, and that was all that mattered to me.

"*I* will officiate," said Sarai, looking too pleased with the circumstances.

She took out a piece of rope from her pocket. Dempsey grabbed both of my hands, holding them as he looked at my face, his eyes flickering back and forth as if he wanted to memorize it. I stared at the rope as Sarai wound it around our hands, tying it together.

"Old sailing tradition," she explained. "And although you aren't getting married at sea, we don't have any salt from the Riverlands or honeycomb from the forest, so it will have to do."

Sarai nodded, signaling that she was beginning. The Lia Fáil gave out an almost imperceptible hum. "We stand here, before the gods, faeries, and humans alike, to witness the uniting of the Clan of Forests and the Clan Amongst the Rivers, through the representation of their only son and daughter."

"They will be together, in marriage, as more than a union of law. Their love for one another knows no bounds, and they will resist and defy any forces that come between them. Their vows to each other will be viewed and upheld by all, an everlasting promise."

Sarai touched my arm. "Say your vows, before all beings, and be held to them for the rest of eternity."

Dempsey

I looked at Willa as if I had never seen her before. From the moment I met her in the forest, hiding amongst the trees like she was a faerie herself, I knew that she would ruin me. And somehow, through some twist of fate and destiny, here we were.

Her eyes were clear, a good sign. All her emotions could always be read on her face, for all to see, even if she thought she was good at hiding them. Gods, I couldn't bear to think about her hiding them all those years, the pain I had briefly been allowed to see. But it was always there, rolling off of her, even from that night in the forest. It was only in recent days that I began to see a difference, no echoes of the ghosts that haunted her.

Part of me feared that she would resent me for this. My father had always been calculating, and I knew I would marry for an alliance, but he had left Willa with no options. After already being trapped in one political engagement, I couldn't see how this was much better. But for some godsforsaken reason, she thought it was.

That was the beauty in her. The ability to be resilient and rejuvenate, even after the traumas and horrors she experienced; she was the epitome of strength.

And now I was hers, forever. I dared to wonder if she would be mine as well, but I stopped the thought in its tracks. She would never *be* mine or be my possession. But she could be with me, and that was all I would ever ask of her.

A tingling feeling spread through my fingertips, and as I looked up, it began to rain. Soft drops, one that you could hardly notice. The kind of raindrops children stick their tongues out at and teenagers kissed in. It was neither humid nor cool, just a comforting presence as we stood there, our hands tied together, as I hoped our union would always be. Even my magic responded to Willa, saw the beauty in her. Since I was a teenager, my magic had been dying, always a trickle rather than a downpour, but there was something about Willa that just sparked everything. *She* was the spark.

Sarai spoke. "Willa, will you speak your vows before the Lia Fáil?"

"I will." Willa's voice was clear and strong, ringing with conviction.

"Then declare them."

Willa took a breath and looked into my eyes. I offered her a smile, letting her know all that mattered was what was between us. Even if she didn't say those vows, I would stay by her side, forever, if that was what it took.

But she did say them.

"I will not shelter from your rain, but embrace your storm
I will not cower in your strength, but accept your bravery
I will not shy from our hardships, but instead resolve our
problems
I will not forget your face, as long as I shall walk this earth
For I am yours, and you are mine."

I blinked the tears out of my eyes, hoping it would pass as the rain. Each and every one of those words was a well-aimed dagger to my heart. The vows weren't just to the gods, but to me, to the story we created together. For the future we were yet to write.

Sarai spoke again. "Dempsey, will you speak your vows before the Lia Fáil?"

"I will." My voice was low, insistent. Nothing could stop me from accomplishing this task.

"Then declare them," she repeated.

I gave a squeeze to Willa's hands before I spoke.

"I will not fear your foresight, but listen to your wisdom
I will not limit the road ahead, but embark on the journey
with you
I will not covet you, but will share you and your joy with the
world
I could not forget your face, as long as I shall walk this earth
For we are together, as one."

And now it was Willa who had tears running down her face. I desperately hoped she knew that I meant every single one of them.

"Now you and your weapons shall bow before the Lia Fáil, the speaker of verity and truth, and hear its judgement," Sarai said.

Willa and I drew our weapons, my great sword and her scian. We laid them on the cobblestones before the great stone pillar and knelt, daring to gaze at the top of the stone, and waited. I felt Willa's palm go clammy, and I wished I could tell her that I was just as nervous.

The stone screamed.

We looked up at the pillar. It was the one screaming, so loudly I could hardly think. I glanced over my shoulder, and Sarai had turned white. I wasn't sure how long it went on like that, the sound that was loud enough to part the clouds above it. I looked up into the ray of sunlight, the gap in the sky, and the whole world went black.

Willa

The screaming filled my ear, incessant, without a break for air or a change in pitch. It was the same one from my dream, the one that had turned into a nightmare, the sound that spoke of ominous things. To my side, Sarai looked confused, as if she had no better knowledge of why it had started and when it would stop.

Then there was a tug on my wrist.

I looked down to my arm, where I was still tied to Dempsey. His eyes were closed, and he was slumped to the ground, his hair falling over his face as his chest barely rose.

The rain went ice cold around me, and I couldn't think as I stared at his body. I knew what was happening – I had seen this story before, knew how it ended, the handsome man dead on the floor.

"It's not supposed to happen this way," I murmured. "I don't understand. He wasn't supposed to die. There was supposed to be no more death. Not him, not this one." Hysteria crept in. I scrabbled to untie the rope tangled around our wrists.

I looked at Sarai. "Wake him up. Do something, do one of your spells."

Sarai shook her head. "That's not how it works."

"What is *wrong with him*," I shrieked. This was supposed to be our marriage day; we were supposed to say our vows. How could Sarai just be standing there, not doing anything? We had to fix him, had to get him back.

Sarai shook her head at my shaking hands, unsheathing her knife and sawed at the rope between our two hands, severing the connection we had just made.

"He needed to return."

I looked at her, waiting for more, waiting for an explanation I could understand.

"Return *where*," I said, my voice cutting like a knife.

"Willa. How many people do you know who have the powers of storm and weather? None. It's never been heard of before, and there's a reason for that."

"But no one has heard of my gift either," I protested.

"That's different. Your gift is… it's an offshoot, of what Kelz and I do. Communicating with the gods in general isn't something that's new. It's been around for hundreds of years." Sarai took a breath and continued. "There's a reason you and him were so drawn to each other."

"Don't you dare say 'were'," I threatened.

"You are a portal to the gods, an entryway, and you can slip into each realm like opening a door. Dempsey has the spirit of *Lugh* within him, a reincarnation. Last night, that is what I saw in my vision. If we came here, to the place where the gods dwell, it would tempt his soul too much. The gods took him back, because he never belonged with us in the first place."

I sat perfectly still, trying to understand what Sarai was saying. Lugh was a storm god, an entity of light and sound, of rain and peaceful chaos. He was a trickster and a jack of all trades, and I couldn't fathom how he could be contained inside Dempsey's body.

"But… then why was he here in the first place? Why give him to us if they were just going to take him back? He didn't even have a chance to do anything –" My voice broke, my throat drowning in sobs.

"Why do the gods do anything?" Sarai asked sadly.

"He's still breathing. Maybe he'll come back – maybe there's still a chance!" Incredulous hope broke through my panic, only to flounder at Sarai's expression.

She touched my arm gently. "He's never coming back." She looked around the meadow. "We should leave, before our presence is no longer welcome here."

"No."

Sarai looked back at me. "What?"

"I'm not leaving without him."

"Willa, I know you're upset. I'm heartbroken, too. He was the only family I've ever loved. But we can get through it. I'll speak to Barra, pledge my forces. This journey won't end here. You're my family now, too."

My wrist brushed something hard in my pocket. The gods, their magic, always whispering to me.

"How did you know? You would be able to speak to the gods yesterday?"

"I saw it in an omen, and when we got to Kelz's place, I knew he had the crystal garden. They can open anyone's senses to the Otherworld, but particularly witches."

But why had I held it in my pocket for the past day and the gods had revealed nothing?

"They just... appeared? Why haven't they said anything to me?" I asked, searching for answers, my hands running over the pocket that still held a piece of the stone, unbeknownst to Sarai.

"You place it under your tongue. Something about becoming a mouthpiece of the gods. And then you truly become a channel – until they're finished with you. Why?" Sarai asked.

But Sarai was too late with her question as I placed the rock under my tongue, noticing the flash of shock across Sarai's face. I laid down next to Dempsey and grabbed his hand, still warm. I thought of all the promises they had made to each other. *For I am yours, and you are mine; for together, we are one; it was always you, since the moment in that meadow.*

I turned my black flecked diamond ring on my finger. His

promises incarnate. It tore me apart that I never was able to give him a ring.

"You can go and tell Felix what I'm doing, but I'm not leaving here without him." I closed my eyes and let the summoning stone wash over me.

CHAPTER TWENTY-SEVEN

Willa

When I opened my eyes, everything was the same, but it wasn't. The meadow was the same, the Lia Fáil still ahead of me and Dempsey still motionless. Sinking disappointment hit me; I was in the same place and the stone hadn't worked, when something danced before my eyes.

Not something. Someone.

A Sheela na gig danced before me, a type of faerie that looked like a creature made from the depths of a riverbank, muddy and misshapen. I didn't dare move in fear of scaring it away.

"Are you here to help me?"

The faerie nodded coyly in response. It grabbed my finger and tugged on it, urging me to follow. I traipsed across the field. Everything here was beautiful beyond my imagination, glowing with vibrant color and whispering. It was truly the land of faeries and the gods, and I wasn't sure if any part of me wanted to leave. The Sheela pointed me down a path, curving towards a tumbling stream. The Sheela skipped through the banks, rejoicing in the mud and the water, and I giggled along with it, at the absurdity of the thing.

Faintly, as if it had been waiting for me to be within its grasp, music began to play. Not the loud, raucous type I was used to hearing at feasts and celebrations. No, this one was a delicate thinking, waltzing on the wind and crooning in my ear, beckoning me.

I looked at the faerie, knowing that this could be a trap. We were in the Otherworld, a land not bound by human laws. It played tricks with mortal's minds, and could make one crazy on a passing whim. But the Sheela smiled, a wide grin that was meant to be encouraging.

And so, I followed it, walking amongst the banks of the river, until I saw it – until I saw him. The Dagda sat before me, playing his harp. He looked larger than life, and I wondered how exactly he fit here. He had curly brown hair all over his head and a beard that stretched to his belly, framing his twinkling brown eyes. It was my first time laying eyes on him, yet it was like I had always known him. I supposed that was right. The Dagda had blessed me with my gift, it was him that sent me the visions and omens; even Boann said that the Dagda had sent her. I wanted to laugh at the idea of this man playing my guardian.

I stood there, frozen, not sure what the next step was, not having thought this far. One wrong move, and I lost all chances of getting Dempsey back. And... I couldn't let myself think of that. I couldn't go there, otherwise I would collapse here at this spot, because I couldn't imagine a life without him. He was as essential to me as breathing.

"I've been wondering when you would come and see me."

My head whipped up, at the Dagda, father and king to the gods, speaking to me.

"I will give you my council. Sit, my dear." He patted a seat next to him before the fire.

Numb, I walked over to where he had motioned. I wrung my hands together, twisting the rings on my fingers.

"I thought you wanted us to protect the isle." My voice was surprisingly steady. It showed no hesitation or fear, a stroke of luck that I counted as a blessing.

"I wish to protect all the land that I have made." His answer was stoic, unrevealing.

"Then why? Why let the Sectarians invade? Why..." My voice trailed off, unable to finish my thought out loud.

"Dear girl, I have no power to change what happens in your world. I may have created it, but I am not Fate. Do not take my omnipotence for meddling." He continued. "I have provided you with tools to defeat the brutish invaders. Is that not enough?" He frowned, as if thinking about taking it all back.

"My love." Boann appeared from the shadows and placed her hands on the Dagda's shoulders. "She is not just speaking of the Sectarians."

The Dagda raised an eyebrow.

"Dempsey. You... you took him back, the part of him that was a god." Resolve hardened in my eyes. "I want him back."

The Dagda barked a laugh. "Oh yes, I remember why I like you," he mused. "Why should I?"

That was a question I was unprepared for, but a thousand reasons whirled through my head.

Because I love him. Because I need him. He is my air and my rock and my water and flame, all at once. We need him to win this war. Because he wasn't finished yet, because he hasn't lived yet. Because you promised him life, and then you took it away. Because I choose to believe this world was made for good things, and he is the epitome of good. Because I will collapse without him, and this island will collapse without him.

I ran through the excuses, each as important to me as the last, but none of them seeming right enough to say out loud.

I twisted a ring off my finger, and held it up to the air. Our promises, given solid form. The ring sparkled in the light as the imperfections contrasted against the world around it, showing the good and the bad can be beautiful together.

"He made a vow. Several times over. He needs to make good on it. And even you, the father of the gods, cannot break a vow made before the Lia Fáil."

Dempsey, or Lugh, or whoever he was had made me promises. Everything he had ever said to me, going all the way back to the beginning of summer, had been promises. And he gave them to me, encapsulated in this ring, for me to wear and keep forever. Not even the gods could break a vow.

Something inside me laughed. Maybe Dempsey was Lugh the trickster after all.

A smile blossomed on Boann's face. "Well, even we cannot interfere with a vow that needs to be fulfilled." Her hands danced across the Dagda's chest as she stood behind him.

The Dagda sat there, his face like stone, refusing to disclose any of his emotions. Boann leaned in and whispered in his ear. "Come now, darling. You remember what it is to be young and in love."

The Dagda chuckled, his laughter boisterous and infectious. Tears formed at the corner of his eyes as his cheeks turned red.

"Ungrateful son of a bitch doesn't even want to be here." The Dagda wheezed. "In the land of immortal milk and honey! It's – wow, it's really too good. Take him! Take him if you want each other so badly."

I slid a hand over my mouth, unbelieving of what the god before me just said.

"He will be waiting for you when you awake at the Hill of Tara. But, Willa?"

I looked at him.

"Losing against the invaders could spell the end of my world and yours. Do not lose." He stared into my soul, all laughter erased.

I nodded, understanding the gravity of the situation. And yet, my heart was soaring. I turned and ran back through the forest, along the river and to the meadow. Dempsey was still there, asleep. I laid down and closed my eyes as I laid my head on his chest. In a few moments, I told myself, we would be in the Hill of Tara, and his heart would be beating the strong rhythm that was so familiar to my ears.

CHAPTER TWENTY-EIGHT

Willa

A steady beat filled my ear. I looked up, wiping the tears off my face. And there it was, that smile tugging at his lips that I loved. I looked around me, but Sarai was nowhere to be seen.

I shoved him as his eyes opened.

"You *jackass*," I seethed. "You leave all these riddles around for me to piece together? As if you don't give a *shit* about being here with me? What happened to us?" I ripped the engagement ring off my finger. "What the hell happened to this? *You and me until the end?* What type of bullshit is that?"

Dempsey plucked it from my fingers, twirling it along his palms.

"They weren't riddles. I wasn't supposed to leave this place. This, here, me," he gestured to his body, "Was never part of the plan. But neither was falling in love with you."

"I don't understand," I murmured. I wrapped my arms around my knees, holding myself together.

"Being placed in your world was a series of trials for me, like finding that faoladh in that woods. But it was always going to end in me rejoining the Otherworld at the Hill." His expression softened. "But then you fought for me."

I nodded solemnly. "I'll always fight for you."

"I said those things, I gave that ring to you because I knew I was going to have to leave you one day. I wanted you to know that while I was here, all of it was real." He slid the ring back onto my finger and intertwined my hand with his. "I still mean it all."

Dempsey slid one hand onto my chin before moving to kiss me. I grabbed his hand, afraid that he would leave me again. That would always be a fear of mine now, him being whisked away in the middle of the night, leaving me alone.

But I let him kiss me, because I would never stop needing him. I would never stop needing his mouth on mine, his broad hands gripping me, those crinkles at the corner of his eyes, the shallow dimple in the corner of his one cheek.

I pressed a finger to his lips. He stopped, waiting for me. "Husband," I whispered.

He grinned. "Wife," he growled. Dempsey moved in a cat-like motion, prowling over me until I was laying on the ground amongst the flowers. Daisies tickled my skin as he left a trail of idle kisses starting from my ear down to my neck.

"Should I call you Lugh?" I asked suddenly.

Dempsey chuckled. "No. Lugh is merely a facet of my personality, something within my soul. Unless you would like calling me that for other reasons?" He lifted an eyebrow as his hands drifted towards the inside of my thighs.

I grabbed his hand. "We're in the place of the gods," I mocked. "I know many who would consider *that* sacrilege."

"All the more fun." Dempsey sucked my neck right above my collarbone, causing my toes to curl. I wanted to lose myself here, let Dempsey and his coaxing win. My mind protested at what my body wanted, knowing that we had two very dear friends waiting outside, not knowing that Dempsey was alive.

"They still think you're gone. We should go and see them."

Dempsey looked at me, exasperated. "I think we'll have time for this later," I teased.

"They wouldn't notice me being gone for a few more moments," Dempsey grumbled, but he got up all the same.

We grabbed our weapons from the Lia Fáil and took one last look at this strange place. As we walked towards the bridge, the Lia Fáil strengthened its silent call and tugged on those threads of magick, crying at the loss of Lugh, beckoning for him to come back.

If Dempsey felt the magick emanating from the stone pillar, he made no indication, instead gripping my hand as we walked away from the meadow with the twilight sky. The flowers wilted as we walked away, stems drooping a little lower, like they were sad to see us go.

Dempsey and I walked back the way we came, moving over the bridge. I stopped before the arching stone pathway, the very one that would lead them back to the underground tunnel and to the gate.

"You're sure you want to leave?" I had to check, knowing all he was leaving behind.

"You're my home," he said simply. "You and Felix and Sarai and even my father. I can't leave you, not today, not ever."

I nodded, and led the way into the tunnel.

The gate shut on our way out, almost laughably swinging as if it were protecting nothing more than a garden. On the other side of it was Felix and Sarai. They sat back to back, neither of them speaking a word. Felix's head hung heavy in his hands. Upon the creaking of the gate, they both looked up, equally incredulous looks on their faces.

Sarai let out a scream that rivaled the one the Lia Fáil let out. Felix rose to his feet, and started to move towards us, his mouth silently forming words. I laughed as Sarai jumped on Felix's back, causing him to career sideways, shrieking.

"How did you do it?" Felix asked. "Sarai said… she said you were gone." I could tell by his careful choosing of words that Sarai had told him everything, about the reincarnation of Lugh and myself diving into the Otherworld to find him and bring him back.

"Willa saved me, like she always does." Dempsey casually strung an arm across my shoulders and pressed a kiss to my head.

Tad came leaping out of the bushes. His energy was almost enough to knock over Dempsey, and he kneeled down, wrestling with the dog who had somehow felt his absence.

"But you were…" Sarai's voice trailed off; unwilling to say it out loud. She turned to me. "They let you take him back?"

I smiled. "Apparently even the gods have a soft spot."

Sarai made a movement mimicking vomiting. Despite her joy at getting her friend back, apparently even she had limits.

"We should get to the Hollow. There's so much that needs to be decided," I said. The task before us loomed, monumental in size.

"A war to be planned," finished Dempsey.

I looked back at the Hill of Tara, a destination that had been our goal for so long, that had held so many horrors and joys within. I shivered. If I had to go back in, it would be too soon, I decided. There was something unnatural about the place. Most people claimed magick to flow through all living things, even going so far as to claim that magick was a fifth element of nature. The elders preached that it was as essential as breathing and the island couldn't live without it. As much as I loved the man next to me who was living proof of the goodness magick held, there was something ancient and wicked about that place that held no regard for mortals.

The way to my childhood home would be fast. It shocked me how close the Hill lay to the Hollow, the harboring of this magick so close to me all these years. I led the way, my mare stretching out her legs underneath her. I knew that she could sense that we were on our way home, too.

CHAPTER TWENTY-NINE

Dempsey

T he camp that once belonged to the Forest Clan was now flanked by makeshift tents. A sea of them had been constructed at a moment's notice, and we had to wade through the rows in order to get to the edge of what had been the outer edges of the old camp. The blue Riverland sigil flew over the southern part of the camp. My shoulders slumped in relief. They were here – the troops made it. All of it, the sacrifice and deaths, had been worth it.

Willa navigated us through the camp, her feet on the path they had walked so many times before. When we finally stopped in front of the granite war table, her family looked up as if she were a ghost. But she wasn't a ghost – not anymore. She was more alive than I had ever seen.

But there were no words to cover the reunion, and Willa's mother and sister didn't try. Instead, they showered her in hugs and tears. Viktor, on the other hand, had his words ready.

"You brought home friends?" His voice was dry, displeasure running through it.

I wondered if they received the letter that Willa sent. It explained everything, from Callan's death to our journey to the

Hill of Tara. If they didn't... this was going to be a bigger conversation than anticipated.

Willa laughed, not sensing the danger of the conversation. There wasn't anything in her but joy at the reunion. "Yes, I brought home friends." She paused, looking at us.

"Callan died." The halting sentence caused an inaudible reaction as shock, grief, and sadness all passed over her family. Yet there was something in Fiadh's expression that resembled relief, perhaps at her sister's freedom from that engagement.

Her parents nodded. "We received your letter," Viktor said.

Would he hate me? Would I care? I had taken his daughter as my wife, without so much as notifying the man. In terms of breaking marriage traditions, especially amongst a chieftain's family, it was unheard of. It would break Willa's heart if he wasn't amiable to it.

"I spoke to Barra, and was able to get him to pledge the Riverland's support."

"I'm proud of you, Willa. I know he's a difficult man – sorry, Dempsey – but you managed to get us the numbers we needed," Brigid said. I began to wonder what sort of conversation Brigid had with her daughter prior to her departure.

"It came with a cost." A knife to a gut. It wasn't meant like that, but that's what it was. Willa looked at me and corrected herself. "No, it came with a contingency. One that I gladly agreed to." She grabbed my hand, and gave it a squeeze. That rip of insecurity repaired itself. "I – we're married."

Brigid let out a small noise while Viktor remained expressionless. He spoke once more, his voice tight. "Yes, we received your letter."

Shit.

Fiadh spoke for the first time, her voice strong and commanding. "This is what you want?" She intoned the question as if there were things she could undo, strings to cut and this marriage would no longer be tied together neatly. Fiadh gave me a threatening glance, no doubt imagining her scian at my throat.

"Yes," Willa said vehemently. "I know it's... soon after Callan, but... I never loved him. And we needed the troops and Dempsey –" Her voice broke off as she looked to me. "He is good and kind, and more than that. He's my friend."

"I always feared that was the case with the Cliffs boy," Brigid murmured. Fiadh gave a curt nod, as if the answer was satisfying enough and the evaluation of the threat passed.

"What took so long?" Fiadh asked the question with her voice cracking a little. A slip in the queenly mask she put on, perhaps showing how much the Sectarian attack rattled her confidence.

There was a hesitation in Willa's response, and I gave a slight dip of my chin. I knew she would catch it, me telling her that she could share what went on inside the Hill. Even the memory invoked the bindings of magick, begging me to go back. But that wasn't where I was needed.

"We said our vows before the Lia Fáil."

Viktor's fist landed on the table with a dull thud. Fiadh's eyes looked up, confusion blossoming in them. It highlighted the darkness under her eyes, evidence of evasive sleep.

"Why?" It was a command, not a question. Viktor's face barely moved as he asked it, and for a moment the warrior he once was returned.

What about the Lia Fáil would bring this reaction? Why couldn't his daughter face the gods when they whisper in her ear? Questions unfurled faster than they could be answered.

"It was a contingency of the betrothal. If we were to receive approval from the gods – if the Lia Fáil found our vows to be true, then Barra would send his troops."

Viktor let out a shallow laugh.

"Of course he did." Brigid said the words bitterly, as if she had been waiting for this.

Willa's brow furrowed as she looked at their faces. Once joyous faces were now masked with pain, confusion, anger. There was something untold – perhaps the price of being the youngest, the one they thought destined to live and die inside the camp.

"That was the sound." Fiadh spit out the words as if riding herself of poison on her tongue. She drank from her goblet, burgundy sloshing over the sides. A drink to make her bitter.

"I don't understand." Willa's smile faltered.

Sarai spoke for the first time.

"It does seem that your parents are upset at the vows before the Lia Fáil. The screaming isn't just a declaration from the gods of their approval." Sarai fixed a gleaming eye on Viktor and Fiadh. "Most circles who subscribe to the old ways, who truly believe in the gods and fate and the mythos cycle, believe that when the true king and queen of Eiram are presented before it, it will scream in approval. The scream is a sound that travels across the land, fills everyone's ears."

No one dared respond.

"Apparently," she added, "We weren't the only ones to hear the screaming. Congratulations." Sarai smiled slowly, as if reveling in the discomfort from the information she had already known to be true.

"There are no kings and queens here." I shook my head. I didn't want this – that cycle of history had been left a long time ago. It barely stirred a memory in the echoes of my immortality.

"There are. Rarely, every few hundred years, but when the right match comes along..." Brigid's voice trailed off.

Willa looked like she wanted to run.

What kind of religious zealotry was happening for her parents to be so disappointed in this information? For them to already know the history, their refusal of acceptance or approval... it didn't make sense. Hatred radiated off Fiadh. Willa pressed into my side.

"I think this a bit much for us all to take in, and as much as we enjoy a reunion, it has been a long journey. I think we will retire. With your leave," I added. Even if my words didn't betray the lack of an option, I let my hand drift toward the hilt of my sword.

Thankfully, Viktor nodded.

"Your tent is still there, with everything how you left it." Brigid sounded apologetic, but Willa avoided her gaze. Tears dripped down her face, and I placed an arm around her shoulders as we walked to her tent.

When we were within sight of her tent, sobs wracked Willa's body. I collected her in my arms, cradling her head to my chest, walking for both of us. I sat on the bed with her in my arms. Her hair tickled my nose as I tucked her under my chin, waiting for the storm to pass.

It would pass soon enough, and I knew that. My hand trailed up and down her back, just like I had done every night before sleep found us. No words needed to be exchanged. I saw the hurt and pain – she didn't need to explain it, now or ever, if she wanted.

At some point, Felix and Sarai entered the tent. Sarai pressed a small hand to Willa's arm, and Willa opened her eyes to the sunlight filtering through the tent. Sarai perched on the edge of the bed, waiting for the approval to say something. Felix stood in the back, fiddling with the things on Willa's dresser.

Willa gave a shuddering sob.

"Can I say something?" asked Sarai, gentler than I had ever heard her. Willa nodded in response.

"I've had scouts reporting for a while, and I admit there was a time when even I didn't believe them. But I never brought it up because... well, I never thought we would get this far." She eyed me.

"Because you thought I would die," I added dryly.

"Yes, that."

"I don't understand." Willa repeated those words that broke her in front of her family.

Sarai gave her no-nonsense look. "Sai and Fiadh's marriage was arranged not just for stability amongst the clans, although that's what they marketed it as. I have it on good authority that your father wanted to present *them* to the Lia Fáil, that he believed their power and lineage could produce a screaming."

I tilted my head, musing. "It makes sense. The screaming would produce a stronger claim to leading all of the clans into battle against the Sectarians."

"Their marriage was planned before the Sectarian attacks," Willa protested.

"The clans have known of their stirrings for a few years now. Nothing concrete, but there have been whispers," Sarai said. "Besides, I don't think that's the sole reason why your parents wanted to present them to the gods."

"I don't understand," Willa repeated again.

"Power. It's a cruel, harsh thing, and it would allow them to have a monopoly on it. Who could dare reject their claim when they're playing into the very system that dictates our way of life? I have to admit, it's very clever." Felix frowned.

"That's not my family," Willa protested.

"Isn't it though?" asked Sarai. "Why else would they leave you to drown in a relationship that wasn't necessary for any type of strategic alliance? Why tie you to a dead clan?"

"Your gift is too powerful, and you are too good, Willa. It's why we all love you." Felix offered her a smile. "But when it comes to a game of politics, you are an outright liability, and your parents handicapped you by trying to marry you to Callan."

"No," Willa breathed. I could see her belief in her former life crumbling, and I hated that Sarai and Felix were the ones to tear down the bricks. But right now, the evidence was too plausible to not believe it.

"We all saw what you were going through with him. And –

your gift has never been stronger since you two ended." I danced around the truth that Callan died. "Since that weight was lifted, you've spoken directly with the gods on multiple occasions. You are undefeatable. You are a queen, it's undeniable." I held her gaze for a moment, begging her to see her own strength. *See the truth.*

"You knew? You all knew?" Willa asked incredulously.

"Gods, no." Sarai got up from the bed. "I barely put it together while we were speaking to your parents. I was surprised Felix figured it out just as quickly though."

Felix scowled.

"Then why did Barra send us to the Lia Fáil?" That part couldn't sort itself in her mind, refusing to click into the puzzle.

"He suspected what your parents were doing. Heard whisperings of it at the wedding ceremony. And Barra being Barra —"

"With his overly large, inflated ego," I cut in.

"Yes, with that, assumed no one could be more powerful than his son. And some blind faith he had put in you. So, he decided to beat them at their own game," said Felix.

Felix seemed to notice the questioning glares he got. "Which I all just found out when I spoke to him, after the scene at your parent's war table."

"Why didn't your parents try to marry Fiadh to Dempsey? That's what I don't understand. Why Sai?" Sarai's brow was furrowed, not understanding the obvious choice that sat in the room.

I chuckled. "My mother had no lineage and ran out on her kid and husband. I don't think that screams royalty. Plus, not everyone knows about the," I smiled and motioned to my body, not voicing what everyone was thinking. *The reincarnation of a god.*

"Not even your father?" Willa asked.

I tweaked her nose. "No, he doesn't. The journey to the Lia

Fáil was pure vanity. I wasn't supposed to make it out anyways, and he would never want to lose his most important asset."

Willa rolled her eyes.

"Sai's family has led the Mountain Clan for decades. Before the Sectarians, they were the strongest out of all the clans. Not to mention that Brigid doesn't trust Barra," Willa offered. Her parents, it seemed, had miscalculated.

Willa looked around the room at her fiercest protectors.

"So what now?"

Felix let out a long breath, his eyebrows raised at the loaded question. "Barra did want to have a chat with you both."

Willa laughed. "I'm sure a chat is all he wanted."

"We need to watch your parents. I hate to say it. I'll set a scout on them, see if anything is up." Sarai knelt, looking Willa in the eyes. "You need to be prepared for the fact they may try and use you, or manipulate you. They know you like the back of their hands, and you have everything they have been working for."

I knew she spoke the truth; however painful it may be.

"Willa, we need to make a decision." Willa craned her neck to look at me from where she sat in my arms. "We need to decide if we're going to rise to the throne."

Willa turned out of my grasp, looking at me fully.

The idea of rising to the throne was one I never considered, never wanted it to be an option. Part of me wondered if it was a twist of fate, if it was something that was always destined for us. Maybe it was the reason why the gods let me return – why they let me touch the earth at all.

"I don't understand." Willa caught herself repeating those words again, and took a breath. She attempted the sentence again. "I don't understand how it would work, or what it would mean for us," she clarified.

I took her hands in mine. "It's mainly symbolic. The clans would still exist, still have their leaders, but it would be a sort of fealty system to us. We could live in any of the clans, start our own. We could build an entire ringfort somewhere if we pleased."

"And if we didn't?" Willa dared to ask.

"Chaos would ensue." Sarai picked idly at her nails while she said it, earning her a glare.

"Not *chaos*. But you could expect some fighting for power. Without us, it would be like a hole opened up."

"And you could bet my family would be at the center of it." Willa filled in the blanks of what I was unwilling to say.

"Everyone who has ever wanted for power, for *more*, would be at the center of it," I corrected. "You shouldn't feel obligated to do this if it's just because of what happened with your family. They do not decide who you are or where your destiny lies. You are not responsible for their actions."

Willa sat there, studying the rings on her fingers. "Can I think about it?"

I nodded. "Of course. But the longer we wait, the messier it's going to get."

Willa flopped back on the bed and pulled a pillow over her face. I chuckled softly.

"We'll leave you two to think on it," said Felix dryly.

Willa slowly tugged the pillow down over her eyes, daring to peek out. I smiled, before slowly prying her fingers off the pillow and setting it aside.

"Overwhelmed?" I asked.

She nodded.

I sighed. "I'm sorry. I know it's nothing like what you wanted or what you had imagined." I paused, thinking of my next words carefully. "Do you regret it?"

"No," Willa said the words vehemently, erasing all doubts in my mind.

"Do you know what you want to do?"

It was her decision. She could walk away from all this, ask to leave the isle, and I would let her. I would man the ship that would let us sail away. Anything to be with her.

"I think we have to do it," Willa whispered. "If we don't, who will guide us to the right side of history?"

I nodded. "I think you're right, as always."

Willa let out a long breath. "You'll just have to get used to it," she said nonchalantly.

I moved so I was hovering over her. "Is that so?" I nudged the bottom of her chin with my nose, asking her to expose her throat to me. She moved, and I leaned in and sucked on the delicate piece of skin below her chin. Goosebumps erupted on her skin, just like I knew they would.

Gods, I loved that I knew her like that.

"We probably have a while before anyone comes back," Willa said while my hands roamed her body.

I nipped at her neck.

"Is that an order, Your Majesty?" I asked.

"Close the doors. Now," Willa commanded. I obeyed, moving to tie the flaps of the tent together, shutting us off from the world.

My shirt came off as I walked back, eyeing Willa sprawled on the bed.

"It's been a while since we've had a real bed," I murmured. I thought about the cots and bedrolls we slept on our journey.

"Is that important?" asked Willa as she untied the laces of my pants.

I caught her hands, bringing them up to my mouth so I could kiss them before placing them on my neck. "It adds a nice touch," I said before kissing her, her lips parting to give me access to her tongue.

I brought my hand down the front of her, tracing the shape of her underneath her shirt. One by one, I undid the laces on her leather pants before kneeling to slide them off her legs, the fabric a second skin.

"Lay back," I said. Willa listened without question, and I hooked her legs around my shoulders as I planted small kisses to the insides of her thighs. My lips trailed up before settling in between Willa's legs. With a sigh, Willa wound a hand through my hair, subtly controlling the pressure.

I licked her, kissed her, teased, and played while her hand wound tighter in my scalp and her hips began to move. But I didn't want her to finish – not yet. I wanted to give this small piece of bliss to my wife, and I placed a hand around her hip, pinning her into place.

Willa gave a small cry of protest.

I looked up at her, an eyebrow lifted. "What? You don't think I can make you finish on my own?" I added a finger, and Willa gave another cry, this one entirely different from the first.

"Do you want me to stop?"

Willa gave a shake of her head.

"Do you want me to continue?"

"Yes, please," she gasped.

Her permission was all I needed to keep going, leaning back down to settle into a rhythm of light licks, building in pressure. *Gods.* I didn't need the Lia Fáil to tell me the woman before me was worth a queenship; I knew that. She owned my heart and soul and pride and every other piece of me.

Willa's moans began to leak from her body, and I wanted to give this to her. I wanted her to be physically, thoroughly wracked with happiness and pleasure. She grasped her breasts as she let out a hoarse cry, and I felt her walls flutter around me while her legs clamped on either side of me. I released the hand that was holding her off, letting her ride me until sated.

And when I sat back on my feet, there was another command for me to follow. "More." The word was barely a whisper, but I pounced as soon as it left her lips. Willa flipped over on the bed, eyeing me as I crept behind her, taking her hips in my hands.

I slid into her and my eyes shuttered at the feel of it. Willa slowly pushed up so her back was pressed into my chest, and I wrapped a hand up to her breast and the other at her hip, pinning her in place.

"I love you," I whispered in her ear. Willa's reply was wordless, only a slight murmur leaving her lips. I nipped at her ear in response.

Lust and love mingled in the tent as we both got closer. But it was slow lovemaking, the kind dictated by love and caring and adoration. Willa slipped a hand over her mouth as she cried out and collapsed against me, before rolling off and onto the bed. A shy smile crept onto her face.

"Satisfied?" I asked with a grin.

"For now," Willa eyed me as if she already had things in mind. "I don't want to leave," she admitted.

I knew what she was speaking about. I didn't want to leave the tent at this moment either, when everything was so simple. The second we did, an entire new chapter would start, one we couldn't take back.

I moved under the covers, waiting for her to do the same.

"Maybe we don't have to, just for a minute." A minute of peace, however meager, was all I could give her right now.

Willa wriggled under the coverlet, pressing her body against mine. I cradled her, and let Willa enjoy the minute of peace.

Chapter Thirty

Willa

The afternoon light dimmed as Dempsey and I walked towards Barra's tent. Riverland warriors flanked the path there, clapping Dempsey on the back with congratulations. The smile he wore on his face was genuine, and I could tell the happiness he felt to be back with his people once more.

The love was mutual. Each and every one of these warriors held respect and admiration for Dempsey, and they knew he would lay down his life for them. Despite division within the Riverlands, the different villages and outposts, those inside and outside the ringforts, Barra and his family bore the power well. They yielded it graciously, and their people were happy. My mind drifted to my parents and Fiadh.

I had never considered them power-yielding rulers, never hungry for more. Maybe I had been blind all those years, unable to see past my own self to what was going on around me. If my marriage with Dempsey had never happened, if we had never traveled to the Hill of Tara, what would have happened? Would the stone have screamed for Sai and Fiadh? Would they have taken power anyways? Ambition led them to corruption, not power, and perhaps that was what scared me the most. Ambition knew no bounds, had no limits, and I could not see the stretch of it in Fiadh's mind.

We stopped to disarm in front of Barra's tent, keeping a single weapon on us. It was an old tradition to allow your enemies and friends one piece inside, as a show of respect and insurance against a knife in the back for them.

"You can't tell my father about what happened in the Otherworld."

For the first time in a while, I saw fear in Dempsey's eyes. He continued. "I don't know what that would do to my father, his tribe, or the reactions of others. We can't risk it."

I nodded. "A secret until I die," I promised.

Dempsey pulled his shoulders back. He grinned at me. "Game time."

As we entered the tent, Barra and his advisors went silent. He must keep himself surrounded at all times. It felt like an entire production line bustled inside his tent, always stewing on something.

Barra stood, clapping. "It appears I have a new daughter." He opened his arms wide, beckoning me in for a hug. I chuckled at the theatrics but obliged him.

"Nice to see you too," said Dempsey coolly.

"Perhaps if you weren't so tart with me, I would look forward to you returning as well. Willa, on the other hand, is excellent company, and we have all missed her dearly."

I saw the look Fintan gave me when I walked in and seriously doubted Barra's claim. It seemed that my new marriage and alliance to the Riverlands had done nothing to change his opinion of me, and I was sure there was some other mix of advisors who agreed.

"So?" prompted Barra.

"We said our vows before the Lia Fáil. It screamed." Silence struck the room. Fintan's jaw dropped, while the other advisors choked on their drinks.

Barra cursed under his breath. "So you did it. Congratulations, my boy." Barra sported a small smile, as if he had suspected this was his son's destiny all along.

"Is that why you sent us?" Dempsey's question was pointed, cutting through the smiles and pleasantries.

"Not that I have to explain myself to either of you," Barra shot us a stern look, "But I wanted to make sure the girl was serious about it all. And it wouldn't hurt if the stone happened to yell." Barra said it simply, like he was explaining a hand of cards to a fellow player.

Dempsey eyed the advisors in the room. "Can we speak to you in private?" Barra's eyes gleamed. Something told me he knew what we were going to say and had already planned out this entire interaction.

"You lot, leave. Fintan, stay." Barra waved his hand and his cronies responded, not a remark of protest amongst them.

Barra took out four wine glasses and uncorked a bottle. "Red, I assume is okay with you, Willa?" I realized he must already know Fintan and Dempsey's preferences.

"Yes, please."

"So, come tell me what you really wanted to gossip about." Barra sank back into his chair, enjoying the vintage in his hand.

"We're going to ascend to the throne," I said. I took a sip out of my cup, the wine full of acidity, stinging my throat as it rolled down.

"Good choice. Fintan and I had a bet on whether or not you would."

Fintan blushed. "I said you might think about it carefully and decide it wasn't a life you wanted for yourself."

Barra waved his hand. "He said you didn't have the balls." He added a jab of his wine to accentuate his point. I bit my lip to prevent myself from smiling at Fintan's deepening embarrassment.

"We debated about it, to be fair, Fintan."

"I don't think Willa's family was... *elated* to hear the news." Dempsey chose his words like he was picking a sword for battle.

Barra and Fintan exchanged a glance. "We thought they might react that way," said Barra.

"But they're accepting of it, right?" Fintan furrowed his brow, no doubt thinking of the complications and crossed alliances if my family wasn't.

"They don't know our final decision. I would hope so. But if they aren't..." Dempsey's voice trailed off.

"It would spell war."

I looked at the three men sitting before me, incredulous at the conclusion. "Would it? With an invasion on our doorstep? When all three clans are so close to fighting together?"

"What better time for a coup than in a time of chaos?" A maniacal look took over Fintan's face. "A slip of a sword, a misplaced dagger, saying the stone made an accident, a sister who might play a natural successor?"

Barra nodded in agreement. "So much easier to only have one child," he sighed.

"But, time will only tell," said Fintan briskly. "When will you announce?"

"Tomorrow. There are a few people I need to speak with yet," I answered.

They nodded. "The quicker, the better. Less time to plan and make things messy."

The four of us sat there in silence, finishing our drinks and mulling over what could be. I wasn't sure if I should laugh or cry at what my family had come to, the brutal power games I was now playing. When I was a child, I had always thought that love had no place in politics. It was the only way my own betrothal had made sense at such a young age, and if there was love, that was sheer luck. That's what Fiadh had with Sai, luck. But I had never imagined politics invading my family, replacing the love that was once there. *Or was it ever there?*

Love has no place in politics, but sometimes it has no place in family either.

T swallowed, my mouth suddenly dry. The moment I had been dreading finally arrived. I stood outside Bowen's tent and couldn't bring my feet to cross the threshold, my guilty conscious weighing me down. A shadowy figure moved inside, evidence of Bowen being home.

A mixture of guilt and pain rolled in my gut. I may have come to terms with Callan's death that day on the riverbanks, but speaking to a grieving parent was a different sort of battle. An attempt to heal a forever gaping wound.

Before I could debate on it any longer, the flap to the tent moved aside, and Bowen stood in the doorway.

"I wondered when I might be seeing you." Bowen offered a tired smile, with no light reaching his eyes, his face empty. He looked to have aged years during my weeks away. Grey hairs peppered his scalp and weary lines folded into his face, like his own aging accelerated so he could see his son sooner.

I opened my mouth and closed it. Words chose to fail me at that moment. "I should have visited earlier." The truth, at the very least. I was right, I had wanted to see Bowen earlier. *No, not wanted,* I told myself. *But I should have seen him nevertheless.* Cowardice held me back.

"Come inside. Sit," Bowen stood back, letting me pass through the folds.

I took in the tent, trying to remember the last time I was inside it. Not since I was a teenager, at least. Not since Callan was a teenager, still living with his father. Nothing much had changed, save for the absence of one bed, now replaced by a particularly beautiful bookshelf and matching chair and settee.

I placed myself on the couch, examining the book titles, trying to stop myself from wringing my hands together. My father once told me Bowen had brought books with him when he fled the cliffs. The strange man with the odd accent valued knowledge more than material goods, and he had let family jewels be captured at the expense of the tomes that were now housed in the glass menagerie.

"I'm sorry." The words sounded so empty, barely taking up any space inside the tent. Not large enough to reach Bowen's heart.

His eyes looked distant. "How did it happen?"

I loosed a breath. Thoughts scattered across my mind, trying to figure out how to piece it all together.

"I don't think it makes sense. Or at least, I can't seem to figure it out. Maybe you know something, know better than I." I broke off, waiting for Bowen to say something. But no sound echoed through the tent, only a silent, curt nod as he motioned for me to continue.

"Right." I ran my palms down my pants. "We were on our way to the Riverlands – we were so close, only a few days' ride away. Callan told me that he scouted ahead, and that the normal path was cut off by a felled tree. He led us down another path, one that took us to a bog. To *the* bog." I didn't dare speak its name for fear of inviting some dark spirit into the tent. I examined Bowen's face for some inkling of recognition, but only those blue, unfeeling eyes stared back in response.

"We were crossing the bog when they came. The bog bodies, that is. A bog body attacked us, and that's how he died. He died fighting." The image of Callan's split head pasted into my mind, the look of brain matter and blood exposed to the elements, the shock that passed over his face as if he couldn't believe he had finally been defeated.

"And the bog body dragged him back into the marsh. Said he was *payment*. And they let me go free." My voice sounded small, something that would come from a child. Tears traveled down my face, and I couldn't bear to wipe them away. I let them stain my cheeks, as remembrance for all of my trauma.

"And –" I didn't know how to phrase the next part of the story, the part that hit like a gut punch. The part of the story that would make me sound paranoid. "I was on my way back with the Riverland warriors, and they took us to that spot we had been the day before. Right to the point with the split in the path, except we didn't come from the bog. We were on the trail that was supposed to be blocked by a tree. None of the Riverland warriors knew what I was talking about, they said that the path was never blocked, they never sent a patrol to clear anything, and there were no felled trees that I could see. No major storms for evidence of a tree to be destroyed."

I rubbed my hands on my face. "So why would he do it? Why send us through the bog knowing which one it was? When the other route takes just as long but is perfectly safe? I don't understand it. I can't come to terms with that piece of his death – that he sent himself to it."

Bowen weighed a book in his hand as if he was justice himself preparing judgment.

"Perhaps he was just a foolish, young warrior looking to prove himself," said Bowen.

Those words pierced my very soul, had me moving across the couch to place a hand on Bowen's wrist. "Don't say that about him. It isn't how he deserves to be remembered." Such pretty lies coming from my mouth. Like a tragic death equates forgiveness for years of hatred and misery.

Perhaps it does, I dared to wonder. Maybe people forgive when people are no longer around to answer for themselves. Maybe I forgave when there was no longer a person to blame.

Bowen's eyes glittered back at me, full of pain, matching his son's eyes, what they had once looked like. He shook my hand off, not wanting any of my sympathy.

"Why," I pressed.

"Would you like a drink? I'm afraid I don't have any wine, but I do have cider. Your favorite, if I remember correctly?" I was slightly phased by the deflection but recognized my misstep at once. How could I grill him about his dead son? How could I pressure a grieving father who didn't get to bury his son? My brief foray into politics had hardened me, forced me to turn a blind eye to feelings. Resolve hardened in me; I would not fall victim to the emotionless state that I so often saw my parents in.

"I would love that." There was something simpler about his offer, a beckoning back to earlier times. A reminder of what had once been before the world got so screwed up.

A half dozen memories floated through my head while Bowen poured our drinks. Playing with Callan as a child, him being just as serious as ever. Ordering me and my dolls about, *because one day he would be the leader of the clan and people would do as he said so*. The memory felt hollow as it clanged about, full of empty promises once more.

A stolen kiss had occurred behind the flaps of the tent, where we had thought no one could see us. Back when I had hope for us. That night had been my first kiss, and Callan had pried it from my lips with whispered sweet nothings and a bouquet of lilacs.

My first time had been in this tent, too, when we were still teenagers. It had been awkward, and bittersweet, and I spent the week regretting it and praying to the gods I wouldn't become pregnant. Fiadh had found me crying in the willows, and had shown me the herbs that grew on the backside of shady oaks that would prevent unwanted children and stop monthly cycles.

And for as many happy memories there had been, so much pain seeped through this tent as well. Anger, hurt, a whole kaleidoscope of emotions had passed between us. Our first fight happened before the tent flaps, about something I couldn't care to remember.

Once, when I was seventeen and headstrong, I had broken up with him here. I had yelled at him, saying his head was stuck too far up his ass, and the second he could retrieve it was when he could speak to me again. That hadn't lasted long before my mother sat at the foot of my bed, explaining why a breakup would never be in the cards for me. Callan showed up on my doorstep the next day, a false apology on his lips. I refused to accept it. It was too easy to tell that his father had crafted those words, so painstakingly selected. It wouldn't be until years later did I recognize the engagement once more. After that was three years of fights, of pain and a dulled world, slipping deeper into my anxiety, flinching at every raised voice and avoiding my betrothed at all costs.

Maybe none of those memories were happy. Every one of them were tainted with melancholy and reluctance, with tears and rage. Maybe I hadn't known happiness until after his death. Or happiness had found me at the river, with the friends who had saved me.

Either way, none of it would help Bowen now. None of it would help grieve his dead son. I stuffed the memories deep down, laid away in a box in my mind, where I hoped they would slumber, forgotten.

Bowen turned around with a glass of cider in hand and a small smile on his face, telling me my prying from earlier was forgiven. And so we chatted, and I indulged his stories, allowing him to reminisce about his golden boy. It was his only child, and it was likely he would never have another. His love had died when the Sectarians had originally invaded, and Bowen's eye had never drifted, his heart never reaching out either. Loyalty ran through his bones, so much so that it broke my heart, that he knew that love and it lived on inside of him.

Callan had never spoken about his mom, not that he had much to remember her by. Callan was around the age of six when she died, when they had fled, and his best memories of the cliffs had been fleeting. There was a phase when he was around ten years old where he would make preposterous claims about his homeland, telling the other children that mermaids bathed on their shores and the faeries lived amongst them in the caves.

It was that image of Callan, the round-faced boy who always had a fight to pick, that made me stay there and indulge in talk. Because I knew that was who Bowen was remembering right now too, the young boy who did no wrong, the boy who would never be held in his arms again.

And for what? My mind kept returning to that singular, unanswered question. For all the fighting Callan did, based on his pure need to survive, to excel, walking into the bog was the antithesis. It went against common sense, survival skills, *religion*.

I sat there stuck inside my own mind while Bowen droned on, occasionally nodding my head or interjecting with laughter. A bright smile plastered on my face, mastered from years of misery.

Would I really destroy the image of a dead son in order to get my answers? Was it worth that much?

I sat my glass down on a small side table, making a puddle of condensation.

"Bowen, why did Callan navigate us to the marsh?" I asked softly.

Almost imperceptibly, Bowen's eyebrow twitched, the slightest of movements. But I recognized it. For years, I had sat at my father's war table, watching, waiting, learning. Whenever Bowen was aggravated about an issue, when a debate didn't go his way, he would make the same motion. Small enough to go undetected, large enough to defy my father.

"Willa, I honestly could not tell you." He shook his head, as if he had nothing more to offer.

But I saw it. I saw that little tell. And gods be damned if I didn't figure this out.

"Did you give him the map? Was it old?" I persisted with the questions, waiting for another piece to drop, something to click into place.

"No, all of our maps are up to date. Besides, a map like that wouldn't have shown a fallen tree cutting off a path. They aren't that detailed." Bowen spoke slowly, the same tone he used when explaining to children.

"Right." I gave a quick smile and bat of my eyelashes. "Felix, I think, mentioned that he told you guys about the fallen tree, right?" My stomach twisted as I asked the false question. I knew very well that Felix never gave them a map.

"Right," agreed Bowen.

And there it was. I got what I needed. Now I needed to get out, undetected.

I picked up my glass, waiting for Bowen to realize the mistake that he made. Waited for him to say something, but the only sound inside the tent was the cicadas singing their shrill song.

"Well. I'm sorry if I've upset you, but I should probably be off. It's been a long day." I smiled apologetically.

Without daring to look Bowen in the eye, I placed my cider glass on the table once more, the glass sliding in the water ring on the wood. I went to stand, but a tanned and sun-spotted hand placed itself on my knee.

"Stay for a while yet. I'm afraid I haven't had much company recently."

The look in his eyes was so sad, so tragic and full of tears, that I found myself nodding, bowing to authority once more. "Maybe just another drink," I agreed.

Bowen took his glass and mine, moving to replenish them. I scanned the room, hairs raising at the sheer emptiness of it. It felt like we were in another world, the normally busy camp quiet outside. The sky was a velvety navy blue, causing me to wonder how late it really was.

"Did he say anything? Before he died?" Bowen's question took an odd tone.

"No, he didn't." I paused, not sure what else to say. "He went down fighting. There wasn't much to say."

Bowen let out a sharp laugh. "So he didn't tell you?"

I studied Bowen's back, still getting us drinks. "Tell me what?"

Bowen turned, neither of our drinks in hand. Instead, he turned a silver dagger over in his hands, his thumb testing the tips of it. Like he might just break the skin to see the red bead of blood. I went cold. I knew I had pushed it too far, that Bowen had noticed his slip earlier.

His eyes were cold and cruel as he studied me. "He didn't say that you were the one that was supposed to die?"

CHAPTER THIRTY-ONE

Willa

I went numb. I twisted the rings on my finger, my nails catching on the corners of the diamond, thinking about the ring that used to lay there. Thinking about what the giver of that ring had planned for me.

"I'm sorry?" My voice was clear, level. Surprisingly strong, given the circumstances. I eyed the exit of the tent, but Bowen stood directly in my path. I wouldn't make it without hand-to-hand combat, and even if I had been training, Bowen was much larger. I could try and slit a hole in the canvas of the tent, but the fabric was double layered and strong. Most of all, I didn't trust turning my back to Bowen, not for a second.

I could scream. That was a definite option. And yet... part of me needed to know why. So I stayed.

"My boy," said Bowen with a shaking voice, "was never supposed to die in that bog. It was you. It was you who was supposed to drown in that marsh."

My mind was racing. Maybe he meant I was the weaker of the two, and logically, I wasn't supposed to be the one that survived. But even as the thought entered my head, I could see in his face that this was not what he meant.

"How? Why?" The questions poured out of me.

Bowen scoffed. "Callan knew the alternate path to the Riverlands was still open. He wanted you to go down that path, to the marsh where no one dared lay a foot. So he could kill you there, and leave you to rot."

"Someone would have found me."

"Would they have? Your beloved clans have convinced themselves the godsforsaken bog has a curse on it. That setting foot inside equals death. If they did find you, it wouldn't be until much later, until your body was in such a state of decay they couldn't tell what happened to you." His lips curled in distaste.

"So Callan knew." It was half a question, half a statement.

"Of course he knew. He hated you and this clan just as much as I do."

"Why?" I repeated the question.

"Why?" A slow smile appeared on Bowen's face, a teasing grin of malice. "Because I have forsaken your clans and your peoples, and they can rot in hell for all I care."

"So what? You're going to kill us off one by one? Line people up outside the bog? It's absurd."

"What's *absurd* is your parents turning a blind eye to the decimation of an entire people. What's absurd is the clan leaders refusing to fight for our territory. To allow an invasion and just sit idly, watch them come in, gut and massacre *my* people, *my family.*" Bowen went absolutely still, like his mind was in another time, twenty years ago.

"I watched my wife die, ripped from throat to belly, saw her bleed her life onto the floor. I begged on my hands and knees for aid, and Viktor and Brigid have the audacity —" Bowen's voice softened to the sound of knives singing, of cruelty and pain, "They have the audacity to offer me a two-year-old. For marriage to my son who is still crying about his dead mother. They tell me they have no intention of moving forces, of fighting at all. That their gods hadn't spoken to them about it."

"Bowen." Even if I hated him, hated his son, I could not stop the sympathy from creeping into my voice. Empathy at the utter pain and brokenness laid before me.

He held a single finger to silence me, and I listened.

"Your *gods* abandoned us. They deserted us when we needed them. What happened to goodness and piety and grace? What would your witches and leaders and your *foresight* say about that?" Bowen spoke as if he was only uttering curse words, venom on his tongue.

And for the life of me, I didn't have an answer. All of the things Bowen said, all of the things he felt, I understood. I pitied him for it. In another world, if he had come to me, confided in me, things might have gone very differently.

"So you tried to kill me. For revenge?"

"So your parents could finally understand loss. Loss like I had experienced. And what better way to break a strong leadership like theirs than the death of a child?"

"What then? What was going to happen after I died? It's tragic, so what?" My voice hardened, trying to pretend the subject wasn't one I had floated across my mind half a dozen times.

"With the death of a princess, the empire starts to crumble." Bowen smiled. "Without strong leaders, the Forest Clan is weak. The Mountain Clan was already caught unawares in an attack. We were never close to those Riverland brats anyways; it would be simple enough to convince your parents to cower from aiding others once more."

I cocked my head to the side and stared at him. "What would they need aid for?" The question was quiet, making Bowen notice it.

His smile grew.

"From the Sectarians, of course."

And there it was. A shock heard round the world. Now was the time to leave, to get out and *run*. But how to do that, was a better question.

"How long have you been working with them?"

"Long enough." A defensive answer.

"Since their resurgence, I'm sure? You planned the mountain attack in the spring, right?"

"Yes."

"And the attack in the Riverlands?"

"Yours truly."

I looked at him, taking it all in. All that evil and hate, born out of pain. Born out of love. I knew I needed to keep the conversation going if I was to make it out of here alive. Maybe compassion was the way out.

"So what's the next step?" I asked casually.

His eyes fixed on me. "Killing you."

I rose from the couch, knowing I was target practice sitting there. I started to take steps backwards, out of the seating area, into the open where he couldn't trap me.

"What if we could work this out? Find an equitable way to move forward, rebuild your clan? When I rise to the throne, I want it to be different." *This all started because of your clan.*

Bowen let out a soft chuckle. "Willa. You aren't going to be surviving this."

I glanced behind me, looking at the wall I was next to. It would only take a second to make it there; I could make it in time. I locked eyes with Bowen. My eyes darted in the opposite direction, trying to throw him off my scent, buy me one more split second before I ran.

I sprinted for the wall and crashed into it with all my might, but the tent was too tightly posted into the ground and the fabric held taut. I went to pull the scian out of the sheath around my leg. One long swipe and the fabric would rip in two, I would be free, I could run across the camp and get help from anyone.

Unless he has supporters. How long has this insurrection been building?

A cool knife caressed my throat. Bowen gripped me tightly behind it.

"Scream and I slit your throat right here," he threatened.

Terror leapt into my throat and at that point I couldn't scream even if I wanted to. He outmaneuvered me and I had let my guard down too much.

I tried to jerk of his grasp, just to give me a bit of space that would allow me to fight, but he refused to yield, only pressing the dagger further into my skin. I felt a sting as it began to cut across my throat.

Would my friends hear me scream? Would anyone see the trail of blood leaving from the tent? Bowen would have to deposit my body somewhere. It was the dead of the night, no one would see him. I would be gone tomorrow. Would Dempsey figure it out? Would he think the gods took me as payment instead?

My parents would probably blame the Sectarians, scour the entire isle before calling it a lost cause. My mother would never be the same, and my father would turn into that façade of rock. And after a few years, no one would notice my absence, having never left a mark on the world.

"Bowen." A voice entered the tent and I almost sobbed with relief. They were here. I was going to be okay.

Bowen wheeled me around, knife still against my skin. My terrified eyes landed on my sister, standing before the entry of the tent.

"Fiadh," I said, my panicked voice breaking on my sister's name. As I spoke, I felt the knife's edge prick my skin. A scratch began to sting.

Fiadh's eyes moved slowly across the scene, taking it all in. The threat laid bare before her.

"Bowen, let her go," Fiadh said slowly, threatening him. She was wearing her scians, a wedding gift from our parents. She could beat Bowen with them, I knew it. My sister would save me.

Fiadh took slow steps towards the two of us. "I *said*, let her go. Now." Her voice was no more than a whisper, laced with promises of death.

The knife lifted off my skin and he shoved me forward. I ran to my sister, to safety. I grabbed Fiadh's arm.

"We need to go," I warned. I had learned too much during my time in this tent, that we needed to alert our parents. To hell with Bowen, he could escape for all I cared, but we had to get out of here and get to safety. We could deal with him another time.

Fiadh's gaze didn't move from Bowen. "Did you think you were going to kill her here?" Her voice was incredulous, shocked at the audacity of it all.

He remained silent, refusing to answer Fiadh's question.

"And then what? So the entire clan could hear her scream? And know that you did it? So the sentries could see you drag her body into the woods?" Pure rage was on her face.

"It would have been fine," muttered Bowen.

I looked between the two. *Did he just say–*

"Fiadh, let's go," My voice sounded timid, uncertain as I shook my sister's arm.

Fiadh grabbed my hand. "Willa, we aren't going anywhere."

"He's not worth it. It's not worth it," I argued.

Fiadh pressed a finger to her temple. She looked at me, her eyes as sharp as razors. She kicked out her leg, sweeping my legs underneath me, stunning me momentarily.

And then Fiadh was on top of me.

"No, Willa. You aren't walking out of this tent tonight."

I blinked once, twice. My eyes widened as I realized what Bowen's words meant earlier. *It would have been fine.* He was reassuring Fiadh, telling her that he had it handled.

"Why?" I croaked.

Fiadh rolled her eyes. "Shut up." Bowen handed her three pieces of cloth. Fiadh was methodical, stuffing the gag into my mouth before she rolled me over to bind my hands and feet.

How did it come to this? I dully pondered the question in the back of my head, but I had no real answer. I stole the throne from my sister, and it was as simple as that. Fiadh didn't need more of a reason than that. Like a child with her toys.

Bowen picked me up and heaved me over his shoulder, an impressive feat of strength for the older warrior. Fiadh led us out the front of the tent where two horses were waiting. Fiadh mounted one and Bowen slung me across the back, tying me to the saddle so I wouldn't fall. He climbed atop the opposite horse, and the two set off at a brisk pace.

Each bounce of the horse made me feel like I was breaking my ribs, slamming into its back. But what did Fiadh care if she was only to kill me the second we got to a clear spot in the forest? Despite all the fights I had been in, the grueling training I had endured, all skills that might be a lifeline fled my mind. There was no desire to live within me. I was beaten, and I knew that. I was a novice at the game of politics and all I received in return was my death.

I wasn't sure how long we rode as I watched the blur of grass pass by, and by the time we stopped I was laughing. Some part of me worried I lost my sanity on the way here, but it was funny to me. Ironic that in my grand dreams of turning the isle into a place of justice and righteousness, I failed to see the rot.

Bowen and Fiadh dismounted and walked away from me. I laid my temple against the horse, one that I had raised. The familiar scent of alfalfa and barley filled my nose, bringing me back to the days in the field when I was too shy to look at my own shadow. I could see Bowen and Fiadh out of the corner of my eye, pointing at a fire pit they had made to roast me alive and scatter my ashes to the wind. Maybe they would give me a small act of mercy and kill me before tying me to the spit.

At least I'll be here, in the forest. Maybe the wind will scatter me to the Riverlands, and I can be with Dempsey. A breath caught in my throat. In the midst of my spiral, I had forgotten about the person who arguably mattered the most to me. But with the memory of him, the faint recollection of the sea and salt and soft eyes, I decided to fight. For him, for just a few more moments with him. To fight for him just as I had done in the Hill, I would do it in this reality as well. It was the ending we both deserved.

I willed my breath to still, to calm and allow me to breathe and think. I begged my mind to snap out of this dream state and find a way to save myself. It was only on the brink of death did I realize how much I truly wanted to live.

The sound of a blade scraping against its scabbard caught my attention. I strained my neck to get a look at Bowen and Fiadh, sure this was when they would come to deliver the final blow.

Instead, I beheld the sight of my sister wielding her scian, the silver shining in the night. The blade sliced through the air, arching in a time that seemed longer than what was real. Fiadh's scian landed on Bowen's neck, slicing through that life-containing artery, severing it as blood poured out of his neck. Fiadh withdrew her blade and wiped it on the corner of her cloak, turning and leaving Bowen where he stood.

Bowen grasped at his neck, trying to stop that flow of blood. It was no use, and soon the front of him was drenched in the almost maroon liquid, his tunic limp with blood. His face was pale, even more so than normal, and I saw his eyes glaze. Bowen wouldn't be leaving the forest, and I knew how far my sister was willing to go.

I was next. I was going to be slaughtered like a pig at a feast and placed to roast over that fire, and that would be that. It all screamed my sister, really. Executed neatly, no loose strings.

I closed my eyes. *Boann? The Dagda? If you were ever there, if you have ever thought of being here for any of us, please, let it be here and now. Save me. Allow me the chance to save us all. I just need to get out of here, make it out of these binds.*

Please.

The prayer floated across my mind and into the world, and I hoped it would find its target. My sister was striking a piece of flint, trying to start the fire. Taking a cleansing breath, I reached into my heart, tried to open the portal that dwelled underneath, the thing that I spent all those years trying to keep shut.

Something was next to me on the saddle. No, not a thing. I wanted to laugh and cry when I saw the little mud-grey body next to me.

The Sheela na gig appeared to answer my call. For the briefest of moments, I pondered what really made up a god, because in that moment I would have called the faerie one. With two quick movements, the Sheela had my hands free and cut the ropes tying me to the saddle.

I blinked, and she was gone.

I slid silently down the back of the horse, landing softly on my feet. I didn't dare to breathe as I slipped the bindings off. The gag in my mouth released without hesitation, and I closed my eyes, just for a second. Part of me knew I needed to prepare for what was going to happen.

At my side was my scian, a twin to my sister's. I withdrew the blade slowly, hoping it wouldn't make a noise. I stepped out from behind the horse, ready to face fate.

Fiadh rose from the fire pit. Bowen's body now laid on the flames, beginning to crisp and burn. "How?" Her eyes searched for a reason, but couldn't find one. Fiadh shook her head. "It doesn't matter."

The twin scians that were once a wedding gift slid out of their scabbards and twirled in Fiadh's hands.

"How could you?" I couldn't help but ask the question.

Fiadh rolled her eyes. "Easily." Another flick of her wrist and the rotation of the scian. "You can't handle it, Willa. You're weak, and useless. Your entire life has been spent running from Callan and herding horses. You don't know a single thing about ruling or politics." She smirked. "I'm doing you a favor."

With a few simple words, all my insecurities were laid bare. "The gods *chose* me. And you would really slit my throat, all for the sake of a crown?"

The silence was answer enough.

"The gods chose the man you ended up marrying." Fiadh rolled her eyes.

I flinched. Out of all the accusations my sister could have thrown, that one stuck because there was some part of me that feared it was true, that the Lia Fáil only screamed for Dempsey.

My free hand dangled by my side, itching for one of my weapons.

"No." My voice was strong. "The gods chose me, because they couldn't bear facing a future with a tyrant like you, who is incapable of caring for anybody except herself. There's more to politics than just power, Fi. It's about the people, in case you forgot."

My arm went arching through the air, flinging one of my favored darts across the meadow. The dart was a blink of white, flying across the air before finding its mark.

Blood poured out of a gash on Fiadh's shoulder. "Bitch." Fiadh closed the space between us, slowly circling towards me. I wished I had my bastard sword on me, something with a longer reach to combat the dual blades.

Fiadh started to slowly swing her scians in slightly overlapping ellipses, creating a guillotine if I were to step in front of her. I inched as close as I dared.

I dropped down to the ground, slashing out my blade, aiming for Fiadh's ankles. She jumped backward and went for a downwards stroke, looking to make the killing blow early.

The shot made me think of my battle with the Sectarian

guards so long ago, how they kept trying to make the same killing blow at every chance. A battle strategy fueled by hate.

The hilt of my blade drove upwards, aiming for the notch in Fiadh's wrist. Hit it correctly, and Fiadh would drop the scian, even out the battlefield. Hit it incorrectly, and she would lose a hand.

The blade hit that sweet spot of tendon and Fiadh cried out. The scian tumbled to the ground. My sister's face filled with pure rage. There was a split second of stillness, and then Fiadh went on the attack. She slashed her way forward, placing me on the defensive, forcing me to back up.

I caught Fiadh's blade with the bottom of mine and held it there. I looked at Fiadh, into her eyes where her body language could not lie. "Let it go, Fi," I warned.

Fiadh's answer came in the form of a thrust. She slipped her scian underneath my blade, aiming for the center of my chest. I let out a squeak as I spun while slashing my blade, feeling it hit skin.

I readied myself again, preparing for Fiadh's attack once more. As children, Fiadh was always too aggressive in swordplay, never knew when to quit. She would rather place herself in a dangerous situation than a smart one.

Not much had changed since then.

We battled in the middle of the night, no one around to hear the clanging of steel. It was an even match. As much as Fiadh was experienced with her scians, I was right there with her, where I had sat for the majority of my life, silent and unnoticed.

Fiadh fought with anger and resentment, while I fought for my clan, for hope, for love. For two people who had been raised the same, we couldn't have ended more differently. I wondered how my sister got here, how the power had corrupted her so. The idea of might was a drug in her veins. But Fiadh had never known the dark side of things, and there were dangers in floating too close to the sun.

Fiadh and I dueled, battered and bloodied, equally wearing blood and cuts on our skin. Fiadh had lost one of her scians at the beginning of the fight, now buried somewhere in the grass. I still had a bag of darts at my side, but Fiadh would never let my hand drift close enough to use them. My elder sister fought with such force it took me two hands on my small blade to beat back the power.

But for all of Fiadh's cunning and planning, knowing it would come down to this moment, that she would have to murder her sister in order to take the crown, she forgot to plan out her killing blow. I could tell from the way she kept parrying, focusing on making large attacks, never quite finishing her deadly strokes. The idea of *winning*, of victory and triumph, clouded her judgment. She couldn't see past each parry, put too much of herself into the riposte, and that was where the fox became outwitted.

If Fiadh was aggression and might, I was deflection and fluidity. Buying myself time, not wanting to make the cuts in my sister's skin but delivering the blow nonetheless. Each of my strikes was a half-beat behind, waiting for Fiadh to yield, to apologize. But none came, so I continued deflecting each blow and waiting, watching the pattern forming before me.

When I looked into Fiadh's eyes, I no longer saw my sister there. It was a person of malice and hate. The girl I once knew was corrupted and empty, her body no more than a shell.

On the next parry, I spun wide, lifting my scian to clear the top of Fiadh's. She turned to meet me where Fiadh thought I would be, ready for the next blow, slicing my blade across where my stomach was supposed to be. But I wasn't there. Instead, I had stopped short at her shoulder, backhanding my scian after lifting it over Fiadh's head, slitting my sister's throat.

CHAPTER THIRTY-TWO

T he pool of blood was a stain on the forest floor, dripping over the grass. Fiadh's hand rose to the gash, knowing it was there but not quite believing. Her face was the part I couldn't stomach. Fiadh's face was a mixture of surprise, hurt, confusion, panic.

My feet stood rooted to the spot, not sure whether to go to my sister or flee. Whether to face the consequences of my actions and the guilt I would need to live with for the rest of my life. In front of me, Fiadh's color was dropping away from her face and she swayed in place as the blood left her body.

I gently removed the scian from my sister's hand and lowered her down to the grass. Fury echoed faintly in Fiadh's eyes, even if she was moments away from death.

Tears dripped down my nose. "I'm sorry."

Fiadh opened her mouth to speak but nothing came out, only a muted gurgling noise as blood pooled in her mouth. Drowning in her own essence. Her hands shakily rose before slipping off a ring, placing it in the palm of my hands. We locked eyes. Fiadh mouthed something, and I could swear my sister had said 'me too'.

Her blue eyes dulled and those endless sparkles in her irises winked asleep, and it was over. I brushed my hands over them, not able to handle the lifeless look of my sister's face.

I wasn't sure how long I sat there, but no part of me knew what to do next. Finally, I shifted Fiadh's head out of my lap and began to scour the grass. One by one, I pulled out the wildflowers I could find, the bluebells and daisies, and braided them together. My hands were surprisingly steady and I tied the knots, repeating the same pattern of *over, under, over, stem, tie, repeat*. I went on until the pile of flowers were no more, the small clearing I sat in picked clean, all of the beauty in the night in the circlet I made for my sister. Just like it had always been.

After placing the flowers on my sister's head, I got up and looked at the fire, tilted my head, and added a few more logs to it, waiting for the blaze to burn tall and bright. Then, I picked up Fiadh, so impossibly small and light in death, and set her on the logs that were meant for myself.

I stepped back and waited, sat there as my sister's beauty turned to ashes, until her laughter was no more than dust on the wind, her soul sparkling embers floating up into the sky. I wondered if I would see her one day, walking in the Otherworld as I had known her in life, impossibly light and happy. I wondered where that had gone in our own world, what had gone on behind the closed doors to make Fiadh change.

I stayed there for hours, knowing Dempsey would be worried. Something wouldn't allow me to move. I stayed there until all of my sister had faded into ashes and the logs had faded into faintly glowing embers. I kicked dirt over the fire, putting out the rest of it before tying the two horses together and riding home, leaving my sister there to rest amongst the forest trees and nymphs.

Shock set in on the way home as my heart slammed in my chest and my breathing increased. Imaginings of the inevitable conversation I would have to have with my parents played out in my head as I prepared for the anger.

What will the clan think of me? How could a clan accept a ruler who had killed her own kin? My actions had been traitorous and bloodthirsty, and I didn't know if I recognized myself anymore.

Who had I become? Who had the politics turned me into? Perhaps it was the same exact toll it had taken on Fiadh. I was simply a reflection of the corruption on the winning side of things.

By the time I entered camp, I was entirely living inside of my head, not noting the curious stares of the warriors on guard. The entire world was numb, my senses dull, the only thing echoing through my brain was the self-hatred rising in my gut.

My body moved as if another controlled it. I faintly watched as I brought the horses to pasture, unsaddled them, and walked slowly back to my tent where a light glowed within. Waves of nausea racked my body while I vomited again and again, sick of my entire being, disgusted with myself.

Pale and shaking, I brushed the hair out of my face and went to face Dempsey. His tall figure was seated on the bed, awake and waiting, no doubt worrying about my safety. The faint irony of what could have been struck me, and I dully registered my laugh.

I pulled back the flaps to my tent to see his tense face. Scians clattered out of my hands and onto the floor while Dempsey raced for me. His eyes went wide, taking in the cuts and blood that crisscrossed my skin.

"What happened?" Dempsey kneeled, waiting for an answer.

"I killed her." I heard my answer faintly. Somehow the truth was spoken as a question, like I was unable of believing the actions myself.

"Her?" Dempsey scanned my face, not understanding what I was saying.

I slowly sat on the ground, my arms cradling my body, holding myself together. I looked at Dempsey's face that somehow looked so innocent in the firelight, even though I was well aware of his own list of kills. I tugged on my now double-stacked pinky ring, one for me and one for my sister, and told the story of tonight, starting at Bowen's tent and ending at Fiadh's funeral pyre.

Dempsey let out a long string of curse words after I finished. Silently, he walked to the washbowl, his back to me. The sound of water filled the tent, and when Dempsey turned around he had a bowl of water and a washcloth in hands. Tenderly, he washed the dirt from my wounds as if he could erase the stain of what I had done. But we both knew what I did tonight would stay with me forever, haunt my memories and dreams.

"It won't be the last time you'll have to kill in order to survive with the crown. Are you still sure you want to do this?"

My face filled with pain. "Isn't it a little late to turn back now?"

"Do you still believe in what we're trying to do?" With that question, Dempsey ignored my pain and self-loathing, the betrayal of my family.

The rings on my hand stopped turning.

"Yes." My answer was the truth because, despite all the pain and hurt I had seen tonight, I also saw the root of the cause. It still all traced back to the killing of that clan many years ago, the genocide of an entire people, the root of corruption it had seeded. And maybe, just maybe, one day I would be able to justify the murder of Bowen and my sister. Even if I wasn't the one to slice the blade across his neck, his death would forever be on my head.

I stood, my legs still unsteady underneath me. "I – I need to tell my parents. About tonight. I need to tell them that we're still going forward with the coronation."

Dempsey grabbed my wrist, loosely, giving me the option to leave if I truly wanted to. He always gave me the option.

"Why don't we tell them tomorrow morning, together? Nothing's changing between now and then."

I nodded, knowing he was right.

I looked around the room. All of my things were exactly how I left them no more than a few weeks ago. It felt like years ago, a different girl in a different lifetime. Dempsey's warm body welcomed me into bed, cocooning himself around me, a silent promise to chase the nightmares away that would inevitably come tonight.

"Do you think I'm a monster?" I whispered, revealing my deepest fear.

"Never for a second could I believe that about you. The girl who defied the gods to save me because of love? Never," he told me softly. "I think this is bigger than us. The Sectarians recruiting Bowen? Him allying with your sister? It's more of a network than a cause and effect."

"How deep do you think the network runs?"

Dempsey paused, hesitating. "Much deeper than we know. Every single movement the Sectarians make is because of those insurgents. *That* might be a bigger war than battle with the Sectarians."

I cursed.

Dempsey nuzzled into my neck. "No one said wearing the crown would be easy." He was joking, but I knew he was right.

Sleep evaded me that night, and I was still haunted by what happened in the forest. When I finally did fall asleep, I dreamed.

The Otherworld surrounded me, full of its oddities and bright colors, the feeling of magic turning through the air. In the middle of it all was my sister, wearing the dress from her wedding day. Fiadh was beautiful, and bright, and happy. There was no evidence of her last minutes of pain, no gash across her neck, no malevolent spirits in her eyes. It was how it was supposed to be, but never came to fruition.

CHAPTER THIRTY-THREE

Dempsey

Morning light filtered through the pasture as Willa and I sat amongst the horses. During my first visit to the Forest Clan, I had asked anyone and everyone about her. Through those quests, I discovered that this herd was hers – for use by those in the clan, but the responsibility and raising of the animals fell solely to her. Willa announced the names and traits of each one, revealing their personalities and ticks. With each explanation of the horses, she also revealed herself, the work she put into the creatures throughout the years, the glue that held her together.

She avoided my eyes when she explained the bargain she made with herself, that as long as there was something she could take care of, she had something to live for. Her voice grew quiet as she exposed her weaknesses, one by one.

I sat there and listened to it all. Word by word, I took it in, silently and without judgement. I waited through every hesitation, every stutter, every stumbled and rushed word.

"But mainly I decided on the horses because they bore most people to death. There is no glory that you get from fighting, no pride that our cooks share in, no lasting monument like the builders. It's quiet and solitary. It's a hiding place."

Anger flared in me. It always did when she talked about *before*. Before she escaped Callan's grasp. Before she was allowed to flourish. I'm not sure it would ever end, the anger.

"Did no one care?" I dared to ask, the words squirming out.

Willa gave me a soft smile. "Dempsey, no one knew. I think that's the thing that was worst about it all. I was wasting away, every piece of me haunted by this unhappiness until it festered, until I hated myself as much as he did. And I was so worried about everyone else that I kept it hidden."

Willa saw the questioning forming in my eyes, and answered it before I could ask.

"My parents are so busy they don't have time to look that close. Not until the cracks began to show, but by then I was already so broken it was damage control. To make sure a fracture didn't turn into a break." She took a deep breath.

"And Fiadh... Fiadh and I shared a tent up until a few years ago, did you know that?"

I shook my head no in response.

"We did. We had beds just a few feet apart, and every night we would gossip until one of us fell asleep mid-sentence. When my parents started to groom her for command though, it started to change. We were still close, of course, but it wasn't the same. No more midnight talks. There was a degree of separation."

Willa scanned the horizon like she was afraid of her ghosts appearing, as if she could speak them into existence once more. Her voice turned hoarse, and she spoke tentatively. "In those years I learned how to cry silently. I would wait until she fell asleep, which didn't take long, and I would let the tears come. A hand over your mouth, to try and keep the sounds in, a hand on your chest to keep yourself breathing. It's really all in the breath control, to keep it from turning into sobs. Sobs... sobs are noisy; those will wake people up. But if you keep your breathing steady and let the tears pour out of your eyes. When your back is turned to someone, it just looks like you're sleeping. Rhythmic breathing and all that." Willa absentmindedly picked a handful of daisies and began to braid them together.

"She never knew?" I asked.

Willa cocked her head. "I don't know if anyone knows. Fiadh got engaged not long after, and she moved to her own tent. I mean, my parents started to notice I was slightly less. Withdrawn, I guess. But I just blamed it all on the gift of foresight."

"And no one thought to see past the nightmarish dreams you said you were having?" I kept my face carefully composed. This was not my story to impose my feelings on. I was not here to judge. But I could offer her myself, so she would never have to sob silently in the night.

"They really did end up getting bad, especially right before Fiadh's wedding. But I think my nightmare was in real life, not in my dreams."

I wanted to yell; I wanted to draw my sword and fight the ghosts that plagued her. It stung – no, it felt like a knife to the gut that this was not a battle I could fight for her.

"If I could strike them all, right now, I would. Banish the demons."

She looked at me, her eyes wide as tears slid down her cheeks. "But I did," she whispered. "They're all gone. I killed him, and I killed her."

I didn't need her to speak the names out loud. I knew what she meant. What I didn't know, was how heavily those deaths hung around her shoulders – especially Callan. But that was the beauty of her soul, the ability to care and love.

I gathered Willa to my chest and let her cry those loud, shuddering sobs, hearing every gasp of breath and each piece of pain.

"They dug their own graves. It's not on your head or your conscience." I said the words quietly.

Willa began to quiet. "I think what was most fucked up was

that they were the closest thing I had to family – they were my family."

I gave a tug on her wedding ring. "I have one I could provide for you," I said with a small smile. *Felix, Sarai, Barra, even Fintan.* A found family pieced together through love, respect, and loyalty. Bonds tighter than the broken engagement or the frayed relationship with her sister.

"Come on." Willa stood up and pulled on my hand, dragging me up with her. "We have things to do."

Willa walked over to one of the horses nearby and ran her hands over its backside, calming it. She guided it and a speckled gelding out of the pasture, securing the loop around the gate, leaving me to hurdle over the top of the fence.

Willa hauled herself on top of the horse, using the paddock fence as leverage. She sat straight, smiling into the sun as she looked at me.

"Planning on a journey so soon?"

"No. We're going to the Hollow." She took off without another word of explanation, leaving me to gallop after her as we thundered into the village.

In another life, we might have ridden into the sunset. This might have all been a bad dream, and we could live happily. But there were expectations weighing upon our shoulders, a screaming that occurred, a death that marred the landscape. We rode into the Hollow to settle the whispers and begin our reign.

I had accompanied Willa to her parent's tent earlier that morning to tell them the news of everything. Throughout the entire tale, I stood behind her, hands on her shoulders, silently offering myself as support.

Viktor and Brigid were grieving, but it could have been worse. Killing of kin was no light offense, and their hurt and emotions could have easily turned against Willa.

But instead, Viktor let that cold-faced expression take over his features, one that was practiced from years of being a clan leader and making kills on the battlefield. Brigid was equally strong, if not more admitting of Fiadh's faults. Brigid reported that she knew Fiadh was upset – but weren't they all?

Their family agreed it was a shared fault, pushing Fiadh too far, too single-mindedly, forcing her to create a destiny that wasn't meant to be hers.

Perhaps most surprisingly, Willa's parents apologized for all of the pain this summer. They apologized for Callan, for Bowen, apologized for Fiadh's greed and lust for power, the pain of killing one's own sister.

Willa and I rode into camp high on our horses, commanding attention from the second we reached the outer limits. The village fell silent, no doubt from the gossip that spread like wildfire. I heard – and I didn't care. I would defend us until the last stroke of my sword, and even if this crowd of people turned against us, I would find a way to get us out. Get her out. I would go to the depths of the Otherworld for her, as she had done for me.

As we headed to where the bonfire burned at night, the crowd gathered naturally. A throng of people followed us, tentatively at first, and then with more urgency once a crowd was bolstered and people knew they could blend into the blur.

I spoke, just like we had practiced. Every piece of this, down to the words and pauses, was carefully scripted in our bedroom this morning. Practiced and repeated until perfect, until we created a strength that no one dared question.

"We know you are all curious, so gather round. Hear what we have to say, cast your judgment before the gods." My voice was one of a prince, so formal it almost sounded like Felix's court advisor's voice, curt and lined with civility, edged with the promise of brutality if crossed. I gave Willa a small smile at the joke I left there – allowing the people before us to think that the gods remained in the Otherworld, waiting to pass an unbiased judgment. In reality, this was the closest to a god as they would ever get, and I knew that the gods played favorites.

Willa cleared her throat. "I have no doubt you have all heard of our marriage by now." I placed a protective hand on the horn of her saddle.

"Three cheers!" someone cried in the crowd, no doubt placed there by Barra. Willa waited patiently for the cheers to die down before continuing.

"Thank you," Willa laughed. "And I know you all heard the Lia Fáil scream, just as we heard it on the Hill. We journeyed to the place where the gods meet the earth, and they gave their approval of our union."

I spoke once more. "The Lia Fáil has not screamed in hundreds of years, not since the like of Eochaid and Tea Tephi. The Coronation Stone is alive once more." A hush fell over the crowd as they waited for what came next.

"We have decided we will ascend to the throne, the seat that has not been filled for hundreds of years. We will provide ourselves, our skills, our services, to you all, and live at your aid until the end of our time." I looked at Willa, waiting for her to continue.

"But since we have come to this decision, there has also been treachery." Willa cast her eyes at the crowd before us, unsure of their reaction. "We discovered two traitors in our midst." Gasps echoed throughout the meeting ground.

"Bowen, formerly from the Clan o' Cliffs, advisor to the Clan of Forests, betrayer to us all, was found to be working with the Sectarians to undermine our leadership and existence. He wouldn't be satiated until the fall of our society. He has since been killed in battle. May the gods decide where to take his soul."

If anyone asked me, I would tell them exactly where I thought his soul should go – but now wasn't the time for accusations and enemies. No, Bowen was a friend to the clans when he was alive, or at least he appeared to be. People would be shocked by his death, and we didn't need them questioning the tale, however true it may be. People could be murderous when it came to traitors, and it wasn't always on the side of the just.

"The second betrayal wasn't just a betrayal of our clans and authority, but of kin and family. My sister, Fiadh, is guilty of attempted murder. She tried to murder me for the crown, and was working with Bowen, with knowledge of his deeds to do it. She challenged me to combat, and lost. She created her own death with the decisions she made. There will be no mercy for betrayal of us and our clans. *If anyone* decides to follow in either of their paths, they will be dealt with in the same manner."

Willa was quiet for a moment, letting the weight of her words sink in to the people before us. My imagination had prepared me for protests, accusations, violence. But there was none. There were only our people before us, shining in their devotion to Willa and I, the children of their clans, who they believed worthy of their love and loyalty.

"But Fiadh was one of us. We grew up loving her and hoping she would become one of us, one of our next great leaders. I'm not foolish enough to believe she won't be grieved. We will all miss what she could have chosen to become, the promise of herself."

"So there will be no coronation today. Today is a day of grieving, for all we have lost. We have all lost a sister in her. Let it be a warning, that such behavior is not tolerated, but I am not heartless. Let today be a day of loss, and tomorrow we will continue onward."

Murmurs rippled across the crowd. Uncertainty – but this was the right move. For years, our parents had preached that emotion was weakness, and maybe that's why Fiadh was groomed for command. It was also what led to her death. Our rule would not become the same.

Willa slid down from her horse, waiting for me to do the same before wading through the throng of people, weaving our way out of camp. Stares came, along with the words of compassion, deference, words of hope, fear, and loss.

We had almost made it out of camp when Viktor turned Willa around with a tug.

"What are you doing?" he hissed.

Willa stared back at him coldly. "You heard what I said. I'm not taking back any of it." In the many variations of today that we played out, we had expected this possibility, too.

Brigid's concerned face appeared over Viktor's shoulder. "Willa, I don't think you fully understand the potential consequences of what you just did—"

"I understand it just fine. For all that my future may now entail, I'm still a *person* who lost a sister, just like you two are parents who lost a daughter. You can't pretend it didn't happen."

"Darling, we aren't pretending—" Brigid's soothing words were cut off by Viktor's growling voice.

"Do you understand the weakness you just showed? The liability you just created? We now live in a world where traitors are mourned?"

Willa's voice rose. "So let the people see it! The *gods* didn't seem to have a problem with it. You are so concerned with creating the image of an unmoved leader that you forgot the people you rule over have feelings too. They have emotions, and that is precisely what got us into this mess. Twenty gods-damned years ago, you refused to acknowledge the emotions of people who had just survived a *massacre*. You refused to save their lives and their lands and their way of life and it rotted Bowen from the inside."

Her eyes were blazing in a fury, and she hardly stopped for breath as she continued.

"Your obsession with control and being this stoic leader was the death of Fiadh. She was so engrossed with this idea of what she had to be, what you made her into, that she lost herself. She was willing to *kill* for it. That's not the Fiadh I knew. That's not the Fiadh I grew up with.

So gods-fucking-forbid if I decide to take my time as queen of this isle on a different path. I want to care for the people within it, and I'm not afraid to let them see it. Maybe it will inspire their loyalty. Maybe it will be my downfall. But all I know is that I will not fall into the traps you laid decades ago, and I will not continue to let this isle fall into it either."

Willa looked both of her parents in the eye, straightened and collected herself, and plastered on a steely voice. "I thank you and understand your cause for concern, but it is not necessary. I'm aware of what I am doing, and I can promise you it is intentional. If there is any more on this subject it will be dealt with accordingly." The threat hung in the air between us.

Together, we turned and guided our horses out of the village, not waiting to see their reactions. Viktor and Brigid weren't just the problems – it was in Meili and Barra, too. The old way of things, the way of ruling cobbled together in a time when they almost lost everything. But that wasn't our world anymore. So we left that perfectly crafted veneer of clan leaders shattered behind us. It had to be done. Our world would no longer thrive in that coldly crafted façade.

CHAPTER THIRTY-FOUR

Willa

"I really think that could not have gone any better," Felix drawled.

The comment earned him a punch from Sarai. "Really, Felix?"

"I think, all things considered, it went well," Felix added defensively. "No one challenged it, no more deaths! A good first day, if you ask me." He took a swig from his glass of whiskey.

Sarai rolled her eyes and walked over to the bed where I was laying, staring at the ceiling. "Felix might have a point. I don't know if you could have handled your parents in a different way." She scrunched her face as if trying to imagine the tea leaves revealing our future before her.

"I feel... like I have no clue what the future is going to hold. I've blown every essence of tradition up." I lay on the bed, spiraling after the argument with my parents.

"One day at a time." Dempsey leaned down and spoke softly to me. "Coronation is tomorrow. We focus on that, and then we'll take the next day."

I groaned. "There hasn't been a coronation in over a century. We're literally playing make-believe at this point. What does a coronation even entail?"

"Crowns?" suggested Felix.

"I happen to have a friend, who is what we mortals would call omnipotent. I'm sure he was around at the time and might be able to shed some light?" Sarai cast a pointed look at Dempsey.

He winced. "*Was* omnipotent."

"Still," argued Felix.

"It's mainly a ring ceremony. A dance between us two, followed by a feast and revelry, of course. If the gods find it particularly blessed, they might send a sign. We could change the entire thing though, and no one would be the wiser," he added with a devilish wink.

"It just doesn't feel real. What if they object to it all?"

"A fight to the death occurs," answered Felix. Sarai shot him a glare laced with venom.

Footsteps shuffled outside the tent, obviously overhearing the snippets of conversation. The entire tent immediately went on alert, shifting to their weapons holstered at our hips and thighs. I flipped over so I could face the entrance.

"You may enter," I called out.

A familiar face entered the tent, characterized by his sharp jawline and jet black hair threatening to hang over his face it had grown so long. I hadn't seen Sai in months, but the time hadn't been kind to him, faint shadows hanging underneath his eyes, bruising his pale, almost perfect skin.

Grief. It was grief written on his face. And I couldn't blame him. Fiadh had a quality to her that made people fall in love with her very essence, possessing the ability to make anyone feel like a fast friend, like they were the entire world. The man standing before me had loved Fiadh with all his heart, and I had broken it.

Out of the corner of my eye, I noticed my friends grip the pommel of their weapons. I held up a hand silently, letting them relax. "Sai," I said, by way of greeting.

"I – I was hoping we could talk." The words were neutral, no evidence of malice within them.

Did he mean it? I had killed his wife, broken his world. If Fiadh had hoped to take my place in the Lia Fáil, what had Sai been hoping for? I drew the scian at my hip and placed it on my lap, knowing what it would remind Sai of. Gods knew it reminded me every time I drew it.

"Go ahead," I answered softly. Noticing his gaze, I added, "Forgive me, but the events of the past few days have left me on the defensive."

Sai gave me a sad, small smile. "I would expect nothing less."

"Well?" prompted Felix coldly.

Sai glanced at Felix, their eyes meeting in some form of contact that I could not decipher.

"I came to apologize. I didn't know... the full extent of Fiadh's ambition. I didn't know what it had turned her into. There's no way I can prove this to you, but I hope you can understand. Willa, I once viewed you as a little sister, and I hope we can still be there for each other."

I studied his handsome face, the trust that had once been so easily given lacking.

"What did you know?" The question escaped my lips, but I had to know the lengths of mutiny that ran through the camps.

Sai ran his fingers through his glossy hair. "She would tell me of her goals, to unite the clans, lead them as one. It was nothing more than a daydream, one that fit us well, being from two clans."

Except it was more than just a daydream.

His voice got quiet. "I didn't know she was meeting with Bowen, that she thought she could usurp you, that she planned to kill. I... I didn't see any of it in her, and maybe that makes me a fool."

"None of us did until it was too late. Maybe that's just as much our fault as it was hers."

"How are we supposed to do this? With our clans falling

apart from the inside, the threats from the Sectarians. How are we supposed to last beyond the year?" Silence rippled through the tent as I laid bare our weaknesses.

"You build the most powerful court the isle has seen." Sai grabbed the sword at his waist slowly withdrawing it from the scabbard it lived in. Within half a second, Felix and Dempsey drew their swords completely, and Sarai had a dagger held high, ready to throw. Sai smiled and shook his head while he knelt.

"I would like to offer you my sword and my service, if your companions will allow me to keep my head?" He raised an eyebrow at the threat around him. "I will ally my sword and self with your reign, as a warrior, as heir apparent to the Mountain Clan, and anything else I can offer you."

I looked at Dempsey, unsure how he would take this new addition to our fianna. Although his face was unreadable, he gave a slight dip of his head.

"I accept your allegiance and your oath." I walked over to Sai after he sheathed his sword. "You can always be my brother," I said, enveloping him in a hug.

"I hope to prove that I'm worthy of such a title." Sai nodded his goodbyes and left the tent, not meeting the eyes of Felix as he went.

"So who's going to explain?" I demanded.

Sarai snorted and sat down on the bed. "You've just invited a piece of history back into our mix."

I assessed the reactions of Felix and Dempsey. Dempsey stared back with a cool face of faint amusement. Felix, on the other hand, looked as murderous as I had ever seen him. Even in the middle of battle, Felix managed to keep a flawlessly unbroken courtier expression, prepared for any trick or maneuver.

That same advisor now looked positively off-kilter. He hadn't taken his eyes off the door where Sai had left, and I watched his knuckles go white around the sword hilt. The distant look in his eyes was no doubt imagining what to do with the sword if the offender had returned.

"Sworn enemies? Jilted lover? Betrayal or simply two egos sparring?" I asked, narrowing the cause down to two avenues.

"All of the above," answered Sarai sweetly. "You might know Sai as your sister's man, but he's a bit friendlier than that."

A dart went flying through the air, landing directly in the pillow next to Sarai's head. She sat up in a fury, narrowing eyes glaring at the open pouch at Felix's side.

"Man is a bit generous of a term," Felix said. "Spineless sycophant might be better."

I quickly grasped the depth of the hurt in Felix. I forced myself to adjust my tone, keeping it lighthearted. "Well, there's not much we can do. We need allies if we're to survive this."

Felix raised an eyebrow. "Interesting one to start with."

CHAPTER THIRTY-FIVE

Willa

"Truthfully, I never expected it to get this far," said Felix at breakfast, never one to mince words.

Sarai rapped him across the knuckles with her butter knife. He scowled back in response, rubbing the redness away from his hands.

"You know, that should offend me," I pointed out.

"Did you really not expect us to take the throne?" asked Dempsey.

"Oh no, I was referring to way earlier than that. I mean, Willa proposed to you. Gods above, I never thought she would have the balls on her to do it."

I smiled primly. "Thankfully, myself and my balls did do it." Dempsey leaned over and kissed me on the neck.

"It's rude, Felix. It's rude. How you manage to get around a court session is beyond me," said Sarai.

"I find that saying rude things makes the fun of it." Felix took a swig of the sparkling bubbly beverage before him, a drink he had declared as his celebration earlier.

Sarai stood and cleared the plates before both her and me. Just as I was about to protest at the food being taken away from me, Sarai tapped her finger twice on my head. "Time to get ready," she trilled, pulling on my hand to guide me into the tent where my things lay.

Sarai dug in a bag elbows deep. "Dempsey saved this dress for you. Thought you might want to wear it today, not quite sure what other occasion you'll have for it."

She triumphantly rose, holding a cascading length of emerald fabric. I stepped forward, gently grabbing the fabric and letting it slip through my fingers. "Shit," I whispered.

Blinking away tears, I turned to Sarai. "This was from Fiadh's wedding, when I first met Dempsey. Gods, that seems like a lifetime ago."

"Full circle, isn't it?" Sarai asked gently.

I nodded absently, removing the dressing gown I wore in exchange for the newly revealed dress that lay on the bed in front of me.

A knock sounded at the door, and a familiar shadow lay on the other side. My mother walked through the door, her face pinched with worry and concern. I knew what it was from, without having to ask. As much as I worried about things, my mother worried about me tenfold, and the events of the past days didn't make it any easier.

I went to gather my mother in a hug, but Brigid stepped back.

"I need to apologize. For everything we put you through. For everything we forced your sister in to. It was too cutthroat, it seems, and it wasn't right of us. We never should have assumed ambitions onto either of you."

Brigid shook her head. "I hope today is of your own will and accord. Say yes, and I'll leave you be. I just want to make sure you know the power you're accepting and the future it holds."

A sad smile sprung to my face. "I know, Mom. It is."

It didn't need to be said, but we both were keenly aware of the empty space in the room, air that should have been filled by Fiadh.

"I brought you something." Brigid's slender hands dug into

the folds of her gown, pulling out a stained cloth. She unwrapped it to reveal a small silver circlet.

It was similar to ones I had seen in tapestries and storybooks, the metal so delicate I was afraid that if I touched it a piece might break off. The silver was molded into the shape of leaves, the diameter so thin it would barely show through my thick hair. Blossoms of gold and copper mingled amongst the silver leaves. It bore no jewels, for none were needed. The circlet was a thing of great brilliance and beauty, and it mimicked the ones the queens of old wore.

Brigid placed it around the crown of my head, intertwining it among the strands to hold it in place. "There," she said tightly. "Now you look a real queen too."

I squeezed my mother's hand, not knowing what to say or how to put it in words.

"Are you ready for them?" Brigid asked.

I nodded, letting my mother guide me out of the tent and into the sunlight, ready to face our new world. We walked to the clearing where all feasts were held, except it was almost unrecognizable. Two thrones made of woven wood stood at the center of a dais, their backs to the willow trees, facing the camp, ready to watch the scenes unfold before them.

A path was clearly marked, paving the aisle with petals and leaves. I turned around, my mind already full of questions only to see my friends smiling, walking towards me. There was a similar crown resting on Dempsey's head, a thick work of silver with strands of copper and gold weaving through, runes imprinted into the thick metal, the story of the clans incarnate.

"How does it all work?" I asked, shaking my head.

"We've asked a friend to perform the ceremony, who should be getting here shortly. You need a witch to officiate, of course, but I'd rather not spill my little secret just yet," said Sarai.

"I have rings for us to wear, and there will be vows to exchange." Seeing my concerned face, Dempsey hastily added,

"Nothing to memorize, you'll just have to repeat after Kelz." His eyes sparkled with amusement.

"And after, we party until the sun rises," Felix finished.

"Well if it's that simple," I said.

Felix and Sarai made excuses about preparations to see to, leaving Dempsey and me alone in the clearing.

"Do you remember when we were first here?" I asked him.

"The little nymph girl in the clearing? The one that insisted on taunting me by dancing circles around me, or the one that pulled me under a willow tree to scream bloody murder?"

I scowled. "I did not scream. I think we simply had a conversation."

Dempsey pulled me into his arms. "Some conversation," he murmured.

I rose up onto my toes, reaching to kiss him.

"Willa – I want you to know that this life, with you, is the happiest I've experienced. I don't know where the strands of fate will lead us after this, but I'm not going anywhere without you."

I became acutely aware of my own mortality and the lives Dempsey would live after he left this earth.

"You're being silly," I whispered, my voice suddenly caught in my throat. "You'll be tired of me by then, and you'll do just fine living in the Otherworld, being amongst the gods and the divine."

His hand caught on my chin, lifting it up so he could look into my eyes. "*You* are the divine. *You* are my day and night and planets and constellations. I would rather live amongst the stars, watching the world you have blessed, than retreat away."

A breath escaped my body, possibly the last one I had, because the only thing I could know at the moment was the stinging of tears in my eyes.

"You are my world." And when Dempsey kissed me, I could feel that he meant it. That kiss held all the things he had whispered, the sparkle in his eyes and the warmth of his soul, and his passion and adoration all wrapped into one action. "But for now, I'll settle for making you my queen."

Slowly, reality returned to us and the hum of life rose. I let myself savor the feeling of being completely still in his arms for one last second.

"It's time, isn't it?" I asked. Dempsey gave me a smile and nodded.

People filled into the clearing, anxious murmurs heard all around. I couldn't blame them. There hadn't been a kingship in over a century; Dempsey and I were certainly nothing like they had expected.

Sarai and Felix gave us a quick hug as they guided Kelz to the altar, the little witch practically hopping with excitement when they saw me. I laughed and gave them a hug, wondering if Kelz had known they would be in this position all along.

Somewhere a stringed instrument began to play, and the crowd quieted. I looked at Dempsey before hovering my hand in midair, waiting for him to place his hand underneath it. When he did, we slowly glided down the aisle.

We knelt together at the stairs of the altar, waiting for Kelz to begin.

"Those that claim the kingship to this isle kneel before me," they said, in a voice more serious than I had ever heard. "The Lia Fáil screamed their righteousness, and they are here to accept this claim. Does anyone see fault to this?"

Kelz paused, and whether it was for ceremony or in seriousness, I could not tell. But, no one spoke, and so they continued.

"Repeat the vows of the kingship before me, the gods, and the people you seek to rule over."

"I see, hear, and believe in the gods. May they right me on my path, and whisper words of guidance to my ear."

Dempsey and I solemnly spoke the words after Kelz.

"I shall use justice to reign over my people, or they shall use this justice unto me."

We repeated the words again.

"It will be my sole mission in life to protect this isle, from threats of invaders and the threats internal."

The air began to hum around them as Dempsey and I spoke this third verse.

"May the spirits of the nymphs and sprites join me with the nature of this isle, the power of the gods connects me with the Otherworld, and this body connects me to the innate power of our clans."

The undeniable feeling of magick rose through the clearing during the last verse. I glanced upwards to Kelz, the image of them with arms raised striking against the twilight blue sky.

"You may rise. Do you have the rings of your court?"

"I do," Dempsey spoke, his hand holding a small bag that came from our smith.

"Place them on the middle finger of your left hand, never to be removed during the time of your reign."

Dempsey slid his own on before taking my hand and sliding the ring, a replica of the crown I wore on my head in miniature.

"It is my honor and privilege to preside over these vows today. May you both have a long reign," Kelz spoke directly to us before raising their voice to the crowd. "Long live the king and queen!"

The crowd that stretched far beyond my naked eye erupted in cheers and good wishes as Dempsey and I walked, hand in hand, toward the feast and celebration.

It was both alike and unlike the ones we had been to before. There was the large bonfire, and people dancing, and the cook hurriedly maintaining the feasting tables. But there was also something different about it all now, something I couldn't quite place. Something in the air had changed, and Dempsey felt it too.

Sometime later, as the party continued with the cries of

dancers and the crackle of the bonfire, Dempsey and I found each other in the clearing, not too far from the spot we first met. I was laying in the middle of the late summer flowers, smelling their cloying sweetness, knowing that soon they would turn crisp and return back to the earth before showing again in a year's time.

"You know, strange men could find you out here," teased Dempsey.

I hummed. "I've had to deal with worse." I turned to him, a smile on my face.

"So the deed is done," he said, turning the ring that sat on his finger. "How do you feel?"

I stopped, thinking of all the things I probably should be feeling. The ceremony, the honor of our position, was enough to intimidate and inspire anyone, but none of those words and feelings were right.

"At peace. I feel at peace. I know that probably sounds crazy, but we made the right decision. This is what we were put on this earth to do. Whatever happens, this is the beginning of it."

Dempsey took my hand, laying down in the flowers next to me. His thumb stroked broad circles over the back of my hand. We laid like that for a while, staring at the glittering stars above us, the divine mingling with the mortal.

The End

If you enjoyed Willa and Dempsey's story, please consider leaving a review on Amazon and Goodreads.

ACKNOWLEDGMENTS

If there are any readers who have made it to this point in the book, thank you. I always hoped that you would be able to experience this world, and I hope it lives on in your days and nights.

Thank you to Sam, for being better than any book boyfriend. (Yes, dear readers, they do exist). Thank you for encouraging me to write and not calling me insane when I first described the world I created in my head to you. Thank you for having me speak my book into existence, and never letting me put it down. I'm sorry for never using snakes as a plot device. You may never read this book, but your love is written through every page.

Thank you to my parents, for enabling my book habits. Mom, I remember the laptop you gave me in the fifth grade, and you telling me that it would be good to write my stories in. It only took a decade and a different laptop, but I finally did it. Thank you for all your love and support. Thank you for my education. Thank you for giving me the chance to go abroad and discover the world of this novel.

To my grandparents – thank you for always having a book in the car for me. To Yamma – thank you for biking me to the library every summer and allowing me to fill tote bags full of books. It made more of an impact than you will ever know.

To my sisters – I love you. I promise Fiadh's character is not based off any of you. I hope you get to read this book one day.

This book wouldn't be where it is today if it wasn't for all the beta readers that I found via TikTok. Thank you for letting me trust you with my book baby, and for loving it as much as I did. Your feedback was invaluable.

Lake Country Press – where to start? Brittany, thank you for everything. You are a force and I am in awe of you and your work every day. Thank you to the team that works behind the scenes. Thank you to the author family I have found at this small press. I've never had writer friends before, and I feel so lucky to have found you all.

And lastly, to Kodak, my inspiration and my buddy. You may not be a wolfhound but you are the best companion I could ask for.

ABOUT THE AUTHOR

Ashley is obsessed with storytelling: written, on the screen, or word of mouth. Daydreaming in the middle of the pandemic about her time abroad in Cork, Ireland led to her first attempt at a manuscript. This passion project resulted in her debut novel *Reign of Clans and Gods* publishing November 22, 2022.

A student of history and political science, telling the dramatics of government and power calls her name. When not with her laptop, you can find Ashley wrangling her dog or re-watching her favorite TV series. Ashley resides in Arlington, Virginia with her boyfriend, but also calls Boston and Southern California home.

CPSIA information can be obtained
at www.ICGtesting.com
Printed in the USA
BVHW041309141122
651890BV00007BA/148